I0612486

Cerulean Codex

◆

Ω

Credits

Story: Guy Maybriar
Front Cover Art: Christi du Toit
Back Cover Art: Mark Cooper
Interior Art: Jeremmya Devin
Interior Art: Tristan Jurolan
Interior Art: Pon Pratchayanan
Interior Art: Vincent Kristianto
Map Art: Jog Brogzin

Contents

♦

Introduction

Today is April 6, 2025. Currently 12:05PM. And I'm astonished. I'm.Still.Alive. It's been sometime since I've done a long form story, and honestly, I never thought this one would ever see the light of day. Like all my stories, it starts with music. Then, a soundtrack. Then, the main thought of, Do I proceed with this concept? Give it the creepy green light? I reviewed older material like "Miasma." What a mess. I can honestly see why people don't take me seriously but just like the quote I entered at the end, if I stop writing, give in to the restlessness, and become nothing…then what's the point of it all?

And that is where the danger resides.

When I first got the ball running on this back in 2014-2015 I was excited about my first World-Builder story. Fast forward to 2019 on January 26, 2019 at 12AM, where I first start jotting down ideas in a burgundy steno book. Then, delays. Had to get other stories off my chest first. Felt right at the time. Looking back now, it was definitely the right decision to make. I had so much to learn. I still do. God knows I have so much to learn. My memory gets foggy and distracted very easily when then depression kicks in or I've stagnated for too long from a project. I didn't start penning (literally) the first pages of CC until November 6, 2021 at 03:42AM. Only 12 incomplete pages.

Why? I was struggling with weight issues, trying to understand if life would ever get better, and too many rejections from the opposite sex. Something real dark clawed its way back into my head. Something I thought I exorcised long before. Suicide. Paraphrasing, since I can't remember the exact words, but it went along the lines of, "I can't do this anymore. None of this matters. There is no one. There never was. Therapy never worked, my stories collect dust, love doesn't exist, everyone is fake, and I'm just so tired. Let this be my final story. Doesn't matter if people love/hate it/me.

My heart hurts, my eyes are dry and I haven't cried in years, there's nothing to look forward to, I have terrible migraines, and I cannot sleep soundly anymore. Maybe I psyched myself into believing I am a 'writer.' Nothing of great value will be lost. A benefit to society with my permanent absence. I'm constantly told I am being overly dramatic when I do speak out to vent. People hate me on a natural level. Terrible skill to have; pulling it out of them with ease. It's getting harder to breath. Let this be the final…"

Embrace chaos.

That was the mindset I started to embrace as of recent. Everything is burning all around me. Everyone has their own issues, but I won't let them take me down. No. Never ever ever, baby! I realize there are some real bad people out there. Dark and murderous. But not me. I'm odd, but I'm lawful. Sure I have a great deal of anger inside of me, but I keep it leashed for the right times. The appropriate times. It's all dark humor from here on out. No reason to take life serious at the moment. Too many grey hairs sprout. I am on the path of going nomad by building up some wealth to disappear from New York. For good. You should leave your current environment if it deals harm to you: physically or mentally. There's no guarantee I'll find peace wherever I go, but it's better to try than to stay and give it all up without ever wondering, What if?

We lost some of the greats along the way, who personally affected me growing up: Val Kilmer, Gene Hackman, Michelle Trachtenberg, Carl Weathers, James Earl Jones, Quincy Jones, Donald Sutherland, Terry Funk, Paul Reubens, Tony Bennett, Alan Arkin, "The Iron Sheik," Jerry Springer, Raquel Welch, Billy Graham, Lanny Poffo, Tony Todd and to top it all off, David Lynch…who died on my birthday. They say never form para-social relationships with celebrities—which I 110% believe in—but that doesn't mean we can't love them for inspiring us to be better. For me, it's creatively. Still I mourn for them, their friends, and loved ones. I also lost some close to me these as of recent.

But at least there's art.

Despite having a soundtrack readied a decade prior, I tend to have issues filling in certain parts of my work. The meat and potatoes. Which is why I am glad to have delayed this story and worked on it through piecemeal or a bit by bit system. I discovered some bands that immensely helped bring not only this story but future lore events into fruition. The first major band, and album, to really push my creative juices for CC is called Sermon: Of Golden Verse. This album is 11/10 to me. Blows me away every time. So many scenes drawn up. The Distance is my personal favorite. Coming in second is Kardashev: The Almanac. Again: 11/10. Are you guys kidding me?! Incredible! Beyond Sun and Moon is the favorite. Last band, that I discovered recently, is Dawn of Ouroboros. From their album Velvet Incandescence, the song Rise from Disillusion really powered me up. Their newest album Bioluminescence is fantastic and something about the song Dueling Sunsets makes me want to live.

Other bands have helped me garner the courage to live as well like YOB with Beauty in Falling Leaves off of Our Raw Heart is so powerful. Ghost Bath's album Starmourner is a tour de force with tracks like Seraphic, Luminescence, and Principalities. The track Cleaning Out The Rooms by Sea Power did something unnatural to me. Grandiose detox on my tarnished soul. And, of course, Devin Townsend—my #1—coming out with PowerNerd and hitting my soul with songs like Glacier and Goodbye.

To live among giants...

But music and art wasn't the only things that pushed this story forward. It is highly unfortunate, but I did it as an experiment, but I did delve into many (legal) substances to see if anything would unlock inside my brain. I honestly can't say even after indulging in copious amounts of alcohol and edibles. I drank so much beer that I'm just disgusted by it, and switched over to wine. Then I started pairing the wine with the edibles and that got me too distorted and almost died from a few blackouts in my home after crashing unconscious while circling my living room, with my headphones on, and forcing ideas to come out. It worked once or twice…I think. When that was getting old I started to ponder on how to really relax myself, but still enjoy the freeing experience. I subtracted the edibles and the formula that works now is one glass of wine and a spoonful, or two, of citron marmalade with a mint chocolate protein bar.

Groovy and relaxing.

So that's that. I'll delve more into other things in the closure and let you have fun with this book that I have come to love in all its wonders and flaws. I cannot express how much I love how this one turned out!

Be well.
Be safe.
Make love.
And tend to your own garden.
Let the butterflies come to you.

With all my love,
R.K. aka "Guy Maybriar"

In memory of:

Michael Damiano

&

Anthony "Tony" DelGuidice

Special thanks:

Devin Henderson

Cerulean

CODEX

A Story By
Guy Maybriar

Prologue

†

Afterimage

April brought unhampered skies with warm rays and
gentle winds. Soft blades of green swayed side to side with
adjacent neighbors; the choreography was impeccable. Virgin
snow, from distant peaks, thaw to create malleable change.

Overlays of mud glossing the earth, and for every bit
of yesterday's frost came cool refreshments for nature's
denizens. Those with wings and puffed chests bathed
jubilantly while whistling their tunes. Of those small and
significant; hoof or paw, took to hydration to satiate thirst.
While some returned to their nests, others ventured off to
various trails searching for berries among the brambles.

Distant voices kept them alert to their surroundings. A
dwarfed cottontail holding its gaze on a nearby hill inhabited
by one lone tree, visited by one lone soul, approached by one
lone stranger.

"Should've known to check here first before running
around the school to come find you," the stranger greeted
the lone soul. Ignored. No response. Not out of
rudeness, but because her mind was already
preoccupied with memories that once were.

All those colors, transmutations, and
natural phenomena. All that blood…

She sat there on the soft grass, leaning
against the trunk of her silent companion, who felt

each strand of her red hair the breeze blew onto it. *Was this made in our land or the queen's?* With dreamy eyes, she stared past the blue heaven.

So many books to study, she thought.

"Sadie!" the stranger shouted.

"Oh…hi, Mary. My mind was elsewhere."

"Either you were meditating or in another realm."

"Funny you should say that because—"

"So anyway," Mary interrupted, "I just heard the craziest thing!"

Crazy; now there is a word that would be stamped on her forehead if she had a chance to talk about her story—post-certified. Sadie turned her head back to the sky, this time *willingly* ignoring her colleague, shutting her eyes to the darkness. The very same that played transporter.

Express to ruin.

Darkness. No calm. Storms and heat. Elements gave rise to contrasting sounds. Barriers introduced. Delicate hands roved over them to discern. No slate. No stylus. No raised bumps to translate. They tried to push outward for air or light. No such luck.

Welcome to panic. *Panikos.*

The animal's mind knew it was trapped. Pores wept silently. Oily. Glands working overtime. Cry us a song. Weeping lachrymal pair. A muscle of life, swelling with love, awaiting the coup de grâce of casualty; *The White.* All ends lead to light. Wet were the cheeks, but soft eyes saw true as sky blue flames conjured before them. A shy tongue took up courage and mimicked the emblazoned words aloud: "Seek the *composer* in the *Menes Spire* or die in this—"

Greenstone split the words in a jagged formation. Soggy, wrapped, bitter, and crude. This ax was gluttonous.

Bits of solid darkness brushed against the face. Ravenous tool; it finally freed itself to allow a slit of light to enter, and with it came a leering eye.

"A young maid in the closet?!" a baritone voice exclaimed, unable to keep down his excitement, "The *Primes* bestow me treasure worthy of many ruby blades!" Large, smelly, and oafish summed up what had now torn off the door from its hinges.

The darkness swelled into a small cottage. Feverish shades; drunk flames; insurrection. The giant idiot of a man licked the corners of his mouth. Staring at his prey without so much as showing signs of blinking, only to ask, "How's about a kiss for your rescuer, freckled maid?" Exercising a smile revealed his chapped lips weeping red.

Sadie shrieked, like a woman of the fairy mound, quickly skittering through his legs, trying to evade his calloused hands. Fortunately, the door to the outside was already open for a quick getaway. Heaven knows what he had planned for her.

"Come back, my love," he began while retrieving his impure tool. "I only wish to be your tipping bull!"

And *now* she knows.

Jumbled, all-too-familiar sounds of noise all made sense now.

This was a raid. And no one was spared.

A simple village of timber hay and heifers, razed by marauders with boisterous laughs, greeted by simple folk with terror clogging their throats.

How did I get here?!

She was in the center of the fray, trying desperately to avoid capture. Possibly worse. Men on horses sprinted through the unleveled soil while dragging the young through it. Thick bondages of rope bound their ankles. Cutting in the skin just right. Making the flesh docile. Torn clothes. Their backs, rawly exposed, by sharp rocks and upended roots that tattooed their skins like wet parchment. The fair sex and their little lambs were segregated into dense wooden cages. Wrought iron clasping both neck and wrists. Resigned. Blubbering children. Baying women. Only a few able-bodied adolescents tried to play defense with offense—immediate failure.

The ferocity of the marauders was akin to the various animal skins that adorned them. Each personified predatory behavior to the once-breathing beast that armored their skin.

One beast—well alive—trampled through with no remorse for any one person's safety. Ally or not. It could not be characterized as anything normal, but fantastical. The same could be said of its rider: pale skin, reptilian yellow eyes, and large tusks protruding from the cheeks covered with bronze rings. His eyes surveyed the chaos until they met Sadie's.

One brief moment of silence.

A doe to headlights. The beast rider took advantage of the situation, initiating the charge. Meters. Feet. *It's over*, she thought.

Her body was pulled off the ground, not by her own feet, but by a gargantuan hand.

"You're mine now, love." It was the giant oaf again. "Now…about that kiss." His dim-witted sense finally noticed the pale rider, but much too late to evade collision.

Unable to contract his arms fast enough into a suitable defensive position, his body absorbed the full impact of the charge. Sadie was only blown back a few feet away, where she toppled over crates. They outpour clucks. She sat there on the ground to hold her head from the disorienting event. Spinning images. Where did they keep the acetaminophen?!

"You're coming with me, red!" a marauder shouted at her, beginning to unsheathe his crusty dagger.

Sadie quickly looked side to side to find something—anything—to use. The outpour wants attention. Gambling on them. They were the only things at her disposal. Silly as it was.

"Put up a fight and I'll—" his intimidating tactics were disrupted. A fat hen launched to the face. Its barrage of pecking created the proper diversion for Sadie to make her exhilarating escape. Silly as it was.

The damage from the pale rider was profound. No giant oaf to be seen, but the rider…atop that battered hill. Still, his eyes caught Sadie's through the fire and debris easily this night. Another advance is in the works. To prove his serious intention, he removed the war banner from his back and directed it in her direction. Even she knew she could not win this game of joust.

When will this nightmare end?!

Not too far off, rage echoed across the fields. The giant oaf stumbled about. Swinging. Human typhoon. That ax had little regard for who it might connect with. A young boy, no more than eight, was on the same path as the enraged oaf. Greenstone neared the child's small frame. Sadie screamed for the child to run away, forgetting her own life would soon be forfeited by her already charging opponent.

HIC JACET SEPULTUS: The girl with blazing hair.

Stumbling. Creaking. An elderly man came between the child and the wild brute. "Please, not my grandson," he begged. "Have mercy on him!" The giant raised his ax steadily. His eyes narrowed in on the feeble elder, and he spoke his poison.

"THEN *YOU!*"

God, Almighty, where are you?!

The old man quickly embraced the boy. His back was carved through with no effort. Slow. That's how it felt to her: time. Watching it unfold. Murder. Forever etched. Forever burned in. The old man: forever dead. The giant oaf—no, slayer—resumed his march towards Sadie. The pounding earth caught his attention. He bolted likewise towards her.

"She's mine, you cur!"

Tears wept onto the old man's still-warm skin; another child losing a loved one to banditry.

Sick. That's how she felt. Cold, disoriented, and wheezing. To see murder in real-time. To feel the heart overclocking. A horrible sensation of shaking hands—uncontrollable. She has seen the graves, the cemeteries, the war pictures, and the open caskets, and read the stories, so why was this any different? She wanted to raise her fists, skybound, like antennae, as if sudden inspiration took hold, ready to evoke doleful melodies.

Memories. The flashing of life before the eyes. A little girl: teased and bullied by her peers, ran home, doing her best not to whimper as the tears flowed. Ashamed to be seen in such a state.

Mother consoled her until the father came home. The little girl stayed strong and true to her mother, but when she saw Papa…endless rivers. Father was her hero.

Always was. Always will be.

Stiff upper lip. That's the kind of man he was. He restrained himself from coddling her. He had his comfort tactics: stories. On the fly, making up his own fables, but she always loved the historical one about the "Fortress People." At least, to her, it was non-fiction by the way he declared it. Mighty people, that dad said, they descended from. She wanted to be mighty too. It always ended the same: they disappeared without a trace. Nonetheless, he made up his own ending, saying they stumbled upon a portal, leading them to "another realm."

"Where is it, Papa?"

"Who's to say, my love, but if I were a betting man, I'd pay top dollar on *Sueno's Stone.*"

"When can we visit it?!"

"I got some money on the side. Maybe we'll make a trip on one of your birthdays. All three of us could use a bit of escape to the countryside. Always good to see where you come from," he replied. "You'll be strong for me, won't you? Pay no mind to those dingbats."

She nodded excitedly, forgetting all her troubles.

"That's a good girl. When your dear old mum isn't around, I'll show you a couple of moves that'll knock the wind out of those pests. And keep the boys in their place."

She agreed, going in for a hug. He never denied a hug from his daughter. That would be too cruel. Those moments, like seeing the beauty of the sun rising over the horizon.

I want to see those bright rays. Over the treelines, the mountains, the swamps, and the houses. The sun…will it rise again?

Golden lights bloomed from the soil, glowing brighter and brighter. The small bubbles of luminescence surrounded the old man's body, entering his wound. A miracle was being performed.

"Heel!" shouted the pale rider, forcing an immediate stop. The giant oaf, however, did not cease his pursuit. "Fool! You were so close. Now it is I who claims victory!"

Famous last words.

From gold and passion did each light sprout forth from the soil of malnourished history to take hold of their designated mark. The cacophony of sinister laughs transitioned into dull groans and pained moans. Bright, solid beams erected throughout the village, bringing mayhem to those that wrought it.

A hit to the gut, a blast to the chest, a vision to behold.

Some were rooted into the ground, others held in oblong positions; the last bit of supernaturals contorted around their chosen marauder. To struggle meant only to cause a tighter binding.

All had ceased to resist.

The pale rider was too far off for capture. His piercing eyes of sick yellow scouted with such fervor, trying to find who was responsible. Impatient. Angst in his lungs. Cold vapors lifted to their cousins. Still, nothing new to his vision. Only that Sadie had not changed the direction of hers since the illuminated beams came into play.

Her fraught eyes were replaced with awe.

The rider pulled the reins of the great beast, moving around a bend of the hill, anticipating a better visual. His neural network analyzes who was responsible: *A member of the F&C? No, they relied mainly on the physical. C&P? No university is established remotely within these parts. Sanshan warrior? Far too costly to bother with these peons. The Ternion Pilgrims? Never face the nomadic heroes alone; report sightings of them immediately back to the Prime Aeolid. The highest of priorities is to capture one of the Barangda—especially one with the birthmark of the leader. Just who, or what, could cast these miracles?!*

"Too close; all better now," a male said, examining the figure. "Does it still hurt?" A body, familiarizing itself with frigid stillness, began to rise in temperature.

The youth gasped, clutching his hands onto the familiar tunic. Warmth—met by life—greeted by the soul.

The elder rose; body made whole.

"By the composition of red salt...I am alive again!" The grandfather shouted.

Red salt? What a strange thing to say, Sadie thought, *but he's alive! There's just no way!*

Her linear thoughts were interrupted, and the very foundation quaked beneath her feet. The eyes found new interests: reinforcements, under the banner of banditry, stampeded into the village. They rode horses that seemed stricken with rabies. Wood and stone prepared for leveling. Sadie's new mask was replaced by the old one.

The young resurrector held out an open scroll. A small, indistinguishable figure leaped onto his shoulder, where a soft glow of light started to appear. And, for a split moment, her eyes—or maybe it was mind tricks—saw what looked like an apparition behind the reanimator.

Golden.

Shrouded.

Veiled.

A woman like no other.

Another glow. This one came from the young male's right wrist. Something about it amplified the scroll. The sound of a whirring gear. A small sun, born from parchment. Spheres echoed around it, booming with great luminosity. It defied gravity. Levitation within the hands of the caster.

Sadie looked on in amazement.

As did the lone pale rider from afar.

Discreet gestures of the caster's fingers flicked about. Each echoed sphere of light blew into the wind, only to disappear into the ground. The wild savages were too erratic—or maybe too well composed—for hesitation.

Some had already removed their banners to impale the young caster. Others simply revealed large barbed gauntlets to gut him from belly to sternum. Still, he remained focused without faltering. This was not his first time among the dead and sticky red mud.

The pungent odor of both riders and beasts became too much for Sadie to bear. Her legs buckled suddenly. Circulation in the quads, down to the calves, slowed to a crawl. A stabbing sensation rebuked her right to walk.

Acrimonious liquids of slobber flew back on the cheeks of the beast. Its pupils were incredibly focused.

Personified pin needles.

Maws ready to swallow whole.

The attack was made.

No longer malleable beams, but hands of gold giants. Wave upon wave of amplified power clutched easily both rider and beast. A single determined wave; a single fell swoop. But, somehow, a single shadow remained unopposed.

Appearing without notice or sound came the giant-once-upon slayer before Sadie. His rage fixated on her. Enough *was* enough, as his crimson-stained extension pulled back to assault its new intended target. Too dumbstruck to register the impending violence. Stasis invaded the nerves.

Frozen vertebrae.

Curious eyes.

Idiocy all around.

The ax dropped to cleave *only* disturbed earth. Its many fractured cracks yearned to anoint the nubile's dome; at the very least, it wished to kiss her brow.

Giant for a Giant: the hunter, hunted by auspicious gold. Raised high like a toast to the many that sat upon the celestial pantheon. He struggled. Roaring, unable to break the fingers, and the grip became much like a vice. From rage to whimpers, he called out ineffectually for help, "Primes! Please!" The young caster remained unmoved by the pleas, and now, peeled eyes simply became lifeless whites.

His final struggle admitted defeat.

The shaggy crown bowed.

The caster turned to her.

A young, distraught teenager faced the frontal features of an unknown. Shades of black, gold, and sepia. This *person* no longer resembled a resurrector. Fires raged still. Buildings burned down. Before her door, an animal, with gold to beck and call—surely he has swallowed the sun and made it his slave.

I'll take the giant over this, she thought before passing out.

Chapter 1

†

Balance

There is nothing like fluffed pillows, clean sheets, and soft blankets to ease stressed minds to sleep. Dreams? If they weren't *too* excitable, then the door to the gray den is left unlocked. Optional—sometimes forced—supplement of the subconscious.

Now a mattress, at the very least, must be plucked from the clouds: softer than any linen. It must be as smooth as a cat's paw, the wool on a lamb's back, or the small cotton puff of a rabbit's rear, but it *must* be soft!

Pat! Pat! Pat! Thump! Thump! Thump!

Soft. Wait. Wait a minute. What is this "soft" sensation patting me on the head? Sadie thought.

It made spattering sounds on her skin…and it is *not* fur!

Her eyes struggled to open, and the ears picked up tiny stamping movements by her head. Vision was blurred but coming into focus, and with it, a small figure overlooking her. Strength returned eagerly to one arm to raise the torso. The body shook off the small coma. Sight regained fortitude. Two visions.

Face to face, but this small figure had no orbs of its own.

Woodland creatures, near and far, heard her shrieks of terror. It shrieked with her but made no sound. Mimicry. Her hands gained enough sentience to push her away—*very* far away—from this otherworldly homunculus. Mud and grass were flung about. The wretched thing became nearly lost under a castle of dirt. Its size was considerably insignificant compared to hers, for she was the giant in this scenario.

"You'll wake up the dead with all that screaming," the young caster said, approaching her. Sadie refused to look away from the creature trying to escape her frantic moment, and if this wasn't bizarre enough, it turned itself into a ball. Rolling towards the caster and up his body before going back to its original state. Despite the lack of eyes, its face was filled with emotional worry.

A worry that gleamed over the caster's shoulder.

Sadie released her focus to move on to the next, taken aback by the new vision. *This can't be the same person who cast all that magic, could it? Is this the lion that devoured the sun?* For he was too handsome to emit such a foreboding aura. But killers come in all forms…

"Got a name, screamer?" he asked.

"…Sadie."

"Right then, the name's *Milos*; you've already met my traveling companion *Enzu* here," he said, pointing to the bejeweled clay creature. "Your clothes are too refined for this village; uncommon for traveling merchants. So I have to ask: Do you reside within a *mark*, or beyond the *pelagic*? Do you have a composer, *aristarch*, or both where you're from?"

Magister? Doubt you're part of the *Naturals*."

She could not make heads or tails of what on earth he was going on about. Mark? Who were these probable musicians? What was that unholy-looking *thing* latching onto his body?! More importantly, how did she arrive here? Earth—let alone New Hampshire—must be a universe away from here! All she could do was stutter, and before he had a chance to say more, several hooded riders drew near. Dark leathers, reds and tans, cured and distressed long coats. Their mounts resembled an amalgamation of horses bred with bulls. *This is not Earth,* Sadie thought.

The one to lead held a red banner and tossed Milos a sealed scroll.

"Do I not get my reward?" he asked. It sounded harmless, but anyone could feel his deep-seated annoyance.

Another rider pulled alongside Milos with a spare mount. An immediate frown from him, and he began to smack the scroll repeatedly on his palm like a miniature bat.

"Before you ask: no, I won't go. Does he intend to berate me with every invitation he bestows?"

The lead withdrew their hood to reveal a tanned woman with short black hair that was partially shaven. Her frown stifled his.

"Do you object to his honor?" she said sternly.

"Are you completely daft, woman?!" he yelled out, arms in the air. "He still calls me a thief after I gave up that profession long ago! All with a smile on his face, no less!"

She looked over to the satchel on his back and asked, "Did you return the Cerulean lot? If so, I am positive he will disassociate you with thievery."

Milos

Sadie looked to see the color of his face changing to a deathlike pallor. His eyes flashed to the ground, blinking uncontrollably, "...You know I can't." Fear trembled off his tongue, "It would mean my execution, and her *Ornate Alephim* have not given up the hunt. I can feel their elemental teeth nipping at my heels whenever I use one of her scrolls. Should I accidentally rip one..."

"And yet, you confuse our composer for a tyrant. Despite offering sanctuary? Now who's daft?"

This argument continued without showing any signs of letting up. Irrelevant. Unwanted. Sadie fell deeper into the category of unseen. Any third wheel passing along would have more renown than her. Her stomach demanded attention with a roar loud enough to attract the arguing duo.

Dirty bastard.

The lead cocked her head to the side to observe Sadie with a raised brow. "I thought your heart was *lost at sea*? Is the pelagic too deep for you now to continue your effort?" she said to Milos.

More bickering.

"It's not like that," he replied, turning to Sadie. "She was caught in the skirmish. Right now, you caught me in the middle of questioning her whereabouts."

"Unfamiliar apparel on her, and red hair to top it off. Peculiar. Might be a rogue from Somdir."

As if you were one to talk, Sadie thought, *and I'm no damn rogue, rude tomboy.*

"Well, you know how vast in knowledge our beloved composer is," she continued, "I'm sure he can figure it out— lest she be uncooperative."

"I'm no one's trophy to claim, and not to be scrutinized with judgment!" Sadie blurted out.

Mortified by her bluntness.

An internal panic settled in.

You idiot, did you not just witness—more so, standing in the middle of—fantasy and fiction?! Now you have the gall to act brave towards spellcasters with strange familiars and warriors riding strange beasts?! You deserve everything you get!

"Fire bellows from her lungs," the lead said, approaching Sadie. "I respect that. *Slightly.* Do you have a name? Or should I just call you by the color of your hair?"

Milos began to slowly creep away with Enzu as Sadie gave her reply. "*Aruna* is mine," she exchanged back, "One moment, Sadie."

The swarthy lead quickly pivoted and brandished a pair of blunderbuss pistols hidden under her sleeves. They expelled a ferocity of red energy towards Milos's feet. After the smoke had cleared, nothing but small craters were left in the ground.

"You killed them!" Sadie screamed.

Aruna sighed and concealed the weapons again. "If it was that easy, I'd have taken over *Lusura* or *Klaring* under my banner—wretched monsters."

"If you were to prefer constant death marches or having those disgusting *Vermis* under your flag, then sure, why not?" Milos said from behind Sadie. She jolted to one side from his sudden appearance and screeched as Enzu leaped on top of her head.

A heart attack is inbound for the young teen.

"I've never seen him become so fond of new acquaintances since I introduced him to *Kosey*," Milos nonchalantly said while walking past the frantic girl.

"To which I am glad he does not travel with you during these unusual times," Aruna replied, "So…are you willing to meet with him? Or shall I test the limits of that damnable manacle of yours?"

His belly felt the end of one of the pistols pressing in. "Never one to be civil, eh? Fine...let's go then. Any clue if he's whipped up a fresh batch of cakes?" he asked, holding his hands up.

Milos mounted one of the large beasts. An expression of indifference. Aruna still held one gun on him with a smirk. She turned her attention back to Sadie to see her still frantically flailing her arms about, trying to get the playful clay man off her head.

Only *he* could hear her stifled laugh.

An instant flash of light from atop the beast emitted. Milos now stood behind Aruna, playfully placing his chin on her shoulder, returning her smirk, "Oh! I never thought the day I'd see the reserved Aruna produce emotion. How engrossing!"

She was wide-eyed. Fury in her veins, and, looking close enough, a heated blush on her cheeks. Another pivot, with guns drawn, but another instant flash, and he was back on the beast once more. "Alright! No need to get so testy. My word, no wonder you and that shrewd ogre get along so well," he exclaimed with a sly grin.

"Sadie! To me, *now*!" Aruna barked.

The young girl stopped her relentless air thrashing immediately. Aruna's voice became as commanding as any emperor's.

"Must I?" Sadie asked in a timid tone.

Milos pointed out to the now shackled bandits, asking if she'd prefer taking her chances going solo in these lands with things much worse than these men. He continued about erratic goblins, the rat nation known as Vermis, and giant tusked monstrosities parading around the air as culinary disciplinarians. The latter seemed *too* descriptive since Aruna barked at him to take back the insensitive comment.

He. Did. Not.

Enzu rubbed Sadie affectionately to try to calm her. A small shock in her spine from the unusual creature, but she went along with them.

What other choice do I have? I'm a stranger in a strange land, and all I have are my wits. Risk is my only move. Home is my journey. Reality is my priority.

She rode with Aruna. Her curiosity kept asking her to ask *the* question: How did Milos survive her assault? "Teleportation from that bothersome bracelet of his," she replied. Sadie looked over to see the said object but could only see it briefly whenever he lifted his arms. A good spot to hide under those long-strapped sleeves. However, she just *now* noticed he wore an identical coat that Aruna and her other riders wore, albeit much lighter in color. Milos briefly squeezed his ankles and lower legs to get the beast to move forward. Aruna followed while the other riders stayed behind to chain-link the bandits as prisoners.

New labor for the realm.

Far off on the hill, still, the pale rider watched as Sadie was being escorted by Aruna and Milos. He spat a large glob onto the ground with disdain. Pensively, he began to rub the rings around his tusks. Although it wasn't The Ternion Pilgrims, he was apprehensive about confronting them—for the time being. A full report would be made instead to the Prime Aeolid.

The tyrannical ruler of Lusura.

Chapter 2

†

Chromatherapy

ountains at almost every turn. There were some speckled forests throughout, but the hills reminded her of home. Nothing like a good hike amongst the giants of the *Presidential Range*, like Washington and Jefferson, or even…

"Clay," Sadie said to herself. Aruna asked her what she was mumbling about. The young girl started to talk about certain mountains where she resided. One of which was named after Henry Clay and his given title.

"The Great Compromiser? I've never heard of such a man in these parts," Aruna replied.

Milos turned his head back to them, "Maybe she's mixing this fellow with *Grand M*? Now there's a champion I won't tangle with again, even to spar. I learned my lesson once."

Sadie tried to explain her home, but the United States was as foreign to them as she was to their world.

Milos slowed his mount back to Aruna, whispering, "She speaks of places too homely. Don't you think it would be wise if she didn't see 'you-know-who?' She might die at the sight of him."

Aruna ignored him, thinking, *He's so dramatic.*

Enzu's gems glowed, shapeshifting into a miniature statue on Sadie's shoulder. "Oh no, please, Enzu, any other president named on the Presidential Range other than Franklin Pierce; awful, just…awful human being."

Like a bolt of lightning striking her, she realized Enzu had transformed into the statue based in Concord. A statue in her world only. She tried asking how it knew of people from her universe, forgetting that the little creature was voiceless.

Milos looked surprised by his transformation.

"I'll be, I guess, the girl is from beyond the veil."

He pointed out to her that Enzu can read images in a person's mind so long as they appear lucid.

"My liege will definitely want to speak to her now," Aruna said.

Sadie asked her about the ruler, but Milos insisted she would surely die at the sight of him. He described him as a demon. An overgrown stomach. A quadruped who wears a silly puffed hat, a monolith of fire and brimstone!

Shots fired.

More blinks of teleportation. His ride became agitated.

"Careful there! We wouldn't want to injure this fine *jumart*," he said with a chuckle before noticing Enzu jumping onto his face. His hands tried to unlatch the clay man; head shaking profusely in a comical manner.

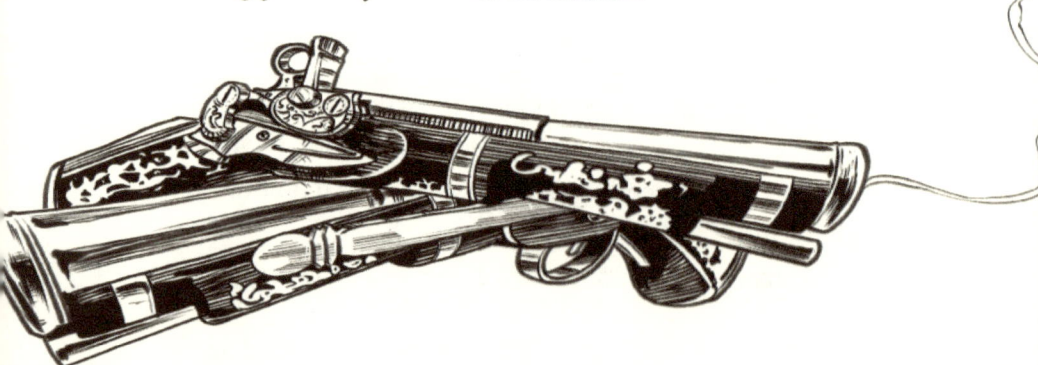

"Serves you right," Aruna said.

Sadie giggled but stopped abruptly when she noticed they came at the base of a massive broad mountain with gentle slopes. Aruna warned Sadie to hold her tight to avoid falling. Her eyes noticed gas expelling through the pitted cavities of the rocky terrain. She could not distinguish the many compounds of smells wafting below her, except that of sulfur.

"The horses seem okay," Sadie said.

Milos withdrew from one of his pockets an egg and cracked it over the surface. The yolk and whites sizzled, deep-fried, and blackened into ash. More noxious air into her nostrils. "Not horses exactly. Born from a bull and mare. They're natives of this land, and so their hooves—and much of their bodies—are immune to heat and flame. It also helps that there are no nerve endings on those cloven feet of theirs," he replied, "Can we get this over with before my last stick of butter melts over my remaining rusk?"

Aruna kicked her heels into the beast, causing a sprint up the slope. Sadie held on as tight as she could, praying she would not jettison onto the dangerous terrain. Gravity felt heavier the further they soared up the slope. Somehow, these slightly slanted hills betrayed ignorant eyes. The steepest of roller coasters couldn't hold a candle to these hills.

She tried to yell out something of great importance to Aruna, but the sheer speed of the animal kept interrupting her speech. The thought of biting down on her tongue was a sure thing, but it still needed to be said.

"A-Aruna! I can't—" Sadie shouted before her hands somehow unclasped themselves around the rider's waist. Her petite body propelled in reverse. Shrill screams expelling forth. Aruna tried to reach her hand with the banner, but it was too far to reach her.

Milos sucked his teeth. A quick flash to Sadie in mid-flight.

"Something tells me I'm going to be saving you far too many times," he said, grabbing her body to teleport back onto the jumart. She was at the forefront now. "I'll let you take the reins. You needn't worry about flying back this time."

A small blush on her freckled face.

They reached the top of the flat peak with Aruna trotting over to them, "My, aren't we the hero."

"You knew this would happen, so why didn't you let her in the front?!" Milos barked.

"A test," she responded nonchalantly.

Sadie and Milos were not impressed by this rebuttal. Enzu plopped on Sadie's shoulder, trying to cheer her up with fanciful movements. Fortunately, it calmed her. Still, would there be more of these dangerous tests? What purpose did they serve?

Aruna pointed out to the distance a grand structure. Large billows of smoke came out of its top, similar to a volcano. Sadie pointed out the resemblance, adding on about how its appearance seemed like it was carved from one.

"That's because it is," Aruna stated.

"And very much active," Milos added.

This was their destination.

"Welcome to *Udalann*, and that there is the Capital: *Raksag-Ni's Mark*," Aruna said aloud, "We shall meet with its leader: *Birati Milu*."

Everything was made of either stone or clay. Accents of colors ruminate throughout each slab of cut labor. No bland designs. No sextant abandoned. Architecture. True and honest to the artisan's soul. Held in the highest regard. This was a renaissance!

The residential district's houses donned red material. Mars is personified. Fortifications, as did the barracks, had brassy to golden-yellow components. Buildings, reminiscent of houses of worship, were glassy black with attractively marbled silver and gold veins. The splattered hues of reds and yellows adorn the marketplace. The commonality of each zone is blessed with dimension stones of impeccable trims, cuts, and shapes of a variety of sizes.

"Let me get half a dozen unwashed eggs," Milos asked a trader.

"That'll be one *floriah* and thirty *florhils*."

Sadie looked at him, bewildered—really, utterly disgusted—she had to ask why he would even consider buying a foul product.

"Prim and proper are we?" he replied, bending a bit down to her, "You go on long trips with no rivers to fish, forests to hunt, or even fertile lands to pluck some fruits, and you tell me how that works out for you."

He exchanged a few bits of fossilized coins for the eggs. Transactions continued on as he started to explain the significance of leaving the protective coating on the shell. Left intact, this helped to prevent air and bacteria from entering the egg, extending its lifespan up to six months. Left in his possession, they never made it that far. Too many cracks. Too many leaks. So much laundry to do!

"And just like your world—don't lie—currency *is* king," he said, holding one of the coins to her face. It had a delicate blue color to it with a strange symbol almost resembling a zodiac sign. More questions from her. She might as well grow some cat ears and a great bushy tail. He was becoming exhausted with her game of curiosity but decided it was a necessity on the off chance she was in their world to stay.

"This coin is known as a *geodi*, the most common currency we have below the deathlands of Lusura, aka *Blood North*. Every country has its own name for it, including the lower denomination, strictly for cultural purposes. Luckily the value is exact wherever they're accepted. This particular one is made up of odontolite, the lowest of values. It is bone turquoise. Soft and fragile material that is difficult to cut and polish. They're the most common to find, *especially* up north, with the apatite and vivianite leaching into the countless unmarked graves. They can't be found naturally in geode stones, the *'Ministry of Commerce and Industry,'* or *MCI*, acknowledges them as having *some* value for coinage— very rarely does a beggar go hungry."

His informative explanation went on about how every land was consecrated with valuable geodes before any race's recorded history.

Sadie & Enzu

However, cracking the spherical hollow stones to extract the minerals for monetary use was no easy task. Each broken stone produced violent shots of energy that tracked whoever cracked them open. Fatalities from this action were common among the starved and irrational. Only certain races, two exactly, had an innate ability to extract the resources peacefully for distribution. They were the *Mairu* and the Barangda, otherwise known as the war-loving giant ogres of Lusura and the talented beasts of *Kotsudas*.

And they hated each other.

Sadie asked what race Enzu belonged to since he was practically covered in gemstones, and he was neither ogre nor beast.

"The little troublemaker is known as an *Essent*, or 'conjured being,' but he's a unique one since no other Essent has been seen with enchanted jewels so far. Those born with the ability to conjure them are known as *Breyjan*," he replied.

"So, where did he come from?" she pressed.

He was quiet. No hints of telling on the small being's native whereabouts. His eyes started to dart across the ground just like before when asked about the "Cerulean lot."

Aruna had finished chomping on several figs before answering, "*Celanjung*, where Mister 'I'm not a thief' is afraid to return to." She described Celanjung as a country of rich resources, forests brimming with bounty, and all other sorts of wonders. Sadie knew better; it was too good to be true, stating it must come with a caveat.

"None may enter the country unless personally invited by the prevailing queen. Those who try to enter by sea, land, air, or even teleportation will face her loyal army's wrath. Her personal royal guard, known as the Ornate Alephim, never rests. They're without appetite, and they pursue tirelessly," Aruna continued, seeing the fear build up in Sadie's eyes, "Probably shouldn't tell you about those *Vicara* that overwatch her lands."

Again, Enzu tried to calm Sadie down.

This world of fantasy—mimetic to the Middle Ages—came off as more dangerous compared to Earth's WMDs. Those young-adult fictional books of sword and sorcery were all too puffed up with cute talking animals or gleefully dancing elves in Renaissance clothing.

It's all a damn lie!

But fantasy *is* the greatest lie.

Or was that the politician's tongue?

A party of four finally arrived. *Clay? Concrete? No, something new, something stronger about this structure,* Sadie thought. Entering the castle, Sadie's fears quickly subsided when she began to sniff the aromatic smells in the large halls. Mixtures of sweet and savory flavors. Her senses were enslaved. She almost felt like her body would lift up.

Too many Saturday morning cartoons consumed.

Milos provided some sustenance previously: rusk, or what she decided to call "teeth-breaking biscuits," but it wasn't enough. Considering how he went on about his dirty eggs, it would seem his stomach was well-equipped to handle long periods without food compared to hers. Aruna's was just the same as a few figs were enough to keep her well alert.

Nomadic life would not find her if she had any say in the matter.

"What in the name of all things holy are these?!" Sadie said.

Gigantasophobia never felt so real to her. The guards wore daunting pieces of plate armor adorned with pisolite patterns. Tall as any fully grown grizzly. Even their breathing was enough to make bears tremble. Strangely, though, none had swords, halberds, axes, or any sort of weapon on them, just banners in their hands, much like Aruna—when the guns weren't drawn. Yet hers was distinctly more decorated compared to theirs. Sadie also noticed their hollow buckles at the waist.

"Deserters of the Lusuran army. They once had carved lithophysae seal stones in the shape of a shell to show allegiance to the new king, or should I say Usurper," Milos whispered to her.

A serious tone about this ruler. Images of *the* slanderer: *Diábolos*.

Two females approached Aruna to greet her. She pointed to Sadie, "Have her bathed and brought to the dinner hall." Milos pointed to himself, asking if they were going to prepare him one as well. "You can draw your own, wayward son, and don't even *think* about asking me to draw one for you, else it's the iron pits for you like the prisoners!"

Left in a huff.

"Eh, maybe one day, right Enzu?" Milos said. Nowhere in sight. Not long before he noticed the small creature still on Sadie's shoulder, waving to him as they were making their exit. "Traitor," he quipped, making his own leave.

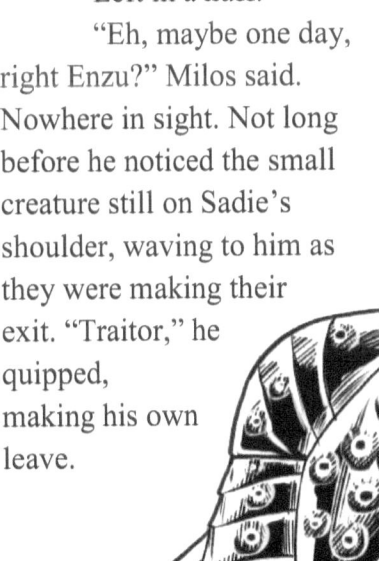

The two women asked Sadie their own game of "Twenty Questions." One asked her about her uniform. The other asked if she was from *Somdir*, a secretive country. A powerful country. Sadie was so overwhelmed by the influx of questions that she couldn't keep up with her answers. She needed this bath to clear the mind of impurities. And her uniform. Also her shoes and socks. Great, there was caked sediment in places she hadn't noticed until now.

Do they have a hot spring? And where's the toilet? Jesus, please tell me they have toilet paper!

But there it was: a small thermal spring.

One down, two to go.

They wanted to help undress her, but she quickly refused their help. Too soon for girls' night. No latent qualities either. They took their leave, but not before picking up Enzu.

He had a look of disappointment just like Milos.

He definitely is a boy, Sadie thought to herself before relaxing in the natural hot spring—a perfect 75 degrees.

A great degree of pleasure from sloughing off dead skin for new. Envious of all snakes who molt. Collapsing onto the bed, Milos remained motionless. Too many thoughts to align. Linear order looked impossible at this moment. In here remained an old friend: sadness. It welcomed him. *They* felt it. His uneasiness. So, they tried to help, in their own way.

Voices, transmitting into his mind.

Too many colors.

"Isn't it nice to be home?" A deep, sultry voice said.

"Maybe. I don't know, Aub," he replied.

"Do you need us, sir?" asked another.

"Always, Aqua. Everything feels caustic."

"Be free," a vicious one said, *"I'll trap your aggressors!"*

"Never one to be sweet. Eh, Mul?"

"You better eat REAL food this time," one ordered.

"Only because you said so, Col."

A little golden apparition, pretending to be a rabbit, hopped around the bed frame. A mute of benevolence. She stared at him. Smiling under her veil. It was his favorite smile next to the one in the sea. He missed *that* one something awful. Too long away from his first. The little golden rabbit saw his distress. Tilting her head, she placed her hands, in a folded fashion, underneath her cheek.

"Yeah, I do need to sleep this off. Thank you, Gold."

And the voices stopped.

And the colors dispersed.

And all he wanted to do was fish.

And sleep.

His eyes drifted around the room; his old expanse. A place always welcoming him back to the fold. But it came with a banner he did not display as his own.

Hard knocks against the bedroom door. His heart skipped several beats. *Please, not now; I'm so tired.* He hoped it wasn't the lord of the castle wanting an audience to discuss old matters. Or a chance to scold him. A voice called out to him to permit entry: Aruna's.

"Decent as one can be," he answered.

She saw his lifeless posture, "Not so lively as you were earlier."

A sigh emitted that he tried to play off as a yawn. "I'm too tired for the dinner bell," he said. "Just leave me a plate over the fire or give it a heated bath or whatever pseudoscience all of you use here."

He rolled on his side and closed his eyes, feigning slumber, hoping she would take the hint of making a quiet exit. Enzu rolled over to Aruna. They stared at each other. An awkward brevity until he began to jump up and down. He wanted to be picked up and held, like a child. She willingly complied. The clay man nestled into her cheek. Milos opened just one eye to see the wholesome moment before going back to playing possum.

What kind of mother would she make?

"When Birati heard about the village raid, he was sure you would show yourself once he sent us out," Aruna started, "So sure, in fact, he knew you wouldn't have done it for the geodi. No casualties, no villagers missing, and more labor for the pits. Even with most of the land destroyed, it can be rebuilt without much effort. My men are testing for known deficiencies in the soil so we can help speed up refertilization. It's a good thing we have excess amounts of magnesium sulfate and potash for emergencies like this. Thank the Primes, we have arable land."

Milos rolled on his back. A belly laugh like no other. Condescending tears. His gut couldn't take any more from what he considered asinine small talk. This agitated Aruna.

"Good thing? A *good* thing?! Evidence points to you being the daft one!" More laughter. More tears. More patronizing. The bracelet went into overdrive as he blinked all around the room. Anger splits his mind. Serenity is excused from this table talk. Those *colors* wanted no part in this rhetoric. Not even the vicious berry.

"How is it that they had no defenses lined up? Not a *single* Essent to patrol the grounds to warn them? What's more is that somehow a band of mere marauders—IQs to room temperature—went unnoticed through these lands to sack a village of no distinguishing features," he ranted, teleporting right into her face, "You know, as well as I, this whole debacle was a setup. Did you not notice *Ashokara*'s personal scout on the hill?! Had the bird and bull emissaries shown up…" He slammed one arm against the wall behind her, their noses practically touching. "I bet you found a hefty satchel of *blood-knives* on your new laborers…"

A punch into the breadbasket sent him kneeling on the ground. The gasping was as violent as the hit. His lungs begged for air to flow back at a steady rate. Surely his atoms needed rearranging. Small hands. Deceiving hands. Tungsten hands. Well-trained vision.

A long, thin razor, made entirely of ruby, was placed under his chin to lift it up.

Aruna's eyes ignited into golden flames.

And the colors demanded reprisal.

"You mean one of these ready to spill out your life?" she said lightly, nicking him.

Animals, caged in their manuscripts, wanted out. Hungry to subjugate. The quiver rumbled. Enzu tried to calm her, but she completely ignored him. Ignoring Milo's portable case.

"You're quite slow with the bracelet when your emotions take hold. You should really take better control of that anger of yours when you're in my personal space," she continued, dropping the knife to the ground, "What would your sweet *Natalina* think if you couldn't control your emotions?"

He wiped the dribble from his mouth, composing himself.

"Everything you've said has validity to it, but it is not I who will answer any of them, but Birati, and you *will* attend dinner. It might surprise you, but he is overjoyed to know you are home after being away for so long."

Before she took her leave, Milos was able to string words again, "Peanut obsidian walls and amber wainscot. How eccentric."

She shook her head, tossing him his quiver of assorted scrolls, speaking with judgement, "I heard them. I don't know how you made them stronger, but keep them on a leash."

A gentle closing of the door, and only an injured man, with his companion and colors, left to repair his pride.

Stillness. If only.

Meats, fish, and confectionaries littered the robust dining table. Known and unknown. The centerpiece was an oversized salmon. Salt-baked. Four braziers guard the corners of the room. Pungent, sweet-smelling scents intermingled with the delicacies present.

There was one smell that invigorated the new guest. Its charm reels in the curious sniffer. Her delicate hands clasped over the onion bottle. Through the air, over the turbinates, inhabiting receptors, and prodding nerve cells, it was a wonder she didn't collapse from the exciting stimulation. More nosing. This was a necessity of the *highest* form! It invoked strong associations and memories of late Saturday nights with her mother and friends. The images came on strong: pinot, riesling, prosecco, and sweet, ever-so-loving sparkling rosé! All paired with charcuterie, the enjoyment of girls' night at home, and strawberry shortcake to end it all. This particular spirit was something otherworldly—Sadie had to have just a taste while no one was looking.

A taste of divinity!

Veto in play.

"The young lady would be wise to place the liquor down. You are far too young for something that strong," a booming baritone voice exclaimed behind her. The voice alone startled her, but how could she not notice a presence from behind? She heard no steps after all. The room was so well lit she didn't even see a shadow anywhere.

How could this be?

Sadie turned cautiously to prepare herself for *whoever* addressed their weighty personality.

This cannot be!

Doom. Glorious doom. Larger than the bannermen. The skin's color showed off what looked like the affliction of jaundice. Immense curved tusks protruded out of the cheeks. What taboo sex brought this humanoid to life?! The piercing white eyes had only a thin lining of dark color to show pupils existed in the sockets. That deep brow ridge steepened the art of intimidation. The regal clothing and a ruff around the neck. Her eyes could not look away from this talking monolith.

She began to hyperventilate. The pores started to weep again like when she was inside the closet. It came on too fast; too cold. Her body wanted to tremble and fall, but the gravitas of this unknown entity spellbound her in place— a small burst of frightened excitement took this opportunity. She always scoffed at practitioners of "crystal healing" when they talked about someone's aura, but in this plane, it truly meant something more than a "gentle breeze." Excitable capillaries bursting with excitement. *I never thought it possible.* Blood trickled down the philtrum, and her heart was on the verge of a seizure.

The giant's brows furrowed when he noticed how suddenly ill she looked. He gently placed one of his rings against her forehead. She could feel warmth in her body again. The sweat started to subside. Sadie felt the presence of home.

She was no longer afraid.

The giant removed his puffed hat and brought it to his chest, assuring her, "I did not mean to startle you. Would you please forgive this old man of the flame?" He genuflects but still overshadows her.

Her head nodded at its own volition. He smiled and erected. It was then she noticed two things in particular: the hat and that his feet did not touch the ground—he was levitating by some inches.

"Are you...Birati?" she meekly asked.

He placed his hat back on, chortling, "My reputation precedes me! Yes, I am Birati Milu, and I am at your service." He reached to the table to provide her with a burgundy napkin so that she could wipe herself clean.

"How did you do that with just a ring?" she asked.

"Of alchemy and chroma, welfare resides in my rings. I have heard from my right hand, Aruna, that you are from another realm. This sort of thing must be completely foreign to you," he responded. She could only describe it as a mere fantasy in her world. He scoffed at the word. "How illogical to think *Iberitus,* or your world, would be the only plane of existence; more's the pity."

Iberitus. Now she knew the world she had somehow become a guest to. Still, too surreal. Still, distraught. Still, no recollection of the "how." Underneath, a necklace, and its symbol, never felt more needed.

When I am afraid, I put my trust in you.

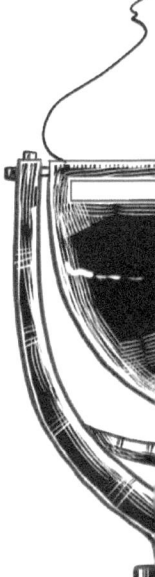

"Tardy as always, Milos, but Aruna, I expected more from you tonight," Birati curtly said to the duo making their entry into the hall. Aruna remained quiet, knowing not to rebut her lord.

Accountability was her best quality.

"Before you begin to 'expound,' she and I were discussing sensitive matters," Milos snapped back in the same brusque manner. Birati's eyes zeroed in on the scribe. Milos rolled his. Sadie felt the tension thicken, and they hadn't even sat down yet.

Does a fight break out before napkins are set onto the laps?

Milos quickly sat down before everyone. His elbows on the table. Eyes intoxicated, looking over the dishes in stupefied delight.

A prize fish for a prize winner!

"Redo yourself, Milos, and pull the young girl's chair before your bottom collapses on yours," Birati nearly shouted. Candles went out on this level…and some of the adjacent floors. Milos pinched the bridge of his brow. He stood up briskly, approached Sadie, and gently pulled her chair out. She appreciated the kind gesture, but it was very off-putting to see him act so childishly. A timid thank you as she sat down. Part of her was embarrassed. Milos cocked his head to Birati, but he wasn't looking at him. Instead, he saw the huge ogre pull out Aruna's seat for her.

Once she sat down, Birati looked sternly at Milos, "Do not do kindness for the attention of others' validation—*now* you may sit."

Four at the table: Aruna and Milos side by side in the center. Birati at one end and Sadie on the other. His guest of honor, as he described. The other side contained two rolling carts with smaller braziers, keeping the contents atop warm with trays beneath to catch the ash.

One of the corner braziers was abruptly extinguished.

On-the-spot. No warning. This immediately caught the attention of Birati. Despite his large size, whatever power that surrounded him gave him great speed through the air. A finger prodding the center of the container. Cold, wet, a sampling on the tongue. A small cloud puff was discharged upon tasting. Crystals of ice slivered on the buds.

"Nucleation…" Birati whispered to himself.

"The food is going to get cold; can we just start already?" Milos said.

"My food *never* gets cold," Birati responded, only to whisper after, "Unless an outside force meddled with it."

Unscrupulous Essent.

He hovered his hand over a nearby cresset to manipulate the fire. A thick stream of flame spiraled downward back into the container, and the brazier relit again. The lighting in the room increased. Like his temperament. He prompted them to eat before him—urgent business to attend to. Abandoning his guests.

"Quick! Eat as much as you can before he gets back!" Milos blurted out to Sadie.

"There's plenty to eat. So why rush your insides to a painful extension?" Aruna asked. Milos pointed to Enzu— while stuffing his face—to make a certain shape. The little clay man turned into a chomping mouth with legs. It waddled around the table pretending to eat everything. Milos burst out laughing. Bits of food ejecting. "Don't compare his old ways of overindulgence to his latest reforms," she snapped back. "You are not too far off yourself, indulger."

It was true; despite his lean frame, he ate ravenously.

"Been too long since I've had trout, and that!" he replied, pointing to the centerpiece. Many plates went untouched by him except fish-related ones.

"Seafood a preference?" Sadie asked him.

He described it as his go-to superfood. Moans of pleasure with each bite. He couldn't get enough of the stuff!

Then, an old memory returned: tusks and silver hair, yelling at him, "You want to be fat like a pig?! Then keep eating like one! Eat consciously! It didn't die for you to vomit back up! I'll turn you into a dog and have you lap it up! We never waste food!"

Then he stifled a tear back.

The fork drops, and hands overshadow the eyes.

"By the composition, how I miss her..." his voice trailed.

"Who?" Sadie asked, showing deep concern at this quick twist. He kept quiet. His interest in food no longer appeased him. He leaned back, staring blankly at the ceiling, lost in thought.

Old memories come back to haunt. Enzu rolled over, hopping onto Milos's chest, performing a small hug. "My first love—not intimately. I lost her to the North," he whispered. Aruna walked over to pour that strong liquor— that Sadie almost imbibed—into his chalice. "You'd do best to remember her sacrifice," she said. His appetite slowly came back. Hypertension eases off. Muscles in the jaw relaxed.

Welcoming a modest consumer.

Sadie tried being slick, "Think I can have a quick taste of whatever's in that bottle?" Aruna paused, *almost* saying no, but she had sly plans of her own. Another glass was filled for the young girl. Overflowing. Then she poured her own.

"Why not, realm-traveler?" Aruna responded, clinking cups, and away the liquids went. Sadie's eyes opened wide with delight, asking for another. Drink chaser. She will forget modesty. Misunderstand temperance. Inflammation will humble Sadie. Or impoverish her. Transforming the uniform into rags. With nothing but holes in her pockets. Emptiness in her bowels. Reluctantly eating discarded handouts of grain…bestrewn with weevils.

What's the harm in another cup?

Dereliction of self-governance.

"I wouldn't recommend it," Milos warned her.

Aruna told the young girl to pay him no mind. She poured her another. Another delicious gulping down the throat. And, again, another poured. *Heaven above! This is a gift from God!* Possessed by some corrupt misfit, Aruna kept pouring the fancy "baptismal aqua vitae."

Carouse for Alba! Caledonia! Scotland!

Sadie flew up from her seat, chalice in the air, attempting to propose a toast, but she was cursed with those insufferable involuntary contractions: the hiccups.

"Look what you've done to the poor lass. She's deep in her cups," Milos said to Aruna. Sadie tried hushing Milos, saying her heritage made her hardy—alcohol was like milk to her. The black descended upon her. Lulling her senses to failure.

Sadie turned to Aruna, flushed, "Gabh mo leithscéal!" Then, she collapsed onto the table, snoring so loudly, with brief pauses.

Aruna ate without so much as looking at the sleeping drunk, caring less if she had apnea, speaking without remorse, "Strange tongue on her; maybe she could read the ancient texts. A *veil* in the making."

"He won't like this one bit," Milos said to her.

"That's why I'll say it was you who did it," Aruna responded.

Incoming. Marked. **SPLAT!** Painted. A flying fish head smacked across her face, but not by Milos.

"I guess I'm not the only one who needs an attitude adjustment," Milos laughed. Enzu danced around on the table, preparing another assault against her.

She withdrew a pistol, angrily grinding her teeth, "I'm taking those jewels for my own, clay-child!" It freaked out hysterically, jumping off the table to run away, while she gave chase, shouting strange obscenities. Milos went back to eating. He looked over to Sadie, thinking about her world.

"I'll make you a plate for when you wake up." He sipped his drink, looking around the empty hall, pondering about the old giant's whereabouts.

Wanting to thank him for the much-needed rest.

Cracked, itchy, frigid; many skins yearning to drink holy oils. They came with no clear indication through the courtyard. Vicious winds. This abnormality had everyone on full alert. Soldiers marched around trying to figure out the cause. Jumarts, neighing with anxiety, inside the stables. Some started to break parts of the walls. Others tried to escape frantically. Any animal cornered doubles in strength, speed, and stupidity.

Her auxiliary found the scent.

"Tend to those beasts before they do more damage," Birati commanded one of his armored giants.

A commanding officer approached Birati, handing him a telescope, exclaiming, "Look to the sky, my lord!" His finger denoted the cause: a formation of crystallized snowflakes, duplicating, one after the other in a long line. Every strand that formed crept closer to the castle. Slow, but sure. Its underbelly wept. "We've never had freezing precipitation in these lands before!"

"And we never will," Birati responded, closing the telescope with orders, "Send for my *adapter* immediately!"

The officer rushed into the castle to retrieve Birati's personal scribe. He looked cautiously to the sky. Visual analytics searches for the best course of action.

Found.

"Yes, it will go this way," he said to himself. With the palm of one hand facing upward, conjured flame spewed forth, transforming in shape, like an anemometer, spinning. Violently. Heated waves traveled across the sky. The crystal-vein configuration, reconstructing a new course: far away, to Lusura.

The commanding officer came back with another man. "Quite a chill to the bones tonight," the adapter said aloud. Birati watched the sky to make sure everything was going according to plan.

"I require you to write another message to that troublesome queen," Birati commanded him.

"Is that what this is all about? Should I write out another plea to spare him, sir?"

"No, this one will be more assertive. Write that if she has one of her Alephim enter, or uses seekers in my realm, it will be seen as a direct act of war," Birati said, turning to the adapter, flames spewing out of his eyes and fists, "Because I will no longer tolerate this brazen behavior!"

The adapter scurried back to his quarters to prepare the message.

But not before cleaning his partially soiled trousers.

Birati felt the movement of a small ball spiraling around his body to come upon his shoulder. Enzu reformed himself to look at the irate giant king. They stared at each other for what seemed like hours before the little Essent did a small jig. Birati bellowed out a boisterous laugh after seeing the ridiculous creature's fanciful movements.

Enzu smiled and continued to dance until his head was consumed by the barrel of a gun. Trouble.

"I've got you now, you little misfit!" Aruna exclaimed, appearing out of nowhere.

"Good health to you, Aruna. Best keep those shooters sheathed when they're so close to *my* face," he said, retrieving Enzu.

"Apologies, sir, but this miscreant fancied himself a food fight. I intend to finish it," she snarled, before looking up at the sky.

"That damnable witch's right hand is practically defecating on my land. It is very close."

Aruna knew how dangerous the situation was. One of the Alephim could easily wipe out scores of mercenaries. But to have her personal creation boldly breach into their territory meant something much more.

"Do you reckon she's becoming more desperate?" she asked.

He hesitated to answer. Thinking. Expanding thought beyond the realm. Revelation.

"I must speak to the girl; is she still eating?"

Aruna shied away from the question. He asked again…stern in tone. Pulling rank. She stated how she deliberately got the girl drunk. He let out an exhausted sigh,

"Despite giving you command over my armies—second to me—you still haven't let that buccaneer persona go. Did you not learn anything good from the *Phorcuson* that rescued you in your youth?"

Tomorrow he would learn of Sadie using his most favored skill. For now, vision to the stratosphere. The snowy crystal formation was no longer in sight. This relieved him.

"One day—and I hope soon—*Evren* will cease her hunt for my boy," he said, cracking one knuckle, "And when that day happens, these fiery mountains will break forth in song."

A historic day that is nowhere in sight.

The world spun round and round. It was nauseating, but it came with pleasant smells. A rust bucket was deemed necessary. At least something that could catch the impending projectile of aromatic liquids sloshing inside the soft belly. Panicky whimpers fell on nearby ears. They tilted the soft head, blessing the lips with a clouded water.

A small task of comfort.

"What are you giving me?" Sadie groaned out.

One of the maidens said potassium water. She helped Sadie drink the liquid while preparing a cool washcloth for her. Dabbing around her face, she couldn't help but ask if Sadie was from Somdir.

"Like I said, I'm not of this world. I don't even know how I got here! One minute I'm resting underneath a tree, near my school—like I always do, once the weather permits it—and then the next, I'm fighting for my life! Hoping not to be some smelly large man's concubine!"

Abject fear of strenuous intercourse.

The maiden calmed the flustered girl. She only asked since red hair is a treasured characteristic in said country, renowned for its sorcery.

Chroma.

"There used to be a powerful sorceress there," the maiden explained, "She had vivid red hair, like yours, and her eyes were even redder. Incredibly peerless blue pupils. Even her lips were naturally blue! A sign of innate magical power: overflowing."

Sadie asked what happened to her. The maiden explained she disappeared from the throne without a trace. Her contorted, three-faced familiar remained in the castle, briefly, droning on about the "*Lost Divide*," before it too vanished. A realm without one unified flag, but many. A realm where many obscure female aristocrats inhabit. A realm where many men enter but never return.

A realm of hedonistic death.

The continued details reminded Sadie of Sybaris.

It was late into the night. The maiden offered to show Sadie around the castle grounds to offer fresh air. Despite the long ice trail in the sky receding hours prior, the air was still brisk. This actually comforted Sadie, who preferred cool nights with a light jacket, but she had none of her own. Just a school uniform that was starting to gain its own odor of personality. The maiden offered a similar type of apparel, much like that of a robe.

"The cerulean is a favored color around here," the maiden pointed out, "Even if it is a taboo color to show off."

Sadie could not wrap her head around a color being taboo.

They walked up to the peak of the castle, a domed tower above the others. There was a large table, a kiln, a pile of limestone bricks, sealed barrels, a large telescope, and several alchemical apparatuses. Sadie looked over the alchemy set, noticing a familiar smell coming from a rounded flask. It was inside another glass container holding an ice-water slurry. She wafted the fragrance. Almost obsessively.

The maiden pulled her back.

"Didn't get enough at dinner—or lack thereof—did you?" she said. She pulled out the round flask to show off the liquid, "From this distillation are the contents of Birati's personal spirit: *Scoria*. Affectionately named after the volcanic rock."

It was dark, it was spicy, and it satisfied the young girl's sweet tooth. She *had* to have more!

The maiden saw Sadie slowly reaching for the flask. She grinned, pulled her hand back, and gulped down the remnants. Sadie wanted to fume, yet she knew what would happen if she had any more.

"Your constitution is too frail at the moment. You need something to sop up that mess in you," the maiden said. She walked over to the kiln to see if it had anything left over. Not to her surprise, it did. She saw a tray of recently made food and extracted it using a pair of tongs to place it onto the table. Sadie's mouth watered, watching the fresh braided bread being sliced. It oozed out a vanilla cream; the slivered almonds on top looked festive, and a divine smell exhaled from each individual section. The maiden put the nearby mortar up to Sadie's nose to smell; it still had some of its crushed contents. "Taste," she said. The young girl sampled the confection. It was sugar and saffron—delightful.

A moment to forget troubles.

Sadie could see the peerless stars. Without any light pollution, everything was illuminated in the sky. Impeccable. The telescope invited more to show: strange planets with even stranger lands. The maiden pointed out the cratered northland of Udalann. Sadie could see encampments of many dangerous-looking creatures clad in armor. A deadly battle takes place between giants, beings that appear human, rat men, and creatures far too big to behold. She had almost forgotten she was separated from Earth after the current pleasantries. She withdrew her vision when she saw one giant tear the viscera from another.

A moment to remember troubles.

"They'll come here for certain if they keep this up!" Sadie shrieked.

The maiden calmed her. "They have tried, and they have failed, numerous times. Here, at the Capital, we are not so easily beleaguered."

Lusura: a land of constant battles known as death marches. Each soldier vied for a place among the strongest within the kingdom's Capital. It was not only described as caustic but—ironically—a country of some of the rarest elements, making it surprisingly a bountiful country for any who can survive the blighted lands and sparse forests. Only a select few knew of its ruler on personal grounds. It held many titles: The Prime Aeolid, *Palatial Usurper*, the *Deserter* of the Pelagic.

Its true name must never be uttered within Udalann, else it would blister Birati's ears, and that would come with absolute castigation…

Sleep started to take hold of Sadie. A stomach of sweetbread to ease her into bed. They made their way back into the lit halls where warmth greeted them again. Not far from Sadie's room was Milos's. Strange sounds within. The room's door was just barely cracked open for a peek. Soft sobs emanating. The eyes caught glimpses of shimmering colors around the room. Some whispered calming words, but one thrashed their tongue without remorse.

Who would be so deserving of harsh temperament?

The door swung wide with Birati standing in the frame. Sadie's view was almost completely blocked by the intimidating figure.

"Tend to his mind for the duration of the night," Birati commanded the maiden. Regardless of the giant's presence, Sadie was able to peer briefly past him. She felt her vision betrayed her; a witness to colored female spirits surrounding Milos's bed.

Maybe Jerome was right. I guess we do receive, from birth, guardians to protect us.

Several maidens, present with basins of water and strips of fabric, dried the sweat from the sleeping man. Enzu watched over him diligently. Its many gems shone bright. The giant king gently closed the door behind him before turning to Sadie, "Not something a young girl should see in the dead of twilight." He decided to escort her back to her quarters.

"What's happening in his room? What were those things?! What—" Sadie asked before being interrupted by Birati, putting up his hand to stop her.

"Learn to control the disquiet," he said, "I will answer your queries, but I have several of my own to ask."

Like the hydra, when she finished off one question, the following doubled. Each answer piqued his interest, yet still, he couldn't fathom how she was thrown into his world. That was until she brought up the message summoned before her.

"The Menes Spire?" he said, rubbing his chin. "To seek the composer would prove to be fatal. Not only for you, but for Milos most especially."

When she asked why, all he could reply was that death would be most certain for him. "Have you witnessed his capabilities?" he asked. She described the village ambush in vivid detail. "Then you know, firsthand, how talented he is, despite his halfhearted composition—how I dream of him becoming culturally poised. His mood, however, is too much like quicksilver."

"You seemed very angry with him in the dinner hall," Sadie said.

"Did I lash at his skin? Peel away the nails? Inflame his body with sulfuric acid? No, what I gave him was well-intended honesty that has tried *endlessly* to puncture through his mentality. I have promised lost kin to protect him until my very psyche is no longer present. That is my sworn duty," he explained.

"As...his lord?" she asked, hesitantly.

He opened her door, stating, "As his adoptive father."

Birati Milu

Wishing her farewell, he returned back to Milos's room to check on him. So many questions unanswered until later. The verbal hydra, building, doubling, tripling even, in her neurons.

She saw a plate of food on the writing table with a note next to it: *Remember to eat. Water closet down the hall. -M*

At least this world has functioning bathrooms.

Stand proud when the king and queen are in your presence! It is always a triumph to know they are alive. They walk with purpose.

To be so young and to be born into an exemplary household. You are the envy of every young maiden in all Iberitus. Can any man, in your land, hold your hand?

None so far.

You cannot have peace without war, as it goes the other way around.

You can't help but say aloud, "Why here? Why them? Why *us*?"

Fragile alliances with the Mid-East wouldn't allow reinforcements to aid the realm—pinned against their own invasion. Old East.

After the fall of the Myrtle Kingdom.

Gory teeth. Thirsty weapons. Promises of honed incarnadine currency. Blood North. Traveling by land, through desert and mountains; slipping into the night from beaches to small waters, across the swampy strait; bearing arms, numbers, and terrible-sized monstrosities.

All in the name of alchemical experimentation.

Steadfast to his kingdom, the king cleared every advance on all that encroached on his soil. Triumph—it seemed certain—only temporary. Faced against the champion of black sulfur, from one of the darkest depths of the pelagic.

He, who respected the noble metals, fought valiantly against the cunningness of brimstone. Fate had other plans. He could not thwart against unknown weaponry that transmuted instantaneously.

And so…the king fell.

The gaze of the champion, unimpressed, at the lifeless body at its feet. *How could you fall so readily from such an infantile attack?* Sights set on the Capital: *Aureate's Mark.* The sheer brilliance just begs to kneel to the champion's might. It wanted only knowledge, though, unlike its own ruler, who craved dominance over the region.

It signaled its corrosive dual swords at the castle.

One final assault.

The besieging monstrosities howled. Sheer bliss. Trampling through the bountiful forests, displacing all wildlife, and urinating on anything that blossomed.

With the country's forces eradicated, what could stand against such a devastating campaign?

A final moment of quiet desperation.

She respected the Chroma; even when she did not know all of its secrets, she still gave thanks for its wonders. A wish made to pass upon primaries, secondaries, tertiaries, and beyond.

Argent answered the call.

She appeared in the sky—boundless—to welcome the invaders with a tumultuous parade of scattered light, piercing through their very beings. Spectral arrows. Leaving behind undamaged, lifeless bodies. Deceptive darts. Each volley displayed impaled souls before dispersing into the air.

Pinning down souls?

Unscathed bodies?

This must be the Rapture!

A full retreat was signaled by the champion before it too succumbed to aether's wrath. Triumph, finally, but the Prime of Argent required compensation. To take, one *has* to give back, according to this chroma's contract. So, the well-wisher, the queen, was its sacrifice. A trade. The country could prosper again.

But it had no leader.

Only a lost and scared princess who had no choice but to inherit the throne because of regicide.

The cries for mother and father went unheard.

"Casualties of war," the councilmen spouted.

"Necessary sacrifices," the priests of Chroma proclaimed.

She raised her hand in defiance. Dispelling them all from her land. These were not normal screams of rebellion heard. Symbols of both alchemy and color were torn down. The elements of absolute nature were erected in their place.

A new philosophy came about: isolationism.

A new age.

She would not aid those she considered too weak to aid her doting father, nor consider listening to the counsel of any who worshiped the pantheon of colors. Even willing conscripts were disallowed into the kingdom. Her mother's sacred grove was never intended to be used as a means of violence. Sacred office. The queen would surely disapprove of the new usage, but she was gone; what difference would it make?

A new power was discovered nearby. Underground. Danger within shadows, metal, and brick. Help from a Prime, Her Messenger, and the sacrificed. The Vicara were erected in the corners of the land, the Ornate Alephim came to being, and previous philosophies were tossed to the wind.

The only thing kept, of bygone years, was her mother's handwritten manuscript, anointed by the power of Sky Blue. No man, woman, or beast would ever dare enter Celanjung—much less the Menes Spire—to steal its power.

Until a certain thief came upon its existence.

Only cursing himself…

Soft sensations patted the head. She recognized these from before. Blurry-eyed. They opened to let morning's first rays of light in.

"Morning, Enzu."

She had become acclimated to the world of fantasy with tremendous speed. Recalling memories from a life that never existed. Enzu, cheerful as one can be, smiled at her as she sat up. He rolled out the door, letting others know of her waking.

Knocks and words on the other side, "Not to rush you, but my lord requests your presence, so make haste," Aruna said.

No time like the present, but another conundrum for the young girl. "So...how's the dental hygiene around these parts?" Sadie asked shyly. Aruna balked. She presented the young girl with a small moving tendril. *What Lovecraftian horror is this?!* The sheer sight of it was so grotesque that Sadie's morning appetite had gone to the bucket. Never had she imagined seeing this sort of cosmic mythos.

"Put it in your mouth, and don't swallow the damn thing!" Aruna ordered her. She tried to put it into the young girl's mouth, but Sadie evaded it with great agility, it looked as if she had been possessed by a martial arts master.

Sadie wanted a toothbrush. Paste and all. Preferably new.

"The old ways, huh? I suppose we can make do." Aruna ordered one of the maidens to retrieve said items. Sadie heard giggling in the background. Aruna, meanwhile, threw the disgusting-looking tendril into her mouth like a piece of candy. She stood in place, arms folded, staring at the young girl, all while the animated object wriggled around her mouth for less than a minute before plucking it out. She showed her her teeth, and they were *absolute* pearls.

"We get these creatures from the Phorcuson in the southeast," she explained. "They trade us these cirrus creatures—which eat away the harmful bacteria—and we provide certain materials."

A maiden came with the supplies to hand to Sadie, holding back a stifled laugh. "I don't see why this is funny to everyone."

It was explained to her that this was an archaic invention. Even the poorest could afford a cirrus, whether by currency or barter; the pelagic provided an overpopulated commodity below cost.

"Now that you have your bristled polyamide stick and dentifrice, I expect you to do what is needed before Birati becomes irritated with your tardiness," Aruna said brusquely.

The domed tower awaited her once more.

Fine, I'll keep an open mind about the wiggle worm next time. Second thought. No. To hell with that!

"Good health to you, young Sadie," Birati exclaimed. He did not mind her being late. "It is quite fortunate we still hold alchemy in the highest regard around here. When I heard of your reasonable requests, I thought to myself, 'Ah, the combination of abrasives, detergents, and fluorides with plastic and nylon…how nostalgic.' Long gone are the days when I first discovered these components. Nature has provided much more that is no mere proxy." Chuckles were produced here and there.

He waved her over to assist him. A vibrant spread of ingredients was displayed on the table. The kiln blazed, which worried Sadie. She asked how it was possible to create anything edible without turning to a crisp. Waving his hand, the fire relaxed, a simple capability of his, "When you study under the Chroma, their Heralds offer unique abilities."

Again with the word chroma. The purity of a color. Now, Heralds? Are these their gods? Color is a religion? Best to continue listening.

He discussed how even simple ovens of clay were still around, but those were mostly for Naturals, fanatical

Alchemists, or those with no interest in respecting the Chroma. This upset her.

"Everything seems so advanced, and yet, displaced. You and your people laughed at me for asking about something as simple as a toothbrush, but stone-age ovens are still a thing? Doesn't sound like you have a wistful affection for the past. On top of that, you know beyond basic chemistry and plumbing, but no electricity?" she complained.

They say that when someone becomes too riled up, their intelligence diminishes. Too emotional. The girl knows but still dares to cross certain lines. Maybe the liquor was still plaguing her mind. After-effects. Too emboldened. What could go wrong?

"Did you enjoy the sweet bread last night from my athanor?" he asked, not paying any mind to her rant. She stood in place, bewildered by the question. Birati turned to her with the mortar and pestle, placing it under his nose to inhale. A sigh of comfort. "Additives have a complex olfactory profile. The sense of smell picks up on these ingredients, which—objectively—have their own distinctive personalities. But," he explained, "the nose is an entity of its own, not just a tool. Yours is much too curious. Learn at a pace before something—or someone—tears it off for its curiosity. Everything can be explained, but to force information ruins the significance of even the slightest detail."

She felt the throat squeeze. Best let the experience of the ride explain everything. Easier. Less conflict. Innocuous.

Birati began instruction on the meal they would be prepping. Aromas building up, like the stories he had for her.

Let's rouse and cajole those ears to listen.

And keep that tongue under both lip and tooth.

Sealed.

Udalann is the youngest of the countries, freshly established only a few decades ago. It was once an extension of Lusura and its only ally, Klaring. And before that…independent.

"Now put the collagen trussing like so," he instructed her. Food wraps multiplied on the table. "I used to lead quite the force in the North," he continued on.

Hundreds of years old. From grunt to tactician to leader.

The latter by escape.

"I have seen death in countless forms. There is no justifying it," he said. The condition for "justice for all" always came with blurred lines. Sadie asked how he became ruler of this particular realm. "Eradicating old comrades who lived for bloodshed, establishing a shaky treaty with *Gottlir*'s leader, *Leandro*, and using all accumulated knowledge of the arts to take a stand against old alliances."

Too many death marches can turn a sound warrior towards the path of pacifism…or warmongering.

They completed the meal, but he pointed to the telescope, "Don't move it, but tell me what you see."

She took her small bites before concentrating on the set display.

"Is he okay?"

"He has never been at peace."

A forlorn watcher sat on a cliff, overlooking the ocean, his nose down, no hints of contentment, prone to dejection.

"He tortures himself with false solitude. Surely, he is afraid of abandoning his nomadic lifestyle. More so…afraid of proclaiming adoration to the one he has met in the pelagic," Birati said. Sadie wanted to look away, but again, her curiosity kept her glued to the sight.

What troubles ran through his head?

Rogue waves of grief...

Sadie decided to disclose the dream she had to Birati. It felt right to share it. Odd, but still, something to get off the chest. Maybe a thought? He did not react.

His eyes looked out to the cliff where Milos was, murmuring to himself, "An additive..."

She did not understand him.

"Let your curiosity teach you, but don't let it control you."

Birati gave her a satchel of supplies for the future endeavor.

He began to think of Milos's childhood. He *knew* Sadie would have to go through possible traumas that may await her beyond the castle. If the Menes Spire was her destiny, then it was also Milos's as well—no matter how much he avoided it.

Many pieces of her pneuma will crack. Never to return.

"He comes," Birati said, looking out to the cliffs. Sadie saw in disbelief Milos gliding through the sky on a vapor trail towards the tower. Skysurfer. "Just remember: this world is as real as yours, and there are those who will do much more than harm a young girl like yourself."

He placed a bracelet around her wrist as a parting gift. "Don't let the basalt outer shell fool you. I have imbued it with the power of my own blood. If you ever come across any grand dolmens or megalithic tombs, give thanks to the Chroma of Alaea and make a wish. If you come to respect its power, it will bestow some of its own unto you. The Prime of Alaea is a curious one and a wraithful one," he warned her. She remembered the bandit screaming about Primes. The question was asked, and Birati quickly answered, "*The Creators.*"

Milos flew into the tower to grab food off the table. The lean piranha ate with gusto—ignoring the two.

Birati was not pleased and did the unthinkable.

They heard it, Iberitus, as a whole: the earthquake.

"Blighted by black sulfur, he's on foot!" Aruna shouted out. She raced up to the tower to see what had caused Birati to stop levitating.

"Can you for once make a proper entrance?!" Birati yelled at Milos. His booming voice parted the clouds in the vicinity. Clear skies. Cracks appeared along the foundation. Milos teleported above the dome.

"A bit serious this early in the day, Milu," he said to provoke the giant king using his surname. Flicks of spitting fire came out of the ogre's sockets. Bits of wood singing. Blackened circles. An exasperated sigh to blow them away. Milos laughed, knowing that Birati wouldn't dare to destroy his precious tower when he could easily evade in a blink or fly off.

Swift was the blow that came to his head. No evasive maneuvers here. He lost his balance. Too dizzy to react. Heavy is the body that goes adrift to beckon his near doom.

"I should let gravity become your teacher," Birati scorned him while grabbing hold of one leg. He threw Milos inside the tower near Sadie's feet. Enzu sprawled out of his jacket, looking as dazed as his human companion. Spiral sockets. Sadie picked him up, trying to help the Essent regain consciousness. A bucket of ice slurry was tossed on Milos. An instant reaction of awakening in an unpleasant manner.

"I think next time we should humble him," Aruna said, holding the empty bucket, "Or maybe next time I should take the shot."

Birati levitated again. *It's too early for contention.* He floated over to Milos to pick him up.

"Next time, say your greetings to all present before you engorge. You could've avoided all this, young man," Birati calmly explained.

He placed his hands on Milos's sides, lightly drying his clothes with a comfortable heat with his hands. It wasn't all blaze and glory at his disposal. Temperate sorcery had its seat at the table. Milos looked down at the floor before apologizing. *There remains an innocent child inside him.* "Aruna, can you take our young Sadie to the shrine and please show her how to give thanks to the Chroma? I need a moment with my boy…alone," Birati instructed.

When will you find the sky that overlooks your place of sanctuary? Soon? Never? Don't think this can lead to a wondrous life. The king of Udalann has warned of predators that far exceed mere bandits. Some lurk in the daylight with noses lifted high. *Strive to live.*

Birati clapped his hands. This summoned some maidens to him. "Wrap the cakes," he commanded, "Pass one over first." He gave Milos a thick ball pastry that resembled cheesecake with cream on the top.

"Go on now."

Milos ate it slowly. Birati poured him a drink to wash it down. "Listen closely to what I have to say, son. The girl speaks of the Menes Spire, more directly, of its infamous composer: Evren."

Milos looked at him from the corner of his eyes cautiously. No flames in these sockets, but colorful energy. Concentrated.

"Aruna interrogated some of the prisoners working the salt pits. The catalyst for the raid on the farm was our dear Sadie—allegedly. That 'gentle' oppressor, Ashokara, somehow caught wind of her impending arrival. The prisoners don't know why he's after her, if that's true or not, but now I'm told there's the matter of a certain Tarwini who planned this invasion on my realm, undetected," Birati explained.

Milos crushed his cup—several small cuts on his palm. Small trickles oozing out. *"Olu-Zad..."* Milos quietly said. Birati could feel the strong anger from Milos. His scrolls were lighting up, waiting for their powers to be conjured at a moment's notice. His bracelet emitted a whining sound with the small gear spinning uncontrollably.

And he heard them: the voices of color.

Concerned. Angry. Vicious. Authoritative.

The intermediate, between red and blue, screams. She was the most unhinged. Deranged by the grand ceremony of sacrifice. Discovered purpose in him. Overly attached.

What becomes of her and her sisters if his ghost is stolen?

"Temperance, son, or become a victim to the black sulfur. I fear Ashokara is still trying to get you to convert to its ways," Birati said, placing a hand on his shoulder. He looked over the many scrolls in the quiver. His eyes studied the largest.

"The Auburn seal is still intact on the converted Cerulean."

"I've yet to use such a devastating power," Milos responded.

"Isn't that a good thing?" Birati concurred it was, but to be prepared for the oncoming journey. "Aquamarine, Cobalt, Mulberry, and...Argent? How could you have found such dangerous parchment?"

Birati immediately pulled out the scroll to read, but the sight of a screaming silver woman burrowed into his retinas. Temporarily blinded. It remains sealed. Milos used the same scroll in the village to heal the burn marks around his eyes. "Always keeping Goldenrod close to the chest, I noticed," Birati said, patting his eyes. Several blinks. Several floating women looked on. Quickly dispersing. Milos placed the small scroll back under his jacket.

"You should know that certain Chroma are too taboo to read unless it has blessed you," Milos explained, "Even a Mairu, like yourself, is not immune to divine flames." He told the giant king of being led to the argent power while venturing on an island east of Somdir. Milos knew full well of its power and has since refused to use the scroll, knowing it would require his servitude beyond the stars.

The giant king heard her transmission: *"Suffer! Obey!"*

She was no sister to the others.

Each, except innocent Goldenrod, wanted her paper torn and burned to ash. Gold tried convincing the others on numerous occasions: there *has* to be another way to bring peace.

She'll never give up.

"But have you noticed? Look what I've finally discovered," Milos said, revealing the diamond-like crystal attached to his bracelet. Birati looked it over but could not figure out its significance. "Isotropic, adamantine luster, transparent—is it not an ordinary diamond?"

Milos smirked, stating it appeared that way, but only to the untrained eye. He concentrated on the piece, holding out his arm, showing a slow transformation forming over his arm before stopping it short.

It stopped at his shoulder where a mechanical pauldron had formed. Pain rose, heart pounded, skin contorting, and an unintelligible ancient voice whispering in his mind. Legendary. Too great a power to wield without surrendering the body and pneuma.

"The Prism of *Sesathoth*! But—" Birati tried asking.

"A hidden tablet that had broken off from the original. I discovered it some years back in a random cave. The same cave I last faced against Olu-Zad…"

A few trips back home, and never a mention of this possession. There was still an issue of trust that needed mending.

Birati asked how it was possible to even carve it down to simple-looking jewelry. That is when Milos pointed out to Enzu being the only one capable of doing the impossible.

"*Prime Matter* material, and an Essent that can manipulate it. Evren is a formidable Breyjan. Speaking of her," Birati said, again looking over the quiver, "It would be wise to surrender those Ceruleans' in your possession— they're slowly attracting her right hand…it is no mere Essent."

Milos scoffed at the idea, asking how he could return them, sneak past the Vicara, say he was sorry, *and* survive her wrath.

Birati had only a simple response: "Escort young Sadie—alive and well—to the Spire, and perhaps her presence will keep you alive. A 'Unity of Opposites' to pave the way to sanctuary. Better for her there than to be stolen into the Usurper's realm."

What a disastrous idea, Milos thought.

"It's time for you two to part. Take great care of her; she's your responsibility…as *Katya* was to you," Birati said.

Milos bit his lip, tearing up at the mention of this particular name. "Enjoy the cakes; the second box is for my dear boy, Kosey. Send him my warmth, as I have given unto you."

He personally escorted Milos to the outskirts of the castle. Citizens from the torched village had started to set up camp. Many gave him their thanks. He could never get used to praise.

Never felt deserving of it.

Aruna arrived shortly after with Sadie. Shaken by the ritual.

"The ossuary caught her by surprise," Aruna mentioned.

"Loyalists to the kingdom, dear Sadie, you needn't worry too much about the skull and bones," Birati chuckled. He examined her bracelet, satisfied with the glowing result. "Now you can conjure a small flame. What a grand survival tool at your behest! Keep giving thanks to the Chroma, and more wonders shall follow. Let *her* be your sword in the darkness. It was a pleasure, Sadie; you're always welcome here. Good luck finding your way home."

Sadie, Milos, and Enzu rode off on borrowed jumarts. Birati stared for as long as he could into the distance until they were no longer in sight.

"Do...do you think I was better this time, Aruna?"

"You didn't scorch his rear like last time, and not once did you refer to him as a thief. I'd say that's a win," she replied.

The corners of his lips creased up a touch.

"Send two messages: one for Gottlir's, Leandro, and another for the witch of Celanjung, Evren. Yes. Another. Tell the *King of Lynxes* to be on guard of intruders from the North—specifically from Klaring. Milos may not see it, too desensitized, but war has arrived with Olu on the prowl. I'll spare what I can.

"As for Evren, state that if my son should fall, in her realm, by one of her Alephim, or even so much as one of her Vicara drops a single leaf on his head, I will personally hold her responsible and cross over the pelagic, fight through the violent maelstrom monstrosities in the *Sea of Akrav*, and see to it enough magma coats her crystal palace that only gabbro remains—not a threat; sheer warning."

He floated back to the palace with Aruna, pondering.

A being from another world. What consequences would her presence have on this land? Who could say? This seems like the appropriate time for a new epoch. What if she's not what the Usurper is after, but something else? Good on me for giving up my own prism. No need for words. I trust the veil to do her part to safeguard. She deserves this freedom after what happened to her…

The Father disciplines the absent son yet still bestows him with wealth. How could he expel him from his life? Too many tribulations occurred at a young age—a war orphan. None of the Chroma or any Alchemist can revert the traumas—or heal. And now he travels back to where he first entered adulthood, but not by choice. An uneasy ritual where one must take into account their mistakes. Most would rather die on the hill of cowardice. But the Father only wants what is best, and in doing so, hopes his only son will return with better judgment and—most importantly—alive.

The very earth will fissure so deep that not even the unfathomable depths of the pelagic will be able to endure his fire…

Chapter 3

†

Deutan

South and to the west, the adventurers traveled. Galloping far and away from everything, olivine green, burnt umber brown, enigmatic gray, and malleable clay, to the border where hunter green and zaffre blue painted the terrain in natural hues.

It seemed never-ending. Going over stock and stone; rest was required. It was quiet all throughout the ride. But once the beasts of travel stopped, the questions began…again.

Curiosity: to be killed for getting too close or saved for having been well prepared.

Who can say with this girl present?

"No more damn questions! I need to get some sleep! Just…ah! Look! A grand dolmen! Enzu, escort her; I need sleep!" Milos said, exasperated, pointing out to the standing stones surrounding the tomb. Sadie sighed, walking over to the area with the little being on one shoulder, and brushing her hands against the tall grass.

"I can't figure him out sometimes. He can be lackadaisical one moment and fiery the next. Must be bipolar or something."

Enzu had a worried look on his face. It wasn't her remark but what he really knew about his main traveling companion. He looked out to see Milos already settled on the ground with a small campfire lit. His eyes slowly closed, trying to ease into slumber upon his quiver, yet still alert with one eye partially open.

The young girl stood before the open tomb. A stark contrast to Birati's temple: oddly shaped, jagged standing stones, lush grass cropped around each one. A stratus cloud formed overhead, and light rain anointed their bodies. *Too ominous*, she thought, but nothing should surprise her *too* much in this world. She could barely see a thing once she entered, despite it being such a small and primarily open tomb.

Deceit at large.

She concentrated on the bracelet and on Aruna's instructions: be calm, ask for help, and give thanks to the Chroma, before and after summoning its power.

You got this.

A small flame began to twirl around the fingers. *Sweet Jesus!* Growing larger. Ballerina in her palm. Finally, a torch levitated above the digits, fully brightening the area. She squealed in excitement. How exciting to conjure fire without burning oneself. In a brief moment, she thought she saw a woman's face in the flames.

Whispers in her mind. Transmitting.

Clapping. Inches from her personal space, accidentally dispelling the flame. Panic sets in, even more when she hears a small laugh nearby.

"Try again, fill the room!" an androgynous voice exclaimed. Enzu's gems began to glow, helping to amplify Sadie's new power. The flame came back—brighter. And with extra help, unbeknownst to the girl. But there was no one around.

"That's it, you got it now. Isn't that wonderful?"

Voices in the air. Sadie turned in every direction, wondering where they could be. Nothing outside, nothing above, and certainly nothing inside.

"Where are you? What do you want?!"

She backs against the stone wall.

"I am everywhere where I am needed. You called me after all. Silence your troubled mind; count me in as guardian—I've been alone for so long in these parts," it responded.

Sadie noticed her shadow stretching opposite of her.

It did not mimic her movements, though.

"How's this? Better?" her shadow spoke. She was beginning to hyperventilate like when she encountered Birati. The shadow tried again. This time it transforms into the shape of a dog. It even became a solid figure once it emerged from the wall. It wasn't ordinary of course. Just a solid dark blue color. Its dark blue tongue hung off the side of the mouth—a "not so" golden retriever.

"Perhaps patting my head will put you at ease?" it spoke. She looked at Enzu, and he approved the request with a nod. Her hand slowly reached for the makeshift shadow. A few pullbacks out of caution. Its goofy, happy face pants in excitement. Gentle rubs initiated. No bites or barks came back to retaliate.

Tranquility took hold of her finally.

"Isn't this wonderful! Or maybe the flame was better?"

Its gaze saw her fiery guardian: silent, wanting to explode, should a sudden attack be inflicted on the girl.

"Who are you?" she asked, still petting it.

"Phthalo, you may call me Phthalo, and yours?" Still panting. She gave her response, and the two conversed.

Phthalo answered each curious question without hesitating. This was its shrine; it was a Herald of its particular Chroma; it was also a very young one at that.

"How come I couldn't hear the Herald in Udalann?" she asked.

Phthalo looked back to the guardian. No desire to talk. Or made known to the girl. *A veil that won't communicate with its companion? And can act independently?! This is peculiar. Dire. That bracelet...it isn't right...far more powerful than it looks.*

It lifted its nose to point at Enzu. "Was the Essent with you before?" She shook her head. "Well, that explains it then," it began, feigning ignorance with truth, "All Chroma can speak to respecters. This Essent, despite it being a mute, is an adapter. Chromatic translators. Without an adapter, or learned experience, it would be impossible to hear our tones. Our native tongue. Your adapter is quite the adept, but he doesn't belong to your traveling companion. If he doesn't return to his Breyjan, you too will be between the hammer and the anvil. I fear Cerulean has already marked you. So let me guide you."

Its snout touched Sadie's bracelet. Little by little, Phthalo's form dispersed into the air, and soon...he was gone. The young girl called out the Herald's name, worried it had abandoned her.

"Take heart, for I am still here; gaze upon my gift, and think of me," its voice echoed in the air. Sadie did as was requested, focusing on the bracelet. Envisioning. Rings of energy circled around her hand. A celestial sphere conjured before her. "No land, no road, no mountain, no river, or any path is unknown to you now. Whenever you are lost, ask for aid, and the safest passage will be shown. Whenever you are within the vicinity of danger, an exit will be shown. Whenever hunger or thirst beckons your attention, a trail to nourishment will be shown. This will guide you to your stars. I hope I did okay. Goodnight."

The rain stopped. The clouds diffused. The air was cool and moist. But Phthalo's voice was gone. It did not respond to Sadie anymore. It was a strange moment for her. A wave of emotions colliding with one another. It was as if she had made a near and dear friend...just for them to disappear as quickly as they came into her life.

The whole event turned funereal.

Stepping outside, her eyes noticed they were on a cliff overlooking the sea. Each wave glimmered like diamonds in various blue colors. Offset by white. She thought the wind played intricate melodies, but it wasn't until her eyes met the form of a shrouded female at the base making the sounds. Humming softly into the night. When she finished, Enzu began to clap enthusiastically. Despite the sounds he made being next-to-impossible for any ordinary person to hear from a distance, the shrouded woman looked over and up to the two, high up on the cliff.

"Send him my love, Enzu!" the female shouted. She waves to him excitedly. As Enzu waved back, she disappeared into the gleaming ocean.

"Enzu, who was that?!" Sadie exclaimed with excitement. The little clay man smiled at her but rolled up for a hasty retreat back to camp. Sadie stopped short of chasing him to look back at the now vacant tomb. No lights or goofy pups—in a singular color—to be seen. She embraced the side of the smooth wall, closing her eyes, thoughts ruminating. A small sharp rock was nearby. Taking it upon herself to show more devotion to the friendly Chroma, she sliced off a few strands of her fiery red hair, placing them in the exact spot Phthalo sat.

"It's not much, but thank you for helping me get closer to home," she whispered. She looks back a final time, waving to it.

It's not all devils or caustic furies around every bend here. There is warmth too, and when the way home is in front of me, I'll forever dream of this world.

So many interactions; so many transformations.

The morning cock's roost was nowhere near as loud as Milos's when Sadie described the event that took hold at the dolmen the previous night.

"Of all the places in the Iberlands, an obscure Herald divined *you* with a map and strategy to everything on this planet?! Do you have any idea how valuable this is? You alone can escape any situation, track down more powerful dolmens hidden away, locate any precious geode that can be traded in to turn you into a queen overnight; the list goes on infinitely! You can even find out a way to navigate through the impossibly guarded Sea of Akrav! Why go the long way through Gottlir when it can just cut us a path through?!"

"Because the path through there cannot be crossed until Sadie's journey has met the right conditions," Phthalo's voice echoed through the air. The rings of light summoned on their own to reveal the dog's face hovering about. Sadie and Enzu were excited to see the Herald again, but Milos was not. Moreover, the bad news of no such shortcut through the most dangerous terrain on the planet.

"The more value of a particular destination or resource, the greater the price is to be had until conditions are met. If you and Miss Sadie were to obtain instruction to circumvent the treacherous waters and airs of Akrav prematurely, then the one I answer to would announce judgment on her. Her very life could cease in order to safeguard our artistry," it explained.

Milos asked if it could reveal the conditions, and it obliged by streaming images into his mind.

He saw the pelagic and was told to drown in the choppy waters. He witnessed a codex sheet beginning to shred and was told to abandon Sadie. He watched the ground erupt into a large dense forest and was told to let those who protect the border die and give no aid to them. He examined that same forest's trees beginning to become barren of leaves and was told to embrace a frozen death so the veiled may send word of his sacrifice. He observed a crumbling fort and was told to fall with it. He glimpsed upon burning cliffs and was told to surrender himself to wrath. He scanned the majestic metropolis of Somdir, paralyzed in a thick web, and was told to sleep while it was besieged. He scrutinized the vile deserts of Klaring and was told to inhale the miasma of a foreign blade into his lungs. He saw the hills overlooking Gottlir and was told to sacrifice himself for the land, widow the pelagic, kneel to the aether, and leave orphans behind to fight through blasted lands.

These were *absolute* conditions for crossing Akrav unharmed.

"I warn you, beast, these foul images you have plagued my visage with will *never* happen—don't test my patience with your lunacy." Milos said, grinding his teeth.

Sadie asked about what he saw, but before he could answer, Phthalo interrupted him to never speak of these things, "You could alter the path for something far worse if you speak up. These conditions are the first of many to come with a price."

Milos was irate, yelling at the Herald for not telling beforehand about conditions having conditions. This was just the grim gift of knowledge it endowed.

If you want the treasures of the world, you would have to give up your own treasures first.

Milos bit his tongue, telling Sadie it was time to continue to Gottlir. "We'll head further south and cross over the throat of the Iridos river. We'll release the jumarts since they can't cross over. You'll be flying with me into the city's port and travelling a bit further down, close to Somdir, to visit old friends. I need their counsel as well as Leandro's, if he will see me," he explained while putting out the campfire. "Right then, let's be off, and no more words from you, Herald..."

Phthalo withdrew its presence back into Sadie's bracelet, but not before reassuring her that all would be alright and not to worry. Milos's agitated look prompted Enzu to give him a message from the stranger in the waters by shapeshifting into two strange creatures: a juvenile lumpfish with a spiraled wizard hat and a playful monitor lizard. Milos dropped to his knees, asking Enzu if he had seen *her* recently. The little clay man reverted back, nodding his head excitedly.

"We saw a strange woman last night who disappeared into the waters below," Sadie said. He quickly grabbed her by the shoulders. "Did she have a message?! Anything at all?!"

She passed him the doting words.

Praise be to the Primes, he thought.

He quickly teleported, his back facing them, "It's a good day for flying!" Milos blinked towards the jumarts, smacking their backsides to run back to Raksag-Ni's Mark, and again, blinked back to Sadie and Enzu, retrieving them for flight, "Hold tight now!" he exclaimed jubilantly to her. Sadie screamed for dear life as he lifted her up to zoom across the sky on some fantastical cirrus cloud.

The enamored heart pumps with such zest you'll find yourself straying from terra firma.

Chapter 4

†

Egoity

At great speed, it flew elegantly over colorful mountains and lush forests through an isthmus of odious swamps into prohibited lands, save for its kind.

The stationary titans watched it closely, discerning the content gripped by its six toes, closing in on the pristine citadel.

Though it knew it was allowed to enter the hearth of its arcane ruler, it was far too cautious not to go near the tower's peak. Taboo.

Personal invitation only.

It could not perch onto any narrow railing—as it was a ground-dweller without talons—so it landed in the center of the throne room. Scanning its features. A befuddled sense of how dark and gloomy it was. Only a few beams of light from the paneless windows lit the crystal floor. The slits of light that once showed a way to the world began to disappear. Only a circle shone around the flying guest, deathly afraid it would soon join the departed.

Was The White calling?

"Another courier? And a personal favorite to add?" a distinctive female voice said in the background. Footsteps reverberated. Louder and louder, alarming the guest, causing it to back up some, but too afraid to exit the light. The arms flapped in a panic. Just the very points of fine-looking shoes entered the lit space.

An extended hand came into play.

"Are you afraid, grand one? Of me? You can be if you want, but you shouldn't either. Your kind once called my land your land; you found no better sanctuary than here. Even more so compared to the one you call 'king,' Birati Milu. Might I inquire about his new message, grand one? I'm sure it's filled with more hazardous words against me," she said. Soft and passionate. A voice of silk. The messenger released the small scroll by her feet. Its guard—still up—with the occasional flap. The mysterious figure waved her hand gently like a conductor and hummed a light tune. The scroll carried itself up to her through her gentle vibrations.

When it came into reach, she viciously grabbed it. Parchment swallowed by darkness. The messenger heard her break the seal with a slight growl. Not good. Mumbling the written words to herself with foul intent. Affirmatively *not* good! Finished, and the color of cerulean highlighted the entire room to reveal veiled women, but not its highness, Queen Evren. Shade concealed her face, save for the shape of her figure and the bright crystals that sat on her pauldrons and crown.

One of the veiled asked, "More empty threats, ma'am?"

She handed the wrinkled scroll over for the woman to read. "He tries my patience," Evren started, "If he weren't a composer, I'd have ripped through Akrav myself to extinguish his flames, but…to do that would mean war with the Pelagic Nations, and most are aligned with Somdir, whom I'm still in talks with for an alliance."

Evren knelt down to the flying messenger, extending both hands to it, speaking gracefully again, "Are you hungry, grand one? Stay the night; reserve your energy. You had a long, arduous journey, and Xantho sleeps to give rise to Melano. I would lose sleep if you were shot down for sport by some fetid human or eaten alive by some skulking Vermis. Come," The winged messenger felt her warmth. Young, but it felt the aura of her lineage's old history. This felt right.

It allowed Evren to pick it up. She stroked its feathers, following with gentle rubs on the head, only to fall asleep on her breasts.

Home has many meanings. Many places.

"That disturbed ogre sends his female *grand bustard* with sharply written words, knowing full well I wouldn't retaliate against it. But what of the others? What if it needed rest before its arrival and a huntsman came upon her? What if the natural elements displaced its course and she accidentally steered into Klaring to become a snack for the horrid that live above ground? So many scenarios that drive my being beyond Iberitus," she snapped without waking the bird up, "If the Usurper were not my sworn enemy, I'd have paid with everything in my treasury to have the thief brought forth to me—I can afford a war with Udalann. They have no formal army. Displaced bandits, old giants, and far too many farmers."

The veiled woman turned to her, "But that would mean war with Gottlir, and Somdir is heavily aligned with them, as well as the *Trasno* from *Grenvalk*, and there's the Pelagic Nations…"

Evren shook her head. "For a mere human, Leandro is quite adept in diplomacy. I remember, not long ago, everyone was fighting amongst themselves. Unification hasn't been seen since the birth of this world…when there weren't any Heralds, but the Primes walked amongst our ancestors."

She handed the bustard over to the veiled woman for care, "It stays with us until I have my thief. I don't think it will mind being spoiled collateral for the time being. And since Birati sends his personal messenger, what progress do we have on my personnel: *Jökull*?" Another veiled woman approached, stating it was deceived by Birati and lost track briefly but was back on the course again, so long as Milos had a single Cerulean scroll from her late majesty's codex.

"My dear Essent, whatever shall I do with you? As for the thief, he wouldn't dream of surrendering one of the

Ceruleans up—too fixated on their power. As much as I despise the idea, I wish he would tear *just* one in two so that it would mark him for life…then I would know everything."

The woman continued on about Milos obtaining something of value during a village skirmish in Udalann. Evren asked if it was a new scroll, which she had no interest in, but the woman showed the strange report, made of ice, to her.

"Jökull, how I adore thee. My lovely Essent came to capture one that partook in the violence there, escaping the guard that hauled off the rest to Birati's slave pits. A new party member? And the Usurper tried to grab hold of them before the thief's arrival? I wonder what she is like," she continued to read, "Oh…the mercenary refused to tell of her importance? What depraved secrets are you hiding this time, tyrant of alchemists? No matter, just another trophy sculpture for Jökull; it'll discover everything for me no matter the cost—all of you are dismissed!"

She watched as every veiled woman left the chamber to make sure no soul but hers was present. When the only sound she could hear was her own breath, she proceeded to a staircase behind the throne, leading to the peak. Evren knew she had to cease her internal seething before she entered the top. It was absolutely forbidden for her to let negative emotions get in the way in this chamber.

Words of the Mother.

The thickly fortified doors had no handles. She took a deep breath, resuming her gentle humming, and soon her voice emitted a coloratura contralto melody. Her hands waved through the air with the emotions her voice personified. The sounds of gears unlocking the doors became noticeable. A thick strip of light streamed down the center, and the doors were now open.

A marble-sculpted tomb effigy lay in the center upon a small flight of stairs, and another flight behind it revealed a large opulent mulberry tree. The leaves showed faint tints of silver on the edges. A large rectangular chunk was missing on one side. She walked past the tomb and gave all her attention to the tree.

She knelt before it in brief silence.

"Your leaves have become more lustrous recently, Mother…" she sadly expressed.

Overlooking the tree and queen in stoic silence, a figure of a great man. A casualty of war.

Chapter 5

†

Fulminant

Despite its speed and their altitude, she was neither too hot nor too cold, or disoriented or unbalanced. This means of transportation came with its own bubble of protection, invisible to the naked eye.

Enough for one to enjoy the sights below.

"Landfall!" Milos exclaimed, pointing to the port of Gottlir. Sadie looked on at all the docked ships. Many stalls and vendors were pitching their merchandise to the large crowd of different races. Just as they landed, the gear of Milos's bracelet wound down and instantly tarnished. "Hm, thought it would last longer before needing a reset, whatever," he said without care. She asked if everything was okay, but he ignored her with his eyes searching for something specific in the small market.

"Enzu, find me some stars and a fishmonger," he asked. Enzu rolled off Sadie to get on for exploring. Milos instructed her to stay close and not leave his sight by any means. He explained how marauders tend to hide among the tradesmen, along with other deviants lurking about, who are unable to gain access to the city without proper identification.

Great counterfeiters, themselves, cannot get past the guard thanks in part to tools provided to the army from the mystics of Somdir.

In her awe of taking everything in, she didn't realize, until it was too late, that she bumped into someone of small stature. "Hey, watch where you're going, lady!" a voice shouted at Sadie.

Her sights looked past her waist, nearly jumping at the sight, only to scream, **"GOBLIN!"** She was pointing at the small green man as Milos tried to do damage control since all eyes were set upon them.

"It's Trasno, you inconsiderate strawberry!"

"Here's a few celestite geodi, my good man, as an apology," Milos said, handing him some polished yellow coins.

"Citrines are nice, but I see you got sapphires. I think that'll sort out this mess," the green man hinted.

Milos squinted his eyes and grabbed hold of the green man's shirt tightly. "Don't push your luck, lad. I earned those keepers risking life and limb. Bugger off with your free coin!" The small goblin scampered off into the staring crowd. "You aren't much on subtlety are you?" he said to her. She apologized, still trying to convert fantasy to reality.

He explained simple lore on the races she has and hasn't encountered yet to try to speed her up, "Humans are abundant, but there are different variations, some being devotees to the Chroma, others aligned with the art of alchemy. Chromatics and Alchemists. You might encounter Naturals; they dabble with both but to lesser degrees. Birati is a Mairu: giants, ogres, or whatever is easier for you to remember. They thrive on fighting. Supposedly born from the core of Iberitus. I don't care for lore, but the way it's told is that a rogue Herald wanted to surpass the power of their Prime by misusing their power to birth the species with a *Harbinger* of Alchemy. The story goes that it was Cinnabar, but what do I know?"

"So what's a Harbinger?"

"Well, you already have witnessed—and have one accompanying us, strangely—a Herald. Phthalo. They are direct lines to their ruler, the Prime, who oversees their realm. They're a mystery to us all. Even the most loyal of worshippers rarely see them. Sometimes for the best. A good number aren't the 'happy to see you' type. Primes to the Harbingers are *much* more reclusive and conservative in revealing themselves compared to the more bounteous Heralds. And there are only three of them for alchemy. Don't be fooled, though. Just because Heralds seem generous, they can sometimes require deadly returns for their offerings— forfeiting life is among them."

She looked at his quiver of various colored scrolls and asked what he considered himself as. "They had a name for me once, but we'll just say 'scribe' or 'pending extinction,'" he replied with sorrow in his tone.

Best not dig too deep, she thought to herself.

"So, are there other races like the goblin I saw back there?"

His eyes searched for a specific stand to find as they walked about. "The formal name is Trasno, and they live on a nice big island known as Grenvalk. Gorgeous land, I tell you, lots of good food to hunt, and, for the most part, hospitable. Their women are surprisingly easy on the eyes, but watch out because every male has their eye on one, and if an outsider tries to butter up one, it can be a bit nasty. Can't say it isn't possible; I've seen a few humans with Trasno wives, but they always leave the island with a new scar or two. They're big on ceremonial fights," he replied, "Ah! Found what I was looking for."

They walked over to a stand with various colored powders and a small mountain of paper so thin they were practically transparent.

He continued his explanation of other races. "Right after I try to seek an audience with King Leandro, you'll meet some of my favorite mates at my home away from home, beyond the city limits. Some are Trasno, some are Sansha, natives of Somdir, and…let me ask you: Do you like animals?" She nodded. "Good, you'll meet Kosey soon. He's known as a Barangda. I won't go into details, but he's an absolute lady-killer, trust me."

He told her to choose a color for the journey.

"What are these?" She looked over the assorted palette squares.

"Instant scrolls for non-Chromatics who need quick aid on the go. Splash the powder on the parchment and the power awakens. You can gamble on a color, or I can tell you what each one does, but that'll take too long, or you can hover your hand above them, and, depending on how this journey will go, the strongest color will choose you. They're not possessed by the veil; transcribed by local scribes. composer-made scrolls cost a fortune…and more. These are base colors, so I'll clue you in on some: blue will be good for water breathing for several minutes, green will supply you with emergency rations, and red will allow you to firewalk for several minutes also. What'll it be?"

What did he mean by possessed by the veil?

She thought long and hard; the simplest colors could be the best choice, but what about something else? Sadie hovered her hand above each color. Her irides temporarily changed into the color beneath the fingers—overlapping voices vying for her attention.

I can show you light; sleep well at night. I can give a fright yet be such a delight. I can show the way; no more dismay. Avoid trampling the ice flower; this is my worthy power. A soft voice reached her mind above the rest. The strangest of transmissions.

Some of the scrolls in Milos's quiver sparked excitedly. He looked over his shoulder. But there were no transmissions.

Sadie had made her choice.

"What in the composition is this, trader?" Milos asked.

"Cardinal purple," he replied. A finger in his ear.

"My glorious ass it is, you liar!" Milos quipped, "There's rust pigment in it. What is that? Iron oxide? Is your picture beside the word 'grifter' if I open a lexicon?!"

Milos hovered his hand to try to decipher the color's ability and personality. He saw a veiled woman beckoning him with a lit sconce in one hand, but the vision was cut short when Enzu disrupted his vision.

Couldn't be. Can't be her…

The little clay man pointed to two directions where, in the distance, one can see the stalls that Milos would do further transactions.

But first…

"Are you sure you want this color? Something about it is familiar, and *not* in a good way," Milos asked Sadie.

She then hesitated, thinking he might be right on this one, until the merchant chimed in, "Tell you what. There's not much of this powder anyway, and I can't seem to unload it on anyone. Pick yourselves another color, and I'll toss in the Cardinal for free."

Milos was still unsure, but Enzu gestured to take the deal. He always trusted his little companion's instincts, so he asked Sadie to make another choice—a more assuring choice. She pointed to the base blue.

What would breathing underwater be like?

The merchant wrapped the scrolls, placed the powders in small satchels, and told Milos the final charge, "Thirty galtavos, sir."

Milos raised an eyebrow. "What black sulfur nonsense is this?! We're only getting one color, plus the freebie. The merchants inside the city charge less geodi for this small amount!"

Enzu jumped off his shoulder. He walked back and forth, turning into comical faces, as the two bickered on in a game of barter. Sadie was laughing when she saw the clay man waddling like a penguin. Milos quickly turned to shout, "Will you cease your childishness!" Enzu quickly shapeshifted into a small version of *The Thinker* statue, pretending it did no wrong. Milos and the merchant resumed their sharp words, and Enzu resumed his Grimaldi antics.

Another player caught wind of the situation.

"He's quite animated, isn't he?" a woman said to Sadie, approaching her by the side. She had similar features as Aruna, except she had a full head of black hair, and a pixie cut, but every time a breeze flowed through it, small streaks of red glistened in the light. Sadie agreed with her, studying her apparel.

"You're in awe, aren't you? *Zebecan* with a flair of Somdirian! I knew you had good taste once I saw your hair from across the market," the woman said with a smile, hand on hip. The exotic robe she wore looked like something a bohemian would wear. Jewels adorning her figure. "Where are my manners? My name is Ruby, and you are?" she asked, taking out an intricately braided cigarette.

"Sadie, umm…I'm not a fan of smoking. Can you just hold off for the moment?" she implored.

Ruby ignored her requests. Lighting the tip without a care. She sucked on the end, pleasurably, releasing some of the smoke through her nostrils, and inhaled deeper this time.

"You should try it out; you'll *absolutely* love the taste," Ruby said, exhaling a big gust of orange-purple smoke against the girl's face. Impossible to evade the smoke. Sadie waved profusely. The girl wanted to tell Ruby off for her rudeness, but something overcame her senses. The world turned into a bright field of psychedelic colors, licking at the edges of normality. Apprehended, in a trance, that stupefied her. Lulled into a false sense of security. Portals discovered.

Ruby walked right up to the young girl, putting her mouth to her ear and speaking passionately, "Why don't we go enjoy a nice cup of lime juice? I know some people I'd like you to meet. What a grand time we'll have."

Her tongue lapped against the mesmerized girl's cheek. Sadie couldn't resist; she nodded submissively, holding onto Ruby's hand to be led astray.

They were lost in the crowd.

"Just so you know, you close-fisted skinflint, I'll report you—" Milos tried to finish his tirade but was interrupted by the sweet-smelling aroma from Ruby's cigarette. Quickly turning around, he saw Enzu stamping around in his various comical forms. You could see the pulsating veins in his forehead. "Hey, boy…where's ole red at?" Milos asked sternly. Enzu freaked out when he noticed Sadie wasn't behind him anymore. Reverting back to normal. Showing a face of dismay to Milos. "I know that smell too. We'd best hurry before she gets further from us. I hate this port sometimes," Milos said.

He grabbed his new colors—with scrolls—without paying, flinging Enzu onto his shoulder, and ran for dear life as the merchant tried to chase after him, only to lose him in the crowd once he blinked randomly through it.

The bastard probably stole these powders himself. Where did the displaced girl get displaced this time?

"Now that is a fine thing you've found for us, Ruby," a man wearing a turban and eyepatch said to her.

At one end of the port, a large black ship was docked with intimidating men patrolling it. Split daggers, curved swords, and jagged fingernails poking holes in the wet wood. Some graffitied their names into the loose planks. Terrible script. Amassing illiterates. Slip of the "sword"—liberal displays of typographical errors. Rebel is as rebel does.

When was the last time they opened up a book?

"Much better than the usual women you provide. I'd say she's worth three amethysts, yeah, sixty geodi is my offer," the man offered.

Bloodlust rising. "Not only does she have red hair, but she was traveling with a powerful scribe and a bejeweled Essent; she's worth five opals, which makes it— appropriately—five *thousand*," she rebutted. The man was not having it. He tried to start up his own haggle war with Ruby, but when she further described who the scribe was, the man knew there would be extreme value in ransoming the girl back to Milos.

Begrudgingly, he gave Ruby five impeccably polished coins for Sadie. A collective of colors trapped in bits. The universe was in her grasp. Another man grabbed the girl's arm, forcing her onto the ship.

"Always a pleasure, Mirza," Ruby said, her skin beginning to melt off. Sadie's senses slowly returned once she looked back at Ruby. Her tan skin dripped off, revealing colored patches all around her body: pearlescent skin, trims of gold, purple lips, red eyes, carrot-colored hair, and pointed ears came forth. The metamorphosis was complete when four large fang-tipped wings sprouted from her back with sparkling sea colors. The hellish beauty of an insect. This was no butterfly by all accounts.

Sadie's knees buckled from the imposing horror show, collapsing onto the man, now taking her hostage. Ruby blew Sadie a kiss before making her escape into the air.

Privilege to leave without moral sense.

"Come on then, get a move on, before the scribe finds us!" Mirza shouted out to his men. They didn't bother to finish loading in the last of their supplies, knowing full well they could recoup their losses. A heavy ransom. A heavy burden.

And the ship had set sail into the pelagic…

"A shame I couldn't have her to myself a bit longer, but time is money, and time waits for no being," Ruby said to herself. A natural camouflage secluded the skin, making her translucent.

Over the market, putting distance between her and the city limits, she found secluded comfort in a tree on a nearby hill.

A particular favorite to nappers.

It seemed safe—no question from this vantage point. *No need for the camouflage anymore.* Her eyes stared endlessly at the sight of the opals in her pouch. Another puff. Another huff off the potent braid.

"Ah, this is a good life."

The ears caught wind of an unraveling sound at the base of the tree. Soothing senses told her to "relax, it's probably a rabbit." Whereas the hyper-aroused demanded she be vigilant. Overstimulated from the largesse, paranoia fiddled its twitchy finger on the sympathetic nervous system. Stress. Survival. Fear. Adrenaline. Every rush activated. *Too* aroused. Looking down, she saw Milos staring up at her.

And a sadistic smile from his hovering, veiled partner.

"Morning, beautiful," he said, grinning. Energy poured out of his hands to enter the scroll he surrounded the tree with. A pink-magenta hurricane sprung from the ground, honing in on Ruby. Streams wrapping around her body. Her screams: profound. They solidified into a beautiful crystal before the weight dropped her to the ground.

Head: left exposed.

Milos overshadowed her vision of the sky. Darkness. Palpable emotions brewing—one of his eyes turned into the same color as the scroll used. His veiled cohort leered at the imprisoned bug-woman.

Claustrophobia sets in on his hostage.

"When I smelled the scent of a rare *Mozmina* in the market, I thought to myself, 'Wouldn't it be rude of me not to introduce myself to her without flowers on this fine *Tetri* day?' But I realized I didn't have time to pluck or buy, so I thought I'd settle introductions with my Mulberry scroll.

"Is it tight in there, love? Wouldn't want you scurrying off just yet. Oh no, I need to know where the girl is, and don't even bother to deny it. Slavery always gets a high price. If those opals could talk, well…why don't you speak for them?"

She heard every word. Crystal. They were calm, but hidden under the tonality lay the presence of a judge. And executioner.

This man has seen the horror of the front lines. No, he IS the horror! Those dual-colored eyes. From gloss to matte…

"I've not a clue what you're babbling about! Free me, or face the consequences from my tribe!" she roared.

I think that worked!

He needed a faster way to persuade her. She was stalling. Distance continued to grow between him and Sadie with each passing second. Milos remembered the tactics used in Lusura. The torture. A distinctive ache in his gut. Even the stomach acids aren't as sour to fall into that line of work. Domineering? That'll do with gusto.

"End her," his veiled cohort transmitted.

"What're you doing?!" Ruby shouted out in fear. He rolled her to one side of the hill. What a view of the pelagic.

"Speak now, worm," he sternly asked. His hands held her body from tumbling into the sea.

"You wouldn't dare!"

He looked at her with such a disinterested look. One hand of balance was removed. She saw the Palatial Usurper in him. His other hand wobbled, trying to balance her crystallized barrel.

"Last chance…" he said with a low voice.

Her eyes showed panic. Overlays of water trickle out.

"Zebecans took her! They've set sail to the *Realgar Islands*!"

She started to plead for mercy.

"Thanks for the tip, love," Milos said, smiling at her.

From matte to gloss.

He released his balancing hand.

Ruby screamed all the way down the hill, trapped inside her magnificent prison. Her vision became distorted from all the violent spinning. No better way to turn the brain into jelly.

Enzu came out of Milos's jacket with that same look of despair. "Yeah, yeah, I know…but she *needed* to learn her lesson first."

Ruby's body flew off the cliff with extreme velocity; she could feel herself misshapen. Knotting and twisting. Ready to expunge.

The jewel prison shattered into glitter. Her wings were useless, but Milos flew in, intercepting her in midair.

"A little Essent told me you needed some saving," he coyly said, bringing her back to the cliff's edge, "but I don't come cheap, lovely."

He grabbed her satchel of opals as recompense, but Ruby had her ways to reward as well. All that excitement. To be so close to death. The game of cat and mouse. Her previous stimulation…surpassed.

Demented bug woman.

"Why stop there?" Her voice exuded seduction. She grabbed a fistful of his hair. Bringing her lips to his. It caught him off guard. *She should have no sense of balance from that display of barrel rolling!* Her tongue slipped in with a mind of its own. Inspecting for cavities. All to end with an innocent bite on his lower lip. A sticky, translucent trail dripped between them. Fertile. Oviparous. Marked.

Disturbing species; slaves to hormones. Swapping spit determines the levels of coupling, from strange bedfellow to eternal helpmate. No other determination. Better than sexual cannibalism at least.

"Woman, I am not for you!" Milos shouted, wiping his lips, and pushing himself away. He patted his clothes to ensure he wasn't pickpocketed—too late.

"Better the bane of my fangs than the stingers on my wings," she replied, taking flight. "I guess three opals will do. Have fun rescuing the girl, *Pictfero*. I'll find you again. Don't die on me, *love*."

Milos stood quietly to see her fly off into the distance. He didn't care about the geodi anymore.

She knows his secret.

Regardless, he still had to make haste before Sadie's captors got closer to their base of operations.

"Tsk, tsk, tsk, should've let her drown. Who knows what'll happen once she returns to the mountains?" his associate transmitted.

"Scorn me later, Mul. 'Little Red' needs us."

"I DO have an actual name! We ALL do!"

"And none of you remember anything after the sacrifice…"

"Appease our Primes so we may remember again! Find our Heralds! Our surviving tribes! Unlock our truest potential!"

"In due time…this, I promise."

The gear whirred. Thick vapors called upon. Flight over the deep sea. Retreating into his own mind. Ignoring further transmissions. There would be unscrupulous fellows in need of a beating.

Bright, brilliant days don't always go cheerily.

"It's a grand day, boys!" Mirza shouted out haughtily. The pirates surrounded Sadie on the upper deck. Lecherous words were exchanged. Others drooled at the sight of her— unbothered to wipe the dribble from their chins. An angry itch, inside their trousers, for the nubile. Maybe they'd remember that once-familiar touch from a woman had they taken regular baths. "Someone give me a tune! I feel like a song's coming on!"

And the men crooned. And they warbled. And, horrendously, yodeled. No jaunty artists here. Just the death of creativity. But he became like that of a rabid goblin: smirking from ear to ear, swaying around, sword in hand, dancing towards his latest victim—not with the best of human intentions.

The final hallucinogenic effects were wearing off Sadie, but, at this point, she wanted to pass out. Or have the side effects continue.

When does the nightmare end?

"Oh, don't look so sad, my love. Maybe a dance will set you right!" Mirza boasted, taking her lethargic body close to his. His teeth were yellow; his gums were heavily receded; body odor would make onions blush.

She wanted to vomit.

One of the men went below deck, checking around the kitchen, seeing the cook drinking out of a wine bottle, "Ain't got any cheese, apples, or pears? Mirza, the twat. The dunce had us load up everything except the last of the essentials. The rarities of all things. Would have at least a bit of leftovers if it weren't for the 'extra' cargo."

The cook suggested checking in on the cargo deck, below, to see if he could scare himself up with some hidden delectables.

"Not a bad idea, wha'chu figure? A bit of sword poking?"

"Here," the cook replied, handing him a butcher knife, "Try not to sully up the walls of the hull, eh?"

The man tilted the knife to see his grimace in the reflection—*perfect*, he thought, proceeding further below the ship.

Frightened screams echoed below.

Mirza swayed back and forth with Sadie tight against him. Round and round. Tighter. Grinding. Groping. Her limp body showed no semblance of resisting his cavalier attitude. The men finished their singing, and he tossed her to the ground. Boasting, his ego stroked, once he heard their cheers.

"Worked up an appetite! What do we have in stock?" he asked.

The cook was summoned.

"'Fraid we got very little, Cap'n," he replied, "We got enough for the way back in a week's time, but small rations— left our consumables at the port; plenty of sundries by the by."

Mirza lifted his head up to notice the sails picking up a good amount of wind. "A good gust out of the blue? Are we still favored?" he muttered to himself.

One of the men shouted out to everyone about how clear the water was, droning on about the large bounties of fish in the area. Mirza peeked overboard to notice all the would-be plates they could catch.

"Shoaling fish all around?! By the composition of arsenic, we are *indeed* favored! Get the *grand cormorants* ready for some fishing, boys!"

Those, by the figurehead, had captured and trained many of the birds perched there for times like these. Desperate, ravenous times. The birds were far larger than their great cousins, able to swallow multiple fish in one go. One after the other, each nose-dived into the ocean waters to capture many prey, and as they came back to the ship, they regurgitated onto the deck once the lines around their throats tightened. A process that helped make sure the fish did not go straight to their bellies.

But the wind kicked up a notch, and the boat started to pass by the scores of food. The calm.

"Lower the masts for now! Can't let this kind of feast pass us by. We got some rocks nearby. Can't take any chances of sinking out here with a damaged keel or hull," Mirza ordered his crew.

Sadie managed to regain her composure in a kneeling position. One of the men noticed and pulled her upright.

"Let's take a walk below deck for some spiced Zebecan wine. You and I."

Now, she was able to resist.

Sadie bit his hand deep as he wrapped it around her shoulder. A strong puncture. He cursed out to her once she tried to get away from him, but too many players were around, and another grabbed hold of her. This mate made his own proposition to Mirza: everyone gets a round. "Fine by me, but I'm first then," he said. He wrenched the girl from the crewmate's grasp, leading her to his cabin, looking at her, "I've got too many nagging wives at home; you'll be quite the refreshment."

Sadie was trying, again, to resist, but Mirza was unfazed by her small hand that wailed away at him.

Until the bracelet awakened.

As did *she*.

He shouted out in pain once a portion of his arm was set ablaze, escaping his clutch. "If you were anyone else, I'd filet you into ribbons…but maybe," he growled, unsheathing his sword, "a little beauty mark wouldn't hurt your value *too* much!" He pointed the weapon right at her, beginning his march toward the petrified girl, who had nowhere to go for miles on end.

The fiery spirit, still unseen to Sadie, drew a line of fire to block off the pervasive captain. Multiple fireballs blasted randomly at the crew. Some went overboard in flames. Burnt husks before touching the waters. Sadie didn't have a clue what was happening, but she didn't care, so long as it hurt them!

But the bracelet's power diminished.

And the spirit withdrew to recharge.

Tagging in the newest addition. A thin dark blue line of energy traced from the bracelet to her eyes. "Walk the exact path I've set for you. They cannot see it as you can."

It was Phthalo's voice. She saw a trail of dark blue mist that stopped at the figurehead. She had to trust the newly acquired Herald.

What else could she do in her predicament?

A single tenacious swing from his sword blew out the strong barrier in front of him. "Where could you possibly be scampering off to?!" Mirza exclaimed psychotically, "Almost had me there, but you got too cocky, bitch!" He noticed the way she was backing away from him and the others in an almost serpentine pattern. With the flames quickly put out, the crew laughed at her supposed retreat from Mirza.

Her back stood against the wall.

"Phthalo? Phthalo?! I need more help," she whimpered.

"It's already here," it whispered to her.

Mirza stood no more than a foot away. "I promise it won't hurt," he said, lifting the sword high. "Too much..."

Lead me from my prison, that I might give thanks to You.

"Hey, all the fish are leaving. What gives?" A crewmate said to another. "What's with the ripples?" the other said, looking to the front of the ship, noticing multiple incoming waves. Gifts from the sky king.

"BRACE YOURSELVES!"

The boat was met with a violent torrent. Everyone aboard lost their balance. Mirza slid all the way to the back end of the deck, losing his sword in the process. Another wave crashed against the boat. Tsunamis knocking. Knocking. Trying to create an entrance outside the hull. Too many sea wolves for these little pigs to withstand. Sadie braced against the wooden pillar of the foremast. The waves kept crashing, then, abruptly, stopping. Unflustered.

Just like that, tranquility washed over the waves.

The tidal onslaught disoriented the entire vessel, from top to bleak bottom. Sadie positioned herself against the wall of the figurehead. She thought *maybe* she should at least try to escape through the water, but Phthalo advised her to remain calm and stay in place.

Mirza, regaining his composure, snarled out, "Someone give me a damn good explanation on what's causing this, NOW!"

Birds shrieked forth. All the grand cormorants were released from their neckties, flocking away with great speed. Escaping back to any island, any coast, any beach. Milos sprung forth from the sea. A final tidal wave crashed against the ship.

Quite the entrance.

The quick ambush caught all the pirates off guard. Blinking in multiple directions, smashing his feet, elbows, and fists against each man. Ripples of skin create their own waves. His feet never touched the ground until every pirate on deck was downed.

Quite the feat.

"Sekani! *Sekani!* Get up here, damn you!" Mirza bellowed out.

"You alright, love?" Milos asked Sadie. Her eyes grew frightened at the beast of a man emerging from the lower decks—pointing behind Milos to look.

A dusky bald giant stared at Milos. An incurious look.

Milos looked back at him, equally unimpressed.

Mirza spat on the drenched boards, a fire in his eyes. "Bend'im and wash'im!" he commanded, "Bring the girl over when you're done."

The sound of Sekani's footsteps towards Milos shook the boat; the ship's sides frothing lines of brine.

"Do something! He's getting closer," Sadie exclaimed.

Milos waved a hand in the air. "I want a closer look; it makes it more interesting."

Enzu leaped over to Sadie to watch the confrontation. The two men gazed at one another—sizing each other up. Sekani had a minimum of two feet over Milos.

"Break'ya and drown'ya I must," Sekani finally spoke.

Milos let loose a howl at his words. He cocked his body to the side to look at Mirza. "You running a rig on me, One-Eye?! How much dirt-water has this one gotten himself into?"

Mirza gritted his teeth.

"All brawn with little going on upstairs," Milos began to insult Sekani, "Either too much ingesting of dirt-water or sniffing lines of ruby sulfur has warped things for you. Take a nap while the adults play."

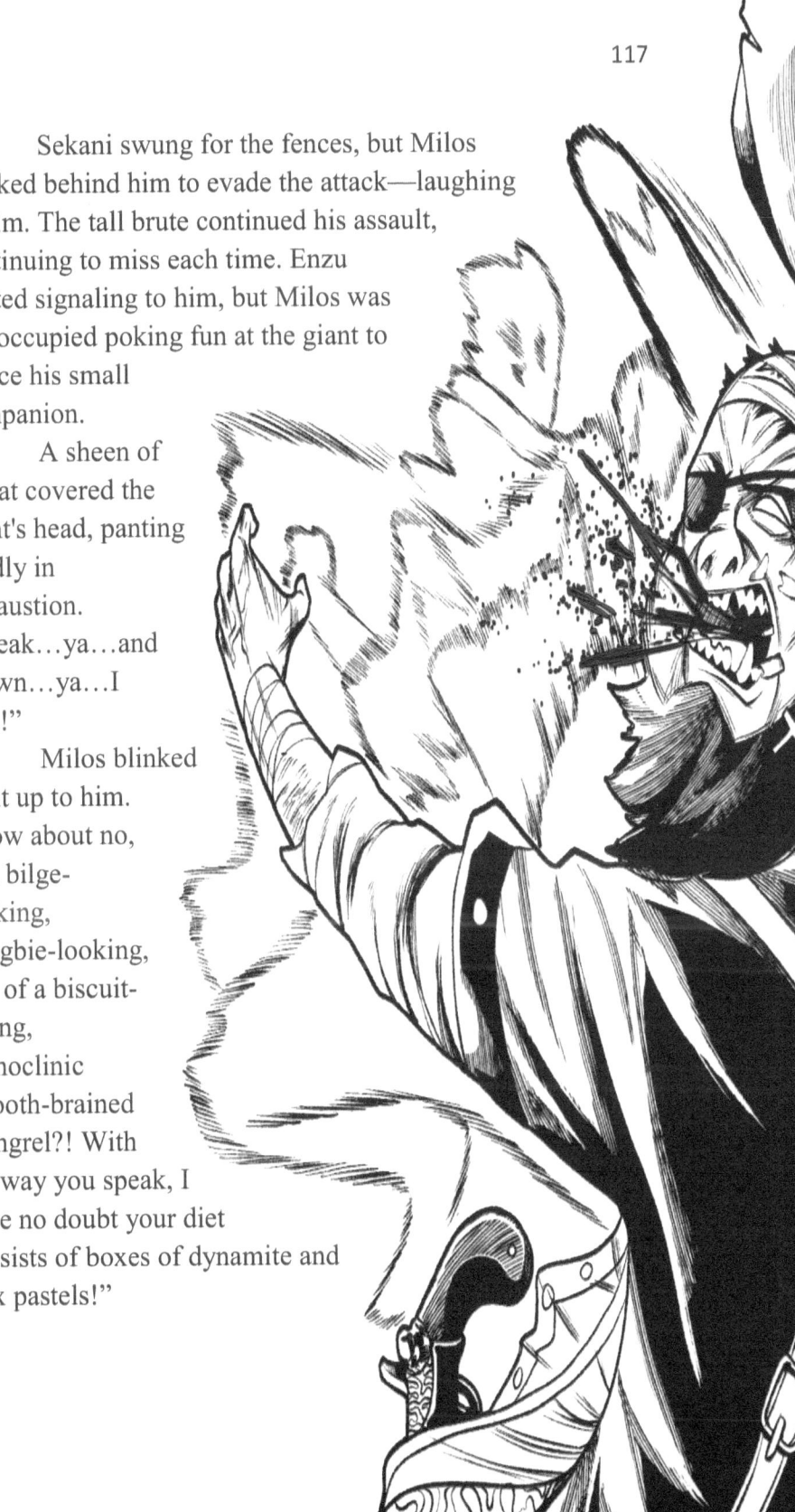

Sekani swung for the fences, but Milos blinked behind him to evade the attack—laughing at him. The tall brute continued his assault, continuing to miss each time. Enzu started signaling to him, but Milos was too occupied poking fun at the giant to notice his small companion.

A sheen of sweat covered the giant's head, panting loudly in exhaustion. "Break…ya…and drown…ya…I will!"

Milos blinked right up to him. "How about no, you bilge-sucking, dungbie-looking, son of a biscuit-eating, monoclinic smooth-brained mongrel?! With the way you speak, I have no doubt your diet consists of boxes of dynamite and wax pastels!"

Sadie tried to assist Enzu, who tried *again* to signal Milos over with his little arms, but cockiness blocked his vision down to horse blinders. Sekani revved up another assault, swinging his enormous right arm back for a mean hook, until a loud pop emitted from Milos's wrist. He held back, briefly, noticing Milos looking over his bracelet.

The gear: burnt out and immobile. Absent of its ability to instantly blink. In need of a recharge.

A moment that cost Milos dearly...

Sekani's hand smashed against Milos's temple and sent him flying several feet across the deck. The giant let out his own howls.

"That's the way to do it!" Mirza shouted in glee. The onslaught became more ferocious when some of the ship's mates joined in on the brutality of a downed man.

Stick a fork in the poor bastard because he's well done.

"Please, stop it! God help us," Sadie screamed. Mirza had almost forgotten about his original prey. That lone eye gives attention to her. He recovered his fallen sword and motioned to Sekani, "Alright boys, let's let ole red here have a say in the final blow!"

The giant brute held Milos's lifeless body over his head.

"So now that we've beaten him, why don't I give *you* the choice on which side of the ship we chuck'im over! If you don't choose, my boy here will snap his back in two, finishing the job before he's given a watery grave. Am I not generous?" Mirza said to the poor girl.

Does it matter what side? Either way...the cavalry is dismounted.

"Choose the left side, where the rocks are," Phthalo whispered into her ear, "Remain calm when they come. I repeat: REMAIN CALM AND DO *NOT* SHOW FEAR TO THEM!"

Who are "they?"

She closed her frightened eyes, going with its suggestion, pointing to the left side of the ship. Mirza peeked over to see some sharp rocks sticking out of the water.

"If we had the time, we could get a little closer to them. A good show. Oh well, Sekani, try to throw the rotting bastard on those pointers; I want to see some blood!" Mirza commanded the giant.

"What about his valuables?" a shipmate asked. "Those scrolls can fetch a good price on the mainland."

Enzu saw some of the men going to steal Milos's gear and scrolls. He shapeshifted into a ball with all his jewels having spiked ends, springing himself at Sekani's face. The giant couldn't withstand the piercing pain that blew back his head.

"Dammit all!" one of the mates bellowed. Sekani dropped Milos prematurely into the deep waters. Nothing to fence now. "All that scribe's treasure: gone," they continued to groan. Sadie leaped to the railing to see if she could see Milos, but he was far too gone to even see a silhouette.

"Get this ship back in motion; I'm bored of this stagnation, and grab that damnable Essent! A shame we couldn't see your scribe get torn up, but at least we know the waters will give his lungs comfort. Now, get over here, girl!" Mirza roared, pointing the sword back at Sadie. Prey against the wall with nowhere to go. A sea of thoughts.

The body sank like stone.

The nose allowed blue death inside.

The heart beats fast before dropping.

The mind descended into a comatose state.

The ears heard familiar voices before deafening.

But the body kept sinking.

And the collective rose.

"I refuse," a voice echoed through the waters. A slender being torpedoed into Milos's body to recover. "They will have the red waters in which they seek…once we free them of their liquid iron," it said, bringing his body up for air and onto the rocks before submerging.

In the mind of the unconscious: *When I drifted, I heard a faint melody. In this vast field of silence, one is glad to be of service. Through the dying light, frequencies were made visible. Let nature take its course as the colors fade into me. Crossing rivers and shores; symbiosis. It all starts from pieces—this life is a beautiful war.*

No fish wandered around the ship anymore. They scattered at speeds unseen by any man or predator. Their masters claim this bounty of marauders. One pelagic nation demanded retribution.

She—*of the crown*—commanded her monstrous vanguard to advance upon the unsuspecting pirates. Take all as property, and if any should resist bondage, let them feel the embrace of cold-blooded bellies.

These were their orders.

"Captain! The ship isn't moving! Something's got us anchored!"

"In vast openness? Maybe a rock wedging us. Any volunteers to go snorkeling?" Mirza asked aloud.

The boat tilted intensely to one side, jolting many overboard. They tried to climb back aboard, but massive scaled arms pulled them back down, into the depths, by unknown entities. Any still standing topside withdrew their swords.

"Brace for impact," Phthalo said to Sadie.

The waters finally parted. Unveiling the great reveal.

"You've no right! None, you protein-filled slithers! We have an agreement with *The Glaukós Imperator*!" Mirza screamed once he saw them. Beastly serpent men lunged onto the ship with exceptional swords and open snake mouths designed on the pommels. One overshadowed Sekani easily. It gazed its white eyes at the shivering brute.

"Attack, damn you!" Mirza commanded.

Sekani smashed his fist into the large serpent. Failure to flinch. Contorted fingers rewarded his failed effort. The serpent warrior returned the provocation with the pommel of its sword. A direct blow into his temple. It replicated the same action done unto Milos, except he garnered wings. The pelagic embraced the massive pirate.

More serpent warriors sprung onto the ship. Their agility was something to be seen for large creatures out of water. The battle royale was in their favor. Sadie and Enzu were getting sucked into the fray.

She, of the crown, emerged from the waters, checking on the wounded sleeper. Her fingers gently pushed the hair out of his face. Afraid to commit more harm to his features. The eyes showed no sign of waking up. She heard the faint of his breath, but she wanted so bad to see his colors. *What are they today?* They were her gateway addiction.

A fire deep within her breasts.

A fire she refused to extinguish.

Using her temperament and power, the surrounding waters bubbled. Although the serpent warriors had immense strength, the pirates trembled further once they saw the seas parting before them. She, of the crown, was the cause. Her hands waved about, conjuring large bubbles to suffocate some of the marauders while simultaneously brewing a tidal wave of reinforcements. Wrath descends upon the ship.

"By the composition, what in all the Iberlands is that?!" Mirza shouted.

The conjurer's face appeared from the highest wave. Impact imminent.

One serpent warrior came before Sadie and Enzu, casting its eyes over them. Fear filled the heart, but she did her best not to scream, remembering the words told to her before by the Herald.

But how long could she hold out for?

"I'll fillet you to bits, sea-worm!" Mirza exclaimed, lunging at the warrior. It grabbed hold of Sadie and Mirza, dragging them into the treacherous waters. The impact from the wave meteored into the ship. Everything had sunk into the glimmering black and blue.

Do you remember me?
I showed you how to smile in the mirrors of my home.
Do you hear me?
You heard my song, conveying my intensity for you.
Do you feel me?
I was your first. Your last.
Do you see me?
It's not raining.

Chapter 6

†

Gold

Gentle pats plopped against his skin. Little arms pushing back and forth for a reaction. Unresponsive.

"Thank you for saving me," Sadie said to the serpent warrior towering over her. He had managed to keep her safe from the violent powers of the one he had sworn to protect. She observed the beach they were brought to: normal sand, but strange produce on the trees.

"Don't eat the fruit unless you're Zebecan—it'll burn a hole right through you," the warrior instructed her. "Eat this instead."

He presented a prickly rock. With no effort, he cracked it like a walnut, and small siphons wriggled out.

She gagged at its grotesque sight.

"*Pyura* is safer to consume," he said.

"I'd rather not, thank you," she replied. A bothered look was displayed. "On second thought…" she said, sheepishly. Taking the eldritch item from the warrior, she slowly put small bits into her mouth; bitter. Is there sentience in the flesh rock? This tunicate?

A stream of Phthalo's power guided her to a nearby box washed ashore from the wreckage. Unable to pry it open, she asked if the warrior could assist her. His nails dug deep into the wood, ripping the top effortlessly. God knows what these same nails have done to man.

A small bounty to behold.

"Limes, lemons, tomatoes, and onions! Maybe this will work," she said to herself. *Real food.* Without thinking, she used his nail to slice the produce, almost forgetting she was using a proud beast as a culinary tool. "Don't suppose you've seen any bowls and spoons around, have you?" she asked him. That same ire again, but his curiosity wanted to see what she was up to. Proud and patient with her ignorance.

His tail slammed against one of the trees. A deluge of that strange fruit raining down. Like the pyura, he cracked one open with one hand, expelling the steaming contents that burned into the sand. *He wasn't kidding about the fire fruit.* He lifted his tongue, shooting water from a hole beneath it, and cleansed the interior shell of one-half before passing it to her.

"...Not sanitary, but better than nothing. I'll just…use my hands to mix everything," she said. Shortly after, she tried the pyura with the mixed produce, content with her simple concoction, putting the bowl up to his face. "Voila! Try this!"

"Interesting," he replied, licking the makeshift bowl clean.

"It's the closest I can make to ceviche to pair with that '*thing*' you gave me," she continued, "I guess you *can* take blood from a stone."

Warriors emerged from the waters with emaciated souls of men, women, and children of different races. Alongside the large beasts were women who almost appeared as human but had exaggerated features resembling they were a part of this sea race.

"Succor the weak!" one of these women commanded the others. Sadie saw one warrior holding a boy who was completely purple, hands hanging down with no signs of movement.

"It's just so cruel," she whimpered.

"What is?" the warrior asked.

She pointed to the child who had succumbed to the sea. One woman, of the sea race, heard her and approached the boy. She placed one hand over his stomach and the other over his mouth. Sweeping gestures ensue. Soon, small jets of water spurted out of the boy's mouth. He coughed gently, taking small gulps of air. Standing carefully, the warrior held his hand as the boy tried to keep his legs from buckling. "Be firm, child, and feebleness will wash from you," the warrior said to the child, slowly leading him to some nearby rocks to rest on with the others.

The sea woman approached Sadie.

"The boy is only fatigued. Have you never encountered Sanshan-bornes? I know they're rare to see outside of Somdir, but not uncommon as say the Barangda," she asked Sadie.

"I'm...from a place far away to have known such people existed," Sadie replied, trying to keep her ignorance a secret. Her eyes were so curious to study the woman's body.

"Regardless of how sheltered your background is, it is not polite to stare as intensely as you are doing now," the woman stated.

Sadie apologized profusely.

They were no different—all these uniquely coded beings—in temperament. A child, with the pigmentation of heliotrope, still maintains the disposition of naive innocence. The warrior, an evolution of sea predators, upheld stalwartness that kept true to its title. Long ears, scaly skin; a manipulator of water. The female was still very much in touch with her femininity. Nurturing the boy was akin to mother and son—despite being extreme opposites in nature.

Meanwhile, another sect of warriors emerged with the captors that managed to survive. Ironic how one goes from captor to captive.

"Where is he? Did they recover him too? Please…" Sadie said to herself, looking about the shoreline.

Too much movement, too many beings going in all directions, and too many ripples to focus on a single one.

But this weather is immaculate.

A splat of clay landed on her shoulder to catch Sadie off-guard. Another screech for dear life. Enzu formed with his cheeky smile. "The novelty of fantasy doesn't interest me anymore. I just want to crawl into my own bed…under my own stars," Sadie sighed.

Enzu patted her cheek as if to say, "There, there."

It started to annoy her.

"Strange Essent," the warrior said, "And bejeweled…if that thing is not from Somdir, you might as well drown in the realm of Hadal."

Sadie inquired about the grim talk regarding Enzu's features.

"Somdir, though highly restrictive to visitors, allows their unique Essents to wander the lands freely. An experiment that allows their creations to become self-aware and—if they so choose—to pass the title of master to any being they cross…if said party is compatible, of course. Otherwise, they relay information back to the kingdom. Same with their other foul familiars," the warrior informed her.

"That still doesn't tell me why I should give up the ghost."

"I never said I was done, but straight to the point: if that Essent is not from Somdir, you have stolen property from Celanjung, and that composer will never cease to free your head from your lovely neck."

More dangerous talks about this ruler, and still, they were heading to her realm. What if Birati was wrong, and she refused forgiveness?

Sadie tried to pry more from the warrior, but he resisted her weak attempts at interrogation. Inquisitor-proof. His best option: pointing off into the distance at two individuals. Starstruck with each other's presence. "Best wait for them to finish their business and not interrupt. Our nation depends on those two," the warrior finished.

He took his leave. Fellow comrades needed aid.

The young girl didn't know what to do. A balmy breeze passed through. The sun, drying out her clothes. They smelled of salt and fish. *Better alive...I suppose.* She stood still to realize this all happened because of her *not* holding her post in the market.

Wanderlust yielded no reward.

Damned insect! Even here there is a culture of romantic stoners draped in gypsy apparel. Thank God they found him alive and well.

Blue trails surfaced from her bracelet. "Nothing wrong with getting close enough to hear without intruding," Phthalo whispered. She hesitated. *It wasn't right,* she thought, *to eavesdrop on such exclusive privacy.* She stood her ground, telling the Herald why it was not possible. "Admirable, but they aren't hiding in secret. Not to mention within earshot of others. Just follow the trail. If you listen attentively, you just might come to understand him more. It serves a purpose to keep you from harm," it responded.

"Harm from what?"

Another trail, smaller, pointed to her right foot. "Dig your hand into the sand; retrieve the item *carefully*. Because while he has his own pursuers, you have given him—and yourself—additional trouble that is now becoming ubiquitous," it proclaimed.

She knelt on the warm sand, slowly digging into it with her fingers, only to feel her joints beginning to shiver with anxiety. One hand had to hold the other in place to keep it steady while she continued her plowing motions. Flashed images of a beast's teeth snarled in her mind. The rabid sounds of a wolf ready to gorge on a little red riding hood.

The hand felt it. *Grab it, now yank!* A satchel, and inside was the supposed cardinal purple, with iron oxide, undisturbed by the ocean, the torrents, the previous disasters.

Stolen mystery follows thief and accomplice.

"Both sconces are lit. Liminality proceeds—no more sleep, just the rousing of his colors," Phthalo whispered, "As we progress, I'm going to need you to try your best to not beg for mercy when the hardships unveil like before. Celanjung's queen has always remained stationary since taking power but former royalties from the Abyssal and Kotsudas are en route—none, so far, can contest their strength."

Most people forget how time works. It's very humorous to see how short forever is when the bad times swoop in unexpectedly.

The young girl was so flustered. She remembered the stories told to her from medieval times: the torture methods used in the *Spanish Inquisition*, the bodies that fell in the *Battle of Towton*, and *Robert the Bruce* cleaving through *Henry de Bohun's* skull during the *Battle of Bannockburn*. The display of violence at the border of Lusura was just the tip of what exaggerated death looks like in these lands of peculiar races with their godlike attributes.

A giant can split you open like a soft bun, but what are these Chroma capable of when used in war?! The Alchemists?! Are they like mad scientists?! Oh no…Naturals. I think I'm surrounded by them. Don't ask! Don't pry! I'll sew my lips until I see safety again!

Iberitus's triumvirate of social-cultural systems is as ruthless as those on Earth. Maybe a little bit more.

Enzu transformed into a miniature jumart and tried to push her legs towards Phthalo's first path. Sadie had forgotten about it. Too much overthinking. Maybe she can still catch the end without disturbing them. Behind some clustered palm trees, she sat in silence watching them.

"She's so pretty," Sadie whispered to herself.

Their feet were partially submerged in the water as small waves lapped over them. They couldn't let go of each other's gaze; neither did they let hands part from one another's embrace. His thumb slowly caressed her skin, trying to be as subtle as one could be.

She smiled with each stroke.

He wore a tired half-smile.

Something wonderful is transpiring here.

"When I saw your lifeless body fold into the depths, magnetized by the abyss, my heart sank, just like you, and I thought, 'If he were no more, then what reason do I have to continue?'" she said to Milos. "But I felt your warmth on me. So fervent."

An immeasurable amount of fatigue sat on his lids as he spoke. "The Herald of Crimson knows I burn for you. Even if the Harbinger, or the Prime of Sulphur, were to take me, I'd know the pelagic would rebirth me back into your arms."

She placed his hand on her cheek. "You speak like the clearness of this water for someone who almost succumbed to it. I found you soaked; now you are burning beyond Crimson. Will you set me alight as well? Speak truths only."

He held her at the waist, one hand massaging the small of her back. "Was I not meant for this? To hold you sacred like water in the palm of my hand in the scarcity of the desert?" he whispered.

"Your eyes still show loneliness, always lost in thought, forgetful of time. Please don't draw terminal breath."

Concern on the cusp.

"Never with you in sight," he responded.

Both of her hands raised to his face, "Then stay with me this time! We can build a home on any island here. You need not carry on into dangerous territories for monetary reasons anymore. Father has approved our day. He still waits. We can finally have a family. I am yours as surely as the day when the sirens intone our vows."

He closed his eyes, letting out a deep sigh. "I am still pursued by the coldest of angers. It would be wrong to bring her wrath to your people."

Rising from liquid blue, a similar human-like male emerged from the waters with several others.

A warrior who commanded with his presence.

"Then let that witch of gems and talking trees come upon us! You speak as if we cannot hold our own against a few veiled women alongside faceless Essents'. We are innumerable. We have faced the Akrav, the Hadal, and the Abyssal! They don't come near us anymore. We are the apex above all other pelagic nations!" he boasted.

"The Abyssal again. Must be a scary place," Sadie said to herself.

The male warrior heard the young girl perfectly. Thick ropes of water spurted from the sea behind him. Much like the woman earlier, he manipulated the water with his hands to lasso Sadie towards the group.

"A Zebecan spy!" he shouted.

Milos looked at poor Sadie tied up in the air. He turned back to the female from the pelagic, "This is another reason I can't settle down just yet. The current mission."

The woman looked up at the young, struggling redhead with curiosity. She saw Enzu also trying to flag her down.

"Let her down…gently," she commanded.

Pride sucked its teeth.

The manipulated streams placed the young girl back onto the sandy beach. She was flustered, trying to wipe the sand off her knees. The female of the pelagic approached her cautiously. Sadie was shocked to notice that her eyes resembled stained glass.

An awkward silence followed their mutual gaze.

"Current affairs have caused me to become this one's ward. Birati suggested it could end favorably for me," Milos explained.

"End what exactly?" she asked.

"Evren's perpetual pursuit."

"This Somdirian is going to negotiate on your behalf for amnesty?"

"She's not a native—or of this world—but from beyond, like the ancestors of humanity."

"Like yours?"

"Who can honestly say…"

The woman extended a hand to Sadie. "If you're going to release my love from endless pursuit, then I offer peace. I am *Natalina*, and the one who released you is my brother, *Duilio*. We welcome you to the *Euphotic Nation* of the southeast waters."

Contact was made with this unnatural beauty. Sadie felt her grip tighten just enough to send a message: be warned. Natalina's smile showed warmth, but the hand's hidden strength was ready to eviscerate.

She was a tempest hiding in plain sight.

Stories were exchanged to bring the new company up to speed. Preparations were finalizing to get back to the task at hand.

New creatures to behold.

From the waters came two that had undressed their camouflage: one slinking its body up Natalina while the other crawled at her feet, bellowing small grunts at her. She picked up the strange reptile delicately to cradle it like a newborn while the other—some strange lumpfish with a spiraled top— studied young Sadie from the shoulder.

"*Kal'i* and *Mar'e* wouldn't forgive me if they didn't see you off," Natalina said to Milos. He wagged his finger at Kal'i, a reptilian known as a *skalume*, before playing the staring contest with Mar'e, a *birubal*.

"You miss *Mod'i*, don't you?"

Natalina

"Every day...he saved me as a child," he replied with a low tone.

"Just like—" she continued before he interrupted.

"Don't. Please...I already went through my blues at Birati's table thinking of her."

"Are you certain you don't need an escort? That damnable prism of yours could give out over the waters, and we can't have you getting caught by other Zebecans or rivals that lurk in our waters," Duilio said, approaching beside his sister.

"I overexerted...Let my emotions get the better of me. Maybe if I tattoo the letter R on the back of my hands, it'll remind me to relax."

Holding his hand up to the sky, the prism reacted to his call, winding up the gear in response. Sadie saw the stream of lines coming together: stratus forming. "I know there's enough juice to get us back to the mainland; come, lass, it's time for our departure," Milos said to her.

He guided her on the strange transportation with Enzu to the forefront of the cloud. She turned her head back to him, slightly shocked, and noticed him and Natalina lip-locking.

Everyone deserves their moments of joy.

"Don't die on me. It wouldn't be fair to journey into paths that I am unable to," Natalina said to him caringly. She didn't want to let go of him. Scared for him. The hazards of his nomadic lifestyle. If he fell in the forest, would the birds relay it back to her? If he disintegrated by some crazed alchemist or renegade chromatic, would the winds transmit it back to her? Would his veils? So many unmarked graves. So many lost loves who never got the chance to say goodbye.

They waved their waves before all became non-existent dots to the naked eye.

"When will you see her again, sir?" Aqua transmitted.

"Who knows…" Milos responded.

"The moments go by so quick," Col transmitted.

"We'll safeguard you; don't worry," Aub transmitted.

Turn your back on a child, and you'll see how quickly they change. They always remember how they were raised.

These two were fond of one another. Of calm waters and community for one. Of trauma and orphan for the other. Maybe in one set of eyes, it was wrong for their impetuous behavior to become enamored so quickly—disastrous results.

But the equations came out harmoniously.

Somehow, they found each other's company.

Breaking their infinite cycles.

Advancing the venture.

Chapter 7

†

Humors

Twins of gold

Accompanying
Wrinkle and nose
Sneering through
dark wood among frost
Sets of hands, rising
Rerouting blue paths of the Herald
To its blind rage
Away from
The Palatial Usurper.

It slithered past craters
Into dry wood
Past the guard
Silent invasion
To steer the boy
Into its imposing domain
To stand by it
To wrest control of any and all
From organic
To Prime
Inviting ascension
With erroneous promises.

False organism
Assassin of the Deep
Advancing the many
Distracting the king of clay

Planning a murder
On the one who broke its mouth
Tore its right hand
Riddled it with scar tissue
Punctured its lung
Producing raspy breaths
Leading the path of brethren
And addled Picti
With the use of a grand egg
Excreting plague bearers
In the name of Antimony.

When diplomacy has failed, the ugliest of all creatures rear their heads out to ensure the beginning of all ends. Ends that only the dead can see.

They arrived back at the port at nightfall. Temperatures fell sharply, flitted nerves, and spazzing muscles. Entering the city proved difficult. The guards are on high alert. Questions were asked in regards to Sadie's appearance—fearing she was a spy for Somdir. Milos had talked them down from further interrogation when he presented an opal from his sack to move towards the Capital with no more impediments and a personal escort. Currency always proved useful in persuasion. A carriage was provided since air travel, on the stratus cloud, was prohibited.

"What's got everyone riled up?" Milos asked the escort.

"Many strange attacks on the northern border," he replied.

"The northern regions are always under siege from Klaring's unrecruited and their wildlife, the tribals, and Lusuran deserters. What's so different this time?" But the escort did not answer. "I hope it isn't what I think it is…" Milos muttered.

Sadie looked at the city with extra curiosity. The people seemed hardier than those she saw outside the walls. They stopped briefly, waiting for an intimidating group of militants to walk across the path.

"An F&C unit…looks like they're making their way to the west gate," Milos said.

"Who are they?" Sadie asked.

"*Flint and Coin*: private military contractors commissioned by the king and Gottlirians only. Usually deployed for rescues, but I'm guessing this unit is on a search and destroy mission," he replied.

"What makes you so sure?"

He pointed out two members in the back that weren't in military garb. "Because they got two aristarch instructors with them. They're the university's top alchemists and also belong to another group known as *Clay and Powder*. Mostly a support faction, usually in helping with expansion or economic projects, but since they're with F&C, I'm guessing they're on support duty. I'm surprised they don't have a composer with them."

The alchemists had an intensity to match the soldiers' piercing looks. On the path, some citizens stepped out on the well-crafted walkways to watch them pass. The boys looked on in awe, with some thinking, *Someday, I'll join!* The girls either shied away, with heads bowed in respect, or tried to garner attention by dropping handkerchiefs, which failed to work on the diligent.

One set of eyes, from the valor, made a sudden glance at one of the fair maidens, but not for its intended purposes. Behind the young girl, a man, in passing, slipped his fingers into her dress and pickpocketed some geodi. The F&C contractor pointed his pistol in her direction and released only one subsonic full metal jacket.

A scream came from the crowd in unison with many hitting the floor, including the maiden. She heard the wincing of a man behind her: the pickpocket. His duplicitous hand had a neatly centered hole; smoking. The guards jumped to action when the contractor withdrew the stolen coins from his purse. Off to the tombs with this one. He'll think long and hard about the situation.

One guard joked that, with plenty of time, he'll get from the adjudicator; he'll learn to whistle with his hand's new wind corridor.

The contractor handed over her money. And her handkerchief. With a quick wink, he returned back to the line, and the detail resumed their march. She was captivated by the strapping young lad. Tormented by the fact she forgot to ask his name.

"Even the most slippery of outlanders never make a career in the city limits. They'll soon find out where he came from and seal up that crack. A little 'physical' persuasion, no doubt," the escort said.

Everyone followed the letter of the law here. Sadie saw the contrast difference between the city and the port. Paths had no debris. Shop displays either sparkled or looked fresh. Signs pointed to fines for spitting, among other bodily fluids that defaced property values or bankrupted public morale. Criers were given strict rules to cease and desist on vespertine's arrival unless it was government-approved. And one crier belted out announcements for military recruitment in the night.

Although you won't find the haggard here, there were prominent displays of quiet anger from the elderly, the military-aged, and those coupled. They wanted the same glory days of expansion their ancestors had. For boasting. For new territory to claim. For new holiday homes. It didn't matter if it consisted of diplomacy or by force.

They craved to extend Gottlir's reach and influence.

"I don't like how some of these people talk," Sadie remarked, trying to hide from their eyes.

"Take the bad with the good. Gottlir was founded on expansionist ideals; that's just how some of them were raised, mainly military and legislative families. A lot of them still feel the effects of losing out on the East to both Lusura *and* Udalann. Of course, Birati reclaimed the lost territory back from Lusura and allied with Gottlir, since it was an independent country before, so they're not *that* angry. Ideologies are nuanced and variable, and the people are mostly affable. All you need to know is you're safe and welcomed here. So put your worry-worn forehead away. That's how you get wrinkles."

No country is perfect, but Gottlir tries to prove they are superior to others. And it's not that far off. Maybe the king should have a walk through the port to see its current state of moral decay. Surely he could spare some of his oversized carnivoran pets to dissuade current and future transgressors.

Onward to the Capital: *Haven's Mark.*

"Are we allowed here?" Sadie asked. They entered the main castle where the king resided.

"They know me," Milos replied. He talked to several guards before reaching the captain, a large woman with muscles to match.

"*Tekla*! Good to see you. Real quick, I need an audience with Leandro on urgent business," Milos said to the woman.

"You're too late for that; the king left earlier to the north garrison with the council, as am I at this moment," she responded.

"...You can't be serious...does this mean—?"

"Yup, war has started with Klaring again, but this time they've disbanded with Lusura."

Broken alliances?

Milos was pleading for someone, with Leandro's authority, to write to Queen Evren for permission to enter her realm, without giving the notion of espionage or being seen as a declaration of war.

"I might be able to assist," a youthful man said, approaching.

Milos quickly knelt both legs on the ground with his head bowed.

"Prince *Ramirus*, I ask your help; name your price."

The prince noticed Sadie, scrutinizing her look, before grabbing Milos off the ground. "There's no need to genuflect, Milos; you've done your fair share for my father and the people. Your proclivity for dangerous work is well recorded. The least I can do is to try to return the favor...so long as you tell me what it's all about," he said, looking again at Sadie. Milos updated the prince on the attack on Udalann, Sadie, and Birati's advice.

Tekla noticed the bracelet on the girl's wrist. "The Mairu composer trusts you; that's enough for me to trust you as well!" She heartily hugged Sadie—feet dangling in the air.

"Oy! You'll erase the pneuma from her being," Milos shouted.

Tekla laughed wildly. "We redheads don't crumble that easily!"

"Did you not hear what I told the prince?! She's *not* a Somdirian!"

"I've heard enough," the prince said, "Send for my adapter." A guard went off to grab the scribe. "Remember, Milos, I cannot forge my father's name, but my own. So the weight may not carry."

The scribe came before them.

"I hope you reconsider this venture because *that* woman will have you torn limb from limb—I see you have multiple Ceruleans on you still. Might be wise to return them by other means," the prince said, "Bird couriers could work."

"Can't take the chance. Better done personally…just have your adapter add that in. I'd rather not deal with the *Assinikoda* when we arrive at the marshlands," Milos replied. Another race Sadie asked about.

"Swampfolk that live in marsh reservations. Very dangerous sort. They don't belong to any nation. They just have a treaty with Celanjung," Tekla said to her. Politics has many boundaries.

The adapter finished writing onto the parchment and prepared to send it via bird. "Do you intend to stay in the Capital until it returns with a reply?" the prince asked.

"Who knows how long that'll take? I'm returning back home to rest for the night before setting out there and hoping for the best."

"Then you should know that Tekla and I are heading north to aid Father, I hope we meet soon; we could really use the help…" the prince said, trailing off.

"The north garrison, *Sarsen's Pass*. What are the chances of it falling?" Milos asked in a serious tone.

"...When the king goes to the frontlines, it's all or nothing. The ramifications, if it were to fall, are too high to even consider. Good luck to you two."

Milos stopped him quickly to ask another favor, not as demanding but of high importance nonetheless. "Birati had made some, but considering I lost most of my provisions in the pelagic, I promised to deliver some back home," Milos said. The prince chuckled and gave him permission to—partially—raid the kitchen. "Take only *one* batch; Father does have his sweet tooth when finishing important work," the prince said, making his exit from the great hall with Tekla.

"Come on, lass, we need to pick up the pace," Milos said, running into the kitchen quarters. She followed behind, Enzu's legs flying in the air, arms gripping her shoulder; more pursuits.

"This, this, and this, oh! Especially this!" Milos was shouting, blinking rapidly around the room to grab multiple bags of food.

"Greedy..." she grumbled. Enzu nodded in agreement.

Milos finished by grabbing a decorated box with gold inlay inside one of the ice boxes.

"What's in the box?" she asked.

"A gift for my little brother, well not biological, but as close to one as you can get. Damn pirates ruined Birati's batch. Better not tell him or he'll blow up every Zebecan island. I like to holiday on some of them. Been some time since I've been home," he said. They made their way out of the castle and realized their escort was no longer there.

"Guess we're walking it until we reach the port; maybe the west gate is closer; come on!" Milos exclaimed.

The west side of the city had more of a raucous vibe to it, far away from the prude academics on the southern side.

Sadie witnessed the majority of denizens leering at her. "I still don't understand the fascination behind my hair color."

"It's rare for people to set eyes on a 'warrior-mage' from Somdir. Their society is on par with introverts or the stubborn recluse. Besides the guard, people here are skeptical of their intentions since they tend to stay neutral to anything beyond their realm. Despite its alliance with Gottlir. You won't find them taking a huge part in any proxy wars except those that've gone rogue. That'll put the fear of the Primes straight into you."

Strange gods…

"Get out, you rotten bastards!" a man yelled out from inside a nearby tavern.

"We're paying customers, you bloated bumpkin!" a high-pitched voice shouted back.

"No Trasno allowed here!" the man shouted some more. The door burst open with three goblins blowing raspberries—except the one wearing a skull—to the owner.

"Forget it, brothers, let's just head back to the village," the skull-wearing goblin said calmly. He and Milos noticed each other.

"Fancy meeting you here, *Sibi*," Milos said.

"Milos! We did it! We finally did it!" the blade-wielding one shouted gleefully.

"Did what, *Daru*?"

"We got the book," the gun-wielding one chimed in.

Milos saw Sibi clutching a thick tome with tentacles slithering out. "You three really did go into an underground dungeon? And came out alive?!"

"Almost didn't; it would've been a shame not to see Grenvalk one last time," Sibi said.

"We came back with a fortune too! But this louse refuses our geodi!" Daru shouted, kicking against the entrance.

The gun wielder noticed Sadie. "I thought you were heading East after that tip-off. How'd you manage to pair with the Somdirian?"

"She's not, *Xamak*, she's…the Heralds must've intertwined our paths, so unless you three are heading back to the village, I can explain everything…AGAIN!" Milos shouted in frustration. He looked over to Sadie, "I'm covering your head; this is irritating me!"

"To hell you are!" she responded.

The goblins laughed to themselves.

"…Sadie, these are the *Newt* brothers: Sibi, Daru, and Xamak. We belong to the same village." More strange allies, but better than encountering raiders.

"We commissioned a carriage for the day; why not show her the countryside as opposed to an aerial view?" Sibi said.

"A carriage? You boys trying to show me up?"

"You won't believe what we fought! But *we* prevailed! Yes!" Daru grabbed hold of Sadie's hand. "So, there we were—!"

He waved his small sword around enthusiastically while telling the tale. She smiled throughout his story; a friendly goblin. Better yet: Trasno. He continued at length while they traveled to the south. Milos talked with the others, sharing the food he procured from the king's kitchen.

Sadie looked up at the sky, noticing the colors streaming about like aurora borealis. There was true beauty in this world.

If it is possible, as far as it depends on you, live at peace with everyone.

"We're back! And we got Milos with us too!" Daru shouted upon exiting the carriage.

"I figured you lived under the sky," Sadie said to Milos. "I do, but this is my true home, where everyone I care about lives," he replied, entering the tavern.

"Kitchen's just about closing! Last call!" a woman shouted. Sadie saw a light purple-skinned woman with a tattoo on her face behind the bar. "A newcomer? Where'd you find this one, lover boy?" she said, teasing Milos.

"Why not say Somdir like everyone else?"

"Any true Somdirian knows she isn't one of us—no offense."

She extended her hand to Sadie. "Name's *Riha*."
Pleasantries exchanged.

"Our Riha is a *real* Somdirian, but she just had to have a taste for the adventure life with yours truly back in the day before leaving the birthlands of the Chroma," Milos said, gulping down a mug of ale.

"Those days are long gone; I like my peace here on the border. I think it's the safest spot in all of Gottlir," she said.

Sadie just stared at the woman. Was she an elf?

"Not polite to stare," Riha said.

"Give'r a break; she's getting crash-coursed into everything these days. Now that she's seen someone from Somdir, she can get an idea of your people, well, the Sansha at least."

Sansha...the same as the boy who was rescued from drowning.

"I saw one of your people, a young child. I wonder what became of him and the others," Sadie said.

Milos filled Riha in on the Zebecans running a smuggling business down at the port.

"And a Mozmina was involved too? *Conation* is ending on a sour note. *Putration* better be grand. What am I saying? It always is!"

Milos looked over to Sadie. "That's the month we're in, and what follows, before you ask; I'll show you a calendar later."

The Newts ate ravenously, save for Sibi, with the other patrons.

"Milos..." Riha's voice trails, "I have a heavy load downstairs of flour I need help with."

She pulls up a trapdoor behind the bar.

"Oh, come on now, I've been run ragged these last few days with raiders, pirates, and—" he tried to continue.

"Stop whining! Come! Kosey! Bring our new guest some stew!"

"Oy, wait! I haven't seen my boy yet!" Milos shouted while being dragged down. No time like the present. The trapdoor slammed, and the sound of locks clinked underneath.

"Hi, would you like fish or meat?" a young voice asked Sadie from behind. She turned, eyes in disbelief, lips beginning to curl, cartoonishly catlike, slightly squealing at the sight before her.

Don't pinch me; don't wake me up; just don't!

This was no time for heavy labor. He disliked basements—or being underground in general. A feeling of abandonment, like lonely hearts wasting away without a body of light.

But Riha had other plans.

"I don't understand why you had to lock the damn door; if you have a secret, just tell me," Milos said. His agitation showed.

"Best to show you…" Riha whispered, "Come out now; I have someone here for you to meet."

Milos saw a moving silhouette from behind the stacked barrels. His scrolls illuminated. The figure scuttled out in full presentation.

"DECEPTION!" Mulberry transmitted.

Milos grabbed one of his scrolls to invoke, but Riha stopped him.

"Have you lost your senses, woman?! What is *this* doing here?!"

"Keep your voice down! He's here to help," she responded.

An aged, grizzled, man-sized rat, draped in a biomechanical robe with various weapons, cautiously looked at Milos and his scrolls. "I seek diplomatic immunity in exchange for information."

"I'm not daft, Vermis; your species has always enacted war with *every* nation! I've seen your kind slaughter children, toss men into the mouths of those oversized monstrosities breeding in your caves, defiling the land with urine and scat, and behead women! What makes your words speak the truth?!" Milos said, gritting his teeth.

"Let me imprison him!" Mulberry transmitted.

"His kind does not do fair play, sir," Aqua transmitted.

"Ready to bludgeon..." Col chimed in.

"It's *Tarwini* to you, Pictfero. Keep those veils in line."

"...Are you in league with the Mozmina, because the one I dealt with recently revealed me as well."

The rat man drew closer.

"Your people are of Klaring's domain. Your mind is...well...more cohesive. Born a Klarinite. Raised as an Iberian. They aren't extinct like others would have you believe. Positively bloodthirsty compared to my brethren. Maybe that is why they hold the first level, only following orders from the bottom where the queen reigns.

"That's right! Klaring has multiple levels! Your mentally unstable brothers and sisters hold the first, the *Rubicund Domain*. Tarwini's home—no longer mine—holds the second level. Pictfero are the ones giving the orders on the atrocities you speak of. The leader, *Ard Rex Calbhach,* and his heir, *Edling Gibroy*, are advancing on Gottlir to claim it for their own expansion purposes.

"They've had enough of living underground. Had enough living with my blood and the deep ones. They found a way past the frozen mountains on the border, bringing large siege machinations accompanied by Tarwini, *Orke*, and Mairu who have defected. The waters to the south are still protected, but they wane like the mountains. A Pict commands the 'Grayskins' onward to Haven's Mark, whereas Ard Rex and Edling will open the chokehold at Sarsen's Pass."

"I refuse to believe I was born from Klaring's blood soil!"

"Whoever your parents were, at least one was a Klarinite and the other from Gottlir or another realm. Your eyes are the evidence. But…I gather you don't know for certain who they were. I can help when the time comes."

Milos wanted to continue his argument on lineage, but Riha insisted he cease this derailment of emotions. It will have to wait.

"How can a Pict lead Orke's if he isn't one?" Milos asked.

"Primor of the Orke Assembly, *Flann Treasach*, contested many on the surface. You know those lesser-minded beings; a little bit of winning and they all hail you as a warrior-king…until someone else usurps you. He has his own menagerie; he rides a *guivre*. Can you imagine a human commanding a wyvern? Status is on his side."

"Tell him how they managed to bore through the pass," Riha said.

That's true, Milos thought.

In a time long before he came into existence, the leader of Somdir aligned with Celanjung's leaders to place an impenetrable ward across the entire mountain range. The water's barriers were recent after the joint attack on Celanjung and the near capture of Aureate's Mark. Whatever lived on those mountains before was now divided amongst themselves.

Hostile pelagic nations as well.

"They say it's a rumor, but I say it's empirical, that a certain Chroma's Herald has deserted their Prime—undoing centuries of division. From here to Lusura and Klaring. The ward is weak, and it is only a matter of time before it falls. Imagine a head-on attack if Klaring's large beasts bore through—or worse—bore under. Fly, even. No nation will be safe from Klaring's rabid creatures, let alone their military.

Each level will vie for a slice of Iberitus before setting eyes on the pelagic. Even the Prime Aeolid Ashokara would struggle against former allies."

So the discord between the two is true. But what's this about rogue Heralds betraying their Prime? Is that possible? It's unprecedented. Are there no consequences? Why does the Prime not intervene? The girl's curious nature is afflicting me.

"If you state this as a fact, then you would know which Herald is responsible. What Chroma do they belong to?" Milos asked.

The rat man pointed a finger at one of Milos's scrolls, the same one that blinded Birati.

"You lie like a rug," Milos said angrily.

"Do you know why you have not been sacrificed to the Prime of Argent? Cerulean protects you from it…for what reason is beyond me."

"You're no ordinary Tarwini," Milos showed civility.

"I hear the messengers; hear their veiled ones; know their price. Cerulean keeps their secret tight. Their Prime might've blessed you. For what reason? A tighter secret."

"...Who are you?"

"I am *Enitan-Navid*, last of my kin, nemesis to the Zad clan, at your service."

Enemy of the Zads! Milos thought.

"Let me tell you what Olu-Zad has been up to, young scribe."

The dawn of a new age was upon the world. To all who slept through it, let it be known that your paradise is coming to an end. For the old founders, cornerstones were on the cusp of breaking, and the new had red in their eyes.

Riha and Milos withdrew from the basement, only to come upon a commotion that had most patrons laughing, while one was embarrassed.

"Please, ma'am, stop," a young voice said.

Milos looked over the bar to see Sadie holding, and squeezing, a young beast boy with absolute glee.

Something off the fantasy bucket list to check off.

"Bout' time you two showed up; Kosey here is about to be snuggled to death," Sibi said with a sly grin.

Milos tried to pry the boy from her arms, looking over to Enzu, "A little help here?!" The little clay man shrugged.

Riha went around the counter with a skull she had hanging on a pillar. "Sadie, was it? If you don't let go of my boy, one of these will come for you!" She placed the display at point-blank range to Sadie's eyes. The girl shrieked at the strange monstrous piece and let go of him.

"I'm sorry, I couldn't help it; he's...he's just *so* cute!"

"Strange adolescent you have with you, Milos," Riha said, raising an eyebrow.

"She's a girl, unlike you. Those arms of yours have more testosterone than what's between a jumart's legs," he teased. Riha threw the skull at Milos, who managed to teleport in time. "Don't be like that, love; how about we share a bowl of cullen skink and call it a night?"

Another skull, with a half design, behind the counter glowed brightly. Unintelligible voices penetrated Milos's mind. He groaned in pain, gripping his temples, beginning to sweat. "By the composition, let up, woman!" His speech started to slur.

A tug at Riha's apron.

"No more, please?" Kosey pleaded.

"Of course, my love," she said, patting him.

The demonic skull subsided its glowing aura. Milos shook his head about, "Bloody schism magic."

Kosey approached him, "Welcome home, Milos!"

Sadie noticed how quickly he went from agitated to calm.

"I got you something, buddy," Milos said, handing him the decorated box, "I hope you enjoy them."

An assortment of plump cakes. The small boy gobbled one immediately, thanking Milos with a full mouth of the cream pastry. He handed one to Riha, the Newts, and finally to Sadie to enjoy. She kept quiet while watching the others converse with one another. She decided to step outside. In need of some fresh air. It was a humble environment. Small cottages spread about.

She took notice of a lit tower over some hills in the distance.

"That is *Eulalia's Watch*, and not too far from it— although you can't see it from here—is *Euphemia's Keep*," Sibi said, joining her.

She looked down at him, disturbed by his look, but not completely by the way he presented himself. "Why do you wear that awful-looking thing on your head?"

Rika & Kosey

He gave her a bit of side-eye action, "Not one to beat around the bush? I'll ignore your crude bluntness…this time," he began, "This frontlet was discovered on the beaches near my home when I was a child. My overly eccentric brother, Daru, placed it upon my crown as a joke when I was trying to learn the arts in peace—he thought my skull would crack under the pressure of my studies.

Visions of the Old World penetrated my mind. Long before this spinning orb was ever called Iberitus. It has shown me my ancestors, their plight against the Mairu, and the cause of weeping that paralyzes each and every Trasno once a year; it is my anchor, and I still do not know its name, but I honor its gift."

"Does it make you feel secure?"

"No, the safety of my brothers does, and that is why I continue to study the arts so that they may never find themselves in deep peril."

The tome under his arm had its grotesque tentacles reach for her bracelet, but she quickly stepped away to avoid their touch. "The book sees the fire inside. Such anger. It also sees your guiding Herald, as do I, and we see its near future displaced, and another material…" he said.

Phthalo showed itself to them, "I intend to stay by this one's side until the journey is settled."

Sibi gave off a low, unsettling chuckle. "Even the Heralds are fallible to us corporeal beings; we see your fate."

He pulled out a card from his robe and gave it to Sadie. Its resemblance appeared like it was pulled from the deck of tarot. "Should death cross your path, tear this card, and a portal to safety will open up to you. Best keep it away from imbued scrolls; the spirit will try to absorb its power and leech unto it tighter than any drum."

"Spirit? A Herald?" she asked, observing the card.

"My people don't normally associate with the Chroma. Not against them; some convert to their ways or associate with Alchemy's Harbingers, but most of our society is traditional in our ways with Nature. That card holds the spirit known as a *Vakienda*, our 'Herald' or 'Harbinger.' Our messengers come in…extreme forms. But unlike the others, they are charitable and can be lent out to those in need. Don't worry; it'll return back to me once used. Only a Prime can destroy them."

She examined it closely, and he examined her veil, which revealed itself only to him. Sadie was completely unaware of the wrathful being behind her. And this bothered him immensely.

"Have you talked to your veil…or seen it?" he asked.

"What veil?"

"…The one that is—"

"Don't interfere, Trasno! I decide when to make myself known to her! Let. It. Go." the veil transmitted with contempt.

"Don't test me, veil of Alaea, but I will honor it." Sibi exhibited his own form of telepathy.

"Sibi, you were saying something?"

"Nothing. Mind and tongue wander sometimes."

She looked down at Phthalo. The Herald agreed with him.

Why this veil? And the hidden material, Sibi wondered.

He advised her to get sleep since she looked too exhausted for someone so young for a lecture. They went back inside to turn in. Her mind was restless, but her body gave in to soft linens.

Other restless minds stayed awake to watch the skies above. A telescope wanders, but not for stargazing. The eye picked up the anomaly—thankfully still too far to make it come morning's light. They needed the rest after what they'd been through, and she knew it wasn't close to over, especially with war breaking out.

"Snowflake veins...such a bothersome Essent," Riha sighed from atop the tavern, "I pray for his health."

The chase never stops until the heart does.

No pattering on the head this time around. No roosting of the cock to wake the senses. Just the stirring commotion of other busybodies. A new day to wake up to. The spare room, in the tavern, had its smells of morning servings invade her nostrils, quaking her belly. Visual conceptions of protein spreads, fatty cheeses, honey jars, breakfast teas, and carbs, carbs, carbs!

Just one serving. Any more, and it's straight to the thighs.

"They're back! They're back!" Daru screamed in the distance. His laughs were practically hysterical. Sadie slowly poked her head out to see how busy the main room was. Still shy around the new.

"You can come out now; morning rush doesn't happen just yet," Riha said, prepping food on the counter.

The young girl asked about the noise outside, but before Riha could answer, a deep masculine voice came into play. "Your water filter is working again, Riha; try not to kick it this time. Maybe learn how it works?" Sadie heard it outside the kitchen window but only saw a helmet walking past.

Curious.

There was always a surprise around the corner. She had grown accustomed to anything at this point. Almost anything. Only temperaments mattered now.

Riha placed a full plate on the counter for her to enjoy. In the blink of an eye, two plates of food were on the counter. Sadie wondered if Riha could blink as well.

Settling on the idea, she missed the quick action.

A trail of blue wrapped around one plate. "Do not consume the other," Phthalo whispered into her ear. The other plate had her favorite dishes of eggs, grilled tomatoes, drisheen, and mushrooms with julienned potatoes. The scent enticed her, but the Herald warned her, again, to the other dish: bubble and squeak.

The finest peasant dish for a long journey.

"It tastes—" she started.

"Better than it looks?" a sultry voice intervened. An armor-clad woman leaned against one of the pillars, making her way to the vexed girl. "Sibi was right, you do have a guiding Chroma," she said to her. The woman overshadowed Sadie, her bust practically against her face before she pulled back.

Women are built differently here. All the boys in school would lose it! Why are there no men here like Natalina's brother?! Or Ramirus? Or...never mind. He's basically engaged at this point.

Her eyes noticed the plates of food transforming. Bubble and squeak turned to the hearty breakfast she desired, while the other...simply nothing.

"Would've been fun seeing you trying to eat air with your belly, wondering why it requires more sustenance with each failed bite."

"You've had your fun, now let the girl eat," Riha said, "Pay my sister no mind; she's always looking for some sort of thrill."

"*Nagy Seltheia,*" she introduced herself.

"...Sadie...Harper."

She noticed the same demonic skull behind the bar was on the sister's pauldron. "The skeiborne: badges of authority we Sansha earn through many tribulations. They take part of our pneuma in exchange for its abilities, like the simple illusion on your senses just now," Nagy explained, "My little sister likes to keep hers on display to intimidate some of the rabble that wander in from the city."

Sadie pointed at the other skull that was attached to the pillar.

"How come that one looks different?"

"That once was a *Khrosgar*. They're the most dangerous creatures on Klaring's surface. Hope you never encounter one of them," the same masculine voice from outside said behind her.

She turned her head to see no one there.

"I'm not that short, little lady," the voice said.

Her eyes looked down to see another goblin; decked out in advanced gear, mechanical weapons hovered around him like spider legs, while his upper face hid underneath a large helmet. Sparks zipping around the assorted exotic array of weaponry.

"Electricity…" Her voice trailed off.

"Only the best!" Daru yelled out, barging in with Xamak and Sibi. They clamored around him like fans.

"My adoring kin are remarkable in knowing how to embarrass me," he chuckled. "Call me, M."

"Oh? Leaving behind the 'Grand' are we?" Riha asked.

"Grand M is too professional in this circumstance."

Too many names to keep up with, Sadie thought. All she wanted was just some breakfast so she could have a functioning brain to start the day. Grand M extended his hand to shake while she introduced herself.

Nagy Seltheia

Grand
M

Although the door was still open, the light from outside was completely blocked by another figure entering the tavern.

"Ah, now the whole party is here. Little Sadie, this here is our third—and last—member of mine and Nagy's group: *Kabir Gen.*"

The giant beast man approached her...slowly. This reminded her of Birati's entrance, but this felt more dangerous. Thick claws protracting and retracting at whim. Kabir showed little remorse for her panicked look. A look made of stone. He did not say anything except stare at her; judgment in his eyes. Her knees felt the metaphysical quakes of thunder. Trying to tear down her foundation. Frayed nerves. Underneath those incredible layers of ectodermal tissue, her bones shapeshifted into jelly, while every organ screamed for an escape route. Her brain warning: before you is a violent miracle. Make no attempts at petting. Instinct has such large teeth.

An intimidating presence is a prerequisite for these sorts.

M and Nagy grinned like deviants. The Newts, on the other hand, made a barricade in front of Sadie. Acting as a final line of defense.

"This one is of our own," Sibi said, his hands glowing blue with the tome becoming restless. Hideous shrieks emitted.

"Don't even think of it!" Daru shouted, brandishing his blade.

Xamak lost his usual grin. Taking aim with his large rifle at the beast man's head.

A quick flash appeared at the forefront. Milos's chest against the large Barangda's. No sarcastic remarks, no quips—just two scrolls in hand, partially opened, Cobalt and Aquamarine, ready to be unleashed.

If so much as a pin were to drop...

Out of nowhere, Kosey ran up to Kabir, embracing his leg.

"Master Gen! You're back safely! A blessed morning!" he exclaimed with the largest of smiles.

Kabir looked down at the boy. "Do you vouch for the girl?" Kosey nodded, stating that besides her oddly *extreme* affection, if Milos trusted her, so should he. "Very well," he said, ignoring the others, to sit at the counter.

Somewhere on Earth, a head-on collision into a brick wall was diverted. A close call.

"There will be no acts of violence in my business, people," Riha scowled. Sparks of energy emitted from her face tattoo. Everyone had eased off, and the day could move on again.

Too many bad things here. Does it surpass the good? No. Less than. Thankfully. Companionship, like this, deters skewing. This is somewhere to be. Away from the sufferings of false fascinations. The morning rush commenced.

Sadie chimed in to help as thanks for the lodging, but more importantly, to learn more about Iberitus. Milos handed her a copy of the calendar, along with a decoder, for the Old World's text and number system that is still used to this day.

Twelve months, but with strange alchemical words, starting from *Calgation* to *Proxir*. Five as opposed to seven days that symbolized matter and founding countries associated with each. Classical elements. *Lux* began the week, and its honor belonged to the color white for Celanjung, followed by red *Madder* for Somdir, yellow *Aureolin* for Klaring, black *Magnes* for Lusura, and, strangely, Gottlir ended the week with *Prisma*—blurred colors or focus. At least there were four seasons, but more strange names starting with *Itzala, Tetri, Diellore*, and ending with *Merah*.

"My head hurts," Sadie groaned from trying to read the calendar. The ancient text and numerical system had no chance of retaining inside her head, and she wanted no part of it.

"Can't say I blame you; I myself barely remember the ancient alphabet, but you never know when you might need it. Take a look at the wall," Nagy said to her, pointing at recruitment posters.

Flint and Coin proudly displayed the same symbols.

"*Ekkehard Singer*, the current leader, has new *and* old recruits learn it as a precaution should they take a job into the dungeons scattered below. No one knows what civilization created the text, but because of the ancient scribes, we have it all decoded. Omitting treasures among traps and murderous beings, it helps to know how to navigate without succumbing to fear or hunger."

Kosey stood by Kabir with a wooden tray halfway up to his face. He couldn't take his eyes off the large warrior.

"It's not polite to stare, little one," Riha said to him, "Why don't you go outside and play for a while? I got everything under control here." The young boy looked depressed but did as he was told. Kabir looked at him from the side, slyly. Noticing the reaction.

Deep magnification. Eyes examine the gear and diamond. Repair work on the small apparatus. A great deal of attention from the master.

"The gear should run smoother now. Khrosgar flesh is tricky to work with, but without it acting as a buffer between you and the Prime Material, I'd fear Sesathoth's artifact would consume your mind."

"Sometimes I…" Milos stops himself from overindulging. He fears that M might perceive him as unstable the more he goes out into the field; better to keep a tight lip about the artifacts transformation. "Thank you, M. This'll prove helpful in case the queen tries to block an escape route. I've only been there once. Stupid of me…"

"Milos," Grand M whispers, leaning in. "If you hear anything other than us, the natural ambience of Iberitus, or 'The Three Orders,' I'd advise getting examined by an aristarch immediately. As for Celanjung, do you think it is a coincidence that war broke out as soon as the girl appeared? She is from another universe. This is historic."

"I don't see the correlation, but what do I know? I'm just a freelancer. I hear things but can't confirm everything."

"We are heading to the north to aid Leandro right after this. I have an idea where the siege machines are hiding. You would be wise to do the same."

"I still don't know if I'm coming back! Damn witch has been wanting my head on a platter," Milos nearly shouted out.

"Easy, friend. Birati is smarter than he lets on. Keep the girl safe, your wits about you, and faith in your Chroma. This war, it's different with the schism between Lusura and Klaring. Many Trasno have enlisted with Leandro; even Grenvalk is sending a group of elites to meet us near the border. Very dire circumstances. I'm sure you're aware that a certain 'guest' below us has updated you on critical cracks in the mountains."

"Riha introduced you?"

"Long before we set out, Kabir smelled him miles away—nearly destroyed the entire village looking for him! You should know that the Barangda are mortal enemies of the Vermis," he explained, drinking his pint, "None too pleased to find him under Riha's watch."

"You're smarter than any I know, M. Blessed by the Chroma of Silver, what are your thoughts on this Enitan?"

The Newt brothers, also present at the table, stayed silent—even Daru. Their respect for their kinsman was of the utmost adoration. There's a lot to learn here. Knowledge comes with rewards. Grand M's words carried heavy weight not only for them, but Grenvalk considered him a folk hero.

"I simply consider him Tarwini."

Without derogatory labeling, those present knew the rat man below was not a threat…yet.

Exhale or hold your breath. Someone hears vermin in the basement. Another hears benevolent coded messages from the elder. Crumble into stale breadcrumbs or expand? Migrate in all directions. That's the key. They can't catch you lying still. Ten steps forward.

This isn't flight.

It's a fight.

There was laughter out in the village. Children enjoy their time with friends. Some with their parents. The boy watched from afar, sitting alone on stone, dreaming, wanting, silently pleading. This is all he has.

A large shadow came upon him. Gently descending beside the boy. Ears offered. They watched in silence. The giant breaks it.

"Why do you not join them?" Kabir asked.

"I'm afraid…" Kosey responded.

"Are they cruel to you?"

"Not like when Milos and Riha first brought me here," he started, "I just hate disrupting their time with their families."

He looked up at Kabir, asking him if he'd ever go back to Kotsudas, the homeland of the Barangda, in his lifetime, to reunite with the people. The island was too far north, and to get there, you'd have to either go through Klaring or Lusura. Klaring supped on any denizen that was from there like a fine delicacy. Only bleached bones remain. Lusura's Prime Aeolid placed a huge price on capturing the beast race alive. Experimental reasons. Their rarity outside the homeland made them notoriously popular. And the seas between Somdir and Kotsudas held a violent sea nation. On par with the Euphotic.

Watch what border you cross. You'll lose more than just a toe.

"We have both been deprived of our community, but so long as we have a sense of purpose, degeneracy will never taint our nous," Kabir explained. He gave the boy a steely look. "Never show fear."

Kosey tried not to argue, but he went on about how Kabir was born with the leader's birthmark on his forehead, while Kosey was born with the mark of a simple laborer.

A symbol considered lowly even among his own.

Kabir spoke passionately about how Kotsudas was born from the laborer's mark: the cornerstone of the society. Titles of all the classes—even those with the leader's mark— were to be seen as equals.

"And never doubt your birthright."

Kosey felt bolstered.

"Time escapes, and duties mustn't be neglected, so remember my words," Kabir said, getting up.

Kabir Gen

Kosey stopped him short, asking him an old request, one that Kabir always denied, "I know I've asked what feels like a thousand times, but I saved more geodi this time to ask again."

The boy presented Kabir with a heavy satchel of opals, celestites, agate coins, and even one ruby blood-knife worth over ten thousand.

"Where did you get this, boy?!" Kabir asked sternly.

"I...rebuilt the Tarwini's sword in the basement," he replied shyly.

Predatory rage came over Kabir, not because the rat men were their greatest enemies, but because of the fact Kosey might've lost his life to the blade he repaired.

Too friendly; it'll trap him when I'm not around.

An ultimatum presented.

"If you wish to connect our nous, you must never go near that Vermis again! Is that understood?" Kabir snarled.

Kosey was taken aback. He showed fear, fully aware he shouldn't.

"Yes, sir..."

You're scaring the boy. Be the mentor, not the intimidator.

"Remove your band," Kabir instructed, exposing his marked forehead to the youth.

Their respective birthmarks are shown to one another. The large warrior roared, energy spilling out, connecting with the young boy, their eyes going white, and memories swapped. The deed was completed, and the favor was initiated. The satchel of geodi stayed with the young boy. He had no wish to lift him of his currency.

Even leaving behind the blood-knife.

Kabir looked at the boy one more time before heading in to reconvene with the others. "I accept your request to find the one responsible for your loss."

Riha stood by the window. A witness. She grinned before being approached by Milos. "Did he finally do it?" he asked her.

"He sure did. It might be the first time he has shown actual love since we met him."

"Strange times," Grand M chimed in.

"Indeed, this might be the last time we all gather like this for a while, but all good things must come to an end. The snow draws closer; time for you two to head west," Riha said to Milos.

Sadie was given her original clothes back, and washed, along with some food. Riha kissed Milos on the cheeks as they departed, "Don't die on us; I special-ordered a nice dress from Somdir for your beach wedding, and I'd hate to chase after your pneuma for a refund."

"Worry not."

The Newts decided to head to the north garrison, while Nagy, M, and Kabir traversed to the border mountains to see where the breach was so they could reseal it.

"Three people can't hold off an invading army if they're caught; it's insane!" Sadie said, as they were leaving.

"Those three are an army," Milos explained, while Enzu latched onto Sadie's shoulder, preparing for the flight on the speeding cloud, "The Ternion Pilgrims have not lost a battle yet."

Out of sight, through the sky, they zoomed northwest towards the marshy strait that acted as a conduit to Celanjung. The queen's face is sure to fulminate once her eyes set upon the once-upon thief.

Empty was the throne of its nation. A battle of constants kept it from sitting down for too long of a time: experiments, research, domination, and the mundane promoting of lesser beings—the cycle repeats.

Its eyes studied the forest.

Where was the one who evoked a sense of disaffected loneliness?

Its mind remembers some of the beings it snuck past. A recent scene stuck out: a simple-minded woodsman who decided to eat some gilded parchment taken from a dead scribe. Her head was struck by his chipped ax. The girl may have lost to the feverish swing, but the oaf was dead from the neck up. Maybe a parasite bored through his ears one night while the flesh crown rested on rotted wood, smoothing out the wrinkles so that any functioning junction burned out without a chance of synapse. The value of stupidity over conscience is a dung show that perplexes cognition.

It knew where he was headed, but so did the blind empress—formidable being that one. It remembered her ability to redirect fated paths. A plan must be hatched to gain an audience first.

From afar, a line of movement. It rushed to the edge of the forest to gaze on the plains. A blanket of shadow had just barely concealed it under the brush. The eyes glared at the moving sight: a caravan. Aristarch instructors in the center; F&C perimeter; this one's plan is ready to hatch.

"The sixteenth shall find offerings here to transplant a new path in my honor," it murmured. Rising above the green, two swords came into play, accompanied by the master's usual disapproved look. "A principle to invoke," it finished, crossing the blades, and advancing on the group with tenacity.

Reroute to remain.

Chapter 8

†

Isotope

Her teeth chattered constantly. It was no surprise that every creature, deadly or not, removed themselves from her path. Pestilence, from the fleeting misty clouds of her throat, stirred great predators to cower in their holes. Some laid paws over their eyes like children in fear. She hated the blackness. Too close to the Primes as one could get without perishing. Impatient youth that carried a spirit of inquiry— the cause. Had her heart not been shattered, there would be no blindfold. A place where tears are hidden.

Remembrance of a time when the boy was waist-high. *Why didn't he just come away from this road?* she thought. *There would be the absence of many, but he would live far greater than now. It was the female Mairu he had grown to trust. That was the reason to stay behind. An unhealthy obsession with being sheltered. Perhaps...*

An unusual guest of the land came across her, high up on a tree. The thick shade of the leaves hid the face like the traveler's eyes. The twins of gold shone upward to the figure.

"You stalk me, Mairu?" the blind traveler asked.

The light was exposed enough to show it was a female ogre holding a large black and green club with a sealed eye. A flick of the tongue to the corner of her mouth to catch an itch. "I can't understand how anyone can deal with this humidity," the Mairu said, ignoring the inquiry. The blind traveler's nose wrinkled in anger; teeth were bare; arms multiplying. Four, exactly. A warped mind like her matted fur. The Mairu looked unimpressed. She jumped down, smashing the head of the club by the blind traveler's feet. Her opposite spat through a torch. Landing on the Mairu's foot. Unaffected. "Cocky for a deformed Barangda," she stated, holding the club over her shoulder. "I don't believe in the lightfoot approach. No strength in hiding in the shadows. Might as well commit suicide should I do so. However, I do have an obligation to my sister-in-arms to make sure her previous ward is safeguarded from any and all."

"Turned against Black Sulfur Ashokara?"

"Nationalism runs through my heated veins…Lusura before the traitor. I never held office—nor did I seek it. I'm in need of a thrill, like when I faced her! She boiled so brilliantly when I held that boy up in the air. Ironic how things turn out."

"Seek the Lost Divide with the other hedonistic whores if you wish for a perpetual thrill," the blind traveler hissed.

The Mairu presented a small prismatic gem to the blind traveler, "I know underneath that rag you know what this is."

Her opposite stood by quietly.

"An invitation to the Divide is in my hand. I hold a rainbow! It is power that begets itself! A makeup of all Chroma and all metals! All that I need to do is answer the call! I only need one man—the *right* man—to make me flourish. To make me understand that brainless emotion you people call 'love.' They say it makes you stronger!" she shouted out. "But not yet. Promises to keep…like keeping you away from *him*."

She held the club to her chest, gripping the handle tightly, blood dripping out of her one good eye. "Make me feel..." She gritted her teeth and swung for the fences. Deforestation took hold. Quakes that rumbled for miles shook nearby structures apart.

"What was that?!" Sadie shouted out.

He saw the explosion in the distance. It would be wise to traverse on land at the moment to avoid possible hostile activity. His bejeweled companion was struck with fear.

"Never mind that, just some volcanic activity," Milos said. She looked everywhere to see no mountain nearby. "Underwater volcanoes in the pelagic," he dodged.

Something was off, a bad smell filling the air, and they were losing light to top it off. The concentration of the foul aroma grew higher the closer they walked to their destination. A cool, welcoming breeze from the edge of the forest invited them to search for sanctuary there for the night. They entered the dense area. Greeted by the sounds of music in the distance. It was calming. The vibrant columns of melodies in the air eased any worry.

In their minds, serenity acted as a caller from the wild, "Come and stay. We have peace and bounties of food. Stay. Forever."

Fireflies danced around the heartwood of many pine trees they passed. Enzu and Milos snapped off branches from fallen logs to collect. The scribe placed the base of one under his nose to inhale.

"Have a whiff," he said to Sadie, handing her the stick.

"Oh...that's divine."

"Fatwood resin," he explained, "Gather some for firewood. We're camping here tonight."

Natural light had completely disappeared, but that didn't stop them from traveling some more. The young girl was instructed to wield her bracelet's fire capabilities the entire time. It was becoming second nature to utilize the power.

Milos pointed out two vibrant orange mushrooms to contrast their differences. "Never eat this one with the gills under the cap. They're poisonous compared to this one here, without the slits, but have small pores instead." He stripped off more of the non-gilled mushroom from some rotted wood to explain they would eat it once they cooked it.

"What does it taste like?" she asked.

"Well, it's called *'Chicken of the Woods,'* so take a wild guess."

They trekked some more until the music grew louder. Enzu patted Milos's shoulder enthusiastically. "I know," he said, observing the darkness. He deliberately dispelled Sadie's fire so that only navy shadows surrounded them. She hated it, clinging to his bag of scrolls.

Sounds of scurrying feet were drawn to their presence. The bushes rustled about. Chittering noises in the trees. Phthalo was unresponsive to Sadie's pleas for guidance. Even her reclusive veil showed no effort to come out. Milos told her to stop freaking out and to trust him to stay quiet, but her whimpers grew louder. Enzu's gems began to glow, and he jumped onto her shoulder to try to calm her as well.

Her heart froze when she heard the chittering sounds by her waist in the bushes. The eyes had not fully adjusted, but she saw multiple heads pop out, looking dead on at her in silence. As screams were about to emit, Milos forcefully closed her mouth with his hand.

"Peace, my friends. We seek sanctuary for the night," he said to the small shadows, "We have a medley to share."

They looked at one another before melding back into the shadows. Shortly after, the music resumed. Candles were lit in the distance where the melodies came from.

"That's our cue," Milos said, releasing his hand. He apologized to the girl. Not everything in the forests is predatory, yet they needed to act with finesse with those who could help. Helpful prey are masters in the art of stealth, and losing aid in the middle of the night, in the middle of the woods, would put them in a conundrum. "When we get to their camp, try to avoid what you did back in the tavern when you met Kosey."

Small cottages—knee-high at most—were strewn around the site.

Yet, no one was seen. Only a bonfire centered with a boiling pot. Enzu plopped down to retrieve some medium rocks. Some of his gems shone brightly in his arms, helping him slice them into flats, laying them down by the fiery pit. "Put all the food you got onto the plates until there's no more room," Milos instructed Sadie, while he did the same.

She did what she was told. Milos said to leave out the sweets—chocolate especially. Soon after, he plopped down, with Enzu climbing up to the shoulder. He began to hum gently while poking a stick at the embers. "You wouldn't happen to know how to sing, would you?" he asked her. Only one, but she hesitated to sing it, saying she always sang in private.

Too nervous.

"Give it a go, lass."

"...Why?"

"We're welcome here, but they're more afraid of you than you are of them. Plus, I want to hear their music some more. You might be a nice addition."

"..."

Sadie saw his face in a different light; somber. His words, sounding almost boyish, bordered on longing. Enzu looked at her with his arms holding against his eyes while smiling.

Maybe it won't hurt to try, she thought.

She closed her eyes, took a deep breath, and released some small melodies. Little notes of cadence. A strum went off inside one of the cottages. Playing along with her voice. Milos smiled to see some of the doors open with their eyes peeking out. The young girl's melodies started to stream from the parted lips, louder and clearer. The acoustic strings followed. The doors opened, and they came out to watch the red-haired vocalist. The acoustic strings strummed out in the open, joined by other instruments. Milos looked at her to realize even though he couldn't understand the words, they were profound. Something about the folk song unlocked old sad memories of those he lost along the way.

Slight watering in the eyes.

Sadie finished the song before opening her eyes again.

Greeted by the silent villagers surrounding the fire.

"Whoa..." her voice trailed off in awe.

Raccoons, rabbits, cats, and many more in rustic tunics, hats, and vests. A small string band, in the mix, assisted her.

This was the anthropomorphic world she had always dreamed of meeting as a child.

The *Wandrians*.

They divided the food from the makeshift stone plates: one part into the boiling pot while the rest was dry prepared. Night seemed a little brighter here. Maybe it was the abundance of fireflies. It could've been the large opening above them without too many branches overshadowing the village. Or it was the warmth of their hospitality. Either way, the cool air calmed the girl's previous anxieties.

"Tell me," Milos began to ask, "What was the name of that song? Something about it felt like...home."

"*An Eala Bhàn* or *'The White Swan.'* My grandfather used to sing it whenever he remembered old war buddies who died for their country after being sent by incompetent leaders. He learned it from his father, who took part in the 'Great War.'"

He leaned back, his eyes fixated on the fires of the pit, emotionless. "War...I guess it's inevitable no matter what plane of existence you're born into," he murmured. "Bloodshed has me desensitized, I'm afraid."

Sadie had no words of reply. That same forlorn look, from when they were still in Udalann, again. Maybe he was more than just a wanderer. The thousand-yard stare held its ground. Food began to be poured into wooden bowls to be passed around. The music started up again, but livelier. Enzu did a jig in front of the scribe's viewpoint of the fire. A common smirk grew back. Sadie tried to talk to the animals, but they chittered back at her words.

"If the queen likes you, she'll impart the knowledge to hear their words," Milos said.

"You think she might?"

"Nah, but to be honest, she doesn't like anyone 'cept these critters. They're originally from Celanjung, so you'd need quite the recommendation from more than just a few of these."

She pouted at not being able to converse with them. Two of them, a cat and a rabbit, passed by them, nodding only. They left the party, heading into the darkness of the primordial woods alone. "That pair has seen war up close," Milos said, finishing his bowl. He burped, thinking it was over. "Oy, I forgot about the others."

A large tray of assorted food came into view for everyone to pick off: meats, eggs, raw and cooked vegetables, seafood, and nuts.

"Get your fill of *salmagundi* now because they only prepare this on special occasions." Milos picked up handfuls of food to gobble.

"I don't understand how you could stay so thin," Sadie said, taking only a small amount.

"Always on the run; the metabolism never stops. Only lazy kings get fat around here. And they're all dead," he replied, laughing.

Sadie noticed the tray was short of one type of item.

"How come there's no fruit here?"

He gulped down a tankard of honey water before stopping to think about how to answer that innocent question. The animals stared at her, and the music stopped. "Most have gone extinct thanks to the Usurper in Lusura…experiments gone awry. He hoards nearly all of them for his kingdom," Milos explained. She brought up the produce from the carts found on the ship she was captured on. Rewards for nasty deeds. Shady dealings occur frequently in Gottlir's port. The guards care not for what happens outside the gates to the city—everyone is on their own.

"*Diellore* is right around the corner. Time is going so fast all of a sudden," Milos yawned out, beginning to doze off on the blanket of leaves. Sadie retrieved the rolled-up calendar to review.

"What are the names of your seasons?" he asked her. When she replied, he turned on his side to nod off, "So this is Spring going into Summer. Sounds nice."

She pointed out the times don't really align considering her seven-day weeks.

"No two worlds are alike. We're all living in fantasy. Reality begins when we die..." he whispered. His small snores showed his resignation for the day.

Does God carry over into this world of living fables? Or is it converted into a Prime of color, science, or macrocosm?

She shivered, unable to concentrate on her deep thoughts. The cool air tickled the spine until some of the Wandrians handed her a blanket and a rattan pillow. Enzu nestled with Milos. The small Essent didn't ever sleep but liked to remain by his side at night. All the others returned to their small homes among the trees, with only a few climbing them. Vigilant in standing guard over the rest in the shadows.

With one more look at the night sky, she tried to hold the image for as long as she could. Fighting against fatigue so this moment of peace can last forever.

Her blurry eyes saw them fluttering overhead: insects. Not ordinary flies, moths, butterflies, or anything seen so far recognized in the animal kingdom. Soft. Tranquil. Celestial. Their movements were practically muted. She wondered if they were part of the Wandrian tribe, as no one, or thing, reacted to them. Enzu didn't notice them. Strange. Their body—almost marshmallow and surrounded by fluff—of differentiated metamerics revealing, briefly, their spectral anatomy. A constellation of symbols paired with jeweled joints and pumping organs.

Heavy. Slipping. Into the black.

Just one more second before I go...

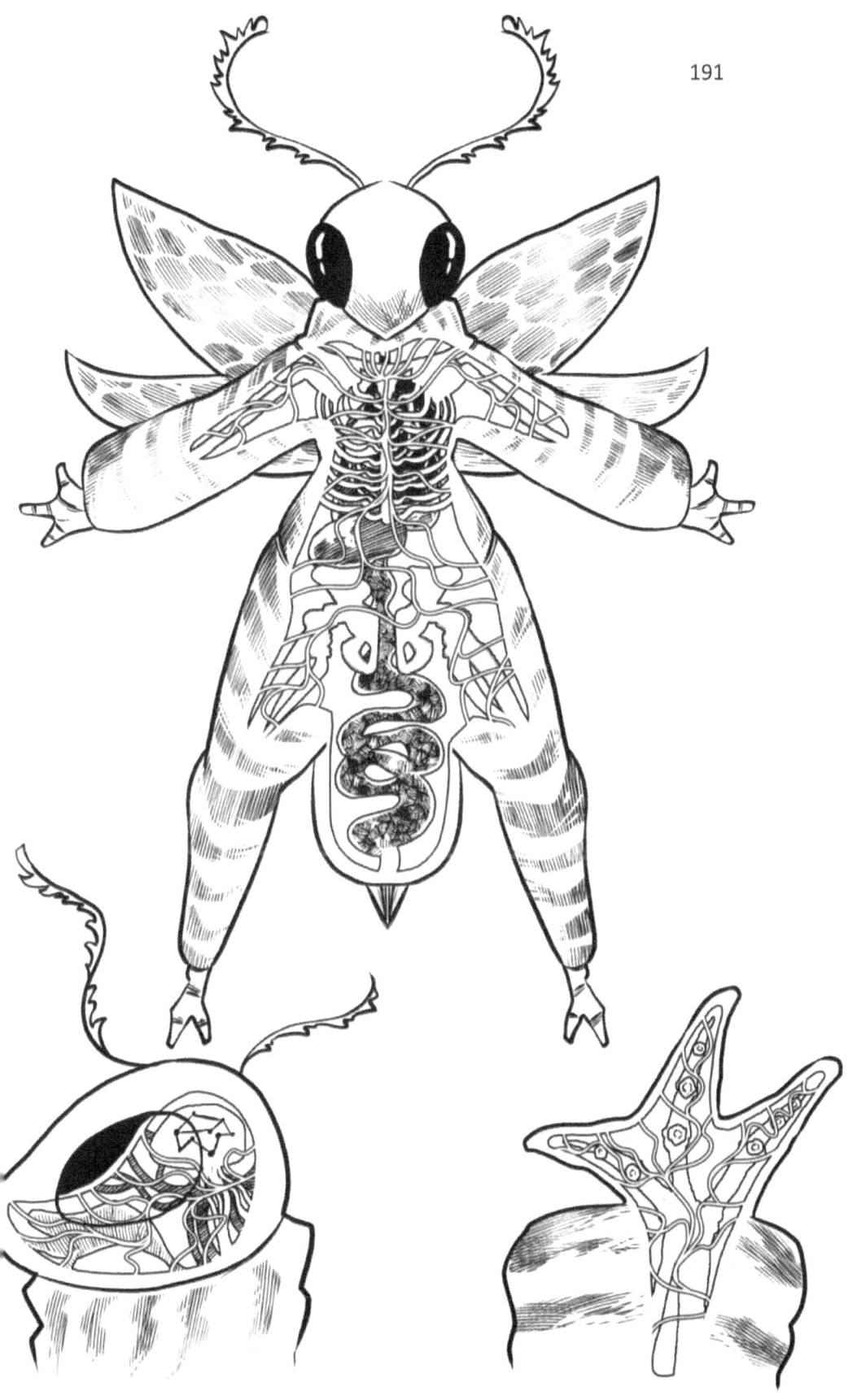

Time slips away where dreams occupy. It was spiked. It flowed side to side. It spread like fire. It twisted in before twirling out. It smelled like honey. It appeared golden. It could be an exotic globe thistle.

"Snap it from the stem, and the garden of opportunity is yours," a female voice whispered into her head. The ears barely picked up the strange message. But it repeated. The eyes strained, opening slightly, revealing in a blur a ghostly being. Shades of Sky Blue. *"Avoid the silvery fingers. Come into the fold, sister."*

The girl wanted to embrace fatigue wholeheartedly. The ghost turned her sights to the sleeping Milos, quietly hovering, observing his peaceful look, sights set on another, transmitting one final message, *"Home awaits us soon, little one."*

Sky Blue's ghostly visage vanishes.

Enzu: emotionless.

Good thing the stars haven't burned out tonight.

The torches' flames grew brighter. Nails from the darkness joined the second pair of arms to gleam. Racing heart. From behind lit sconces came the savagery of a blinded beast to consume the young flesh.

It screamed: ***"WAKE UP!"***

A sharp gasp expelled from her lungs. Her spine bent upward from the dreadful sight. Eyes peeled wide, hoping to see the sun again. *Does it still rise? Please let dawn shine on me!* she thought.

"Easy there! You got nightmares, do ya?" Milos shouted out, standing over her. Sadie shifted against her side, taking deep, concentrated breaths from the belly. The blind beast's face turning instantly into Milos was too real to experience for her. He rubbed the back of his head, wondering how bad the vision could have been.

One Wandrian came by with a fresh cloth for the sweat on her head. A small beaver, in what appeared to look like a wizard's hat, had the girl smiling in no time.

"Is it rude of me to ask if…I can…pet you?" she said to the little critter. It cocked its head to the side. Enzu started to scribble the ancient language into the dirt for it to read. When it saw the message, it chittered, coming closer to her. Arms wide open. She gently squeezed it, rubbing the fur. Milos bent down to her, asking if she was okay. "I just want to go home. I miss my parents so much. I miss *normal*…"

Her voice trailed off, sniffling with red eyes. Several Wandrians came around and, in unison, hugged her in a circle. Her cries wept every heart present. What could mitigate such sorrow? The girl could feel the distance between hell and heaven above, and her hand barely had a grasp on the first rung of the ladder before the great fall. Don't look down.

They waved to their hosts in the distance. The venture must resume. Delays and pauses were harmful at this point. Milos saw mental degradation unfold. It replayed visions from the past; best be shaken off now. He explained they were going back towards the marshlands strait, leading to Celanjung, since the foul odor no longer lingered in the air.

Almost out of the woods.

Enzu stayed closer to Sadie this time.

"Did you enjoy yourself last night?" Milos asked.

"Immensely, I loved the music. It reminded me of *Ceòl Beag* in my world. That means 'little music,' by the way, in Gaelic."

Enthusiasm. This is good. Tucked below the surface, an adolescent still holds on to the child, the good nature. To see the penumbra of her depression is staggering. What lies in the shadow?

She quickly came up beside him to study.

"Problem?" he asked, looking from the corner of his eye.

"You look like you could kinda be Scottish yourself," she said, showing a squishing gesture with her fingers. "A wee bit. You do have a lot of European features…Spanish? Italian? Something about you is so familiar now that I think about it."

"I don't have a clue what any of those things are you speak of. Just your average Gottlirian. Come on, the sooner we get out of these woods, the sooner you get home," he stated, pushing branches out of his face. She wanted to talk some more, explaining the different cultures to pass the time.

Olfaction faculties activated! Attention is demanded by the nasal cavity! Hear, hear! Nay, hark goes the soul of nostrils!

Her nose suddenly caught wind of that same aroma from Birati's table: scoria. Its fragrance beckoned her *much* stronger this time around, and she veered away from Milos suddenly.

Pheromones, delicious sweets and savories, clean linen, robust candles, and incense—none of these could contest this immaculate bouquet's ability to pull. Enzu tried desperately to get her attention, but she was locked onto the spirit. Such exquisite, redolent pleasure from that wine. *I must have it again!* She screamed aloud inside her head. Hoping to reenact drinking the contents one last time…only with a fervor much worse than that night.

Winos would blush at this sort of determination.

It was no use. Enzu leaped off her shoulder to roll after Milos, whose giant steps dampened the sounds of hers.

"My God," she whispered.

Enzu managed to get Milos to release his horse blinders to notice the missing girl.

"For the love of…where has that overly curious redhead gone off to now?" he sighed. Enzu formed into a unique object that raised all the alarm bells in Milos's head.

"By the composition!" he blurted out, sprinting in the direction Enzu pointed out to him.

Something had sucked out all the humidity in the forest. Strange vacuums and eeriness. Still branches; shy-to-fall leaves; black mildew creeping. Fauna and appetite within the locality.

Could he make it in time?

"It smells divine," Sadie said, taking a whiff of it. "This has to be one of the raw ingredients to that delicious drink."

Her hand touched it gently. It responded by unfurling, emanating pride. Small spores dusted off the petals. She further inhaled the fragrance. Shivers of excitement nearly turned the nubile girl into a full-fledged woman.

Temptation had hit its boiling point.

She went to grab it by the stem, but Milos's hand suddenly came into play, stopping her short. He nearly broke her wrist, whispering, almost silently, into her ear, "Walk away from it….*very* slowly."

Sadie didn't have a clue as to why he would be so afraid of a gold flower, but sweat covered his brow. His eyes dared not to blink.

He's so pale. If a white steed suddenly came alongside him now, she knew he was actually Death all along. Bleakness exposed. Inching her back cautiously, resisting to take his eyes off the bright flower, still trying so hard not to blink. An uninvited tear accompanies her. What happens between this space and a flutter? He dared not try to find out.

A loud **SNAP** under their feet from dead wood.

Everything around him had gone black. Milos wanted to cry. His organs *needed* to cry. And they did, starting with the brain. Shards of memories coming together like broken glass. His bladder, the only organ, next to the heart, resisted going weak.

There's no picture puzzle here.

It's only horror.

It's. Only. Pain.

Here comes torture.

Voices, transmitting in unison, *"We're ready!"*

His heart raced when he saw the flower's petals turn from round edges to spiked needles. The stem sucked itself into the bushes. Low guttural noises emitted in the vicinity, thick vapors of baleful breath through the leaves, and sharp talons protruded from under the foliage. It exited the bushes heavily with its eyes on its new prey: all eight eyes.

Sadie's heart pounded so hard the beast could hear it easily.

"Don't do it, please, *don't*," Milos begged Sadie with trembling whispers into her ear. Enzu slipped into the scroll bag. The tail flicked wickedly. It lanced anything in its path. The protruding gems on its joints changed into a myriad of colors. Its head arched to the sky, releasing a thunderous shrill so horrifying that nearby trees were set ablaze, revealing the insides of curly roadmaps of each one's burls.

Khrosgar.

"NOW'S THE TIME, SCRIBE!" Phthalo shouted, shaking him from his seizure.

The enormous monstrosity launched itself at the frightened party. Milos's bracelet took the initiative to evade the attack. Sadie screamed violently when the beast's tail swung in full force to cut down a fully grown tree. Her bracelet ignited suddenly to disrupt its violent path. It had come close to the neck, trying to decapitate her.

Flight took hold, and Milos veered up into the skyline. Sadie had thought they were in the clear until it began to teleport itself rapidly to their location. "It can blink like you?!" she screamed out. Milos didn't answer. His concentration depended on their escape; otherwise, they might have hit a large branch to knock them down.

And that would surely lead them to their end.

"Anytime, scribe!" A voice transmitted to him.

He scrambled to reach the Cobalt scroll to use. Speaking aloud the incantation known by heart. His eyes began to glow, and one changed into the same color as the scroll.

It was ready.

"DIE!"

The beast had teleported directly in their way, mid-flight, with an open wide jaw. It looked bottomless.

Cobalt discharged a humanoid warrior, clad in spectacular blue armor and a pair of twin flanged maces, to repel the beast. It cracked one side of the Khrosgar's body and smashed down the center of its skull. Just when they thought that was their opening, the beast shed its bonelike skin as darts in all directions. Trees toppled over from the violent velocity. The Cobalt warrior defended them but was pierced too many times. Its energy returned back into the scroll.

The veil of Cobalt: silenced.

Shaking its head to regain balance, the Khrosgar teleported again. More tenacious than previously. The shrills disoriented the party.

"Send me in already!" Mulberry transmitted viciously.

"Primes above…" Milos said, trying to reach for Mulberry. Their transportation was slowing down, however. Energy from his bracelet's diamond flowed directly into the beast.

"Bastard! Siphon from *MY* prism?!" The gear winced intermittently, now halting. They were descending steadily, and the mouth of the Khrosgar latched onto Milos's quiver.

Death was *literally* on his back.

It clamped down on the bag. A tusk enjoyed the side of his ribs. A taste of intercostals. Small spurts turned to gushes. The fatal injury steered them straight into the earth. Their bodies rag-dolled in different directions. Milos was losing consciousness. The beast's body, unsurprisingly, was unscathed from the downfall. It crept towards the bleed-out. The eyes scope out its fresh meal. Milos lay on his belly, holding his side to keep the red in, but that was the extent of all he could do. His head tried to lift up to see the creeping death chittering maniacally the closer it got. His bag was no longer on his person.

No more council. Only Goldenrod stayed attached underneath his jacket, but it would do him no good now.

"I pray to the Primes; I give you permanent piles when you excrete me…you freak," he groaned, spitting blood at it.

"How do these work?!" Sadie said not too far from them. The bag of scrolls came into her possession. Enzu rolled around her with rapid speed. Trails of smoke follow behind.

"There's no time for playing, Enzu!" she cried out. But the little Essent's body grew larger and larger around her. Her hands were shaking uncontrollably. She started to cry hysterically. The girl had her own injuries from the perilous fall. Soil clung as bandages to open cuts and random abrasions. All she could do was hold herself since she had no way of knowing how to use Milos's scrolls.

The heart sank.

It all seemed so hopeless.

She would never see home again.

The ears were deaf to everything.

White noise entered her mind.

A trail of blue energy guided her to a secret compartment inside the bag. Three scrolls came out, and she grabbed the first to land in her grip. The Khrosgar noticed her unraveling it. Milos shouted for her to stop, but she could not hear anything except the droning sound. Enzu continued to grow larger. Her veil, watching over her. The Khrosgar decided to save Milos for last—the young woman's flesh seemed more succulent at the moment. It began its sprint, baring tusks and crooked fangs. Her bracelet spewed a wall of flames in front of her, acting as a barrier to the beast. The blue dog appeared before Sadie.

"Rip it! It's the only way!" Phthalo commanded. Her eyes caught Milos's mute hysterics through the flames. He begged her not to destroy the scroll, but she couldn't hear the reason. His gestures slowed down, but so did everything else.

The action: committed.

Time respected this decision, slowing the hands of the clock. Her veil returned back to the bracelet. Phthalo vanished into smoke, repeating the message again, the

Khrosgar leaping through the flames to maul Sadie. Jaws of
death en route.

A scroll of Cerulean ripped in half.

Everything: white.

What comes after ruination?

Life?

Renewal?

Gray lens?

Open sky.

Vast field of flowers.

A garden world.

The very essence of Maytime.

The soft blades of green swayed side to side with adjacent
neighbors; choreography, impeccable.

Bruised flesh regenerated. No longer did the hands shake.
The air soothed the lungs. Give up your grief. Distill fear. It's
beautiful here.

Welcome to church!

Is this a dream? Am I dead?

That same low guttural sound, from before, in the
distance. The Khrosgar stumbled about, trying to shake off
the bright light all eight of its eyes had to endure.

This was still reality. Still in motion.

Spinning violently, the tail searched and lurked,
trying to come into contact with *anything* to guide the
blinded carnivore. The spiked flower ejected more needle
spores into the air. Edgy mechanism. Through calm winds,
the nose would catch that delightful smell again. A forced
sigh of relief from her.

Target spotted.

Why me?!

Why not? Nature is restless. And famished.

It gave chase again, rushing ravenously towards Sadie's direction, hoping to make contact. Hoping to fill its belly. That familiar blind rage shrieked out again.

"Distasteful," a woman's voice said.

Roots erupted from the ground to entangle the beast in place. Its shrill sounded different this time: panic. Zenith to nadir. Those long ivory tusks snapped, horns stripped out, ligaments bent, and the flower froze until it shattered into dust. Mother Nature pulled its enormous body further apart before a woman appeared to the dying beast. She held out a hand to guide a large vine. Wrapping around the neck, forming a fist, and snapping it upon closure. This enigmatic woman made it look so effortless. The body would compost rapidly into the ground. A strange bed of blue flowers grew in its place. Base to apex.

Sights turned onto the girl. This mystery: faceless, her skin appearing like ice, eyes like a ghost, a split gown, pauldrons with large gemstones embedded into them, and a headdress fit for an empress.

"You are marked, girl," she began, "The audacity to rip my family's legacy. You must be accompanying him. The thief. I doubt you could steal away from his nimble fingers. Or the talents for assassination." The Khrosgar seemed less of a threat compared to this woman. "You *will* tell me where he is! Deny, and I'll absorb that nous of yours. Torturing it will be my start. I'll have your corporeal being inside the Menes Spire. After...physical pain."

Dear God, Sadie thought, *the message from the door!*

"Please don't torture me! I was told to seek the composer of that Spire!" she pleaded. The enigmatic woman stopped short of this unveiling. Hesitant to act rashly. Looking over the girl's features.

Coming to only one conclusion.

"You must be the agent of Somdir I have sent for! Sister, embrace me!" the woman exclaimed.

But Sadie took the opportunity to run instead.

Abandoning the post for conversation. An ill-inducing characteristic. No one likes a coward. Especially those on top of the food chain. Despite having no mouth, screams came from the woman's being. The air soon thickened with a cold mist. Frigid needles to the pores.

"YOU REJECT ME?! YOU ARE NOT THE ONE I SEEK AND SHALL BE JUSTLY PUNISHED AS PROMISED!"

A meteor of ice slammed by Sadie's legs, barely missing. More roots erupted from the ground to ensnare her. Quick reflexes outdid them to avoid being turned into a ragdoll herself.

"BRING HER TO ME, NOW!"

Clear skies turned to gray clouds. Church is gone. Forget pearly gates; this purgatory's gone rotten, and hell wants in. What could be mistaken for an angel was nothing of the sort. It broke through the clouds to aid in the hunt. This isn't a paragon of virtue. Something humanlike was gliding in the air to seize the girl for its master. Its elemental wings left a trail of hail behind it. Sadie's heart sped like a rabbit's. No trumpets in this hunt. There was no end to these fields. A root managed to entangle one leg; impossible to rip off.

Closer and closer this faceless entity came. A phantasm high on her own supply. Gliding over the ground much like her faceless angel. The speed was outright astonishing.

Interference from a new player.

A boulder of giant proportions hurled itself across the fields. It shredded through all the vines and untangled the one on Sadie's ankle.

The great escape resumed.

"WHAT IS THIS DEFIANCE?!"

Sadie kept running while the boulder protected her from oncoming attacks. The faceless woman had had enough. A wall of earth protruded all around the girl. Its height was enormous, and it encircled her. Only a small, thin passageway to escape from. Way of the horseshoe. She panicked. She coughed. She felt the burning sensation inside her exhausted lungs. It was too tall to scale, and the passageway only led to the woman—simply staring at her from a distance. The false angel made its descent to the wall's open airway. Its full-speed incline met only the fist of a large golem. Despite being caught off-guard, it managed to endure the enormous hand.

Terrible strength.

A power struggle between two creatures of magic commenced. The golem's back faced her. Gargantuan, with multiple sets of arms, and—more importantly—bejeweled.

"Enzu…is that you?" Sadie whispered.

It continued to hold back the false angel, steadily losing control of its gravity. Its legs dragged backward with mud building up behind.

"YOU ARE MINE TO INTERROGATE!"

"Remember: the card," Phthalo whispered into Sadie's ear.

Of course, she thought.

Her hand reached into her blazer to retrieve Sibi's gift. The golem's knees buckled in defeat. Sadie ran towards the pair, shouting at the false angel, her veil appearing in tow, "GET OFF HIM!" Her bracelet sent a large burst of flame at it. The powerful assault pushed it back several feet—arms crossed over its face in quick defense.

Leaping onto the golem's back, she tore the card in half with her teeth and raised the other half up to the sky. Strange sigils formed above the pair. A pillar of energy hastily transported them away.

The longest three minutes and thirty-nine seconds Sadie ever felt, in her young adult life, to reach sanctuary.

The faceless woman stared into the sky. *"A magister's card worked for a human? She's made powerful allies. And that Essent…"*

She disappears with the rest of this garden world.

She removed the crown from her head. Softly placing it onto a stand near the bed. Meditation of the mind. Vocalization of hums ensues.

Her breath seeks peace and salvation.

"You're in a good mood," a veiled attendant said to her. She ignored the attendant. Opening her eyes, she walked over to the mirror to stare at herself. Fingers playing with the ends. The attendant presented a brush. "You shouldn't fiddle with your follicles too much." She brushed the black hair in even strokes.

Another attendant came inside, bowing and opening the stained glass window shutters.

"A fine day to be alive," the second said.

"What day is it?" the woman asked.

The brushing of hair stopped midway. The attendants shied from answering, heads bowed.

"Magnes, my Queen," a third said, entering inside with a rolled-up scroll.

"So soon, have my Vicara brought news from the East?"

The third handed her the scroll. It had more heft than previous ones as of recent. Eyes sprinting from side to side. Each detail became more and more intriguing. Little whispers of the voice speaking them out without missing a beat. Calculations complete. She moved over to the open window. The light beamed on her face with a cool breeze and warm rays. Placing the scroll on the ledge, she let out a small sigh.

"My heart sings…and sobs. Is everything in this true? Nothing omitted? Stay honest with me. No stray words."

The third approved the information sent to her. An owl flew to the ledge in search of respite. The woman had an attendant sent for water. Her fingers caressed it like her hair, gently.

"How does forgiveness look, little one?" she asked it. It only cooed. A simple animal without Wandrian lineage. She lifted her hand to her face. Searching through the lines of her pale palm. She wondered if having blood on them was the right move.

"It's been some time since the ones above have made their presence known. Notably alchemy. Burned by the swords of black. I wish I could be there to see Her take his nous…and his new female companion."

"If that happens, though, She, the principle of combustibility, will also eradicate her legacy…your mothers."

"Incorrect, the Primes are bound to never begin a war with one another as they once did. Too many planets lost. Iberitus is their longest-surviving yet. Harbinger, Herald, and Vakienda…a different story. A quick and easy retrieval of the scrolls."

The owl fluffed its wings. Agitated. Some whistles, some shrieks, some wavering cries. She stared at it silently, a look of indifference.

"Indulgent is not a quality I shall entertain, little one."

"Those living in the trees continue to sing his name," the attendant spoke, "Even though you purged its nous, many eyes have seen him go against the Khrosgar valiantly. A feat they won't *ever* forget."

"You think I don't know that?! Every day that nomadic thief has a new song to be sung! And yet, they do not see it as a guise for stealing from my family! My mother! Father would have had him under the chopping block. A loose head thrown into the marshlands for those disgusting mushrooms to inseminate."

The sent attendant returned with a bowl and satchel.

"Doubtful," the third said in a low voice.

"DOUBTFUL, *WHAT*!?"

"Doubtful...Queen Evren."

She grinned, "I'll overlook that insubordination. As for Father...perhaps. He had too much goodness in his heart. Had he had some thorns around it...he might've—"

The owl had flown off already. Too scared to be close to the queen's morning rawness. She sighed again, placing the bowl of water down and removing the content from the satchel to study. It wriggled and squealed in a panic.

"You might say 'joy' for another day of living, but one day, all of your kind will finally go extinct. And that day will be the first of many celebrations," Evren said to the small rat.

An explosion happened in the distance where the mountains were. Her eyes closed in on the smoke appearing over the horizon. Foundations of the land dismantling.

"Grand war...again. The slug seeks reclamation. The Hive seeks domination. And the lynx king seeks peace alongside his new composer pet Mairu. Only the beastfolk and my cousins to the south refuse to take part in it—except when defending their lands from the grand beasts. They never take the offense," she said, "a population in sharp decline."

Evren turned to her attendants, ordering them to fortify the Vicara. They made their bows before leaving her chambers.

"Not long now until Jökull gives me *my* reclamation. The girl is an added bonus," she said, dropping the rat from way up high.

Everyone has to do their part in exterminating.

Icosahedron's day shone brightness over the world. But that was its ploy. Lowering their guard and ambushes need very little planning. They would soon encounter a crown of allotropes brought on by one from the waters.

A gamble.

All bets on, enticing the one it lavished over for years.

Tearing the fabrics of an unknown tapestry, she returned to the primeval forest, but alone. If one could firmly describe what atoms feel like rearranging back into their proper order, it would be her.

On hands and knees, and with what felt like a millstone around the neck, a form of asthma took hold. Lungs felt the metaphysical flames. The weight of her neck was too much to lift. Her eyes were set on loose dirt, feeling around to see if anything could help stabilize her before the body succumbed to collapse.

I need to fortify these limp hands and enfeebled knees.

A band of Wandrians saw the poor girl in ill condition. Each raced to provide her aid. They sat her upright against a stone. The presence of ivy in her lungs faded. Still hints of sharp pangs.

Better than one, or both, collapsing.

She gave thanks and looked at her surroundings to notice her compatriots missing in action. One critter provided a stick of hard fatwood for stability. Using the crutch, she called out their names. *This really hurts.* She hoped they would return her calls like a game of Marco Polo. Nothing; nil; zilch; absolute bupkis. Until…an array of whispers came from the edge of the woods—female.

This was the plan originally: to go back in this direction. Maybe a clue will be found here.

More than she could bear to chew.

More than her nose would allow.

Contents of the stomach baptized the soil. The Wandrians themselves almost fled the horrific scene they witnessed with her. The thought of personally witnessing such a sight was never in the cards.

Viewings of grisly photographs seen from the history books before guiltless eyes. This is the very definition of murder.

Charred bodies were strewn everywhere in the open field. Too indistinguishable to tell what they once were. Only the contortion of limbs and warped faces gave way; they suffered a fate worse than some medieval execution.

Phthalo emerged by her side, but not as a dog.

"You're close."

The ears picked up the sound: feeble groans in the center. The Herald made a guide for Sadie to follow. "You need to hurry before *She* comes!" it shouted in fear. More apprehension over the girl. Her eyes looked over the corpses, asking if there was another Khrosgar nearby that did this mess. But the Herald said something far more powerful than any Khrosgar was en route, and the one that did this was merely watching.

Time was of the highest essence.

She leaped over the blackened bodies to where the guide traced. Eyes blurred. Acid frothing in the belly. Chattering teeth, afraid for their enamel, against the corrosive properties. *For the love of all that is holy, don't breathe through your nose!* Her ears picked up small cries of pain. Not long after, she had found Milos. Still bleeding from his fatal injury.

"Damn…blast…sent me…here," he groaned out, "Get the damn…scroll…inside my…coat!" The little creatures came to his side to wipe the grime from his face. Sadie's fingers delicately went into his apparel to retrieve the item without further injuring him.

"Please, hurry!" The same orchestra of female voices transmitted into Sadie's head, but there was no other living soul in sight.

"Who's out there?!" Sadie asked aloud. The Herald told her to pay no mind to the voices, "Just do as they have requested."

Something terrible initiated its approach. The quality of air shifted. Inauspicious clouds form. It had no need for either banners or armies or brigands to convey its formidable nature. It sought a once-missed opportunity.

Reclamation of this dying vita.

"Dear God…" Sadie's voice trailed.

Flowers sprouted from the ground. She thought the Khrosgar killer found them again. Trying to settle the score.

"Worse, so much worse, and far more powerful than she and I," Phthalo said, "I had not anticipated this. This goes beyond my talents! **YOU MUST HURRY!**" The smell of rotting eggs slowly filled the area.

Sadie carefully extracted the bloodied scroll, Goldenrod, to unravel. But she didn't understand how to use

it. She had no practice from what she got from Gottlir. Lost
to the sea…except one.

"This looks so different from the one bought at the
wharf."

"Those are instants. These are composer-made
scrolls; they must be read aloud; only I can aid," Phthalo
responded.

"What about the cardinal purple?! Can that help us?!"

"Primes, no! Last resort if this fails us!"

The failure of organs settling in.

Milos dug his nails cruelly into the wet soil. He didn't
care if it was urine or excrement. He's found a long-lost
suffering. With the jaw beginning to lock, to bare clenched
teeth, she noticed the saliva thickening through with red
bubbles. His eyes sought expulsion to try to escape from the
pain.

"I'm losing!" Milos cried out like a child.

Something about a man whimpering, with the truest
forms of agony, can make anyone's heart crumble. Amidst
his eyes, she saw his colors whitening, reversing, whitening,
and reversing.

The calling of The White.

*I'm useless! I'm worthless! Less than shit! He's going
to die! And it'll be my fault! Why are my efforts so futile?!
God…don't leave this man…I am to blame…I am
unworthy…*

Many Wandrians tried to assist with topical herbs and
remedies while Phthalo instructed Sadie how to pronounce
the words. Milos lost too much blood. The warmth of
skin…gone, replaced by the spill of cold sweat. The traveling
salt, from sea to wind, burned his eyes. Mental endurance
gives up to the cold. A trembling tongue. Calling out for his
love in the pelagic; asking forgiveness from the father of

clay; wishing to hold the hands of dear friends. But something restless seemed to be the only thing drawn to his crumbling shrine, preparing funerary rites.

Ready to display his body on the shores.

Sadie whispered out the cryptic letters into coherent words. Small bits of gold flicked off the pages with each success. Her concentration was paramount, but with each word spoken, a glimmer of the colorful veiled women appeared around the party. Floating. Staring at their fallen scribe. Concern in some. Anger in others. Sadie's eyes saw the other scrolls illuminating like beacons cutting through a fog.

But that wasn't the only thing beginning to show itself.

Not your usual minerals, cells, or extracellular matrix of organic or inorganic components birthed among the living and dead. You won't find calcium phosphates here. There won't be any white steeds or sicklemen to be found as well. And forget your trumpets.

The practicalities of cessation.

Time to die...

"Oh no, the bones are forming! Hurry before the crown appears!" Phthalo panicked. An explosion of two segmented pillars of bone zigzagged from the earth. They were surrounded by more of the peculiar flora. The smell of rotting eggs amplified tenfold.

The veiled women became more opaque as the ritual continued. Sadie's eyes were beginning to hurt. Nice and bloodshot. She did not want to blink and accidentally lose her place. Not knowing if she had to restart the words again if failing just one. The tongue flapped about, but the teeth were mindful, striving not to chatter erratically to pierce the wordsmith.

A Wandrian chittered, noticing the gear on Milos's bracelet whirring violently. The diamond prism started to glow. It embedded itself into his palm. Erratic energy discharging. A transformation had begun, and it slowly made its way up his arm. Mechanical gears, metallic tubes, circular vents, and fantastical symbols, all meld into the flesh.

Phthalo heard another but in the distance.

The observer. The one who committed this atrocity.

"Time to see for myself," it said.

This predator's camouflage completely concealed itself from naked eyes. It sat near the top of the tree zone. The haze added to its concealment. Twin swords dangled by the sides. Dripping red that smelled of rust and iron. Besides the Herald, another was able to see through the predator's camouflage easily. It made its presence known to it, bashing a fist to the tree's base.

The predator looked down slowly.

"That look suits you. Why not join me instead? Your Breyjan perished long ago when I claimed her feeble consort. Speaking of becoming extinguished," it said, returning its bored eyes back to the field.

Another bash on the base.

"I wholeheartedly accept your challenge...after I see *Her* splendor. Fret not for the scribe...I have my ways," the predator responded to his voiceless contender.

The gear on the bracelet stopped functioning.

The diamond ceased its glow.

The impartial transformation reverted.

A curtain call for the lungs.

His head lopped to one side.

A wild expression was imprinted on his face.

Panic sets in.

"— to make whole!" Sadie finished the last words.

"That's it! You did it!" Phthalo cheered.

They rose from the soil: lights of gold and passion. *Just like in the village!* Each beam wraps around the lifeless body to resurrect.

"Please, live," she sobbed out.

Appearing before her was a new veiled woman in gold.

Whispers entered Sadie's mind, coming from the veil of Aquamarine, *"Our dear sir will."*

The injury reversed, new blood circulated, and eyes showed glints of life.

"Almost," Sadie whispered.

But the power of Goldenrod stagnated. The Wandrians scattered upon the arrival of the new guest. Phthalo looked up to see the blinding constellation of a crown, borne in the murky sky, as a yellow haze enveloped their surroundings.

"Master…guide me," it whimpered out.

Sadie and the veiled women looked up to see the ominous event unfold. "Phthalo, what's happening?! Why isn't Milos getting better?!" She saw the towering figure emerge from the portal of flowered bones, "Oh my God…Jesus…please, save me."

Do earthly deities ever congregate here?

As tall as a skyscraper, draped in shrouded regality, displaying the repeating symbol adorned on the head and palms of atomic number sixteen, caressing its feet atop a pile of lemon-colored sintered microcrystals. The ineffable natural beauty of Sulfur, one of the three Primes of Alchemy. Although the deity's face was shrouded, it appeared to be holding an uncaring gaze on the woman of Goldenrod. The other veils hissed, roared, and cursed at the Prime, but not Goldenrod.

Instinctual innocence. Not a drop of aggression. Invisible microscopes: determined to find an iota. None. Only firm in purpose to the bleed-out. She knows it is she who can bid this despondency farewell. A formidable task to repel this oppressive atmosphere. But even kings and queens, in this world, cannot kill the messenger without swift repercussions.

Zero chance of "fool's mate" occurs here.

The Prime lifted back its hood—only so subtly—to reveal the qualities of a woman, below the eye line.

"Nonreactive, just like the rest of your fellowship."

Despite the intimidating aura she exuded, her voice was elegant. Goldenrod caressed Milos's body. Or it looked like it. Unable to physically touch him. She ignored Sulfur. The innocent veil just wanted to finish the process. Dreaming of vitality. Restoring him in full capacity without further delay, in hopes of seeing him smile. Again and again.

But the Prime had other plans for the half-dead scribe.

"Do you see your wings as his shelter? My lap can hold his head for stability—far greater than your 'touch.' It is what I am owed, after all, when the arrow took his voice many seasons ago," Sulfur said, holding out her palm, unveiling her symbol.

But Goldenrod shook her head and "held" him tighter. A ghost longing to be embraced. Poor bunny. It's a shame they cut out your tongue for the ritual…didn't sit well with your Master.

Extinction.

"Too many leaves have fallen over him. I have seen his laborious efforts from those same tired hands. He has served my properties well in the past for someone who stays true to Chroma. Mercury and Salt have been honored as well. Your kind aren't the only ones deserving of such a follower.

Notice how your Masters, or Messengers, are absent…they do not care about him. I hold the heart of his home. Release him unto me. Unburden his grief. There was never an agreement to withhold against a silly acting veil—I can erase you without any breach."

Her harsh tone would rile the other veils. Mulberry and Cobalt acted primal. Auburn and Aquamarine stood with shoulders back and upright. Another—barely visible—playing voyeur. Flecks of silver on her. The Cerulean "lot" remained absent. Goldenrod had a tearful look, her body sheltering over Milos's body, closing her eyes and shaking her head. No budges from this mute bunny.

But the blood kept pouring.

Transitioning back as a canine, carefully beseeching the Prime with a scroll in its mouth. "Please, spare him; I and this one beg for his life to remain here," Phthalo pleaded, dropping the scroll in front of him.

This invoked the Prime's fury.

"A newborn Herald…disguised as a *mongrel*?! **Have you no shame?!** What's more, you present *this* parchment as a bargaining tool," she boomed out, lowering her body to the party, "Why should I listen to a veil that hasn't revealed itself like the others? It has no office here. Do you not understand your precarious situation, Messenger?!"

Phthalo tried for a rebuttal, but the Prime's presence twisted its tongue into many knots. "If you have nothing more to say—like Cerulean—then I will finish my collection," Sulfur said, holding her hand over Milos's body. Goldenrod's body diminished slowly as a yellow haze came to envelop his barely conscious body. All of the veiled women started to disappear with tired, anguished looks of defeat.

Save for the voyeur.

How would she get home now? She knew she wouldn't last a day without him. He took all the chances; maybe she could risk her neck under the ax in his place.

"Can I make an offer?" Sadie spoke sheepishly. The Prime looked at her, nodding. The young girl stood up to make her case, "I'm not sure of what terms you offered him, but what if you made a new contract with me instead? You can take more from me if it means he gets to live."

The haze gave way to some visibility. Sulfur disappeared, briefly, only to stand before her at a normal height. Engrossed by the young girl's next sentence. Slowly encircling her. Gears ruminating.

"Anyone else would be dismissed. Impossible to appease, compared to what this man has to offer for my vivarium. But you…you're not from this plane, and I'd be the fool to pass by an opportune moment," Sulfur said. The Prime grazed Sadie's neck. She leaves behind a trail of soft yellow powder, examining the nape with her fingers, disregarding personal space. Her yellow nail lifts out what has been hidden this whole time.

"I have seen this symbol before. Many seasons ago, when we, the Masters, could walk freely on this plane. But none can tell me its meaning. Safeguarded by planeswalkers: glastum royals and initial Iberians. Share your knowledge," Sulfur asked, holding up Sadie's necklace with a cross attached.

"It is a symbol of faith and devotion to my God…or how people here would call it: *my* Prime."

Sulfur dropped the cross. Chord struck. Taken aback, "It has no science behind it, no hint of pigment, too unknown, never to be seen in the midst of nature—a fabrication of miracle and wonder by the superstitious. Dismiss it, worship under my field of discipline, offer your vita to me, and I'll forever abstain from this man. No objections, no counteroffers, nothing else."

The girl's faith is at stake. If she rejected her religion, it would save a life, but it would cost her so much more. The Prime stated she only had to say yes, or the offer would cease in just a few moments.

Why are some moments an eternity, yet others come as quick as lightning to impale? To be subjected to a speedy inquisition.

Misfortune is a heavy crown, and there is something deeply gross about a forced conversion. Prime, or grand inquisitor?

"This is not right!" Phthalo objected.

Sulfur ignored the Herald. She approached Sadie with a yellow haze to blur out everyone besides the two.

"Embrace my terms by genuflecting to me," the Prime demanded.

Sadie heard Milos beginning to choke in the background. Sulfur purposely suffocated him; life is a fragile impermanence that many take for granted. The girl could only sob in response, kneeling one leg down, preparing to lower the other.

"How do I know you won't take him?" Sadie asked, looking up at the hooded woman.

"You don't."

These words managed to come across distant ears. It was disgusted by this exchange, and it would negate the impending transaction in protest.

"I had high hopes to learn from you. But you're no different from the lessers. Be dethroned," the hidden predator murmured.

Sulfur heard the shambling of feet all around. She dismissed the haze to gaze upon a sight that infuriated her.

All of the corpses rose. Their crooked steps, set in motion, to the forest. Blue flames around them. Her Majesty's rotten haze dwindled away. Her portal, crumbling. She saw through the bodies: parasites of wood and metal frameworks inhabiting them. Their bodies had absorbed the rotted corpses of their sulfuric properties to cleanse the area, robbing her of power. The blue flames of burning sulfur diminished one by one.

The Prime screamed for all of Iberitus to hear. Her gaze locked on the one who caused the disruption, high up the tree line. "Phlegmatic mollusk! Know I will have you judged one day before me!"

She returned to her large original size, gazing down at Sadie, "My short domain of power may be whisked away by another, but not so long as I am still here," Sulfur waved her hand towards the marsh strait. A wall of yellow mist bordered the crossing. "I know where you desire to go, and I'll have you stay on this land longer for observation. You pique my interest, and I *will* have you swear fealty!" Sulfur finished before disappearing into the air. The bone portal crumbled, the crown vanished, and the foul, pungent odors of decay were replaced by sweetness.

Maybe they're not omniscient. But what of Phthalo's...?

Goldenrod returned to finish her job.

Milos gasped loudly, inhaling the fresh air. Now that's a wonderful feeling. The bird escapes the starving cat—freedom. Sadie and Phthalo went to his side to check on him. Besides the obvious fatigue, he returned to full health. "What happened?" he asked them, but they were unsure how to answer. The Herald mentioned how the bodies came back to life and used themselves as portable vacuums to extinguish the high amounts of sulfur plaguing the area—vanishing into the woods. Milos asked if they saw puppets with symbols on their foreheads, but neither of the two could see anything through the yellow haze or blue flames.

"Unexpected, but the result still remains as I hoped," the predator murmured, jumping down to make true of its promise, "I'll raise neither sword, but a hand to your advances…proceed, Essent."

The muted contender held back its large arms and swung with great veracity, as the predator held but one hand up to the attack.

Nullified, without effort.

The once strong husk of the mute's power crumbled like a fine powder. The original format back on display.

"I know one day, you and he will join my kingdom… again," the predator said, looking down at his now minuscule-sized contender, "Go to him; I will see you and the others soon, when night falls, and all that lights the way are her torches, contesting with my radiance."

The predator dissipated into the shadows instantly.

The mute advanced back to his party.

"Where have you been when we needed you?!" Sadie screamed at the ball of bejeweled clay, rolling onto Milos's shoulder. Enzu shapeshifted into a crown with a pair of sconces beside it.

Milos's heart missed several beats. "We need to hurry north; for now, I know of an inn that lies close."

Sadie asked about Enzu's message, but the scribe remained silent. Only thanking Goldenrod for her help.

"At least we tried," Mulberry retorted.

"By having a hissy fit? E for effort, love."

"Better than Cerulean…" Cobalt chimed.

"You need to appease our Primes, sir. It's the only way we can help without incantation. We nearly lost you..." Aquamarine remarked.

"You're right. Immediately after this expedition."

Two would come calling for allegiance. Unaware of the intervention of a third.

The one calling for execution.

Chapter 9

†

Jing

What cheerful warm rays shone on them, belied by the oncoming doom. The light of the skies transitioned into the dull of grays. Light rain passes over weary travelers, and the booming of thunder is not far off in the distance. An absence of ionized air. Evidence of tens of millions of luminous fingers pointing to nuanced directions to the secrets of life. No aim to orient traffic to the very nucleus of the universe: love.

It's all turning to mud.

Within the neutral chroma, the intermingling of white smoke billowed from nearby bloomeries across the grounds. Smelters aid the kingdom with the necessities to keep one held together: couplings, pipes, and garden furniture. The smiths had no grand business on weapons or defensive structures except on a small scale—for a quick geodi. Current surroundings held no abundance of roguish or malevolent activity ever.

An overlook that would repay in kind.

They arrived before the gray masses wept out of the mire. Refuge at "The Gilded Plume." He barely said a word. Cautiously scanning the dark tavern to see if anything seemed unaligned. He had been here dozens of times and knew the regular drunks apart from the unknown.

"It's been some time, handsome, the usual?" a barmaid asked him. He requested a private audience with the owner.

The chandeliers had barely any candles lit. No party-bright patrons here. Inside one's inebriated mind is a notion to pull out some torn cardboard, some skin-staining chalk, and hang a new name for the establishment: "The Penurious Dung." Gliding across the grays, a bird picked up this transmission, somehow, cackling to itself, thinking, *Education's failed this sorry dipsomaniac! Best not to nose-dive the yards to splat on the wretch's head—too easy.* Grog makes fools of us all.

"The nomadic scribe returns to us! And I see you brought company too, a Somdirian I might add," the owner announced brazenly, "Busy lad, aren't ya?" This drew ire.

What fascinating temporal arteritis you have, scribe!

Milos told him to bite his tongue; he simply needed him to listen carefully. Clammy hands withdrew all the geodi from his satchel, speaking in hushed tones, "I'm going to need not only the entire inn tonight but also use of the surrounding land." When the owner asked why, Milos gave scant details, only giving out the possibility of certain "guests" who would be arriving for him. The owner wanted no part of this plan until another patron, from the basement, came into the picture, and Enzu had spotted them. He rolled to garner attention.

A spot of luck.

"I swear no one here will die if you just evacuate the premises for the night! This payment is enough to cover the incoming property damages that are inevitable, but I cannot operate in this weather against the most—" Milos went on before being interrupted by another patron.

"I hear there's some currency to pick up over here," the guest stated. Another introduction to Sadie. Another imposing race. Tall, vivid, and, surprisingly, contemporary in attire. *Woman or women?* she thought. A single body, two arms, two legs, and a regular pair of breasts, all with two heads shackled together by the neck. At the limits of Earth, at the extremity of Heaven, Janus encroaches. This dram shop is an extension of her abode. The one speaking wore goggles. Her opposite wore a half mask over the mouth—dazed. Eyes glazed. Milos saw her badge of office: Flint and Coin. He proposed an offer for services. Again, keeping details close to the vest without rousing too much suspicion from whoever was within earshot. She needed more convincing, suggesting they go to the basement to speak in seclusion.

Musky air. No cigarettes or pipes around, but it stunk. Some noses get used to foul attributes. This *is* the pits. Quick dread, of the girl's mind, wondered if resinous cancer impregnated her lungs. There are worse things than mutagenic and carcinogenic agents to befoul DNA.

Four inhabitants: a carob Gottlirian male, a female Sanshan, a male Trasno, and an enormous male Mairu. Operatives on the scene.

All in modernized, pressed uniforms.

"Another round, on the scribe this time," the goggle-wearing woman said to the barkeep. The half-mask looked tired, but she didn't stop staring at Sadie.

It made her self-conscious.

A glint from her bracelet. Wanting a stare-off.

"What's the Somdirian's name?" the Mairu asked, feasting on a plate of ribs. Smacking lips. Greasy digits. Decorum is not in this man's vocabulary. Milos, leashing back his ire, stated she wasn't from there; the red hair feature was natural.

The Sanshan smacked the Mairu upside the head. "Even I know she's not of my kind. The ones closer to humankind, the flesh-toned or *Krviira-Sanshan*, have red scleras and chromatic tattoos. You know this."

He remained unfazed from the assault, "It's dark here. Fight me. Besides, what about your realm's gold alchemist? I heard she was without tattoos of any kind." She took her ale and walked away, proclaiming that the girl was not a *Bistarira-Sanshan*. Legendary half-breeds. The pale borns: a stark difference.

He huffed before returning back to his sauce-slathered protein.

A crackle from the bracelet. *Milos, do you see this? Little help here.* The half-mask continued to leer heavily. If you hold your breath, you can just barely hear the woman panting underneath. What salacious thoughts blitzed in this woman's head? Are the twin minds connected? Did moral evolution accidentally skip over her? Here's a thought: smitten. The girl is too troubled to think that up. Better this way.

The other head took notice.

"She likes you," the other woman said, "We *Mervigs* never hide our feelings." She gripped the chain to yank the mute's head down, "But she submits to me only."

Thanks, but no thanks.

Smitten. She's going to remember that for a long time. In a *bad* way. It might require soap, water, and all kinds of skincare regimens to feel clean again. Lye isn't off the table. The girl is dead set on her dogma.

She will never entertain the thought of tribadism.

"I have no time for your sadomasochistic nature. Who's in charge here?!" Milos shouted out.

"I am," a male said from one of the tables. Average height, but a wide back. Subtle movements revealed extensive lines of muscle under his jacket. If they should suddenly burgeon, rips and tears would occur. Ego would get a kick. Milos propositioned him hastily and too close to personal space. The members pointed their pistols in his direction. Quickdraw: the first of the prerequisites to joining. Too tight to blink.

Best to conserve the gear's energy.

"Careful, sir," Aqua transmitted.

The secretive man waved his hand. "It's alright, leave him be."

Guns holstered. No standoffs were necessary. Milos noticed the enormous rifle on the table. Realizing who he was talking to.

"Ekkehard Singer…" Milos said in awe. He extolled the man's name. Not often does he show this kind of utmost respect.

"State your business because we don't plan to stay here long," he responded, tipping his hat back. His face weathered. A history of violence, inflicted and subjected. He sized up Sadie. She notices the respect Milos gives. If the Lamb were to suddenly open the first four seals, releasing the riders, going out conquering and to conquer, with thunder in the leader's voice, she felt that this man would prevent harpazo. Seizure will not claim this girl's soul.

Beating the soil. Loosening it. Thunderous and calamitous. Floodgates open from up high. Everything in sight made haste for shelter, either inside the inn or taking their chances in the nearby woods. The river, adjacent to the inn, drifted onto land. Inching upward. No room for mudslides if this keeps up. Heavy was the rain coming down; you'd be deaf or blind to see or hear any approach.

FLINT & COIN

BE A PART OF LEGENDS

Too late to build an Ark.

Here comes the fog.

"If what you say is true, then you can't afford my squad…unless."

"Unless?" Milos replied.

"You take on several of my fifth-level contracts—for the public good—when the need arises. What do you say?"

"Only if I get to decide who comes with me, and we keep whatever is up for grabs that isn't part of the contract. Dungeons hold the best after all. Make no mistake: I will not do retrieval work from them, no matter the price. One ascended guardian was enough for my lifetime."

"I make no bones about that; deal." Singer replied, putting his hand out to shake. Milos responded in kind but heard loud thumps above. Everyone in the room stopped drinking and eating. Breaths held. Singer nodded to his team. One by one they advanced, slowly, to the upper floor. Keeping to the shadows. Milos told Sadie to hide under the bar with Enzu. The goblin was the first to slowly peek his head out of cover. Every patron stretched out on the ground. Cold-cocked. A mist seeps in from the entrance door. He recognized the odor: cyanogen.

Reactivity? Violent reaction.

Fire hazard? Below 25 degrees Celsius.

Health hazard? Deadly…

Don't play with pseudohalogens carelessly.

The Mairu charged past him. A thrilling burst of speed for a large specimen to shoulder down the hefty wood fixture with gusto. Only to be met with crossbow bolts to riddle his body. Milos teleported to the giant to try to heal him, disregarding his own safety. "Jackasses, the lot of you! You think this barrage can kill me?!" The Mairu exploded. He pulled out chunks of bolts from his limbs with barely any blood loss. Envious is the lizard of the Nile blessed by Sobek. The others advanced behind. None could see anything past the thick fog. With the storm, night had washed over as well. The Sanshan warrior's tattoo started to glow.

"They're reloading," she advises.

A great wall of rammed earth surrounded the entire inn. "This should hold'em off," the goblin said after conjuring the large barrier.

Ears picked up violent coughs from inside.

"Sadie!" Milos screamed, trying to return back inside, but the others held him back. The Sanshan held off his power of teleportation, reminding him of the danger that still remained inside.

Glass shattered from above. Figures catapult forth, embracing gravity's pull to the ground. The twin-headed giantess had the young girl in their safety. Stunned, but alive. One big relief for the scribe. Groggy and weary-eyed, Sadie saw the half-mask head was no longer wearing hers.

"Good job, Licarayen." Singer said to her, "Taiwo, Tímea, clear out this nonsense."

The young Gottlirian shot a flare into the sky, creating an artificial white sun, while the Sanshan waved her arms to clear out the fog. Interrelating components of talent. They won't be so easily bested in this turmoil. No yearning for the taste of defeat.

"That's highly unsettling. Your information seems incorrect, scribe. What in the Primes have you got us into?!" Singer asked aloud.

They emerged entirely out of the blanket of darkness. Scores of deranged organs of sight. These eyes do not hold any semblance of lucidity. Modified bodies spewing industrial parts. Scrap metal protruding from their clothing. Behind those peepers remain partially empty brain boxes.

Small amounts of chemical energies, running on a single power line, unstable currents with one directive.

Annihilate.

"Chemical Vermis…he's here…" Milos uttered in disbelief. He could feel it: the tethering. At first, the signal was weak. Vastly superior now. It is an ugly, excited hum. A series of clicks, tones, and lights. Over a hundred trillion configurations, but he's deciphered this one before. No room for permutation. Old friends come to visit.

"*Who's* here?!" Singer shouted.

The malicious unit of rats charged before he could answer. The onslaught took hold with no mercy from both sides. No time to carve timber. With enough disturbed mud, there'll be plenty of holes with red wigglers and grindals and other soil-dwellers preparing to vermicompost.

Wooden overcoats aplenty.

The Mairu was splitting open scores of them, but even lone predators can be overwhelmed by the marching parade of fire ants. Singer was quick with his rifle, but for every shot he took, it seemed they multiplied. The goblin noticed the poisonous gas streaming back into the field again from beyond the simulated light.

Something, or someone else, still held back their presence.

Lightning bombarded down ceremoniously. Many of the unkempt plague bearer rats fell via conduction. Electricity follows the path to their metallic wires. This gave Milos an idea.

"Draw them to the river!" he shouted.

A high pursuit initialized with him taking the lead. *I hope they're as dumb as they say,* he thought. The party lined up in front of the flood.

"I swear, scribe, if you get us killed, I will goad the Primes to torture your nous! Every damn color!" Tímea screamed.

"We weren't getting out of that inn alive with this amount…look," Licarayen said, pointing out to the horde rapidly approaching them. Singer stayed quiet. Only taking shots at the closest ones. The Mairu screamed out a final scream as the frontline leaped into the air to finish them off. Milos reached for Mulberry. Unraveling gently so as to not rip. Asking the vicious princess if she was ready.

"Let's break out the animal wagons!" she transmitted.

Quickfire of the tongue. Incantation complete.

No storm is complete without a hurricane. It erupted from the ground, capturing every single rat abomination in one fell swoop. Milos carefully approached the screaming rodents, holstering the scroll and taking up a large finished pipe from a bloomery. He plunged it deep into the mud. The flood kept growing. Some of the encased bodies were beginning to float. Feet began to sink. Best react now before the sludge hands out pairs of concrete boots.

"Now we get to high ground, and Singer, you can finish the job," Milos said. His hair overshadowed his face, but a rage was there. The veil of Mulberry was excited by this. The others kept silent. There's no role for them here. It's under control. Let fire best fire.

They returned to the front of the inn. Singer loaded a specialty shell into the rifle, aimed it at the pole, and shot. A violent burst of electricity sent shockwaves through the water to kill off their rabid foes.

Flashover burning away at their skins. The smell: unholy. Seeping out of the crystal prisons.

The others cheered except for Milos. He looked towards the forest, screaming, "Come out, coward! **FACE ME!"**

All looked confused, but it wasn't long until something had caused the artificial sun's rays to extinguish. The darkness returned in full, and so did the fog. Wheezing. That's exactly what they heard. That ugly vernacular hum of distortion. A walking apocalypse of tumbled words. It has no inclination for logic, rhetoric, or reason; by the composition, it leads without eloquence! An embodiment of violence.

Ne plus ultra.

Flint and Coin readied themselves again, but Milos advised them to return to the inn, as this was his fight. Any interference could cause great harm to them and Sadie. Duty must not be abandoned.

"No promises; you did agree to our contract after all," Singer said, instructing the others to retreat inside.

The rain started to slow.

A calm breeze passed through.

Ears picked up the ugly rasps.

His gear started to whir rapidly.

"Face me, bastard," Milos uttered.

The cyanogen returned under the guise of the fog. It clouded the vigilance of his veils.

"Get out, you fool!" the goblin shouted from the upper floor. Enzu leaped onto Milos's shoulder, gems glowing, and with some focus, began to push the poison back towards its caster. The scribe could faintly see the silhouette of the ambushing leader.

Noticing he was about to do something risky.

"EVERYONE DOWN!" Singer shouted.

The Mairu shielded the others with his body. A purple-tinged flame sparked and erupted, tracing itself to

Milos. With several blinks, he narrowly managed to escape the flammable gas, but not without damage. Swarms of insects found their way onto his body, latching on, gifting him paralysis. He could feel their aggravating toxins. Each sting injects a personal hell by the master's command. His nerves were intravenously filled with a raw substance. Turning him exceptionally fragile. Disintegrating any feeling. Starting with his hands.

All looked out to see the scorched earth. None could see him. And they feared for his life.

"You...wretch..." Milos strained out, his throat beginning to close. The wheezing grew louder. How long can the scribe endure?

What's next on the prescription? Endurance is fleeting.

The leader finally exposed himself to the downed scribe. A Vermis of foul imagery. Its body was a perverse marriage of matted fur, corundum, and industry. Cautious steps: incoming. Skittish knees. Its pupils were nothing more than continuously spinning swirls. An absolute being of pathological status. Strafing. Circling. Looking for a soft spot around its paralyzed prey. The wheezing was unbearable. Milos noticed its right hand exhaling toxic gas—a hole in the palm. More disturbing was the enlarged decorative egg, hovering over the other hand with insects skittering all around. It cocked its head repeatedly at all angles to ensure Milos could not move or conjure any tricks up his sleeve.

Behold, the heartless. Accumulator of apprehension.

But the rat did notice he was trying to say something. Loud clangs were expelled from the right arm. This furnace has multiple settings. From a toxic flow to now a panacea, it allowed him to speak freely once he allowed the fresh steam into the scribe's nostrils.

Milos vulgarly vomited saliva onto the ground, hefty breaths, before looking up at his torturer in disdain.

"Shocked, the queen let you out of the cesspools, Olu..."

The psychotic rat didn't respond. Its mouth continued to wheeze, inhaling from the pipe attached to a canister on its belly. Still creeping closer, overflowing with paranoia, this time removing a bomb attached to its utility belt. Nails tapping on the device. A sign of glee. He would rather kick the poor scribe into mush for days on end, or free him of mandible and maxilla, or...well...this rat dwells on many horrible thoughts for the scribe.

It'd all end with some act of defecation either way.

"*Sir*..." Aqua transmitted. They felt incapable. Without his words and his hands, they could only watch the torment unfold. If only he...

"My death is certain, but *never* at your hands!" Milos screamed.

Never say never.

Olu gripped his mouth, trying to break it open, but Milos refused with all his might. The pain from the beast's claws sank into the cheeks. Here comes the outpouring of life. Mandible and maxilla it is then. This rat is just about ready to rearrange the poor bastard's uncuttable nucleus of protons, neutrons, and electrons! Subatomic particles be damned! But still, Milos did not give in.

"*Something has to be done!*" Cobalt said to the others.

"*RESIST!*" Auburn, ordered the scribe.

Even as the muffled sounds of pain tried to get him to scream. Even as the tears rolled relentlessly over his cheeks, mixing clears with reds. Dutifully dedicated to the cause. He is still human. There will come a breaking point. So many tears. He's reverting back to childhood...

Goldenrod was in a horrific state of panic.

***"I WILL BURY YOU ALIVE, PLAGUE
BEARER!"*** Mulberry roared. She screamed on and on and
on, trying to rattle the assassin's head. Rich, deep shades of
purple and red whirling like a cyclone around the hooded
dome. Decibels defying the sound barrier. All for naught.
This is a mind that has rejected the Chroma wholeheartedly.
Alchemy too. There is no temple, for the Primes, in this
Tarwini's oxidized core.

Look elsewhere.

"Little sir," Aqua said softly.

A resounding hiss came from Olu's person. The
canister's pipeline: severed. Aid from a steadfast Essent of
clay rolling around his body. There's an evil smile here. The
rat man tried to grab Enzu from sabotaging further
instruments attached, but he was far too quick. Soon the other
bombs were detached and placed inside the hood. Absent of
their pins. A member of Flint and Coin retrieved Milos to a
safe distance.

"Look at me, scum," Singer said in the background,
following the words with a spit of tar. Olu quickly turned to
see everyone pointing their weapons at him. In the sweet
bleakness of his core, he feels a new sensation. Cocking his
head to one side, motionless, there's an obligatory duty to
stand before this firing squad and receive his sentencing.
Those bombs are eager to see the encephalon, thirsty to know
what is in the master's brain. The deranged rat placed an
index finger over his forehead, digging in his discolored nail
as if to say—no—*provoke*: "Look upon this crown of liquid
sand. Turn it into a web of broken glass!"

A volley of bullets ensued on the surprised antagonist.

Explosions erupted. Sublime carnage. Sadie imagined
the sounds to be apocalyptic in nature, as if Heaven and Hell

screamed at one another in competition. The edge of the forest catches the damage. The semblance of dragon's breath scouring the land. A sorry state of collateral damage. Singer and the others looked over the mutilated area, but unfortunately, there was no body to recover.

"He has the queen's egg…he is above Klaring's elite," Milos stated, catching his breath, shaking on the ground.

"A big price on his head, I'm sure. Something I'd like to collect personally," Singer stated.

"So…did we win?" the Mairu asked.

"I'd say so, Benigno. The rats have pissed off. Great job on that fortification also, Mirsad," Singer praised.

The dead of night began to calm itself at last. Flint and Coin looked for survivors but couldn't find a single one. The poison sent each one to their designated Prime.

Sadie rested on the entrance steps, groggy and sick. "I can barely move…Please don't let me sleep here." Her eyes looked as if she hadn't slept in years. Milos looked over Goldenrod, another charge left before the cooldown, and began its incantation. The streams of light flowed around her, and although her body healed, her spirit was not. Threats came from all sides. Without repose, no cell, inside, will manage to maintain any sort of resting potential.

"There's nothing here for miles except wood, water, and marsh, and that sickening Prime now blocks the marsh," Milos replied, "I don't trust the poison to be fully cleared."

"Phthalo, isn't there anywhere we can go?! You've been too quiet this whole time; what's wrong?!" Sadie asked aloud.

"…The plan went awry somewhere. I'm unsure how this ever happened. I keep recalculating, but nothing. I had hoped to find a way before something like this would happen.

I didn't think it possible for me to ever fail like this. I am just as lost as you: blinded. Abandon me. Only black ink covers my eyes," it replied.

Sadie used the Herald's power, but nothing came up. The celestial map was desolate of features. Singer pulled out a map to gloss over. Only forest and forked rivers in these parts. Nothing substantial. No landmarks. No markings of Wandrian settlements nearby.

"We have to wait it out here until the Assinikoda deal with the barrier themselves. It could take days, and the war is leaching into Gottlir the likes of which I've never seen before. Maybe there's a cave nearby," Milos said, glossing over the soggy environment. His legs still hadn't recovered. They refused to listen.

"Or it could take just a single boon to remediate," a voice said in the forest. Flint and Coin did not recognize it, but the scribe did. Milos started to have a panic attack as this was far worse than the battle they had just temporarily won. Better to chew on gravel and spit out teeth than deal with this. Better to feel the thoracic cage implode around the ticker. Slow crush over this. Charge the emotions. Remains of a possible future look so distant. Stygian eyes. It's okay. Cri de cœur.

"EVERYONE INSIDE!" Milos screamed.

Late, late, late, late! The stalker has foresight. All, except Milos and Sadie, were trapped inside oak encasements that sprung from the earth. Only their whites are seen in the perfect molds, holding them in place. The river took their offerings. Now mud's come to claim justification for all the disturbance. And timber made time to coexist with the mire, grateful to the stalker.

"Much better. Now we can talk without disruption."

Sadie imagined this voice to be an immovable force, a cunning serpent, with little respect for those in power, only concerned with the matters of people in dire situations, to bleed dry.

"Don't kill them…I beg of you…" Milos pleaded out.

"You must get up! Try! Soldier on!" Cobalt ordered.

"For us…" Mulberry said, almost childlike.

"For the girl," Aqua said.

"For the greater good," Auburn said confidently.

A director emerges, not from darkness, but in their presence. A chameleon hiding in the light of its surroundings. Unveiling horrible grandeur. Palpitations, small to large, synchronized. With every step the stalker took, the mud below its feet solidified, noses detecting burning odors as eyes perceived pops of fire beneath the heels. Nature submitted abashedly to this speaker. It recognized this authority's ideology with the very despondent who rationalized the use of speed, testable hypotheses and predictions, and turning violence into an art form. A sensible diet.

"How long the days have gone since we last gazed unto each other, dear boy," the figure spoke. Its voice: rich, velvety, dispassionate, "And you travel with a *lesser*. My steward tells me she had something to do with what I seek, but I will be the judge."

"Leave her be…I just—"

"Just what?!" the figure curtly interrupted, "She is a lesser. No more than the excrement my armies scrape off their plantars onto fallen faces. She doesn't even default under the microcosm like your race. She will be your downfall, much like how the world started with desperate savages, long before your kind arrived. Culling them to create bucolic settings. Consummating realms like this pitiful

Gottlir—awaiting its inevitable destruction and desolation. I can see the cycle coming full circle soon."

"Still referring to women as lessers? Tragic," Milos replied. He tried to match the strange antagonist's composure. Millions of neurons work together to handle this hostage situation with aplomb. But his legs still tremble.

Its eyes never blinked. Not. *Once*. Under that mask. Impossible to tell if it was a part of it. This aberration goes beyond xenografting.

Sadie's fingers quivered relentlessly. The cold air slipped over the tips. Her shoes felt like ice bricks. This *thing*, somehow, brought the glacial epoch with it.

How long until the black warped those underlying tissues?

Dear frostbite, find another donor…

"They are evolutionary cul-de-sacs," it replied. "I watched your little skirmish with your old nemesis. Truly a sight that the lessers can learn from. You should've been more prepared. Has youthful knowledge departed from your vita? What would *she* think?"

Milos's brows twitched. An image of old love appeared in his mind. Tall. Dangerous. Silvery-haired. Traveling sister. She'd tell the scribe to lace up and object to this lashing.

"You were close, you know; on the cusp of death…of course I wouldn't have allowed it."

"Vitriol and lies! You are a container of suffering fields!"

Voices stir in his head.

"*Careful, sir,*" Aqua whispered.

"*It's one word away from thermonuclear,*" Cobalt joined.

"Lower the temp. Make it feel important," Auburn said.

"I **never** lie, boy. A weakness for the spineless and entitled that spit daggers into any organism's back when they are unaware. You are well on the path from small order to grand universe. Like me: macro. I see your untapped hunger. Much like how I grew tired of feasting on bluebottles, purple sails, blue buttons, violet snails, and my own. I am the truth. I am medicine. I am the embodiment of forgiveness. I am…"

The figure stood before everyone with two swords in hand, *"The* Prime Aeolid Ashokara. Love is solidified in my vita. Why do you think you survived on those dead fields earlier? My machinations saved you from that wretched stink of Her Majesty. You should thank my armatures."

It sees itself as love, but not in the harmonious sense, but in its actual form: suffering and sacrifice. It imposes these feelings into many mediums. Preferentially physical. With lots and *lots* of incisions.

"I saw you…in my dream," Sadie accidentally uttered, not realizing the magnitude of the situation.

The king of Lusura raised a sword to her throat.

"You have no right to speak to me so formally. *None!* Another word…and I end you. Is that understood?"

She clenched her eyes and wept gently, hoping to stave off its eerily composed anger.

"Realize I wanted a closer look at what my boy is doing with the likes of you. I am *not* impressed," it scolded, gazing coldly. "Know that I haven't slit your trull throat to keep my boy from hating me. You're so close though…test me." The king's chest rises and falls with great alacrity. Maybe some insect will land on the hilt, nudging it. That might just be enough to give Ashokara some failed excuse for penetration. Who's going to stop it from happening?

Ashokara

Sludge and muck bend to its will, the forest is hushed, the mercenaries are entombed, the scribe and his veils know better, and the Herald is silenced. This is all gift-wrapped.

Sadie felt her deep-rooted hairs trying to hit the eject button. Vascularity popping from head to toe with arteries trying to keep the flow from exploding under the skin. Her already wet hair collected pools of sticky cold sweat. Barely able to feel her feet from poor circulation. Her biotic electrical wiring system insists that she embrace the stimuli of the environment's infinite number of microbial activities.

Make it stop! she thought.

"I knew you were coming but cannot comprehend why you came personally. You speak of forgiveness, yet you took a love from me. All you want is to be at the top of the grand chain of being," Milos hurled out, trying to divert attention to him.

The strange autocrat, in even stranger armor, strolled around the area. Muffles and silent roars were produced inside the cases. F&C members struggle to break free. This is far above their pay grade. The king's eyes lacked any sort of empathy—bored by all, omitting the one he spoke to.

"She lives; is that what you wanted to hear?"

"..."

Both swords were raised to the sky.

"Ah! Now your attention peaks! I speak the truth, and she lives high amongst the ranks of my bravest. Abandon this lesser, this…*false* 'Somdirian,' as most confuse her for, and I will lead you back to her bosom. Join my cause, and all is ours. Your 'greater' in the pelagic is also welcome! She will hold an even higher office—should you aid me—despite my differences with her father, the imperator.

"Forget allegiances to wild kittens, malleable clay, and veiled lessers. They would use you for their own selfish purposes. Never have I taken from you by force. Why do you insist on suffocating yourself under a cloche? The best is all I ever wanted for you, long before I took office."

"You mean *usurped*! I know how you dealt with your predecessor." He's putting on a brave face. Milos. Incoming telepathic transmissions. Reminders are needed.

"Sir, stay the tongue!" Aqua barked.

"Let him speak how he wants!" Mulberry retorted.

"He is safe, but not the others…" Cobalt said.

"That foul, rapacious simpleton?! It's truly remarkable how stunted he was in brainwave activity! How anyone could follow such a dullard is beyond me! He had the intellectual depth of a shallow urine-filled crater."

Goldenrod appeared, spreading her lithe arms out in front of Milos. She is utterly afraid a sword will pierce his heart. The golden bunny tries desperately to defend him, futile as it is. She forgets she is just colored air. A sneeze can go through her like the others.

But she wants to try.

The king notices. Well attuned to the Chroma; adept at knowing the enemy. There is old history here. Ashokara stopped to take a deep breath. The scribe catches this. As does Singer.

"That age is over; my kingdom is ripe with opportunities that none could surpass. The king of malleable clay has misappropriated his lands, and the one known to all as the King of Lynxes—what a joke—there is little nobility left inside that so-called royal family. The two share land with sick-minded lesser aristocratic chambermaids, who do nothing more than play around on soft silk and divans, on their backs, legs high in the air, awaiting dim-witted male companionship to devour like mantids. Rotten moll-sacks!"

The Lost Divide.

Milos spat on the ground, "You share lands with the lost aristocracy as well. They keep to themselves at least. The men…only the suicidal addicts venture there. What better way to die than in the comfort of a woman's soft body? The warmth between her legs? I've mingled with the thought when I felt lost and alone in my youth."

No greater way to die than the final climax of sex.

"It's *liberal* thinking like that that needs immediate expulsion, my boy. The lessers infect the minds of men! Without copulation, they are nothing more than mundane blemishes that drive men mad with their hysterics. You found your Hafnium Mairu, your pearl of the sea, the few 'greaters' I recognize. But what of the others that throw themselves at you? Disease does not discriminate. **Reject suicide!**

"As for sharing borders…a temporary setback. The prism guards the land. Even my power has trouble dissolving it. Nevertheless, I will burn it to the ground, eventually. Truly a greater achievement than conquering those erratic tentacles that inhabit the Akrav. But we're getting far from the point."

"Keep its mind occupied. You are its favorite. Make it feel essential, like it believes itself to be," Auburn transmitted.

"Can you spare my comrades and open the path for the girl? I won't swear allegiance, but I can offer a boon…if by reasonable means."

The prime squinted its eyes in scrutiny. It was impossible to tell what emotions lay under the mask. If there were any. It gazed on those it imprisoned, then back to Sadie, approaching her again.

"You spoke of a word that stood out to me: God. Tell me…what is that? I felt a stirring in my nous-vita when I heard it."

Her eyes still clenched tight, her tongue too tied to answer. The Usurper was losing patience. It inserted a sword into one of the F&C's encasements. Loud echoes of pain. The bite of these distinctive blades could easily penetrate the hardiest of thresholds.

"Don't be afraid to scream. Sing for me, Singer," Ashokara goaded. Milos pleaded for his life but fell on deaf ears.

"My world's Prime!" Sadie exclaimed.

Death metal removed.

Attention back to the girl. Swift in motion. "I *like* that word. Something about it fills me with such raw emotion. Maybe *I* should refer to myself as a *God*."

Ashokara enunciated each word like a prize to speak out. Small trembles in the wrists. Exciting vibrations of fear unknown. Its eyes kept wandering as if trying to make the most delicate decision it ever had to make. New ideas reach the corners of the king-usurper's mind. New principles to pursue. New laws to draw up. Diseased. Exciting new ways to inflict violence. New pleasures.

"You remind me of the one I keep away. I was going to take you for myself, for experimentation, but," Ashokara said, sheathing its swords, "this is not the boon I seek, Milos. I'll spare your compatriots if you help your little Leandro to the northeast. You see, Ard Rex and his heir have committed treason. What confounds me is that the queen allows them to continue with their plan. Klaring is never allowed to wage against any realm—except Kotsudas—without a joint attack from yours truly. By allowing this to happen, they declared war on my realm too. This defiance against me, a *God*, will not do. Will. Not. Do!"

An acute, unflinching abrasiveness to the king's tone. The concrete mud under its boots started to melt. A small sound of pain evoked from its being. The king observed its hand.

"My body grows stiff. I know you won't fail; my spies will inform me when it is done. Then travel back on your original quest to give up this lesser to that pale whore of a witch—although both will try to kill you no doubt. Send her my deepest regards. A shame one loses both parents at such a young age, but her father was as weak as a dioptase, so…"

"I would never hurt him!" Sadie shouted. A hint of rage.

The prime turned back to face her, "You, of lessers, carve promises in the pelagic waters. Had my nemesis not made her presence known, I'd separate your head from your body this moment. She is anathema in the eyes of each and every Prime.

"You know what makes my boy so valuable? It's not the scrolls, or aptitude for pilfering, or wielding an ancient's power on the wrist, or its beads that are blessed and accommodated with the hair of a Hafnium Mairu, or the manipulated flesh from a Khrosgar, or even being a King of Skies. No. It's that deep within, his nous-pneuma, he fights to die! Gloriously! It's so incredible that after all is said and done, he fought so hard, he forgot *how* to die! It took a Prime for him to remember his mortality."

A grand laugh for the winds. Unnerving cachinnation. The king turned its attention a final time to Milos, "I do have an insurance plan should you not heed my words: If you decide to venture towards Celanjung first, my armatures, the ones who absorbed Her Majesty's stink, will level Sarsen's under the guise of stealth. There's enough sulfur—a *Prime's* sulfur—inside their bodies to fulminate both armies into a new crater. I'd gladly be the first to plant my flag there for expansion. Think before you act. Until we meet again."

The armor shattered. Almost like Milos's power, he blinked away from the scene instantly. Sadie, for just a brief moment, saw what was under the armor. It was not human. An amorphous blue creature, with large tentacled fingers, countershading its body, back under the cloak of invisibility. Water drips off her nose, onto her parted lips, the vestigial remains of rationality, parting ways. Refusing to kiss her goodbye.

This memory will never evaporate.

"I cannot do this anymore; *I cannot do this anymore*; ***I CANNOT DO THIS ANYMORE,***" Sadie kept repeating hysterically.

Enzu tried to snap her out of her delirium—a lost cause. Her bracelet is cold and lifeless. Merely ornamental.

Flint and Coin's encasements broke free with some gasping on the ground. Benigno pulled up Milos from the wet earth. Still wobbly, but doing what he can.

Something was off about the Mairu after his help: suspended.

The streams decelerated, drops of water freezing in place, the wind desists, and everything had seized in its place. A void closing in. One could not see the tree line anymore. The sky closed off the voyeuristic eyes of the stars, to pitch black. Flint and Coin were paralyzed in place; darkness washing over them.

It desired a private audience. Milos, able to regain balance, steadied himself for the final guest. If you blink, does the void blink back? Or swallow you whole?

"Sadie," he cried out, stumbling towards her, hoping his stilts didn't lose impetus before reaching her, "Don't give up on me now. Come back to us, love!"

But she kept repeating the words. A new coping mechanism was freshly painted over her psyche. Little pieces of her former self, dusted off and scattered. In the back of her head, a system restore point kicks in from previous studies: *Have I not commanded you? Be strong and courageous. Do not be frightened, and do not be dismayed, for the LORD your God is with you wherever you go.*

And the darkness swallowed everything around them. Light, in absentia, except around the still-moving players. And then he heard it: the snarl of something indescribable. The wet mud beneath them turned to stone. Sconces appeared to surround them. The cold departed, and rising temperatures came to be. The young girl's wet hair sopped over her face until claws and black nails wrapped themselves around once rosy cheeks. Hyperventilation took hold. There was no more energy for screams. Only for the tears that spawned. Her internal engine is ready to combust. And the eyes rolled to the back of her head.

Heaven's gates open for this weeping angel.

Ugly cries, as terror zoomed in behind her. It snarled around the sides of her face, baring large teeth of some sort of wolf. Small sniffs from its wrinkled snout. She violently chokes on her fluids. If her overstimulated saliva glands don't kill her, the explosion from her frantic heart will finish the job. A strange ambience invaded Sadie's ears and mind, coming to the conclusion that sure enough, the air was on fire.

All system restore points are corrupting.

Milos knew not to intervene, but Enzu was trying to help.

"She has your same blood," it said to Milos. The sharp nails traced Sadie's neck. A faint aura emits from them.

Healing. The young girl was relieved of her symptoms. No cardiac arrests here.

It released its grasp on her to meld back into the abyss.

"First, death finds you. Then, enslavement seeks you. And now," the enigma said, revealing itself, "freedom awaits you."

A four-armed female Barangda with a crown, blindfold, and two lit sconces in hand.

"Abandon the cause, little pup, as I've told you once before. Leave it all behind. Apprentice by my side."

"Forsake everyone? That was once a thought, but no more. I stand by the Chroma," Milos replied.

"This is not your world! However," the she-wolf snarled, placing a torch in front of Sadie, "You belong in hers. Both of you are displaced. I intend to carry you to a new home. Away from these pox-like Primes or their diseased coterie!"

"I cannot. I have found love in these lands that far outweighs the pain of my youth."

The she-wolf approached him, "Do you not love me?"

"...Many count on me. I cannot abandon this life. I am resolved."

"You leave me with misery in my heart…"

The she-wolf snarled, cracking her knuckles in frustration until she turned her "sights" back to Sadie. The girl tried to run away from her but appeared in front of her from a fine mist. She snatched the satchel from the marketplace.

"You never lost my deadhead."

Sadie had no idea what she was saying until the batch of so-called "cardinal purple" was revealed to her. "Sublimation before nigredo hides under the false color. My way of tracking you down. To know you held onto it this long is admirable…what isn't, however…" she explained before roaring out. Her arms lashed a wave of fire that released Phthalo from hiding. The Herald screamed out as it was being expelled from the darkness. In an instant, the void was quiet again with the crackling sounds of fire.

"YOU KILLED IT!" Sadie screamed.

"Nonsense, I have returned it, back to its origin. Nobody deserves such power from a messenger. Both of you are young, and I have seen recklessness occur should the two of you continue your travels. I am the one who distorted the bonds of your Herald's power, but I am not your nemesis."

Sadie dropped to her knees to weep more. Expelled without so much as a goodbye. When friend's die, do we all go to the same place? Do we truly die when our names are never to be uttered again?

What greater sadness to never see our loved ones again…

"Look at me, child," she said to Sadie.

The young girl hesitantly looked up at the multi-armed terror. There is a sad tenderness in the blind woman's voice. She wants the same things Sadie ever wanted. Long before her eyes were blighted. The blind one evoked those same celestial insects from the forest.

"These are my eyes. They have seen your troubles. They tell me of your innocence. Be brave. Just like the one who resides in your bangle…emotional as she is. Do not let misery overcome you, and do not abandon your condition of discipleship; continue to bear your Redeemer's cross.

"And since the Cerulean scribe won't heed my call, maybe, one day, it will be *you* by my side. This is the time to forego neuroticism. Who honestly requires a victim complex? Forget this repulsive past full of bludgeoned deadwood. It won't help. It never does, to remember things that might have seemed beautiful once before. There's plenty of cruelty in the future. Superfluous. Just like your past that was once alive; that part of you is dead. Don't bother to keep its existence. You're going to be all alone one day. Learn to be an emblem of strength now. Transcend…like *your* Savior."

The sconces blew out. Humidity came into play again. The blind one vanishes, but not without final words in the air: the final trials approach.

The world resumed its leisurely spin.

Stasis: uplifted from the mercenary company. Singer and his crew were unaware of what had transpired. Better this way. Sadie and Milos stood by, quietly, looking at one another. Worlds apart that share the same bloodline. What final trials await? The veils kept quiet.

Milos knew the Usurper would keep its end of the bargain. He had no choice but to believe in the tyrant. If Sarsen's Pass fell, that would be the end of not only Gottlir but all of Iberitus...

More steps coming from the thick of the night. How many more waves could they handle without minds breaking sanity?

Flint and Coin held up their weapons, waiting with bated breath. Milos, Sadie, and Enzu looked on with tired looks. For a brief second, Sadie welcomed the idea of a secret arrow plunging her heart. It might be the only way to wake from this nightmarish tale. But after listening to the blind she-wolf, fight and flight tipped in favor of fight. For now.

The new arrival stood silently before the present company, but not in secret or under any guise. He gazed at all the collateral damage. Two others came from behind. Bewildered by the distressful look of everyone.

Almost impossible to watch this form of melancholy.

Milos squinted to make out their forms, giving a small smile. "If you are an illusion, then my thoughts of embracing you are dashed."

"Then let me hold you as a sister should," Nagy said, wrapping her arms around him, holding his head against her neck. She hears a small and bitterly sharp cry that hides in her skin. His fingers dig into her body like a scared child. Tight. Afraid of losing its mother. It kills her.

Warm and sweet. This is somewhere to be. I am alive.

"*And we will shoulder your burdens, sir,*" Aqua said.

"*Always...*" Mulberry whispered.

"By the makings of natural architects, what has happened here, Milos?!" Grand M said, approaching with his weapons out in full display. He looked upward; the stars abandoned their usual allocated space, gaining some sentience, afraid their own lights could burn out.

Kabir noticed a glint of light in the thick wood. A crossbow bolt was fired. "Pathetic," he grumbled, grabbing the bolt in midair, and crushing it in two under the force of his hand. A lone Vermis still lingered about and tried to escape. The foreign cannon on M's back released an enormous shockwave to level the environment.

The lone assassin was barely alive on the ground. It tried desperately to crawl away, with only its top half. The lower alimentary system was lost in the wild. They gave it credit for still being alive with its loosened midsection and displaced organs.

Nagy casually walked over to it, placing a boot over its neck in place. The skeiborne illuminated.

"Look away, girl," she said to Sadie.

The rat man tried to scream out for help, falling on deaf ears. The Zad clan has no use for those captured or too weak to fend for themselves. The young girl just wanted it all to stop. And stop it did. Her ears only heard a loud pop. Another headless casualty of war.

Stories were exchanged in earnest. Flint and Coin watched in amazement as Grand M used his own machinery to repair the inn completely. Innovation does not sleep.

"There is little we can do for the bodies except give them a proper burial. Allow me," M stated, using more machinery, attached to his back, to dig holes and cover.

Milos explained the sheer madness that culminated one after the other before quickly passing out on Nagy's shoulder. Kabir grabbed him to place into one of the beds.

"Olu-Zad's rage is implacable. Far worse is how the Usurper came on his own accord! And to refuse to clean a Prime's barrier unless the two of you defend the north garrison? I can't tell if it's desperate or if it's a move to put you in harm's way.

"The Usurper must be. It never leaves the castle. We're going to hold off on our current task for the moment to safeguard the two of you until you reach Celanjung's border," Grand M explained to Sadie, "We'll rest until first light."

Her body was covered in all kinds of wet filth. Despite washing away the disgusting mess, she couldn't wash away the scars.

The mind had not a clue whether to call for God to help or a Prime. With Phthalo gone, it was as if she had started all over again with trying to find a close friend here. Her bracelet warmed her wrist again.

What other creatures would try to take her away?

The restless mind exerted too much thought. Overwhelmed with many lights, sounds, and emotions. Encephalopathy, holding hands with dementia, peeking into her subconscious; voracious to change behaviors and experiences. It whispers to Sadie, *Should you allow me, I would love to prod at the memories in your life you would consider most fulfilling so I may hoard them for myself, leaving you with the impression of never having to live a single day.*"

What would be left? A "brand new" home that you've been living in for many years? Adorned with mirrors where you don't recognize your own face?

Go to sleep…My Prime leads me.

Chapter 10

†

Kryptos

At first light, The Pilgrims had finished their deep discussions with Flint and Coin. They decided it was best to keep night watch over the scribe and his ward. Enzu stayed by Milos's side, sitting on a windowsill that looked out to the west. He could just start to see its form, barely, of a place he thought he would not see again.

Would she tear him asunder as well?

Some birds chirped in the distance. Some flew over to the inn to perch. One came by the clay man's side. It stared at him in quick curiosity. Enzu smiled, but the bird flew off to leave him to his thoughts.

It would be nice to fly.

Clattering iron banged about in the main hall, awakening Sadie. She heard the impatience of Nagy searching for coffee. The girl could use tea to calm the anxiety. Or, better yet, a couple of spoonfuls of citron marmalade from the jar before indulging in a bowl of oats full of sliced almonds, strawberries, and blueberries. A dash of cinnamon. Finished and washed down with a cappuccino, plopped with macrofoam.

"How does an inn not have any—" Nagy said in frustration before seeing Kabir holding a tin of fine grounds.

"Bless that nose of yours! I don't care what they say; you're alright with me," she jested. He ignored her and went outside. Grand M tweaked F&C's weaponry to be more efficient. All the while he was creating a large vehicle from most of the sponge iron left inside some of the bloomeries.

Sadie came out to see what was happening.

"A vehicle?" she said in disbelief, looking around to see only bits of junk around on the ground from the fight and flood. "Impossible, unless you plan to create a carriage from those wet trees—again, that's impossible."

"Maybe in *your* world—and somewhat in this world too—but when you've been blessed by certain Heralds, or Harbingers…ohh…the impossible *IS* possible!" he responded with a devious smile.

The machinery on his back picked, melded, and converted; it was endless! The foreign cannon welded parts together. The laser head transmuted useless parts into better qualities. His hands worked as quickly as his helpful artificial appendages. A strange large tractor, with a front drill and backpiece for extra cargo, was the result.

Sadie stuttered in disbelief. She asked how it was even possible to make such a mode of transportation from nothing more than junk metal. He kept it brief: "On my travels I came upon a Herald, and she stayed by my side…until I died. What you see is her sacrifice. What you see is *not* my original body. I owe everything to the Chroma of Silver. This is its grand power. The Prime spoke to me once. And I am eternally grateful."

He pulled out a little device from one of the strange compartments around his waist to insert into the vehicle. It was alive and revving.

Infernal machination purring.

"How do you use those devices on your backpack? Is it psychokinesis? That would be so cool!" Sadie inquired.

"I was born on the day of Prisma. That automatically places my talents under the Trasno architects: *Teks*," he laughed out, "Not some wonderworker! Just your slightly above-average weaver, fabricator, or engineer, if you prefer. I have learned to manipulate my nous with my personal effects."

"We need to move—*now*," Kabir stated, gruffly, trying not to get distracted away from the current mission.

Nagy shouted out from the top floor, "He's still knocked out; give us a hand, Kabir!"

Enzu leaped onto Milos's torso, clinging for dear life. Nagy let out a sigh, "Don't worry, little Essent, we're going to see that everyone makes it out of this in one piece. Even when this one likes to hurkle-durkle. I might join you in Celanjung; seeing a Vicara up close should be interesting." She smooths her hand over the sleepers cheek.

They began to load up whatever essentials they could scrounge before the two parties left each other. Milos remained unfazed by all the racket. A deep torpor welcomed him. Unconsciously charmed by the gloaming, forty winks upon forty more came faster than cognizance.

Singer mentioned trying to find some of his members who went missing from an escort job.

"I...I think I know what happened to them," Sadie said to him.

Remorsefully so with her sheepish tone.

The price of Ashokara's head further increased.

It all started in trapped darkness. Heat suffocating the oxygen behind the door. Riddles prophesying themselves before the ax came down. A world in flames. Abominable riders plowing through the helpless. The visage of death and resurrection before a child. Ribbons of gold flowed from earth and sky to command the field. Hiding behind a tired face.

Full of piss and vinegar.

And still able to smile, to love, to cherish, to cry, and willing to die. An unknown fate of circumstances. The flying nomad, with his insatiable palate for fish. Stranger was his heart belonging to one from the sea. Surrounded by diverse companies. Nearly enslaved by a goddess of Alchemy. Close to death with a mad rat, verging on subjugation from a sociopath playing with ultimatums. An enigmatic oracle playing voyeur to see the world burn from the sidelines. The cherry: awaiting for the thief to return what was rightfully hers.

It all started in trapped darkness...

And all he wanted now was sleep.

Too much dancing.

A pause is necessary to find harmony.

Just a bit of quiet. Maybe a rest under that tree on the hill. It had the best shade. The breeze from the sea felt comforting. The view eased his soul; his pneuma.

Farther from the destination. Closer to the fray. How long till the water wheel dries up and everything withers away?

Her mind drifted to all the wonders she had seen that came peppered with fresh hells. A blank fixture overcoming that wide-eyed, curious look. Antipathy to these deities who have permitted such anguish; purposing it.

"Are the wars in your world tamer than ours?" Nagy asked her. Sadie didn't hear the question until a bump on the terrain caused the vehicle to nearly jump up some inches.

The question was asked again.

She stared out the back of the metal cart to see the environment they were traversing over. The scenery turned into an autumn-esque vibe of orange leaves and bright yellows on the trees. She mentioned what she knew of the two Great Wars, and the distress told to her about Vietnam, Korea, and the Middle East. Kabir turned his attention to her when mentioning the leaders involved: the torture methods they used. The cause and effect on the minds of those caught in the crossfire.

"Sounds like your world is not that far off from ours. Are there no Primes to reach out to?" Nagy asked.

"We have many and call them gods, but…"

"But?"

"They do not appear to us like yours do."

"Well, that's just maddening! How do you even know they exist in the first place?!"

How does someone explain existence or the nature of the supernatural without sounding off their rocker?

She wanted to explain how faith worked for them, and how texts were used as guides, but she was too tired to think of how to refute any argument that could be started. She was still a teenager in high school.

No one had the answers on Earth.

"It's hard to explain—forgive me."

Nagy told her to not worry about it; there would be other chances for a hot debate.

"To think that your world is inhabited by bedlamites like ours is oddly comforting. The day I figure out how our worlds are connected will be the day of my greatest exploration into new possibilities of innovation. Nothing satiates my hunger here. They say portals exist, but I haven't a clue where they're hidden. Maybe the only thing to interpret from this is that I was destined for another world," Grand M shouted out from the front. He went on about trying to find new land for his people. Grenvalk was always under threat from the mainland and hostile nations from the pelagic north of the island, specifically aligned with Lusura.

"Ah, the '*Green Wall*' is close by; let's have a closer look to see the leaves fall. Always a marvel to gaze upon," M exclaimed, steering to a densely smaragdine forest that appeared opposite in color to the rest of the land.

"Your pneuma will belong to me soon," a cruel voice transmitted to the unconscious, but not Mulberry's.

"He's beginning to sweat," Nagy noticed Milos's emerging condition, "Not good."

Enzu's gems started to work their usual charm of amplification; the scrolls in the quiver illuminated, but two silvery hands entered Milos's mind. Suffocating his pneuma. The wrong help was on site. Sadie panicked as Milos began choking, but the others remained in place.

"What's happening?! Help him!" Sadie yelled out. Nagy stated there was nothing they could do; this was beyond their power. Only those in the *"Order of the Veil"* could assist. Enzu tried to expel the silvery hands from damaging the sleeping scribe. It worked briefly, but the power became too much for him to handle. Sadie reached for Goldenrod again but had forgotten the words, and Phthalo was long gone.

"He doesn't deserve this!" Sadie cried out.

The words reached ears far beyond.

She heard them. Echoing. Repeatedly. A chord struck; these were the same words she cried out to her father's lifeless body. Conflicting emotions brewed inside her body while she sat in her garden. Too much to contain. Combustion imminent. Standing up, she paced around the flowers, biting down on the tip of her thumb.

Do I betray myself? I won't feel happier about it.

She could see the young girl, crystal clear, after tearing the scroll. Her eyes clearly saw the raw emotions, the depth of her wrinkles, the fears in her tender heart, and the now: wanting the thought of possibly ending her own life as a means of escape. New strength—from the oracle —already leaves her. It's still too fresh to form this habit. To keep it.

Fleeting rationality…

Commands are sent from the highest of highs. Sky Blue. Messages to the scorned in hushed words. A new belief formed.

Her feet stopped moving erratically. A deep inhalation of fresh air. And the composer sang aloud.

Just this once…

Nagy and Kabir saw the quiver had several scrolls of the same origin, illuminating. Cerulean. A veiled woman who never showed herself—until now—broke back the silvery hands of another parchment. Dissipated. Back into the void. His mind is free again. The veiled woman of Cerulean soothed Milos's condition. Sadie looked up with tears in her eyes to see the veiled one. She kissed the young girl's head and returned to her parchment. They won't believe this. They can't believe this.

But they have to believe this!

Everything is possible for one who believes.

"Impossible…M! You won't believe what we witnessed!" Nagy exclaimed jubilantly, "A veiled woman thwarted another, but not only that, she *physically* touched the girl, and it was Cerulean!"

"I witnessed it, M," Kabir chimed in.

The Trasno remained quiet.

No one can say they've lost their minds.

Nagy, beside herself with happiness, grabbed hold of Sadie's shoulders to reel her in for a deep kiss.

It nearly stole her entire supply of oxygen.

The flustered girl had no idea what was happening. The Sanshan pilgrim stared into Sadie's eyes feverishly, her hands on her cheeks, before pulling her into her bosom.

"She's *not* blind! By the blessing of Chroma, a *miracle!*"

The girl asked why she would lose her sight when nothing bad happened. "Oh, bless you for not knowing what has happened. Veiled ones of the Chroma cannot physically touch the corporeal without their Prime's blessing. If you practiced the dark arts, you could, without their favor, but you'd be seen as an interloper trying to steal their power, like that crazed Barangda running around with her little torches, *Marisha*. She knew the consequences well enough and still went on with her deeds."

So that's her name, Sadie thought.

She inquired about her, "She had no interest in the war or anything on Iberitus. It seemed to me she just wanted Milos and me to live far away with her. Away from where no Primes power reached. She was so terrifying, but that *thing*, Ashokara, retreated from her. Is it a man? Monster, or…?"

"The Usurper? Is there a difference between a man and a monster? I'm joking, of course. Slightly. The Lusuran king is a man in my eyes; if he sounds like one, moves like one, and kills like one, then he is a man. Never took a queen. I heard a rumor that he tried to make one out of his armatures based on one of the citizens who helped him overthrow the kingdom, but that's just rumor and conjecture. Asexual; that's what I think. In it for the power.

"As for Marisha, no one knows her better than Milos. Always had a special interest in him. Even the Usurper—as far as I am aware—cannot fathom the full extent of her power. She may be blind, but something keeps her going. Her power is said to be not far off from the Primes—older than all of us combined for certain. They say she's trying to find a way to kill them for losing her husband prematurely; she blames the Creators. Supposedly he was a human too that resided in pre-Udalann; I forget which kingdom that was. But she took his last name. What was it again?" Nagy explained, tapping her fingers.

"Goretti," Kabir inserted.

Nagy was eager to know if Sadie heard the Prime of Cerulean, but was cut short. "Enough of all that; that's a subject for another time. I see movement ahead," M said aloud. He stopped the vehicle behind a large stone, away from the view of the Green Wall.

To the West, one that has not succumbed to the greatest, saddest trial—reward to some—of being sacrificed to the Chroma pokes at her queen. "I never thought I would ever see you grant clemency to someone you have no ties to."

Evren was in deep thought. With many moments passing, she said what was only necessary to her curious veil, "Release the remainder of my design…This has gone on far enough."

More dogs to track the scent.

Nagy took point, advancing in haste to see a hill that just barely overlooked all sides of the wall. M was pulling out red pellets from one of the boxes on his belt, placing them inside muddied soil, and molding them into bundles of sticks. Kabir heard movement from the forest's edge. His nose wrinkled, appearing ferocious, and he held his staff out in an offensive manner.

"So…the problem starts here," M said, watching them come out individually. Falling silent. These hunched shadows, these loyalists, bring no roses, no gladiolus, no lilies, or forget-me-nots.

They only stir the leaves under their feet. Look hard enough, and they can see immobile darkness wanting to come into the light to play. First, a moment to allow voyeurs to stare inward and show some act of pity so they may pray, a final time, to their Primes.

Sadie poked her head out. Enzu attached himself to the top of her head to participate in the viewing. "Why can't we just travel without a situation?" she whispered.

"I'd stay inside the hold and close the doors. These Grayskins have ideas that aren't exactly benevolent, especially when a young female is around. They get…'riled up'…if you know what I mean," M instructed, not taking his eyes off the Orkes marching out of the forest.

The wind picks up. Boreal's laugh. Caressing skins with a dry tongue. Nothing exists outside of this moment.

Kabir and M looked as they spilled out, but it wasn't enough to be considered a threat to them. The real threat was finding exactly where they came from and resealing it before a platoon turned into a legion. The sound of a debilitating roar came from the darkness. M had his cannon readied. A lone man came out, wearing a bearskin pelt, brandishing two axes, muttering to himself. He screamed out foreign words they had never heard before. Another had recognized these words from his youth. He stood by them to see this new participant. Awakened.

"I understand, but I can't translate all of it," Milos said, studying the berserker.

The ax man's interest further peaked when he saw the young scribe. He continued on in his native tongue. M asked what was being said. Kabir carefully studied to see if any tricks were in the making.

"We're in the thick of it now, boys…That's Ard Rex's Menagerie Commander Flann Treasach. I take it this is his main assembly. Seems too few," Milos explained.

"I smell well over a hundred lying in wait. His guivre must not be far off," Kabir said.

Flann directed his speech to Milos. It is undignified.

"This foul bastard wants me to join him…be reunited with the others as a 'family.' Says…the Pictfero are looking to expand past the domain. *Inside* Klaring. By the composition…this cannot be true."

"It is true, brother!" Flann shouted out in English, "We have heard stories of the King of Skies who controls the colors effortlessly! Stand by Calbhach's side. He might offer you the title of Grand and throw in whatever demesne your heart desires! Come, so that we may reach *Stenness*!" Distant Isles, where the oldest of henge sites reside. Standing Stones from Neolithic times, not far from the coastal stream known as the *Burn of Ayreland* and, not from there, the *Ring of Brogdar*.

More connections to this plane of reality. Somehow.

"I don't know what that is, but I will never side with your kind of tainted pneuma." Milos replied, leaving no room for arguments.

"Should've known better than to try with your type who sees a scriptorium as a temple, a puppet of *Icolmkill*," Flann snarled, spitting on the ground.

Columba of Iona? Sadie thought, *How does he…*

More incoherent nonsense to Milos. Grand M stealthily reached behind, where he kept a small flare gun, to signal for Nagy to double back until an explosion occurred out of the back of the vehicle's cargo bay. Terrible timing.

An Orke was set aflame, trying to get into the back. Soil accepts his offer to give up the ghost. More nourishment. She came out apologizing, "I thought I was using a small amount of power, but I guess I got carried away when I saw its teeth."

Brilliant timing for mea culpa.

Flann's jaw dropped when he saw Sadie. "Another of our kind! So full of life, freckled snow skin, and with red hair. I will make her mine!" He laughed maniacally, stampeding towards Sadie, who in turn dove right back into the cargo, readying another incendiary attack.

During this, the mark signaled to its owner that *this* was the one responsible. He heard the wailing from the child. Old recordings of the orphan perturbed his center. Beneath his fur surged countless electric needles. Each one pinging onto the crazed berserker. Past events conjure up the boy's parents. Slaughtered. Ruthlessly cut down in front of him. Genocide is on the berserker's agenda. Salivating at the thought of bringing heads back, trophies to flaunt to the other levels inside Klaring.

Fires reigned. Embers died. Ashes danced. This grizzled warrior saw the corpses of his brethren: so beautiful, so kind, so gentle; workers and sages, full of talents to share with eager cubs and eager minds; men, women, and cubs...they...they had just wanted life in another land. Bringing new ideas, new innovations, new joys, and games. Willing to give back to those who brought them in. Hunted down. Skinned for pelts. Enslaved to test new theories. Vivisected. And the powers that be carried on, calling them, plainly, "unfortunate casualties of war."

Fresh liquidators born—no room for marginal error.

Guaranteed, as per his promise, even more for his people.

"*You! You* are the one responsible!" Kabir shouted at Flann. Mounds of upheaved earth kicked up, a drawn line sliced, surgically, the beast confronted the berserker, boldly, placing himself between the addled and the motor carriage. Flann didn't have a clue what he was talking about, readying himself to cleave down the beast where he stood.

Numerous Orkes came out of the dark wood. One unified circle forming. With mouths that foamed and teeth that jumbled. Milos and M saw Kabir's forehead emitting a large red aura beneath the band.

"Take them and go, M...This one's nous belongs to me. He is the one that has killed Kosey's parents...and many of my own," Kabir gruffed, as more Orkes surrounded him, cutting him off from the others.

"*Death is assured if we stay here; accept their support. The Barangda will become insulted if you intervene,*" Cobalt transmitted.

Milos and M rushed back to the vehicle while Kabir stood alone in a circle of hostility. Flann laughed at the lone wolf's foolish bravery.

Many minds—on the forefront—are about to be mangled.

Kabir kept calm as they inched closer. He lifted up his staff and, barely, tapped the base on the ground. Every Orke in the circle fell onto their backs by the small force. This is how it starts: predatory hunger. Second nature to Kabir. Second skin. Innate. Reasons describing his birthmark. There's no reaching the tranquil flowers in his mind. As if he wanted out of this soon-to-be bloodied earth of dust. His spine has become a staunch pillar, able to withstand any sort of force, and his palms shiver; they won't stop until they are covered in their fluids and have coagulated. Forming into a pair of gory mitts.

If they listen closely, they can hear angelic choirs singing—beauty from these shaking leaves. Emitting funeral songs.

Flann raced back to the entrance of the forest, calling out for reinforcements. The earth started to rumble. Siege towers, as large as life, started to pour out of the forest. Kabir walked over to Flann, unfazed by the mobile wooden monoliths.

M jumped into the driver's seat and shot a flare into the sky, releasing black smoke. Nagy saw from a distance everything beginning to unfold. Electricity poured from her body as she raced down to rejoin her compatriots. Her body split into two: a clone of herself, darker in appearance, independent from the original, but still ready to draw out blood.

Kabir closed his eyes.

I hear them: the leaves. One floats. It touches the ground.

An Orke leaped from behind. Sword unsheathed.

The staff punished him mid-flight. Sending him afar.

And so, the very first battle of this new war was uprooted here. Supplanting old flags. Who will be the one to write down its details in truth, with no exaggeration?

They encircled Kabir, but his staff swung in all directions, never missing a mark. Speed and power intimidated Flann, making commands, "Open *all* of them!" Mechanical craftworks in action.

When approached by a soldier that they could take down the one beast, Flann remained frenzied, still howling, **"OPEN *ALL* OF THEM!"**

The siege towers opened simultaneously, releasing scores of Orkes to face the lone master warrior. Some advanced on the armored motor carriage for capture, but M bulldozed through, shooting from his cannon and other fantastical machinery.

"I'll get you two as close to the edge of Sarsen's forest before I return back to assist! They won't last without me!" He shouted as bodies flew in the air. Loose teeth hitting the dash.

Nagy had crossed paths with them to begin her work with Kabir. The vehicle became a dot to the naked eye, soon erased. Working alongside her frenzied comrade, their abilities more than doubled. Her tattoo flared, as did her skeiborne, sending many of their antagonists to their unmarked graves. With most missing their heads. The shadowy clone's grimace unsettled her opponents. Taken by surprise. All these two warriors needed was their third to really show off their prowess.

The wyvern made its entrance in the skies.

A storm of electricity chain-linked among the gray Orkes. One large group braced their shields to separate the two to weaken their position.

A lucky, heavy swing broke Kabir's staff, but he managed to continue with his fists. His speed made them practically invisible with each combination he inflicted on the Grayskins. Several Mairu were aiding the Orkes. Shouldering through to break down Kabir's defenses until he was overwhelmed. He roared, colliding his fists and palms to their faces, forgetting about the Orkes to his sides that fatally slashed his arms. One giant smashed his head into Kabir's to stun him. The flying guivre whipped his back with intense ferocity; it blew back some of the deranged soldiers with its tail's end. Adrenaline can only go so far.

This brought the great warrior down to his knees. They pulled his arms up and dragged his body across the dirt to where Flann was. Kabir bled in all places but still remained conscious.

Flann was before him, smiling.

Kabir had one eye open to see him reaching for a soldier's sword. Nagy was trying her best to come to his rescue, but with the guivre attempting to take her down with the others, she and her clone could not push through fast enough.

Grand M calculated the distance he made was enough for Milos and Sadie to be able to return promptly. Sarsens Pass was just beyond the forest aptly named after it.

"We won't forget this, M. I better see the three of you at the Pass!" Milos said, preparing to conjure his prism's power for the cloud to help cover the great distance.

"Don't, you fool! You'll need to conserve as much power as you can when you get there. No telling what those bastards are going to use. Just walk the miles. Good luck to you three. And girl," Sadie looked at him with curious eyes. "A veil resides in your bracelet. That isn't regular magic you're using. You'd best talk to her now; understand her. She is…different. Compared to Milos's. Next time we meet, I'd like to learn more about your world."

His gloves lit up wildly. Makeshift cannons appeared on the sides of the vehicle. The wheels spun incredibly, and, with something that resembled warp speed, he was gone.

If we meet again, Grand M thought.

She looked on, worried. Clutching her hands against her breasts, making small prayers she hoped would reach him and the others. Praying that the inevitable, the great cessation, be delayed, without the utterance of Last Rites. *What must one do to be saved?* Her thoughts try to stay linear; *I can only try.* Looking inward for any possibility, any chance, instruction, guidance, *PLEASE, JESUS ALMIGHTY,* protection to enshrine their lives, for just *one* miracle to happen, on her behalf, she recited the Apostolic Creed.

Consecrated here, this girl-turned-woman, with blazing hair, is now a missionary. Iberitus's first hierophant in motion.

Prepared to be its first universal martyr.

They pointed from their realms, their domains, their lavish seats, pointing at the girl. Jesting. Laughing. Dark Primes. Seeing her as some failed humorist. Oh! If only they could walk the plane again! Just to throw tomatoes and spoiled cabbage at her. More red dye for Sadie's hair and accents of emesis green. Her veil warmed her wrist, watching her from behind. Anguished. Melting even the vicious heart of Mulberry, who looked softly at her, calling her by her new title: little sister.

More echoes from the marked pilgrim.

"You'll bring me with you once the path is cleared, right?" the boy asked the great warrior. Unsure of the future. Xantho sets.

He looked down at him, boldly stating, "I will carve us a route, and you will pave its foundation to bridge our people. Together, we will safeguard our civilization."

And the young boy was filled with gratitude, instinctually, embracing the grizzled warrior's body. Caught off-guard, but not denying it. Reciprocating the gesture. Something he had not felt in years welled up inside him. *So, this is what it is like to have a son.* And Melano rose.

The sword slashed across the chest, sedating time.

His last thought was the boy's face. Innocence. Regretting that he had broken his promise. Kabir's body dropped face down, and with the blood pouring out, he was gone.

Nagy witnessed the atrocity. More electricity exuded from her body. She took flight to retrieve him. Figuring out ways to revive him. Her screams pierced every ear canal in the vicinity.

IT'S NOT TOO LATE! I WON'T ALLOW IT!

Flann had several mages hiding in the crowd, and they noticed her in the air with sparks beaming in all directions. Orkes convulsed when touched by the hateful energy. Spewing out erupted organs that sizzled. A sigil formed underneath. Rendering her immobile in the air. The trap sent the electricity from her body *back* into her with their perverse power. Her screams turned from war cry to an exorcised banshee.

Old loves. Dear friends. Superb liquors. And…

…*Riha…the leaves are so pretty*…

The White had taken her. Her body fell from the sky. Smoke seeped out of her orifices. The tongue slouched out with bubbles of saliva forming. Another soldier fell to grand evil.

Flann raised his axes: a victory for Klaring and, above all others, his level of unbalanced Pictfero. In the name of Ard Rex. The soldiers raised the two lifeless bodies up from the ground to parade. Morale was truly at its highest now. Unaware of the grand architect.

From the distance, M saw what was happening. The speeding bullet started to break apart while he clenched his teeth. Terrible behaviors brewing inside. These were his comrades, his trusted, his family! The cannons shot a barrage of explosive missiles at Flann's army. Fire covered, blanketed, and engulfed; it did not discriminate against the skins that were once held together by bone and sinew. It was cataclysmic. Flann, screaming in his native tongue, made his escape to his guivre once the siege towers began to crumble, crushing all those beneath them indiscriminately. Burning and burning and burning them, alive if need be!

M pulled out the bundle of explosives he made earlier. He saw the primor starting to take flight but ejected, with great force, into the sky, readying a lighter. Lusting with thoughts of becoming a live missile. Longing to see The White come to the coward in flight. Flann heard his maniacal laughs approaching from behind.

"No!" he screamed out in horror. He saw M's eyes in full; a pair of less-than-forgiving lenses. Now, M held *two* ignited bundles in hand. Cackling louder. Filling himself with baser instincts of depravity. Napalm covered the sky, taking down Flann, his beast, anything that survived below, and Grand M.

So ends the hero's journey of The Ternion Pilgrims.

Sadie heard the explosion in the distance; although faint, she was still concerned. A foul mood crossed Milos, telling her to forget the sound and to move forward.

If only they could've had more time together.

"My heart…it can't be," Riha said to herself, holding a hand to her pained chest, tears pouring down her cheeks. Kosey asked if she was alright. She looked at the boy. If Nagy had fallen, there was the possibility that Kabir did too. The sister's connection to her kin was forever severed. She told him everything was okay.

"Milos, what is happening out there…" she said to herself, looking out the bar's window. She removed herself from the tavern to go to the hill that Milos sometimes naps on and sobbed as a child would for the loss of a family member.

The Primes of Chroma heard her pleas, but none answered her prayers. They would not permit themselves to intervene in matters that did not concern them.

It was always agreed that life is suffering…

Chapter 11

†

Lanthanein

Blind leading the blind. The warm rays of Xantho failed to penetrate through this thicket. Troubling. Miles to go. Running on fumes. Low on sodium. Blinking lights on the gauge show the critical low supply of electrolytes. The eggs are gone, the rusks have crumbled into the linings of pockets, too far from the sea for flesh rock pyura; worse when the bowels have been emptied. That's when the bill collector, ghrelin, comes grumbling inside the stomach and abdominal cavities. Cross-examining as to why, oh *why*, its role has not been satiated! These internal and sporadic kicks are not imaginary, and no one is pregnant.

"These damn woods are much darker than I anticipated; how did the others manage to navigate through this?!" Milos barked out, breaking off dead branches in the way, vying to tickle his cheeks, his nose, and cut his vivid eyes. He failed to realize that everything was in full bloom when they entered. Mirages don't work like this.

Anonymity ferments this illusion.

Something alarmed Enzu. His intuitive faculty, beyond normal perception, clanging the tocsin; it is a very small bell, but it still works like a charm. He made his hasty retreat. Rolling into the gloom. Riding into pseudo-midnight.

The only one, fortunate enough, to have boundless energy, without the need for daily sustenance. Revere is proud.

"Where's that little troublemaker rolling off now?" Milos said, scratching his neck. He shook his head and continued in the direction he thought was to the garrison. Still failing to understand the polarity of their surroundings. Could be because of the slow-forming puff bags under his eyes. The blind compete with the insomniac. Sadie tread lightly behind. She kept picking up Milos's disgruntled mumbling. Ignoring his words was hard at best, like watching Edward Hyde's slow, dramatic entrance take form in the sleep-deprived.

This dark wood isn't the only strange case.

Her mind hoped that the others were safe from Flann and his invasion. The bracelet froze over secretly, unaware that her veil is trapped. Trying to relay the danger.
She hates herself for not unveiling to the girl sooner...

A fist smashed into a tree, disrupting Sadie's train of thought.

"I don't get any of this!" Milos shouted, "You'd think after all these years of dealing with this sort of garbage, I'd be desensitized, but no! Always something new and ugly around the bend!"

Punishing, still, those knuckles, to what end?

His barometer forecasts extensive pressure.

"I just wanted to catch some fish in the river—that's it! But no, some screaming little old woman had to come and scare'em off, shouting, 'Bandits! *Bandits!* **Bandits!**' And what do I find?! Fire, carnage, plunderers!" he whined about, turning to Sadie. "And you..."

Sadie stood in place. This is the first time she felt frightened by him. Where does the fair sex go when the safety you once knew turns on you? The cracks are beginning to show.

"Funny how Ashokara and his rider showed interest in you, and then…just dashed the idea just to get me to do his bidding? Is everyone in on this? What game are you playing?!"

Beloved concord: fare thee well.
Vigilance unsubscribed.

"I'm not playing any games! I don't know how I got here!" she responded, her words starting to tremble. A pain gnaws inside, on the underside, and on the left side of her breast. Daggers need only a push.

"Maybe *YOU ARE* a spy for that witch! Are you and Birati conspiring against me?!"

His quiver quakes with angry voices. Aimed at him.

The message is clear: *STOP IT!*

"You're tired, Milos, I swear, I wouldn't do *anything* to harm you!" she teared up. She noticed their words forming small vapors; a chill came over her. Something's not right here. The gloom colludes with his razor words. His blood was so hot that adrenaline ignored these minor details. Ignoring the veils' transmissions to cease, desist, breathe, and apologize. One veil looks on in silence. She feels the essence of home. Too close to ignore. One of the Ceruleans wants to advise, but his mind and tongue are too inflamed. She shares its presence with the others. A cacophony of warnings; he is deaf to them.

"Why did you have to come into *my* life?!" he scorned before turning his back. The veils are silent; crossed.

Frozen in time, like these woods, is where he missed the mark, by instead targeting someone who did not deserve unjust barbs. If only he paused. Just a few seconds—he could've saved everything from the bulldozer, choosing freedom over spasmodic responses.

Choice points do not exist at this juncture.

Her head fell, sniffling up the first stages of the incoming cascade, holding her hands up to her eyes, with great shame, "I'm so sorry…I never wanted any of this to happen. I just wanted to go home. I miss my family!" The young girl wailed miserably.

It was the first time, since arriving, she had truly felt all alone in an alien world. Sense of self: crumbling into granules of doubt. Lost, somewhere, beyond the edge of the continental shelf. Drifting down to the abyssal plain. Tipping, hazardously, toward the oceanic trench.

The hands of Christ fail to pull her up for air. Humiliation cloaked her with invisibility. It is a bleak suffocation of mind and spirit. Too far down to reach his immense soul. Other external hands take hold.

Cool, soft particles landed on her head. When she opened her eyes, it was apparent how they came down, gently, in small waves. It brought back blissful memories of Christmas. The family hands out gifts. Soothing woes, that may be, over hot cocoa, kissed by peppermints and a jolly splash of bourbon. Sadie held back her anguish for a moment to speak, "Does it snow this time of year? It's lovely…"

Milos stood quiet. Paralyzed by the word: snow. Nothing but clear skies before they entered.

When he turned around…she was gone.

"Oy! Sadie! Where are you?!"

The winds relinquish a haughty laugh throughout. His fibers picked up the chill in the air but saw nothing of what she last said: snow. The scribe looked around frantically, calling out to her in a panic, calling out to Enzu, but no one answered. Except one.

"*Should you need me...*" one of the Cerulean managed to get through to him. Her words did not go unheard this time.

The cold irritated his throat the closer he got to one tree. It was robust, but it had no distinguishing features on it. He couldn't help but notice how half of it was covered in pitch darkness compared to the others adjacent. Nerves knocking on the brain to return back to business.

"Sadie!!! I'm sorry! I didn't mean what I said, love! It's like you say, I'm just tired is all. Don't leave me alone," he shouted before coughing from the cold.

It arrived. He felt the same soft particles landing on his head, holding out his hand, and there it was: snowflakes. They didn't melt either. His head turned up to where they came from, his jaw agape.

"By the composition..." he mustered up. Sadie was frozen solid in a cage of ice on the tree. Slithering formations grew below the trunk.

"*Be vigilant,*" Auburn whispered.

"*Such strength,*" Cobalt said in awe.

"*No mercy; none! It won't show any,*" Mulberry snarled.

"*Sir! Look!*" Aquamarine pointed to the pitch.

It came out of the shadows. The expressionless face locked onto the scribe. Its armor shined brilliantly. Fear took hold of Milos's heart. Its malignant hands held it in place.

All it required was the knife to thrust in and twist.

"You...you're one of hers," he said to the enigma.

Silence. Wings of snow and light emitted behind it and rushed into him, but the prism activated. Milos's accessory teleported him to random spots. Volatile. Erratic. His mind and it are instinctually linked. The incredible warrior of ice had no teleportation skill of its own but still managed to come close to contact with Milos each time he teleported. A mountainous snowdrift in the wind. More haughty laughs.

The young scribe lost track of his surroundings as dizziness overtook him. Always a first time for motion sickness. The warrior of ice grabbed both the opportunity and Milos. A vicious assault of combinations ensued on the scribe's body. Milos couldn't react quickly enough to continue evasive maneuvers. Batter up.

He felt his ribs beginning to crack. Too preoccupied with defending his body—admittedly failing—that his hands didn't think to reach for a scroll for assistance. All these women can do is cheer him on.

Trying their best to keep him conscious.

The silent ice warrior summoned a portal above and below Milos, smashing him through one and ejecting him from the other—infinitely until boredom veered towards a new tactic. Blood spilled out of fresh wounds from his head and sleeves.

Milos felt his left arm going numb.

His chromatic veils cursed the quiver's blessed ability to keep each scroll inside, without dislodgement, hoping one of their parchments would eject into his hands.

The enigma grabbed his head and threw his body against a nearby tree. His spine: ready to crumble like a sleeve of wet rusks. Harsh wheezing came with many coughs. Like Mulberry stated: no mercy. The mute brute continued its silent rage without hesitation.

Milos could feel life slipping away again. Somewhere, Sulfur cackled in delight. Ready to seize his pneuma. The ice warrior noticed this and stopped. Its job was to incapacitate the scribe for retrieval. *Not* kill. The mission was halfway completed. Its master awaited.

The great enigma held up Milos by the neck with one hand, silently watching. Milos groaned, trying to open up his swollen eyes without wincing, looking past the ice warrior. The mute saw the reflection in his dual-colored eyes. It quickly turned to face its own trial by fire. One that did not hold back its own barrage.

"*New strength,*" Cobalt whispered.

"*NO MERCY!*" Mulberry shouted.

Milos collapsed before the tree, taking the opportunity to go for his scrolls. "Keep'em busy, Enzu…"

Enzu had appeared as the same large golem as before when protecting Sadie inside Evren's secret garden. The strength it beheld was one of marvel compared to its original format. It refuses to lose this time. The ice warrior, now on the defensive, couldn't evade the damage from Enzu's extra set of appendages. Many hits connected with the head, stunning it. Enzu went in to bear-hug the large warrior in place.

"I heard you," Milos whispered to the scroll.

"*And we, of the sky, acknowledge you,*" Cerulean replied.

No reactions from the other women. Tongue-tied by her boldness. She speaks on behalf of those with residency inside the quiver and on his person, save for the tincture of silver, ignoring social rules that the affectionate should remain coy.

Ambrosia scents the air, calling on warm, sweet, and intoxicating memories once veiled. Old static removed.

Smiling. From the upper crust of the maritime.

Bashful. Born from the unremembered. He's trying to find the words. The *right* words. Stuttering. Follies of the mind wish to corrupt his tongue. She doesn't mind. She knows he is trying his best. His fingers fidget in the grass. They saturate his prints with oils from fallen citron. A sensory modality, longing to ward off noxious behaviors, with pleasant redolence. Scant. Waves crashed against the rocks, hampering his train of thought. She sees this. She *stops* this. One snap, and the waters relax. By her command. Resuming her expression of delight to him.

Melano was bright. Reflective mirrors, from the open sea, traced along her features. Beaming. His heart does not betray him. Warmth, cupping her hands with his, he speaks soundly; the words cascade with intention. Honoring her with better days. In hope of the same reciprocation. In hope of purpose. In hope for a future that won't become a haunted spectre in his mind. An impermissible phantasm.

Awkward, quick-dry, slightly unaligned, but passionate nonetheless. She smells of sensual vanilla and tastes of strawberries; hearth and home. Freeing the worry-worn creases of his brow.

Short-circuited. His body begins to lean sideways, with rolled-up eyes, ready to collapse into the gentle waters. She catches him. Laughing, in a new direction, and falls on top of his torso with hers. It stops. Her hand softly examines his roseate cheeks. She fiddles with his hair. Their eyes fixated on one another and tossed brevity aside.

Two become one.

Hard-pressed with their own bodies.

Purpose found. And the memory fades.

Milos finished his incantation. The scroll transforms into an ice-blue plant. It smells of better days. New snowfields to greet.

"Cerulean take you," Milos said with clenched teeth. Three veiled women rose from the scroll and materialized a fantastic millstone around the warrior's neck. Chains clung from the stone to their necks. Enzu released his grip to safeguard Milos. The warrior struggled to break free, but it could not match the power of Cerulean. The veiled women comforted the warrior to cease and desist.

It had, at last, admitted to being bested.

Milos looked on to see the warrior now sitting patiently on the ground. "Release the girl," he said. The warrior did nothing. This infuriated the scribe. "I could've used any other scroll to send you directly to the Primes, but I *chose* detainment! Release her, Essent..."

A distant voice entered the mute's mind. With stern orders.

"Do as you are instructed."

The warrior lifted its hands where ice-blue energy flowed out of, directing itself to the imprisoned Sadie. Ice to water, melting away rapidly, and she dropped down, with Enzu catching her. She held the large golem and had no more energy for tears. All so tiring.

"I thank you, Essent," Milos proclaimed. He dropped to his side in pain. The veiled women looked at him pitifully.

Sadie dragged her feet, dropping down to Milos, speaking in a confidential tone, "I know you don't believe me, but I do—"

"Don't...I am the bastard that should be apologizing," he interrupted, holding his side, "I'm beyond daft to have accused you of anything sinister. I promise you...I'm going to get you home: even if it costs me my life." His left arm is broken, and he struggles to move the right. Enzu's large frame breaks apart to reveal the small body again. He went into Milos's robe to retrieve Goldenrod, presenting it to Sadie.

"But I don't remember how to use it."

"*We can help,*" the three veiled women said.

"*IMPOSSIBLE! Veils are barred from other Chroma's rituals of invocation! Only Heralds are permitted if they wish to aid!*" Mulberry hissed. Her distorted words echoed into Sadie's mind like a clear picture.

Attunement reached.

"*In honor of his unwavering heroism, a rapport has been established between our Primes.*"

"*Leadership still hasn't recognized us?*" Cobalt asked.

"*Pilgrimages must be made if their words have not reached your pneuma,*" one replied, looking over to Auburn, "*Except you; too complicated. Traitor to us. Honorary to yours.*"

"*She is no traitor!*" Cobalt retorted.

They ignored her, looking to Sadie, "*Listen and repeat.*"

She unraveled the scroll. They guided her the same way as Phthalo did. The same streams of gold were expelled out to mend his many wounds. Enzu amplified the scroll's power more to give him extra vitality. Milos lifted himself up halfway. Sadie's face was next to his. She had this smile on her that was filled with sorrow.

"Maybe…you're the little sister I never had," he said, trying to lighten the mood.

"And maybe you're the overbearing—yet protective—older brother I never had," she replied.

"I hope one day you can forgive me," he said, lowering his head.

"I already have."

Enzu leaped up onto Milos's shoulder to embrace his cheek cheerfully, "Yes, yes, we couldn't have done it without your help also."

Sadie looked over to the warrior who remained impossibly still, asking what it was. Milos stood up to look at it again. An intense moment of silence.

"Evren's elite. I recognize that emblem, on its cape, as one of Celanjung's. Not sure what its name is since it can't speak, just like Enzu," Milos said.

"*Jökull,*" the three veiled women answered.

"Right…Well, let's head to the garrison before the scroll wears off. I don't plan to keep it in my possession anymore," Milos turned to the Essent. "You can keep the scroll once its power has ceased. I ask that you don't come searching for me anymore—I plan to return the rest of the Cerulean soon. Especially the torn. Pass this message to your queen. Maybe she will spare me of her wrath."

Sadie thanked the veiled women for their help and departed with Milos. His veils bring comfort to him, with Mulberry having a look of malaise upon knowing they were probably seen as a roaming band of misfits to their designated Primes. Unworthy of appreciation. Auburn consoles her. Aquamarine remains pensive.

"The Matriarch was right about the girl," the Cerulean-veiled women said to each other. Jökull looked up at them when they said this.

Nomads, leaning on one another, down a new path. It is increasingly precarious. They share a moment of sorrow with one another.

Melding into a cornucopia of emotional debris.

Chapter 12

†

Metamerism

Homeland markings disappeared beneath the heels. Only sparse grains, which permanently stick, remained; always the first at the wake. Some came in their native shade. While others were outfitted in a spectrum of reds. Burgundy accommodated the coagulated. Thousands marched to the front. Thousands fall at the forefront. Morale crumbles.

At least there was daylight. At the very least! She hated cold, wet days that reminded her of early March. Second of March, more precisely. Sleet. Slush. Screams behind the door. Calls for anonymity. Left behind. Broken vows. Idealization. Code R45.851 would like to parlay. Straight, double-edged, and cruciform, it bore itself in passing. Neatly bathing in the warm rays atop the grass. Her emotions are still raw from the ice cage. The shadow of her mind plays images of the sword running through her. Most abusively.

Picking up her horrid vibrations, a quiet gold bunny appears to the young adolescent. And another color. And another. They tell her she is much stronger than she thinks. Advising her to stay the course. Aquamarine has most especially heard the girl's inner thoughts. Words to her Lord and Savior. Words from Scripture. The girl tries to remember. Too distraught from all the clashes, the bodies, the blood, and the mental games. Warmth on the wrist, a subtle whisper, *"Remember,"* A new voice, and she recalls from the good book, reciting to herself: "Be not overly wicked, neither be a fool. Why should you die before your time?" She exhales, feeling confident, and looks at the fortifications meaningfully.

Remembering her heritage.

This "Flower of Scotland" cries, *"Buaidh no bàs."*

Parrying the erasure of composure.

Clan Harper announces its new knight to Iberitus.

Fights broke out in the main camp; tusks sparred with matted furs. Wrinkled, bold eyes watched the small outbreaks from afar. He went back inside his large tent, chortling to himself. Unsurprised, but also amused. "It's no wonder they don't have any grand leaders of their own kind," the old man said. "Don't you agree, Edling?"

He addressed a tall man, still in his youth, on the right side of twenty-two, passing a skean over a whetstone. Far too many times to count. He held it up to a torch. "What else would you expect, Father? The plague bearers, clay-brains, and their less-than-average grey cousins could never aspire to be like our kin."

"Yet, clans, like the Zad, come into play. Worse: the Milu."

"It's fortunate we ended all—"

"But one damnable ogre," the old man interjected.

"NEWS!" a voice shouted outside the tent. The old man waved his hand to acknowledge the guards to permit entry. Entering the tent was a large Mairu. "I bring news from The Mouth!"

Edling pressed his skean up to the giant's neck. "Start over; properly address your sire. *Now!*" The large messenger grunted, but the young assassin slowly dug across the thick leathery neck to draw blood.

"Ard Rex Calbhach," he announced, the blade lowering down, "I bring news direct from the queen."

The old man, rightfully identified as the high ruler of the Rubicund Domain, approached the Mairu. "Well...don't keep me waiting." His hand pensively rubbed the heavy choker around his neck. The chain ends are linked together by a penannular ring. Symbols engraved on it: zigzags, discs, and a V-rod. Assuredly of high status.

The giant detailed how the queen of Klaring released one of her latest eggs, in full maturation, awarded to Calbhach.

Its arrival was imminent.

"Noted," the high ruler said, looking at Edling. The skean quickly sliced off one side of the giant's tusks clean. The pommel bashed against the back of the head, causing a loss of consciousness; the guardsmen dragged him off. "The older I get, the more I embrace the bittersweetness of life," Ard Rex said, clasping his hands behind him.

"Does that bring on melancholy, Father?"

"Quite the opposite. I feel more content. The beast is en route as we speak. From The Mouth to here, my guess is no more than a day. Maturation takes so long, but the value is extraordinary. We'll send the fodder straight towards the gate to scale and breach in one push with the queen's *World-Eater*.

"A shame we couldn't bring our own people, except one—she perplexes me sometimes. Our queen. Flann had best done his part to cement our race's potential," Ard Rex continued, looking at Edling with stern eyes. "Before the beast carves through a victory for us, I want you to present me with a head, preferably one of the crown."

"Wouldn't want it any other way," Edling said, disappearing from the tent. Calbhach glimpsed outside to gaze upon Sarsen's Pass in the distance. Though old, his eyes were sharper than any in his kingdom. One eye clearly saw the king of Gottlir staring straight at him without any expression. A direct challenge. This infuriated Calbhach.

His other eye burned bright.

And two veiled women appeared behind him.

The soft grass started to ebb away the closer they got. Coarse dirt, broken gravel, the abundance of sand speckled about—border scarring. A patrol spotted them from afar. Riders on jumarts raced to their location.

"State your business or be off!" one shouted at them.

Heterochromia gazed at them with extreme malice. The large beasts became too rowdy to handle, ejecting one. He landed on the harsh ground. Abrasions on his knuckles. Dust clogged his sight. A body overshadowing him, "Bring me to the king…otherwise, go piss up a rope," Milos growled out at the felled soldier. Sadie tried to calm him.

He couldn't relax.

"We're literally on the frontlines of a war we *shouldn't* be a part of," he said. Strings of spit popped through the fine lines of his teeth. He didn't bother to wipe the spittle that roped his lower lip.

"The life you seem to enjoy will be forever lost should we lose this fort," Tekla shouted, galloping on another jumart.

"You seem different from last time we met some days ago."

Milos would explain everything if she could get him an audience. She obliged, noting his service to the realm, and provided them with the fallen soldier's jumart she had pacified. "Off your ass and back on patrol before my boot finds a new home in your rear!"

They marched through the large camp carefully. Sadie noticed how many goblins were in the ranks among the humans. Her back felt warm from the large star in the sky. She was grateful to not become a living ice statue.

"It feels good to see the Sun again," Sadie said.

"What's that now?" Tekla asked.

Sadie pointed at it in the sky.

"I don't know what a 'sun' is, but that's Xantho."

Sadie's exhaustion made her forget her place again. She explained that was the name in her universe, only to follow with, "We have the Moon—sometimes called Luna— at night. Yours appears almost the same, but if I look close enough at it, and at your Xantho, their colors are different on the following day. Why is that?"

"I like that name: Luna. But ours is called Melano. As for the colors…ancient history between the Primes. It's too long to get into. I myself am confused by all of it. Supposedly, the Primes used to walk this land freely. Although the Chroma infinitely outnumbers the *Tria Prima* of Alchemy, or Three Primes, if that's easier: Mercury, Salt, and Sulfur.

"They held their own with ease despite only being three. One big clash between the two groups almost destroyed the planet until the Naturals intervened. The grandest war of them all, '*Black Twilight of Lost Souls.*' Grand mouthful if you ask me, and we're not supposed to say that word anymore: soul. Bad luck, allegedly. Your scribe here—no doubt—is more faithful to the Chroma, so pneuma is his word. His lover would say nous. And those high-nosed, lambasting alchemist aristarchs at the universities would use vita."

Pieces of the puzzle finally sewed together in her mind.

"What do you say then?" Sadie asked her.

Tekla smirked, "I say, who gives a damn?! The Primes don't concern me! They could care less if we live or die! At least I'm doing my part to protect this land from being overrun by absolute mad-lads."

Sadie catches a small sting of anguish from her harsh tone. She tracks her gaze. A thick, red ribbon surrounds her left bicep. This wasn't there before when she and the prince departed. The warrior caresses it, looking back past the natural environment to the Capital. Someone dear to her is still there. A farewell to arms. Possibly a beloved that wants the ribbon back. Her veins pulsate with the bloodline to take the front lines—just to ensure victory. One way to return to their side in haste.

Six feet in times of peace, fifty-four in times of war; auspicious to king and country.

Godspeed...

Milos remained quiet, too perturbed, expressing only a somber look. Tekla noticed and jabbed him in the arm to brighten him up. Old scars are surfacing. Too close to previous homes. Loose components leave a trail back to the land of craters: Lusura. They weren't left gingerly.

The bulwark was incredibly monstrous. Much taller than Gottlir's Capital. It astounded Sadie further when she saw how much higher the crenelated towers appeared. Arrow slits, neatly even embrasures, sturdy battlements; everything jumped off the pages from her history books. Ominous howls from the wind blaring through. Just like the dark wood.

An insufferable wave of hot air, accompanied by a foul stench from the deceased. Spotted sheets cover them on the animal carts. Left out under the bright rays for far too long. Bubbling foams of saliva build inside her mouth. Ebullient creatures of water and mucin. On standby, deep within her viscera, predigested matter remains, congregating.

Prepared for a populist uprising.

It's all gone to shit...

On Earth, the skeptics say there are no such things as alien life forms. Even beyond the ocean space. Small minds with a lack of creativity. "Only us and God in this existence. He created us in His image," they would boast. Easily swayed by the upper echelon skilled in rhetoric. *The life here, on Iberitus, has opened their eyes to the impossible, simply because they live it. An experience that no Earthling could conceptualize unless they were touched in the head,* Sadie thought.

Her faith doesn't wane, but...

It sounded beastly, the portcullis when they raised it. However, once it was lowered, those inside the castle grounds spoke much softer, almost to a whisper. Church in session. Only the sluice gate would turn the heads of the unfamiliar. They eyeballed the three entering. She saw a small elephant sleeping nearby. "A *gamijah*? They're only found in Somdir. Why is it here?" Milos muttered. Despite desperately seeking home, something about that mysterious land below Gottlir lured Sadie's curious thoughts. A shiver sent up her spine. It reminded her that death was afoot in all corners. Maybe it was best to leave the thought in the back of her gray wrinkles.

Living was the goal; live to thrive, not just survive.

Tekla announced to the guard about Milos's request for an audience. "The king is aware of his presence and also of the girl but grants it only to him," one remarked.

"It can't be helped. I can find my way up. Can you stay by her side? I cannot explain what has happened in a few seconds, but I—sorry in advance—*demand* she have round-the-clock protection. If something else happens to her…"

Tekla heard the seriousness in his voice—a first for her. It invigorated her spirit. Her father came to mind for a brief moment. She agreed, "I'll take her to the shrines for now."

Enzu went with Milos. It was he who needed a morale booster.

"What're the shrines?" Sadie asked.

"This place holds many factions for the lord and his retinue. Lots of diverse members. Lots of diverse souls. Need to provide solace in times like these, yeah?" Tekla led her to a pathway with three large, segregated rooms. All faiths side-by-side.

The walls dividing them do not burn to scorn the other.

"You've seen it all so far; what's your flavor?" Tekla asked. Sadie pulled out her cross. She wished she had a chapel to attend in quiet solitude. Regardless, a thought reminded her that the chapel to God always remained stout in her heart. And no one could persuade her otherwise. Hellbent goddesses fail to dissuade, she explained to Tekla.

Religion is *not* an immutable characteristic.

It *is* a choice.

Tekla screamed suddenly in a girlish way as to accidentally disturb the worshippers. Apologies were sent all around.

"You *denied* a Prime's request?!" She grabbed the young girl by the shoulders. "I am proud to call you sister then. Can't deny it. Don't know about your beliefs, but that is just…ugh…*STRENGTH!*"

Instantly bolstered. It's been a long time since Tekla felt this way. Sadie further explained that despite her monotheistic beliefs, she welcomed other religions. She would not be one to turn the other cheek, but her ears and eyes were not glued shut either. Denying exploration could deny her keys to her own curious thoughts. More questions than answers were not on her checklist. A double glance past Tekla's frame.

She thought she saw the friendly face of Phthalo. *When anxiety was great within me, your consolation brought joy to my soul.*

"How fortunate to hear there are those open to other beliefs," Sibi said, coming out of one of the rooms. Sadie was happy to see a familiar face, and two more showed up with smirks and teeth. The Newt's assembled. Sadie ran to them, hugging all three in one big go. Sibi was the only one caught off-guard as Daru and Xamak welcomed it. Not exactly the infatuated type, but he obliged. Trasno rarely—if ever—receive physical endearment from females, not of their race. Underneath the helmet resided a reddening goblin.

Seconds to eternity, he felt he could fall asleep here. *Affection…how novel…*

"Make no mistake, Trasno, just because I have little feeling for the Primes does not mean I lack reverence for life," Tekla announced.

Sibi's eyes discharged vaporous streams of energy, enough to cloud the sockets of the skull. "One day…you too will take the pilgrimage. There's so much potential in your nous. It too yearns to become a magister like me."

She remained reticent.

Dangerous truths come out during harsh undertakings, and even the hardiest become victims of circumstance. No amount of narcotics, bottles of rotgut and vin ordinaire, or marathons of sexual degeneracy could ever dilute the truth. Tekla does not mind physical pain. She would rather shift for herself. Independent. It is the present, the *only* truth to her.

Expectations? Unreasonable…

Sadie entered their place of worship to see concrete walls with divergent vegetation, lightning bugs, and a flowing font in the middle with dissimilar skulls around it. Some looked human, while others looked like they came from beyond the pale. Sibi saw that it brought an uneasiness to her—perhaps she still couldn't accept that her own mortality would end one day. He showed her the other rooms: one with incense burning with a small lab table and one that had a spectrum of colors moving—yes, moving—on the walls.

"This must be for those who worship the Chroma," she said, looking at her bracelet, "but I'd like to visit the Alchemist's shrine. I barely understand them."

Sibi rubbed his chin.

"Go inside; I'm going to find this keep's aristarch." He jogged off. The remainder went into the partially clouded sanctum.

The incense calmed her. Calmed her *too* much. Lethargy. Her slave driver. Dozing off before Tekla grabbed hold of her.

"This stuff only makes the most battered fall asleep for recovery. What else have you and that scribe encountered on the way?"

She looked at Tekla, her lips agape, speaking only of the horrors. The Wandrians came to mind, but so did the Khrosgar.

"I don't even know if they're alive," she nearly cried out. When asked who, she spoke of The Ternion Pilgrims.

Sibi returned with a massively muscled old man with a stern look on his face. He observes the young girl. Utterly helpless in her current condition. Gripping his enormous ledger and walking to the small lab table, he begins to concoct a formula from inside the book. Quiet words were exchanged with Sibi, who then passed on the message to his brothers. They ran out of the room with haste. A new task at hand.

Apparatuses bubbled and toiled. The alembic distills a cloudy liquid. "This should do for now," the old man spoke, pouring the liquid into a clay cup. He hands the cup to Sadie, instructing her to nurse the drink. Her vision was somewhat blurred from the slight waterworks, but she thought she saw her grandfather handing her the concoction. Even his voice sounded almost identical to his. She did as he asked. The effects were slow and steady. Her heart fell back to a proper rhythm.

Tranquility brought on by science.

"This is nice; is this chamomile tea?" she asked. He chortled, shaking his head, only to state it was medicine for the vita. *Literal medicine for the soul?* Her frail fingers wiped away what seemed like endless tears from her eyes; properly thanking him with a clear vision and a clear mind.

"I am told you would like to negotiate with science," he said.

It was too silent for him. Grievances spilled out, but his whines flushed with them too. The action wasn't intentional. He was just so tired—more than usual. Gold cannot heal restlessness. Still, he knew this would annoy the king. The liege had his back turned, but he listened attentively. Squint hard enough and you could see the ears stretch back. Catching every vowel. Milos's words slurred randomly. Breakneck thoughts; his tongue is unable to keep up. He couldn't hear Aquamarine instructing him to explain at a leisurely pace. Mulberry winces at the thought of him biting his tongue. Auburn tries to gain his attention by calling out his name in soft, kitten whispers. Cobalt snaps her fingers inches from his face. Argent laughs, but Cerulean dampens her discourtesy. Goldenrod is not sure if she can cure speech impediments.

His majesty felt the scribe's nervousness. His hand gestured over a grand beast to ease the troubled scribe.

The tongue still flapped about without showing signs of exhaustion. Vision—let alone peripheral—noticed the magnanimous creature sitting beside him. A large paw vies for attention on his thigh with mellow mews.

"Milos…pet her," the king commanded, his head turned to the scribe's direction. Milos noticed it: a large armored lynx.

The prince, also in the room, said, "It knows your kindness. Give her a pat, rub her ears, and hold your head against hers."

Hesitation. Milos's hand feared losing itself into the clutches of the massive jaw. Ramirus knelt by the beast to demonstrate. Despite its body nearly overshadowing him in a defenseless position, it purred.

"Go on," he said to Milos.

His hand tried to rebel, but he dashed the thought of weakness.

Soft. So soft.

The other hand joined in. It purred like a well-tuned engine. A smile grows on his face like a child with a new, unwrapped toy. But something odd happened that caught the royal family off-guard.

He started to cry.

Years of surviving. Not enough living. The list of strange encounters. Infinite. Indeed he should have changed for something greater. Perhaps wiser or more mature? Stuck on juvenile. A better writer? Trite. His penmanship is lacking, and his powers are barely honed. Rejected by all scholastics. Too much brooding. The scales between play and brass tacks are irregular. That lost child is still present. Grand sufferer among the silent. Fortune smiled on him with his veils—tragic as their stories are.

The expedition was becoming desperate.

Fixity of purpose reminded him to never let down. The anger was righteous. The child is pure. It's okay to sob.

How much further?

Two heads leaning on each other. Arms wrapped around the majestic creature. It felt his inner pain. Its soft, shining coat helped coax out more of his bottled melancholy.

In his sorrow, words, from the unknown, whispered into his psyche: *unstoppable, affable, composer.*

Pull back. No ordinary kitten. Maybe the neurons jumbled about in pinball fashion. Who cares now? Morale is resetting the dangerously unbalanced knife in his mind. Deep breaths.

The king walked over to Milos in full view.

"Confidence comes from surviving failure."

The dark thoughts washed away. Inside his frame, he felt his pneuma swell. Adversity leads to its meaning. To know its symptoms. To understand its cause. Prevention. The cure. Onwards to health. Alongside, birthed, and coupling, alacrity eager to work with the painful threshold. His back straightens.

His majesty is for the people. Like Milos's spine, they too are the backbone. Without them, there is no country. Just animals led by a diseased crown. Tossing half-eaten scraps on the ground. Invitations for vermin and ill alike.

King of Gottlir, Leandro, also known as the "King of Lynxes," cherished the thought of raising others who were overlooked; to extol faith in oneself. No one in the court was distant from him. Magnetic. He understood what would bring both success and failure to his undertakings. Base sentiments were never entertained. His eminence had a way of drawing out the truth without a raised voice. And when low morale ventured within his vicinity, he would squash it. The loss of social cohesion welcomes the death of civic virtue.

Enzu studied the king. No gimmicks or any sort of foolishness. He knew better than to show the antics of a jester. A silent awe. Inspired. Leandro raised Milos from his sorrowful state, leading him to the terrace that faced the realm of bloody sands. No scruples.

Leandro

They watch the foul entrenchments that snaked miles back into the tired lands littered with mangled tents, burning corpses, and pockets of angry mutinies between fur and tusks.

The only thing honest about Klaring was its awful truth hiding within each grain of sand. Ever-changing dunes that lost memories of self to the arid winds—mutating perpetually.

What secrets do they hold?

Why do they whisper silently?

The monotone features stripped life down to the starkness of pain—a clarion call.

"In my youth, I fought to keep these bloodletters from entering my lineage's realm. I became so overzealous that I led many to The Mouth. I lost too much that day. On most days, this crown feels so heavy," Leandro remarked, his hand tracing the baluster. "If you hold your breath long enough, you can feel the pulse of both realms vying against one another."

Milos placed his hand onto the support, closing his eyes, and held his lungs back of oxygen. Seconds to eternity. Deep reverberations felt on the tips; irregular. The limbic system screams in fear. The lungs resumed again. He looked at the king and prince. Their faces are like unmovable stones. Fear had long passed from their minds.

They would invoke it unto any trespassers.

"Milos," the king said, turning to him, "would you ever strike down one of your own?"

"Sir?"

"Ard Rex, and his disturbed offspring, they are the only two here of your blood, but I know of the ones who still lie in wait inside The Mouth. I have seen them myself—formidable. The Mairu respect them. The half-blood Orkes obey them. The Tarwini despise them. I have seen them conquer *Winzangi* cannibals. Some take several of the blood-snow females as wives. Dangerous breed of man and monster. Again, I ask, could you ever strike one of your own down?"

"In the interest of my safety and those dear to me...without hesitation. I have encountered one secretly crossing through the *Icterine Mountains*. The Ternion Pilgrims aided our escape. I have no doubt they made short work of the poison-minded berserker and his small army of uncultured conscripts."

"Omitting what had to be done in Lusura, you haven't killed anyone or anything since. Only the bounty of nature to keep your belly from eating itself," he stroked his long beard. "Without hesitation?" His eyes, though tired, were filled with profound wisdom. He rested a hand on Milos's shoulder to state he should remain as he is now. The king knew of Ashokara's ploy to withhold crossing into Celanjung before Milos's arrival.

An abundance of spies in his court. Certain measures made in advance to derail the Usurper's plan. He explained this to the young scribe. Milos wanted to collapse and kiss his hand, but Leandro would not have that. The spies brought other news, unfortunately.

"I have some sweets to share with you..." Leandro remarked. The young scribe knew something was amiss. A belly of aromatic indulgences to soften the blow. "Do you care to join us, ladies?" Leandro said to an otherwise mundane wall. Milos saw nothing out of the ordinary. Enzu leaped off his shoulder to examine the wall. His stones glowed to reveal just the outline of their figures.

"Trouble," one voice said.

"Impressive," exclaimed the other.

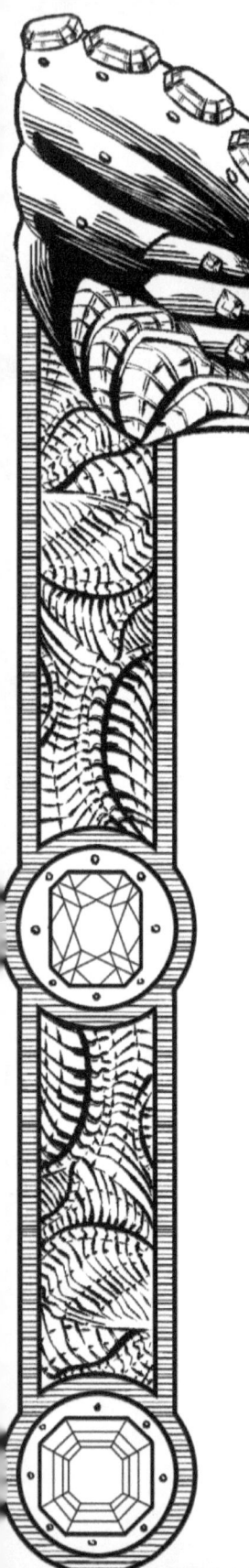

The veils are displeased. How could they protect him, warn him, or guide him if they didn't sense these two close by?

Unfolding from concealment were two female wizards: Somdirians. One picked up Enzu to examine. The other glanced over to Milos, only to shake her head, releasing an exasperated sigh. A black whirlpool appeared behind him. Like diamonds in the dark, it examined his quiver of scrolls, backing off once it laid its eyes on the largest: Auburn. The prince was disturbed by the vortex sentry as opposed to his father. Undoubtedly sangfroid. His cool composure had seen enough in his time within the dungeons of the ancients.

Ancients that were somehow overcome by a human. Each master bequeathed a largesse of reliquaries that would soon help the founding of Gottlir. A bloodline forever cemented into Iberitus. A lineage that rose through the biological hierarchy to give humans a place to stand.

They aim for first place.

The black familiar shifted through the air to one wizard. "Not only do you have an Essent that doesn't belong to you, but you've had a composer convert one of their prized pages," one scolded, pointing a finger at him, "*Only* death awaits for your pneuma! Avoid her realm should we wish to continue breathing."

The second glared at him before Enzu escaped her palm to return to the scribe's shoulder. His clothes become clammy.

The king stepped forward, beside Milos, placing his foot down: "My son told me of the request you made to Evren. Its weight is just as heavy as my own signature—ease your nerves."

While he did not raise his voice to the women, he did remind them that it was premature to utter demoralizing words.

No matter how true.

Leandro watched Milos, genuinely concerned. He knew he didn't want to die. Not like this. He internalizes the scribe's struggles as if they were his own. It is loneliness wrapped in claggy, pox-infected blankets…and someone has tossed him to the bottom of the pelagic.

Where the Abyssal Nation waits.

On the coldest day of Itzala: the sixteenth of Calgation.

Strapped with chains.

Accessorized with fetters.

The loss of something greater than a simple denizen.

Fundamental pain.

Should you crack, let light seep in the antechamber.

They did not apologize. Their fatalistic behavior was to be seen as helpful facts to aid the young scribe. The accuser had her skirt halfway ripped off by the lynx. Running amok with the fabric. Utterly embarrassed, she became a chameleon once more. The other remained in sight to glare at the king.

"My pet agrees with me when I say, 'Leave it be.'"

Esprit de corps proudly reports in. She won't push further.

Milos withdrew Auburn, speaking gently and carefully, "The original was faded when I took it. A near-complete erasure by one from the Hadal. She *begged* me to save her. I didn't know what else to do."

Auburn appeared behind him: strong, vibrant, full of fervor, flames crackling around the eyes. A halo of meteors and comets adorned. Altruistic. Saint Mother watches over him.

The wizard held a finger up to her lips.

For a split moment, a honeyed smile.

"We'll take our leave now; we wish to evaluate the outsider," she concluded before melding back into the environment.

Leandro looks at his lynx, giving itself a tongue bath. Wanting a cleanse for himself after the transgressive behavior.

"Believe it or not, they're just novitiates, but their Order saw them as enough to aid us for the final pushback—dramatics. Something in the mana. Thankfully there's a composer with them. Now, about those sweets I promised."

Sweets are nice, but what about last meals? Forget that, Milos thought. A palpable sense of dread twisted knots. An intangible jester of the Primes hastily polymorphing his organs until they cried out like animals inside an abattoir.

Sweet, alright, and dark business.

Downy. A lightly dampened cloth patted across her forehead. The concoction from before, though a relaxant, did not anticipate the nightmares she witnessed since arriving. It would appear Sadie was starting to develop the first signs of a traumatic disorder—this could lead to multiple levels at the current rate.

And it was advancing without letting up.

Fortunately, for her, the aristarch was able to brew another compound to cease the panic.

"Muscle tension: receding. Lockjaw: recessing. The antibiotics are doing a fine job," he said, holding up Sadie's eyelids one at a time. "Follow the light," he instructs. A small orb hovering over his index—back and forth. Her pupils ignored the first few seconds before adhering to his order. "No signs of retinal ischemia," he muttered.

The illuminated ball started to revolve around her head. First, revealing a glowing skull. The water molecules in her aligned before the ball's speed sped up, and rapidly changed alignment. Now, the upper region became translucent, transitioning into celestial lines to reveal the brain; a hidden power only taught to these high-ranked teachers of science. An image shot into the aristarch's eyes. Proper analysis. The ball dissipated, no longer revealing the gossamer show of wrinkled energy.

The others looked on, worried, notably Tekla. "Was it me? Was I too loud?!" Frantic. This was not the case, he assured her. His biggest surprise was seeing how the girl didn't fall into disarray sooner.

"Will I be okay now, doc?" Sadie asked with a shortness of breath. He nodded; rest and food were her prescription.

"I do not like the fact you are not far—and I do mean *far*—from here! **Sheer madness!** Your body is overstimulated, young lady. It's mimicking symptoms of neuronal excitotoxicity, which is to say your glutamate levels are dangerously high!"

Every second, so far, of wandering, Iberitus has made her pathway narrower and narrower. A tightrope ready to snap. Her nerve cells are suffering. Excessive stimulation. Cellular expiration is the next step, and it won't be a caricature. The grand equalizer where some trek before others. No age limits.

He gave her a small bag of ampoules. "Take one every time you feel despair is about to swallow your vita, but don't abuse them; they are strictly for emergencies. More than one may unlock who-knows-what inside that pretty little head of yours." His eyes scanned the others. One was meant to guard the prince, and the others were volunteers. A finger pointed at Sibi, with strong words to follow. Sadie was still disoriented. The words didn't reach her lucidly. Her eyes only saw him storm off.

Others tend to just wake up before the morning light.

"What did he say?" she asked.

The eldest Newt exited the chamber without answering. He proceeded to the staircase. Leading to the top floor. Where the king and prince were. The elite of Leandro saw the small goblin run with great determination. The tome in hand showed immense agitation with its grotesque tentacles shaking loose. Whiplashing. Snapping at the air. Ally or not. "Invitation only" to meet the king. The other Newts were quite aware of how this would go down, but Tekla knew also.

Duty first to the royal family as she chased behind Sibi.

"Is everything going to be fine?" Sadie asked the remaining brothers. Daru nodded without his usual smile. Xamak withdrew his blunderbuss. Aiming it above her head.

"Don't look," he whispered, eyes glued to the strange phenomenon. That same void creature, of the Somdirians, is in their presence. It watched curiously from above. It made no attempts to hide. Maybe that's why the quiet sharpshooter did not pull the trigger yet.

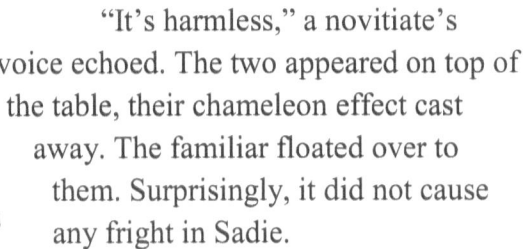

"It's harmless," a novitiate's voice echoed. The two appeared on top of the table, their chameleon effect cast away. The familiar floated over to them. Surprisingly, it did not cause any fright in Sadie.

Daru sniffed the room. "Another?"

A shiver ran down Sadie's spine as the nose caught hold of bergamot entering their personal space.

The novitiates immediately got off the table to bow their heads on the floor.

Sadie, Daru, and Xamak had forgotten to breathe once they saw the figure appear behind the table. Her face was concealed by a large straw hat with a twisted pattern in the center. Xamak nearly swallowed his tongue—this is beyond their league. Sadie ignored the wild clothes, the pearlescent skin, and even the bright, lustrous hair that flowed around the breasts and transformed into the heads of snakes.

This woman was one to execute judgment.

She wanted to ask who this mystery was, but the tongue wouldn't answer the call. Her intimidating presence had the brothers fall under their own weight. The straining of necks ensued, but thin streams of Chroma held their crowns down. Tenaciously. A finger traced the table to examine some of the residue used to help the young girl. Thumb rubbed with middle. Her tongue sampled while her lips smacked.

A beam of satisfaction.

She tipped her hat back to expose one eye to the girl: pale purple. Daru was becoming enraged by this subjugation. His words could only curse the floor. Trying to bounce them into the woman's ears. The spectral color became more opaque around his head.

She walked past the erratic Trasno, looking down at Sadie. "No one provokes me with impunity."

She hummed a bit, examining the girl, and the streams flowed away to release the brothers. A novitiate, looking at Daru, saw how he wanted to advance on the woman, shaking her head as if to say, "It will hurt—a lot." Xamak holstered his weapon. Further explaining to his brother, non-verbally, to ignore the slight.

Daru had no choice but to submit.

"Smart, boy," the woman said, glancing back with a devious grin.

Sadie found her courage again. A finger pressed on her lip before she could ask. "No questions," the woman stated. "It is better to listen."

And listen she did. A spectrum of colors invaded her ear canals, carrying a message only she could hear. The bracelet's power ignited. An imprint embedded into the floor. It wasn't long before the flowing of rainbows ended the transmission. The woman snapped her fingers, with the novitiates springing up to her. She turned to the brothers, "Tell the king we are withdrawing…something wonderful is going to happen!"

And just like that, they were gone. In the courtyard, the elephant creature also disappeared without a trace.

Daru cursed the air.

Xamak feared they had weakened their position.

Sadie…

"We need to escort her away from this before we hit the point of no return!" Sibi exclaimed. Tekla tried catching him, but the book gave him the ability to temporarily turn his body into air. Her large hands, trying desperately to catch an evasive cloud. The prince raised his hand. Tekla stops her pursuit. Sibi made his case to the king, but…

"Your inquiry is reaching the wrong ears, magister," King Leandro bluntly responded, nodding over in Milos's direction. His eyes gazed over the mountains. Intent and steady. Sibi tried to get the young scribe's attention until he saw what he was staring at.

"Look at how they observe us, as we do them," Milos whispered.

The magister squinted his eyes at the cold, bitter wilderness on the left side: Winzangi cannibals and bohemian Mozmina. The tribes watched to see which realm would come out victorious. Front-row voyeurs. Something familiar from this end. Khrosgar, pacified by the Winzangi, kept watch vigilantly. Amenable to greater monsters. Their masters. Aiming sights to the right, where one lone hot dirt mountain stood. Rogue Mervig women watching alongside Mairu soldiers of Lusura. If he had perfect vision, he would notice the Capital of Lusura crawling with Ashokara's machinations and shrewd denizens.

Below, scattered bodies, from Lusura, are impregnated with human and Trasno projectiles: various alloy spear tips, triple-zero buckshot, and crossbow bolts. The ground is dazzled with a seabed of bronze and copper percussion caps. Hammers bang away in the distance, of men and goblins trying to fortify the large gate. They are horribly tired, but the brackets don't care if they break. Nor do the hinges.

One grand push was needed. Then, the bodies will really begin to pile up. The sweat of nations ready to tackle one another. Composed on the green lawn, while those of fang and tusk were placing bets: who could carve the most initials? A gesture of Klaring hospitality.

Is it too late to say goodbye?

A platter smashed in the room in anger. The arrest of the scribe and magister was released. News of the mages made its way to the chambers. The prince, overwrought. Leandro only closed his eyes; nothing to be said out loud.

What a way to end Prisma.

Xamak updated the others. The minds raced for fresh ideas. It was too quiet. Moments later, Sadie appeared before the chamber, only watching, from afar, as the elite guard stopped her. Had their weapons not clashed with the other, mental calculus would have persisted uninterrupted.

Opening one peeper, Leandro saw her: "Let me see what emboldens the 'pseudo-prime' to venture so far from its throne."

Lifting crossed halberd poles, she made her way inside. Delicate footsteps. Too eerie here. All eyes are on her. Self-conscious. *Maybe this was a mistake,* she thought. Self-inserting into heated discussions. But something inside her kept prodding her to push the envelope harder each time. Damnable curiosity. Or…an act of strange courage only seen among drunks who can't take "no" for an answer.

Milos walked over to initiate introductions, but Leandro held out his arm, halting him partway. An evaluation. In his mind, she is the very reason *all* of this is happening. But not a guarantee.

He gestured his lynx over to her. She was technically the shortest human compared to those present. The grand beast prowled around her, taking small sniffs, keeping its nose to the ground, releasing a snort here, a snort there— sometimes a fang showed from its curled mouth. Her skin became slick, but the heart wasn't as erratic as previous fantastical events. *Better this than the Khrosgar,* she thought. Thirty-three bones are at attention to make a strong column. The lynx halted before her. Something about it brought on a new attitude in her.

She acted on impulse.

"Hm, you have an interesting companion, Milos," Leandro said with a dulcet voice. He approached the teen with furrowed brows. One twitches harder than the other. "Like putty in your palms…Good thing you're no assassin," he quipped with a sudden sigh.

His words failed to reach her; she was too busy mushing the large feline's face in glee. A grunt—it wanted out from this detail. Shaking its head, it strolled off nonchalantly, but not before swiping its large bushy tail against her face to cause sputtering. Loose hairs tickle her lips. Snapping her back into reality. Milos exhaled. Enzu rolled back to her side and onto her shoulder again.

The king's voice steered to a not-so-subtle tone of authority. Proclamation that crumpled her backbone; no longer erect. It came as a scolding. Funnels of information made it easier for him to create a profile. A father's disappointment. Overbearing, inquisitive behavior created one too many faults on her end. With every syllable, she could feel her state of being crushed. His voice echoed off the inner stoneworks, doubling back to cram into her canals. Milos felt the need to intervene, but he knew better—it was for her own good. *And* it was working.

The visual makeup of her surroundings was erased until she and Leandro were the only ones present. She tried to avert her gaze. Optic paralysis. A tragic failure when one's body refuses a command. Every chastising word became its own soldier, advancing on feeble prey. So tangible she could see an army forming around him. Flint sparks from the bracelet; temper temper.

She could feel the water pipes rumble around her eyelids.

Two steps ahead: constricted optics; no sudden leaks will spill on this fine rug. Overwhelmed with exhaustion, her demeanor shifted from distress to another that curled the corner of his lip: irritation. The gaze of the two became noticeably prevalent. With her brows crinkling inward, those small hands white-knuckling, bagged eyes drying out, temples pumping out a roadmap of veins—this is exactly what he wanted.

Steam awakened around her. Shatter from the wrist.

The others looked on, bewildered and astounded. A twirling cyclone of flames surrounds her figure. Shape, taking structure behind, with animosity in its eyes: a veiled woman of fire. Alaea. No longer in the shadows. Introversion thwarted by the king.

"Finally," he calmly said, releasing his gaze.

His fingers snapped, and an attendant brought forth a pitcher of water with one cup. He insisted on pouring the contents himself, presenting it as a gift to Sadie. The flames ceased, and soon she fell back to relaxation—no clue as to what had happened. The woman of fire returned to her bracelet. But not before Sadie finally saw her.

Her guardian.

"This power seems—no—*feels* amplified. Stronger than ever. How?" she said, looking at Leandro.

"The Chroma, they have seen your intentions. They have seen your thanks. Birati must've seen this when he first saw you. I saw something else that no one in the land has seen. Your desire for strength. You keep it well hidden. Tears are for after the storm has ended, not during. How I envy you."

"Envy? Of what?"

"You come from a foreign world of war, like ours, and you have not participated in it. Your anxiety leads you, by the neck, until a courage to fight emboldens your spirit. The first taste, when did it happen?"

She thought about it. Scanning the floor. Counting the cracks. Eureka. Her gaze returned back to him to detail what had happened when they first encountered the Khrosgar *and* the one who chased her through the mysterious garden world.

"She knows what you look like now, your every move, but is deaf and blind to those around you unless they too have ripped a part of her Codex—a family secret."

When asked who she was, his words confirmed the same fear in Milos's heart, "Why, Queen Evren, of Celanjung. Have you not told her this?" He asked, turning to Milos.

"I had hoped to avoid this. We've had our fair share of bad luck."

He wanted to make an argument about nearly dying to a Prime of Alchemy, almost claiming him, along with the three encounters at The Gilded Plume, but he didn't want to give any excuses. It is better to keep her in the dark than add another spike to cortisol.

Leandro saw the tiredness in Milos's eyes. His head barely moved, a motion that only his son saw. Ramirus quietly stepped behind Milos. Sibi did not like this, a vein pumping harder on his forehead.

The others: oblivious.

"Milos, the *Commonwealth of Barbonal*—land of Spiders—on the islands west of Klaring…what was their motto again?" Leandro asked, his right hand beginning to glow blackish green. The eyes lit up. Milos tried to react and teleport, but it was too late.

Leandro's hand expelled a shot of the dark-colored energy through the scribe's head.

A reaction of elites stormed inside the room to assess. Ramirus held onto Milos's unconscious body, giving an order to the guard, "Take him away; give him the softest bed available."

The Newts were angry. Tekla silently seethed. Her hands burned white-hot. Sadie was about to join the Newts—minus Sibi—on thrashing words, but Leandro told them to cease their worries. It was necessary.

"Look at his face. Dragged through mud. Through spikes of coarse salt. His face is becoming a wild animal. Bloated. The extension of hairs from his nose greets his lips. There is no hope to be found. Old desires are dead, and he hasn't accepted it. Sleep. Deep and grand. With a trim. That's what he needs. That is what will bury the old hope. It will be mourned. And when he awakens, a new one will come to be."

Tekla insisted on taking Milos's body to rest.

Sadie asked about the motto. "'*We are The Sleep*,'" he responded, "Great enemies of ours that are rarely seen, even in Klaring. Hope you *never* encounter them. Go. Eat. Sleep. Communicate with your once-shrouded veil. She should be more neighborly. Tomorrow, Lux, the day of white and brightness, of the dodecahedron and aether, arrives soon. Entwine this into your story. As others will bleed theirs at dawn."

The king stood outside overlooking the balcony as everyone was made to leave his presence. He saw the diverse tribes still awake, gazing at his fortifications: a deer being mauled alive by two Winzangi men, the Mervig women separated their bodies, and an orgy erupted around a tall bonfire. Strange how these double-headed ogresses were all hermaphrodites, but once they spliced, the dominant side took strict hold of the male genitalia to use on their submissive female counterparts.

It disgusted Leandro; their animalistic sounds reverberated in the mountains. Peak hedonism. Interior thoughts wishing primordial origins could go extinct. *Some cultures are superior to others.* He did not dare to see how the other voyeurs were enjoying the show. Tonight he would sleep further in the fort. Away from the lotus-eaters.

Smoke exhaled from her mouth, alongside her colorful sisters. They laughed without a care. Their own party of herbs and the never-ending flow of liquid spirits. Daughters of the pharmacopoeia. No bonfires here. Just analgesic chasers. And bedfellows to reach new heights of elation.

One too many humid inner thighs.

But not her. She fluttered a little closer to the fort. A bolt, landing not far from the party, pierced solid rock. Excited giggles, from her sisters, after the surprise warning. A vigilant soldier warned her he wouldn't miss next time, as others aimed in her direction.

She raised her hands up, withdrawing back.

A sister asked her, "Why are you so eager for an up-close look? At first light we will finally see if we can grab some land if Gottlir is breached! All that fertile land. So lush. A little spot along the coast for me. Dry up some sailors!" She winks at the Gottlirian soldier who made the shot.

Stroking the bolt's shaft. He remains solemn, reloading his crossbow, and she pouts in return.

The woman looked at the fort again. Particularly the balcony. Another hit off the twisted cigarette. It is tasteless. Splashing spit on the ground in disgust. Her sister rolls her eyes. *Spoiled princess,* she thinks, and resumes gossiping with the others.

"He looks so different. Tired. And bitter. Your pneuma. Languished," she whispers to herself. A hand digs around a pocket to withdraw three opals to inspect. *Do these matter if you are dead?* Vice grip of the throat. Dendrites wither. A newfound pain corrupts her heart. "I can't watch this unfold. If he should…" she began, unable to finish.

Spectral vocals, behind her, crept into her head with enigmatic words, "The door closes on this life you made. He and you? Unrequited. Accept this token…or not. A window, left open for gentry, like yourself."

Quick turn of the head. Nothing except air, stars, and shrouded distance. Shimmering inside her pocket: a prismatic gem. A rainbow. An invitation from the unseen enigma. The call. An easy choice to make. Flight took hold of her. Horrible scenarios loop inside her mind should the fort fall with him inside. Her sisters yelled out for her, but she refused to listen. Better to live an unexamined life.

Better to restart and chase new transient pleasures. Denying herself her chosen helpmate.

Would you ever come look for me? Another life. I'll return. If ever. I don't want to be this kind of admirer any longer...

Ruby traverses a one-way ticket to the Lost Divide.

Leandro's lynx roused itself to an aggressive stance. He knew the threat among them. Nonetheless, he did not flinch or grab his sword or command his pet, or even call for the guard; instead, he offered a drink.

"It" decided to offer itself one.

One dark corner came to life; small flickers of nearby candlelight outlined its form. Blue and white tendrils pour into a goblet. Gently. Delicately. Consuming with bitterness settled in its throat. Pain, exhaling from the contents: the spirit of ethanol. A small laugh accompanied it. The goblet was placed down. Partially melted.

Black vapors rise.

"A masochist all too well," Leandro said, pouring himself a drink to share in the moment.

The figure did not leave its dark corner. It did not need to. "I have to remind myself of pain sometimes. To feel. Something you rot of organisms, get to enjoy. Such luxuries. If only a 'pseudo-prime,' like myself, can partake in," Ashokara proclaimed from its little corner.

"When my stomach acids bubbled yesterday, I figured you were skulking about. I thought to myself, 'The pelagic's trivially named bastard child? Here? Desperation comes calling.' The question is," Leandro continued, walking closer to the corner, "for what purpose?"

The lynx moved itself in front of its king, keeping its body close to the ground, ready to spring in a moment's time—should it arise.

Pearls gazed from the darkness. Its orbits look deep into the large feline. Tendrils, unnaturally shaped, extended forth. "Let me pet it."

The beast roared. The sound of rings tapping against a sword's hilt. Leandro shook his head. His hand was ready to unsheathe the weapon without hesitation. More small laughs. The tendrils receded. "Why don't you come forward…Show me your true form," he said, flirting with animus, swishing his cup about.

"Don't insult me," Ashokara barked. "You can see me flawlessly with those bright tapestries overlaying your eyes. So iridescent. I cannot wait to pry those retroreflectors. Someday. As for my unannounced attendance, I'm just here to make sure my boy keeps his promise."

Leandro squinted his eyes, letting out a disgusted snort. The cup raised to his opposition, "Alcohol is like a fine razor to you, *slug*. Have some more of my anhydrous. Keep marinating. My hunters have secured some stags. Care for the shavings of hartshorn? You come to me, naked, without your humectant armor; medium-rare. Leave a piece of yourself here for me to consume," the king said, barely keeping his poise. His grip generated hairline cracks.

More laughs from the shadows.

"You *tremble,* aristocrat! Not in fear. No. I would've lopped your head off had I felt that weakness. You're excited. We can draw blades now. I'd like that. The idea has fermented into my own nous-vita. Give the tribes, the armies, the Primes, their messengers, damn it all, even the lessers' entertainment before the age of *Pasaran* ends within a day's time! Your anthropocentric movement can end here!"

"I remember a time when you tried making your own 'queen lesser' to see how humans procreate. Tossed her too quickly, I say. Not like the original? Toxic behavior for a gynandromorph. Which half brought it on? Strange biology you inherit. When you close your eyes, does the idea of hopelessness seep into your brain? Here, enjoy more of my elixirs. Let someone else usurp the throne," Leandro almost shouted with a laugh of his own to mock. He offered his cup to the darkness.

The void stares back at its twin monster, elucidating, "'Man of War'…I have *fed* on your ancestors. I can still feed on your novice prince. Inexperienced. Hardly a fight. But to gain one last audience with you, to see your truest potential, would bring me such joy before I take this world and kill myself for the pleasure of knowing none—except myself—could annihilate this body, this mind, this…*soul*."

Leandro took another step forward, lynx in tow, "Such threats cannot move me. To commit regicide would mean to lose your best chance of acquiring loyalty from the boy—*my* scribe. Why not commit suicide now with my father's sword? Grandest of sufferings. I can delay the inevitable. Missing vitals. Scraping around. Flaying. Filleting. Placed in the very darkness, your nakedness hides. Tempting, no?"

"Beg those you deliver prayers to to see if they would permit you to snatch the *very* life from me. If you dare me to come forth from this corner on a whim," Ashokara's words quickened, legs beginning to expose, with tendrils from arms and swords to aim, "I vow to burn all lands *tonight* so that not even the grandest of stars, of Xantho, of Melano, may have any brilliance over scorched earth. And you can keep your cup in hand forever on gutted earth, on burnt timber, a useless king to mounds of upheaved dirt. Your only applause would then come from driftwood. *His* Majesty, Salt, will surely fit you with a new crown! And only *my* boy and **my** scribe would be left to see it! Marisha, herself, cannot dream of stopping me!"

"By what means of spiritual food would you give Milos after all is said and completely undone?"

"Appeasement via artificial induction. My cabinets bloom with all kinds of chromatic caplets, ampoules, and pastilles. Nothing that would deliquesce his mind into mush; a few burned-out, blinking synapses. Enough to avoid supersaturation. A superior investiture compared to the lack of one you have given him."

Induced with a malignant prion affliction. To misfold Milos's brain would be nothing more than an experimental act of zombification. Flatlining him would be a greater mercy, as opposed to forced servitude.

The ambient temperature shifted; it was no longer wet and cold. Phlegmatic nature turned choleric. Modifying humors. Would the *final* commence in this room? All that is left of tenderness in this land…blown out like a candle? What a foolish idea. Why dare a suicide?

It can wait until tomorrow…if the idea still haunts.

It's so hard to be human. Born with the seeds of death implanted. The wind scatters bad thoughts on a hill with only one momentous brilliance that dares not become seized by sad fingertips. Miss a chance, and the ignition is set: undignified suffering. Roll a pair of dice; blow on them; pray to your Chroma, your Science, your Roots, or whatever brings you luck for a night in a soft bed with no worries. Warm love wrapped under both arms with kisses on your cheeks, nibbles on your lips, and gentle sensations on your delicate organs.

War loves crackbrained messiahs, but peace is a concrete sediment keeping the fissure at bay; an epoxy, a resistance, as if daring to avoid the face of God. Because some see beauty in the flames. But the hopeful, they take it one discussion, *one word*, at a time, avoiding aimless palaver, in search of rainbows.

Five seconds of reflection. Add another three for drinking in one go. The Usurper does not suspect a thing.

Leandro looks into the empty goblet. "The world is alive with us tonight. It's not about you. Or me," he humbly begins, "The lights of my country, my neighbors, of land and water, something I don't think I could ever *dream* of living without. Alive. Once a day, the land is silent in its peace without the rumbles of disunity. The strewn dungeon artifacts cannot compare to this kind of treasure—it is bewitching. Tables are set for a family. Friends become lovers. Solitudinarians emerge as gregarious teachers. All pushing forward. Iberitus, always."

"...And of rivals?" The limbs begin to retract into the shadows.

"Irrepressible Messengers smile on disunity—treaties must be forged; temporary, as they may be, all parties lose if not involved."

"Rogue Herald's...nothing more than an undisciplined child. The fact that a Prime Chroma is unable to keep a taut leash on its Messenger is comedy," Ashokara scoffed.

"It is amusing, isn't it? I hear that the rich economy in Lusura has fallen behind to Celanjung after the rogue disturbed your mineral supply as of late. That massive seabed of manganese nodules, full of copper deposits and cobalt *and* nickel. I was wondering why the MCI's report showed the values of the galtavo and galcudo rising exponentially recently. The same goes for Udalann's floriah and florhil. Even Grenvalk's *luzso* and *luzcho* have risen. Imagine that. It's a geodi rush. How will blood-knives fare if this keeps up? Debasement," Leandro proudly said. A barely disguised smirk that only the Usurper could see.

"A minor delay. Commerce can easily be fixed. Whereas you have caravans of displaced outsiders, from the isles, flocking to your towns and cities, showing zero effort to assimilate. Uprooted pathetic ones with their hands out. It won't be long until your people turn on you when the parasites drain your economy. They're weak, but smart. They know if they venture into my realm, they *have* to assimilate. Policy dictates you either enlist, partake on the front lines of one march, or be forced upon Klaring's domain. I enjoy the sights of banishment. We have bets in the Capital to see which kills them first: animal, flora, or wanderer—they never make it to The Mouth. Care for a wager?"

"What're the stakes?" Leandro inquired, pouring another drink.

"Abdication from the throne, Gottlir absorbed, you…chained alongside *The Myrtle King*. He is the last of his kind. I'm sure he would be thrilled to see a descendant of lynx royalty after they denied him help from old management. I remind him, each greeting, about how his realm belongs to a Mairu composer. You should see the animosity in his eyes. Just as the daughter of Celanjung has for me. A meeting long overdue. I'd hate to be human, or ogre, if he escaped."

In the distance, a large section of brass winds droned over the mountains. Every ear, in both camps, heard their song. Humans fell silent. Trasno spat on the ground. Mairu roared in delight. Tarwini were silent but emboldened. Pictfero royalty, from Klaring, slept soundly, while Leandro inhaled the acrid breeze coming in: salt, pitch, and excrement. A small, jolting migraine rapes his right hemisphere.

Ashokara joined in, "I can smell it: World-Eater."

Deeper inhalations, followed by a shiver, snow caps synchronizing vibrations with the Usurper, "Sodium-chloride and shattered dreams. The queen's love is ready to hurt you. Best get your rest, king; it might be the last time you see Melano rise again. You already lost your assembly before I arrived. The royal court is extinct thanks to Klaring's assassins; just you and the prince."

Leandro unsheathed his sword with extreme speed that one tendril was partially severed. It absorbed the cells of the king and his sword discreetly. Stolen power passed through the digestive gland of the wounded ceras. Spreading to other cnidosacs. Stored until they are needed for defensive purposes. An oversight of Leandro.

If only he had cut it completely.

"You did not tell me what *triumph* brings me, aeolid."

The lynx remained silent. No shrieks, howls, bellows, or soft mews. Leandro's eyes: broad and extensive. Overwhelmed with conflicting emotions. Contempt. Disgust. Focused on coordination.

"*One* boon—reserved strictly for Milos. That is the extent of my compassion. ***You will never get anything from me unless you sever ties to Somdir***," Ashokara ended with.

Partial exposure showed the true nature of reality: a face so disgustingly opposite from the humanoid armor. Camouflage concealed the grotesqueness present. Sounds of wet steps making their way to the balcony. A vocal score sheet flew from the table; preparing flight.

Snatched and observed.

"I saw her, your *'lost'* daughter. We spoke briefly before some of the others tried to descend on me. She, like the others, is a cruel mistress of the Divide. Shame about the mother. To die on expensive silk. She described your old self, best: a love written in music, and when the queen passed, the melody set itself on loop. You tried to dance to that same song, over and over and over, never coming to terms. Driving her away with your lunacy. A needle that won't stop skipping on the wax. Should the prince fall, will you follow? I can hear the black and white keys of your grand heart hammer away at your strings. Call on me if it bursts. It is only appropriate that our swords run each other through. Should you lose to another…I will plant olives, apples, figs, and grapes on your site."

The composition flew to the wind. Then…silence. The lynx pawed at Leandro's leg for attention. Strokes on the head. Trepidation in the heart. Never has one seen the Prime Aeolid's true self without succumbing to the quietus.

Three brothers ate alongside their kin. Hardy folk. Determined. They had to be. The Mairu were their natural enemy. Separated by one fortress. So close by simple division. Always on the hunt to capture when doing raids along the borders. Mothers, daughters, sisters, and nieces, were raped by the tusked brutes before heads were brained. Fathers, sons, nephews, cousins, and sages, are eaten alive. Screams from the Mainland echo to the island of Grenvalk and its one islet. Forever scarring every household.

Good thing the tusked ones are poor swimmers and have trouble keeping their grand ships from exploding from the quick-witted mages.

The skull-bearer's ears caught wind of murmurs from some of the younger humans: desertion, fear, surrender. Observing tents of injured youth. Barely audible whimpers for their mother. Young men just welcoming in adulthood. Each one is trying to endure the harsh, constant battle of inner struggle—unable to grapple with their insecurities. A slew of older mentors, slain by the first wave's end. Faith waning. Prayers to any who might be listening. Ideas of suicide toyed among others on a tide of blood alcohol. Many candles begin to burn out. Impulsivity rises. The final wave need not be one of turbulence to lose it all, but a gentle breeze.

"Innovation! Allow my prescription!" the pages whispered into the eldest brother's mind. Erratic appendages turning to the right sheets. Eyes pacing side-to-side. Sentences imprinted into the wrinkles. Remembered by heart. Ingredients within reach, save a few found only in the woods, and an odd rarity he hoped to find. The middle sibling stalked some large game on the trip for succulent protein. Taken. The youngest skinned the hide, fashioning a good-sized satchel.

Taken, along with an empty sporran, gifted by some war kin, the skull-bearer set out in haste to collect the last elements.

Familiar voices, calling from behind, gave chase.

"Where are you going in the dead of night?! We have food to finish and sleep to hound!" Daru exclaimed with profound confusion.

Sibi stamped a foot on the ground, turning to him, a rage in his eyes, "Do you think I just act entirely on random?!"

"I ask out of *concern*, brother! Our cousins might think cowardice of you! What if Grand M saw this? Scurrying to the thicket."

"We don't care what others think of us! We do what must be done, and I have taken up the task to provide a provision of fellowship to our allies. Specifically, those of humankind who have barely grown a single fiber on their chest! Do you not see them? Hear them?! A modicum of resilience left in their nous! They are more capable of handling the Mairu than our cousins, toe-to-toe. There is a short supply of experience in their ranks. Without them…we are surely routed," a suggestion of anxiety hiding in the lungs, "We cannot fail Milos, our allies, or—especially—the homeland."

He is in tune with responsibility. Keeping pride at arm's length. So that his head, and second skull, do not weigh his sights down. Away from proud arrows that may blind his vision from the bigger picture.

"We will hold the burden; you carry the light," Xamak said, grabbing the bags.

An eager nod from Daru.

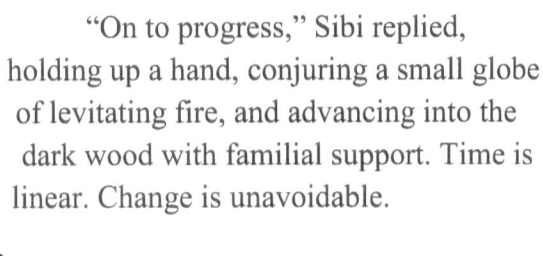

"On to progress," Sibi replied, holding up a hand, conjuring a small globe of levitating fire, and advancing into the dark wood with familial support. Time is linear. Change is unavoidable.

To the East, a cold draft lapped up the spines of shackled laborers, while their deserving overlords watched them like birds of prey with blazing torches. Some mutineers were hauled away by their ankles to toil away in the mines. No water, food, or rest until the assignment is done or a Prime comes calling for them. No work remains insignificant.

The farmers slept soundly in the Capital, knowing their ravaged fields, displaced livestock, and destroyed buildings were nearly replenished. A young boy, unable to get any sleep, looked out to the North, frightened by its residents who never sleep.

A woman of rank approached. "Your nerves shake, but your steely gaze keeps," a hand leading him back to his temporary quarters, "One day, you'll feel the fire inside mature." He asked what it meant. "That you'll make a fine countryman who won't hesitate to defend land and neighbor. It isn't just honor or duty but necessity," she replied.

A worried old man beckons him back to bed, where warmth awaits. Where the community resides.

A rider, coming alongside her, "News. I'm to ask you to return to the castle. His lordship says it is urgent."

She looked north like the boy. Even in the dead of a cool night, the wind picked up its pace, and felt her own axons twanging unnecessarily. On jumart, she rode back to her king's side.

High alert. Giants, in armor, with banners, are being prepared. But for what? A whiny drone of instruments in the distance—to the North.

"He waits in the tower," an attendant said to the arriving beauty.

Drip. Drip. She could hear a leak coming from within the walls. This bothered her. Fire, mortar, and clay are the main residents of this architecture. Drip. Drip. *Someone is testing me*, she thought, ascending.

Nowhere to be found. Empty cartons and a cold oven. Not even a suggestion of mixtures on the table was touched recently. But a sweet smell wafted. She called out to him.

A booming voice, above the dome, "Look, to my ex-blood!"

She approached the telescope.

This was the dread she tried to ignore.

"All lined up and ready to advance on us before first light," Birati said, hovering down to her, "Good mess this is. Your thoughts, Aruna?"

She saw no death marches in action, or practiced, or prepared. They stood, exemplary of the soldier's soldier, next to one another, on the border's edge. Puppets, Mairu, and other equally dangerous conscripts watch the castle from afar.

Two strange humanoids, beastly and cloaked,
embarked on Udalann's domain while the vast armies waited.

"Messages for us from *those* two. I wonder where the
rest of their little club is," Birati said with disdain. "Go down
below. Tell the engineers to be ready to set the valves
as a precaution. I'll snap the usual sign," he
vanished from her sight.

Aruna looked briefly to the West,
wondering if *he* made the journey alive, and with
no detrimental damage.

They faced one another: the composer to
the messengers. Birati waited. Waited. Waited.
Testing him.

Still waiting.

Until…

"Far from the shelter aren't we, traitor?"
one messenger said. Only a long beak stuck out
from the hood. His compatriot watched.
Crowned with horns. What a pair.

Of bird and bull.

"You're on my land; shelter is all
around me," Birati replied, pulling out a sweet
loaf from his pocket to snack on. "Do you
come with conditions? Or should I show you
how well I can handle this handicap?"

"You'll never survive the first wave,"
the bird messenger gruffly said. His
compatriot remains still. Frozen in time.

"A lie. And you know it. Where's
the hermaphrodite? Watching us, I
assume. Feeble slug," Birati said proudly.

The bull-horned messenger took a step forward; a successful taunt. Birati looked past the two to see one wave of militants ready to sprint.

One more push.

"Relinquish your failed kingdom. Your people are fully aware you cannot protect them. A few Mairu to guard the castle and some farmers against Ashokara's armies is nothing but an insult to him. An underdeveloped realm of peons, rocks, and fireworks. Nothing more than a sunk cost fallacy."

Birati looked at the horned one. "Why am I speaking with this 'avian virus' instead of your pale rider? Maybe he sees you two as expendable. Or maybe it's because he realizes this to be a waste of time; giving only his most asinine orders to the least capable simpletons."

Another step taken. And another. And the first wave screamed. Advancing. Birati snapped his fingers to release a large firework into the sky. A scout saw the signal. They blew a horn for the attendants back at the capitol to ring a bell. Instructions for those waiting below in the hottest depths under the castle.

"*Now!*" Aruna ordered the engineers.

Turning. Turning. Valves and pipes and steam and abstract machines acting according to their prompt. Rumbles and quakes. Rocks dancing. Feet unbalanced. But not for the levitating composer. He looked on in all seriousness as crackling veins of fire searched their way to the border. They passed under his body. A grand spread.

Volcanic combustion erupted like a wall all along the border. The first wave disintegrated without reaction. No screams. Only soot from the conflagration. The messengers looked back to see the firewall reaching so high that clouds evaporated. And it wasn't stopping anytime soon.

"Tell the Usurper, your compatriots, and whatever Harbingers, or Primes, aiding you, they are not welcome here—ever. Only my Hafnium sister," Birati shouted, manipulating a small hole in the wall for them to return the message.

The enigmatic messengers had no words.

Only acquiesce.

To the Southeast, in the pelagic, waves clashed against one another. A dense mist covers the angry serpents of the Akrav. Weapons held to the breast; spells engaged in the cerebellum; one Nation, hypervigilant. Eyes emerged, barely out of the choppy waters, to watch the ancient creatures caterwaul before the thick gray concealed them from the natural light of Melano. None could see past the blanket. One head turned to the Mainland to see the inferno barrier. The emergence of civil war.

"Real darkness," the girl said. Fear stirs in her.

Incendiary thoughts linger. Trying to coax her into submission.

"It is, sister. Now we must prepare our own."

They looked at the wildfires, personifying the brilliance of Xantho. Perceiving the wails cloaked in the mist. Feeling surrounded from all angles. How long until other Nations revealed themselves?

Siding? Or against?

Breaking through the water, large and triumphant, a man who has conquered the hierarchy, looking to the fog, silently.

"Father," the girl said, awestruck.

Steady. Unwavering. Resolute. The Glaukós Imperator. A ghastly-looking cleaver of a weapon was held and swung—just once—across the air, calming the waters.

Another screech came from the fog, but of pain, and a splash
followed with incoming waves. He pointed the cleaver to the
fog where his serpent warriors advanced under the liquid
blue. His gaze finally broke to look at his daughter and son.
"Stay away from the outer islets, Natalina. You too, Duilio."

"Father," she approached, "can I—"

"No!" he interjected, fully aware of the same request
he always denies her. "I want neither of you to step onto the
Mainland until they sort out their own affairs. This may be
what you have, these waters, but it is your birthright. Stay far
from those strange *beliefs* of theirs."

"But," she closed her eyes, trying to ignore his
imposing gaze, "he *needs* me! Now more than ever!"
Trembling fists at her sides. Body above liquid violence. She
stands on her metaphoric ground of splash.

Brother at her side. Silently consoling.

The warriors returned, dragging a gargantuan severed
head, under the water, from one of the ancient Akrav beasts.
Entozoon inhibitor, from the stomach of dark waters. Scaly.
Cyclopean. Hyperdontia sea worms. Legendary for their
nutritious properties, should anything claim their grotesque
head. It'll grow back. They always do. Shaming the hydras
into extinction. Birati has offered plenty in return for one
head to be studied: to know what makes them tick. A hint of
who, or what, is behind the perpendicular organic barrier.
Denied. It is the Palatial Usurper Ashokara's head they want
in return. He still strives to fulfill the trade. The imperator
commanded them to take it to one small island within
swimming distance of Udalann.

Proud to know that any advances have been stalled.

The worms are merely startled by the fires. Should
they exceed their own dutiful boundaries, the Nations would
cease. Hadal and Abyssal salivate at the idea of a cataclysm.

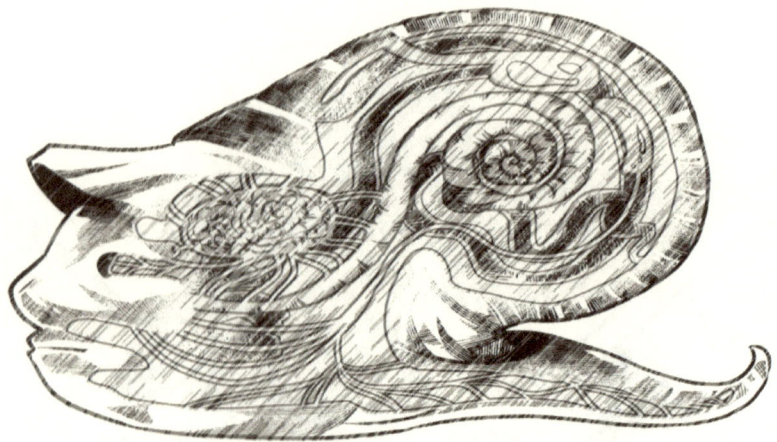

Even if it takes them along. Anything that hollows out the mundane has their empathy. No small relief for the other Nations to know they do not control the wrigglers.

No one knows.

He approached her calmly: "That head will serve as a banquet when he has fulfilled his current duty. These are ruins he *will* walk from."

She had no words.

Only acquiesce.

"Those are all the main ingredients, but this last one…" Sibi pondered, "No simple dye; impossible to find in this realm. It's only found in—"

Click; click; click; click; click. The sound of a broken clock forgetting to tick but only tock. Light to the trees.

Six eyes were wide with surprise.

"Inside! The final component!" the book transmitted into Sibi's head. He told Xamak to shoot it down. Careful. Eye coordinating to align crosshairs to threads. ***Bang!*** A thunderous thud of weight projected onto the earth. Daru poked his blade at it before jumping back in case it was a trick. No tricks here, but neither were there answers to the questions.

"How did this get here?!" Daru exclaimed, reacting by spinning his head to all sides. A swivel couldn't keep up.

"Forget that! What hung it up?!" Xamak chimed in, probing his weapon extensively with rapid thoughts in case of a sudden malfunction. Triggerman's thoughts abound: *Should I tap? Should I rack? Do I go?!*

Sibi dug into its chest, extracting the final component from broken gears, and when all seemed to be over, a new noise awakened. Not of the click; not of the tick; not of the tock. Raspy. Wheezy. Guttural. Inhuman. Buzzing. Bladders tighten. Flirtations with the cold.

"Agh! Gotcha, bastard!" Daru yelped, smacking his neck, a flattened skeeter on the palm. But another pursued for Xamak's. And another came for Sibi. And soon, a green vaporous toxin shifted across the soil-top: rising, collecting, drastic. Sibi was compelled to release a spell of offense, but the tome recommended none of the sort.

Only to wait.

"Don't! Don't! Don't! This beast is too strong for the likes of you three, and you have not come to my most advanced of powers to combat it! Leave its presence to the other!"

Sibi looked at the tome's large eye embedded in the cover.

"This is no time for paradoxical words! Speak plainly, book!"

Bang! A single flash of magnesium shot from Xamak's gun. It cuts through the green, poisonous air. Brilliance illuminated the dark wood with its dragon breath. Skittish triggerfinger. Unveiling a pipeline of truth to the answers. Questions that should be left behind in the drudgery pools of week-old garbage.

He wants to break his goggles. And utterly resign.

Anything to avoid this clear-eyed truth.

Damn my cowardice. Place me in front of the firing squad!

It cocked its head to the side before the toxic air resealed the fired hole. Angry. Bitter. Chattering its teeth on a pipe of corundum.

"***Retreat!***" Sibi screamed in terror. They didn't need to think twice about this. This was no ordinary foe of fur. No ordinary Tarwini.

Of assassins: Olu-Zad.

The deranged rat held out the right hand, sucking them in with its powerful vortex. Turning into vortices. Sibi and Xamak are, fortunately, out of the range, but Daru...

"I WILL RAVAGE YOUR INSIDES IF YOU SHOULD TAKE ME, VERMIS!" He screamed, body held up in the air, blade lodged into a hardy stump. For how long could he hold? The pathological mute's forearm enforced a violent pump that surely any living being would've cramped by now! Violence is his religion and blood lustrates.

Xamak tried to get a clear shot, but the crosshairs wouldn't stop shaking. He might hit his brother. Sibi prepared an incantation, ignoring the tome's previous warning. A virulent predator revealed itself to him with a look of disinterest—halting the spell dead in the tracks.

"Peculiar that you would need my brimstone," it said, pointing at Sibi's blackened fingertips, "Transformation of the vita without fluidity and preservation; I much prefer collecting those from the giants and humans. Looking to shapeshift some poor, fearful souls, magister? Give them courage? Cheating me out of the grandest battle seen in years?"

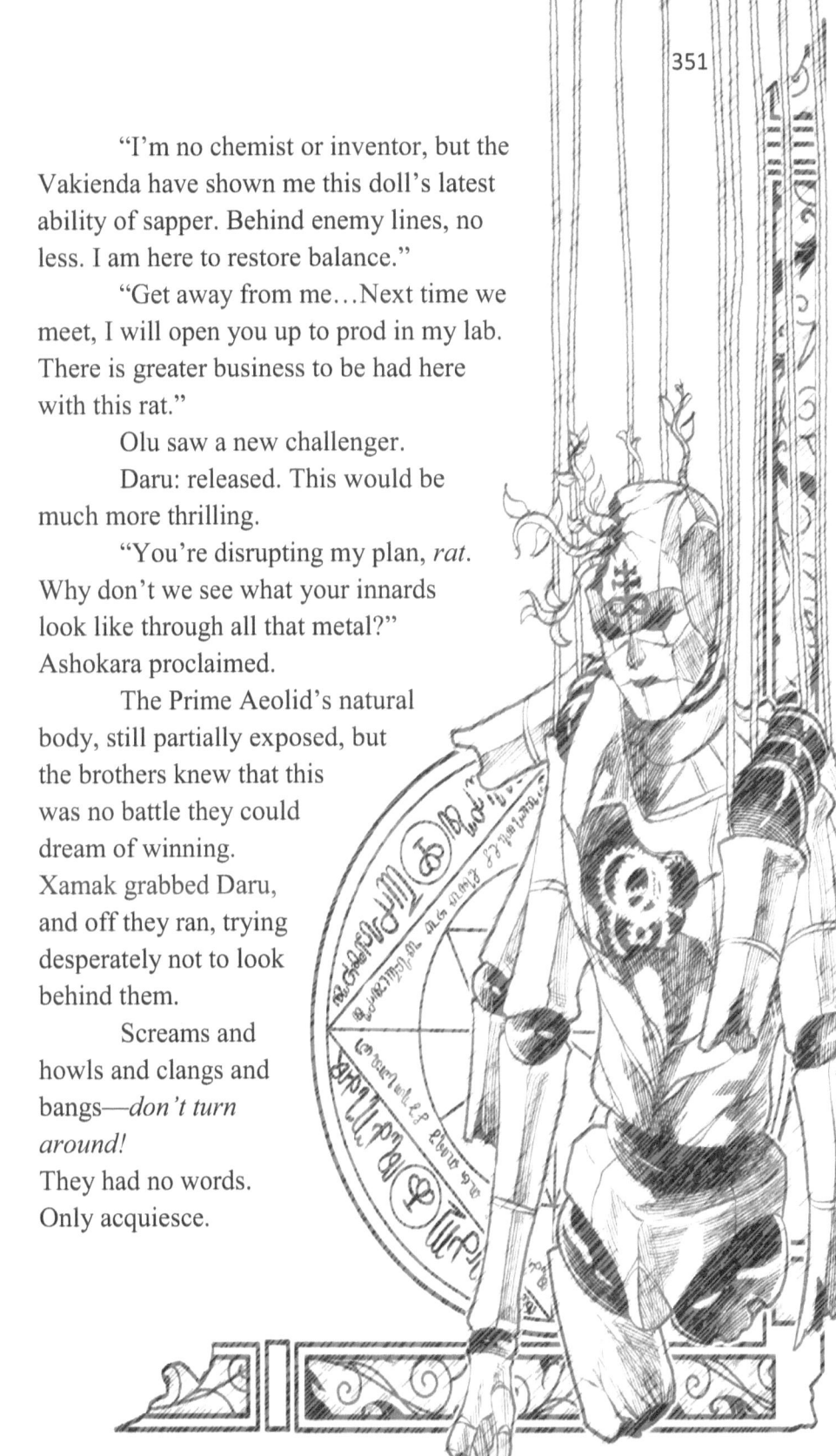

"I'm no chemist or inventor, but the Vakienda have shown me this doll's latest ability of sapper. Behind enemy lines, no less. I am here to restore balance."

"Get away from me…Next time we meet, I will open you up to prod in my lab. There is greater business to be had here with this rat."

Olu saw a new challenger.

Daru: released. This would be much more thrilling.

"You're disrupting my plan, *rat*. Why don't we see what your innards look like through all that metal?" Ashokara proclaimed.

The Prime Aeolid's natural body, still partially exposed, but the brothers knew that this was no battle they could dream of winning. Xamak grabbed Daru, and off they ran, trying desperately not to look behind them.

Screams and howls and clangs and bangs—*don't turn around!* They had no words. Only acquiesce.

Chapter 13

†

Neuroplasticity

They tossed. They turned. Deep sleep for one. Anxiety for the other. Veils comfort the one. Nothing for the other. Except for a confidential voice inside her mind, "*We'll meet soon. All in my land, know you now. What you look like. How you smell. Your fears. Your wants. I have sent word to the Assinikoda, should you cross their path, not to be harmed. You're so close. I await within my spire.*"

Stillness. As soft and as cozy as her quarters were, for a fortress, panic sang its same song and danced again. Frail hands clutching her cross, praying to her Prime—*No! It's God!*—up above, hoping He will hear her silent prayer so that when the light comes and the campaign begins, she does not become a pillar of salt. Last days to remember here. Phthalos is far gone to guide her; this is something already woven into her story—fatalistic as it may seem.

Little song notes call out to her. Inside this *very* room. Ice water rushes through her veins. She is paralyzed, but the tunes captivate her, slowly thawing her out. Sadie does not see anyone or anything; only the lone candle bedside. She looks at her bracelet, trying to talk to the veil that never came to talk to her all this time. It feels different. Soothing. Her blankets feel warmer. Her eyes grow heavier. The candle grows dimmer. No unspeakable sounds were uttered. Just the tunes. They remind her of Midnight Mass on the eve of Christmas.

"More hymns, please," she whispers to the emptiness. Her eyes mist. Praying to see old faces again. Wanting to be with her community, visit her favorite church in Nashua, see her friends, hold her family, and sing her soul out in the wilderness! Touch-starved. She falls asleep with these thoughts. Discouraged by the fact there was no one around to comfort her, except linens and a single bracelet.

Twisting, spiraling; the beeswax candle contorts itself. The gentle flame transforms into a small woman, *"So long as you keep me close and stay honest, no harm will ever befall you, child. We will speak soon."*

And light vanished from the wick.

Something unspeakable is about to transpire.

"THEY'RE ABOUT TO BREACH!" a voice screamed out in the halls. So sudden. Everything in the world felt like it was crumbling down. Sadie awoke to see banners and fire and spears and shooting and screaming, and it paralyzed her down to the very core! The door blasted wide open. She screamed with her hands flailing over her face. Sparks from the bracelet shoot in all directions.

"Calm yourself, girl, it's me!" Milos shouted, trying to steady her scattered mind. Enzu leaped onto her shoulder. He clung dearly to her, doing what he did best, but this was too much.

"Just stay inside! **Don't leave this room!** If you have to leave, go down to the altar of Chroma and pray we finish this today—*everything* today! Celanjung included!" He turned to exit.

But she quickly got a hold of herself to lunge and clutch him from behind, "All of us, right?! Please lie to me and say, *all* of us! Just say the words! **I don't know how much more my mind can take! Please!**"

He felt her warmth pressed against his back, her face buried into his spine, wanting to fuse, afraid he might never return and leaving her here to rot forever.

You will never find another like him in this realm or back home.

Despite all the chaos taking place, he traced over her tight clasp of hands at his waist, speaking gently, "Call me a thief, but never call on me to lie. I promise to all the benevolent Primes of Chroma that hear me: I'm sending you home. Myself. Alive and well. This I swear," A small force to unclasp her; setting out to the gate to assist.

He promised, she thought, *Lord, watch over him...*

Throwing herself on the mercy of a gamble. She hadn't had much luck since coming here. Always crying. Always prying. Always failing. Falling, rather than landing. This was no thrill to her.

A spit of twirling fire sprang in her presence from the bracelet, the veiled woman. *Her* veiled woman. Righteous anger in a bottle rocket! Delegating words only the young girl could hear. Poetry, in fact. Only set for warriors on the go. Raising the temperature in her fast, aching heart. But slowing its pump. A steady dance of rhythms, beats, and grooves.

"We'll burn a path, a way, a track, a round, a course—OF COURSE! Because this finishes with you, him, it, them, and me! No need for blue pups or strange doppelgangers. No worries about bumps or thuds or strange lizards or little green men. I'm the one on the scene now! Frayed nerves? That's a lie, and you know it! You keep

asking the questions, opening all the doors, break the locks—DAMN THE LOCKS! You're a bullet of red chromatic salvation; a revolutionary sensation; give me that fiery elation; YOU BROUGHT THIS WORLD TO FULL ATTENTION! Let's blaze, you and I, for I am always by your side."

Spinning back to its origin on the wrist with pops, sparks, and tangible dangers, she stared at it in disbelief.

A grand smile to behold.

Enzu wished he could speak.

But, alas, he too hit with acquiescence.

The towers came closer. Battering rams: pounding, pounding, pounding. Ladders lean against the walls. Commands from both sides delegating to usurp the other's move.

The young humans were surprisingly bolstered compared to their previous demeanor. A little aid from the magistrate to enter their wood cups around the campfire. Inspired. Some would say the fear was just a fever dream and, in reality, they drank from cups of gold alongside kings of ancient eras. Some even touted that they spoke to the Primes themselves. Shields up. Weapons unsheathed. Spirits are strong.

More magnesium shots project onto the vermin. Furs ignite. Bodies dropping. Goblins shooting in a frenzy. A paroxysm of clashing fits. Spasmodic attacks. Little bodies sure had some heft to them.

But the Orkes seemed infinite. And they too carried that same hysteria with their tusked and furry comrades. Arrows weeping from the sky to route those from Gottlir. Halberds kebobing multiple Trasno in one go. Klaring's towers grow closer. Untold amounts of broken shields.

Broken? Did someone scream, *the gate is broken?*

"Kill them all! Leave nothing for the Primes to claim!" Tekla roared, spearheading to the front; pigheaded as she was, all were following her lead. Her blood could not have been fully human. Her strength was too terrible to behold. Smashing that large sledge of hers with its howling lynx head, Mairu skulls turned to ripe fruit.

Milos aided atop the ramparts, releasing Cobalt's grand warrior, trapping as many as he could with Mulberry, healing with Goldenrod, and using Aquamarine's energy to shield himself, and those in range from danger as often as the power could recharge with the gear on his bracelet, spinning round and round.

A glint of otherworldly light distorted Xantho's rays. The foreign disturbance broke through Milos's conjured cuirass, but not fatally, only dispersing the energy. The pain wasn't bad—bruising at most.

"That should've killed you. Guess I'll try again!" A voice screamed through the air. Assassins are afoot. Invisible.

The Cobalt warrior spun its twin maces in the vicinity. A bark of pain. Critical success on the random landing. The damage unveiled the would-be cloaked assassin: Edling. Rage secreted from his pores. He had his own scroll to use. Quick incantations. Chroma of Rust, expelling the blue warrior. Armor crashed down before it returned back to the scroll. He revealed a second knife, criss-crossing it against the first.

"Try to keep up!"

The gear sparked and squealed. Some black vapor is emitted from the device. Overworked. Milos kept teleporting, but the savage prince kept pace—unrelentless. This was just as bad as dealing with Jökull.

That time was for retrieval for Evren.

This time it meant death if he stumbled.

Opposing Mairu thrashed allied Trasno into the ground. One goblin tries his best to get back up; he has a broken back. Another came to shield his body, watching the tusked ogre preparing a final smash, pleading for the disabled kin's life.

King Leandro's lynx lunged at the ogre's throat. Six jugulars: severed. A barely hanging head. By a thread. Leandro and the prince took part in the melee to boost morale.

"Reinforcements!" a soldier cried out.

Heavy feet shook the hard ground. They came with banners to both unfurl and impale. Leandro saw those familiar pisolite patterns.

"Thank you, Birati."

"Why won't you stand still and bleed?! You think just because we share the same lineage that makes you my brother?! I piss on abject failures like you for fun!" Edling shouted, his arms becoming a blur. Too riled, too sloppy, too uncoordinated with the blinking scribe.

"You disregard the rights of others, fail to comply with our laws and customs, and behave like any rabid beast of Klaring! You are *not* my kind! You and yours don't deserve a mercy killing! But it won't come from me," Milos retorted, his breathing becoming heavy with fatigue.

A near miss to split his sternum vertically, Edling spat out a viscous glob, eyes lifted, buried under the brow, "High and mighty will not work with me! It's true, isn't it? They said you don't kill anymore. Pity. Heard you did plenty of that when you were a crumb in Lusura with the Hafnium Mairu! Was the taste for it too unbecoming, street urchin?!"

Another lunge was taken. Another near miss.

Everything is in slow motion. *I'll knock him out just as he is within range*, Milos thought. The face of psychopathy is near touching.

Suddenly, the stomach of the world grumbled. Feet on both sides of the battlefield swayed, bent, or fell. It came so suddenly. The tribes, watching from a safe range, retreated without a second thought.

This was not in the cards.

"The Usurper was right…" Leandro whispered, gritting his teeth.

Some of the humans and Trasno feared for their lives. Many began to toy with the idea of withdrawing. "Don't even think of it or I'll strike you down myself!" Tekla shouted, seeing the fear in their eyes. But she had no clue on how to proceed. The aristarch manned the back.

Calculating the remains of a possible future.

Ard Rex smiled with grand smugness he decided to join in on the assault. He released his own scrolls that were enhancing the capabilities of his armies. Milos, trying his best to stand straight, managed to catch Edling off balance, and threw him off the rampart. He watched the beast from afar in all its terrible wonder.

A World-Eater…

Tusked, chained, and armored. Its size rivaled the fort's. Klaring's forces continued to grow in size as now they unleashed everything they had at their disposal. Even the injured joined in. No resource was spared.

All was lost.

"I have no choice," Milos said.

He sprinted to higher ground, conserving the energy in his bracelet for this final desperation. "I'll have to do this without Enzu's help," he huffed. Invading Orkes tried to cleave through him, but assistance came from below, the Newt brothers covering his retreat. Leandro, too, saw his need for help, sending Tekla to assist as his vanguard. "By the composition…" Milos's voice trailed, trying to decide which of the two intact Cerulean scrolls to choose from. The choice was made. "Katya, please let this work." Incantations begin. Secrets unfolding. Ancient power rising. Cerulean unfurling its wonder. Words of old passing through his lips delicately so as not to blunder and start again. Soon, it started to levitate, disintegrating into a liquid, roots of light rising from the stone.

Far to the West, she felt the grand conjuration.

"Another reading so soon?" She stepped outside to look to the East for anomalies. She still couldn't see him. Years of wondering what this man looked like that evaded her grip. A veiled woman, standing by, announced, "The Vicara says today is the day Gottlir falls."

Queen Evren looked disappointed.

Will I not have my justice? I will not compromise with the Primes.

The fort was losing numbers. The prince made his retreat back inside, but Leandro stood his ground with the others, shoulder-to-shoulder. Blood trickled down his body from numerous lacerations. Bolts sticking out of his back. Ramirus tried to pull him back inside, but the World-Eater's slow, yet heavy, steps continued to falter everyone's balance, save for Klaring because of Rex's incantation.

"What is...that?!" Ard Rex exclaimed, looking to the top of the fort. A multitude of threads of sky blue light glide across the sky. It looked as if a composer had joined the battle. He grabbed a telescope to see what was causing the strange power.

"That...*wretch!* I want him dead! **NOW! NOW!!** *NOW!!!*"

The scope shattered on the ground.

Sadie concentrated hard to keep some stragglers from coming into her room. The prince was with her, aiding her and Enzu. Her newfound ease helped her control the flames, even imbuing the prince's sword. The smell of burnt fur wrinkled her nose, but she persisted through the violence. A cloud of smoke appeared inside. A silhouette within. The prince advanced to strike it, only to be struck fatally instead. A ghastly cough of red and foam excreting from his mouth. Unconscious on the floor. Spurting out copious amounts of blood.

"A pleasure to meet you," Edling said to the young girl. She screamed, trying to ignite him, only to lose. A dagger's hilt connected to her head. Rendered like the prince's condition. Smoke explodes again, blasting back Enzu. And they were gone. Leaving the Essent.

Alone with a dying heir.

Lines upon lines strewn across. Hands guiding them. The wind blasted back his long coat. Both eyes: Cerulean.

The incantation is nearly complete.

"Agh!" Tekla and the others screamed as a horde of Mairu tackled them out of the way and off the top to a deadly drop. A follow-up of Tarwini archers taking aim at their target. Down below, Birati's elite unfurled their banners, singing out in song to ward those who came to finish the job on her and the others. The aristarch hastily concocted potions on their broken ligaments and spilled gore.

But not all could be saved.

"This is it!" Milos exclaimed happily, ready to unleash the scroll's power. A violent antidote. An unquenchable marvel. The remedy.

"*Fire!*" a voice ordered from behind.

The scribe turned porcupine. A volley riddled his back.

"No…please…Not like this…" his voice was weak. Spitting out red life. Collapsing on his knees, the scroll's final words were left hovering above, out of reach, waiting to be uttered. Vision receding. Heart slowing. Skin-numbing. That same sensation before.

The denial of redemption.

Goldenrod can't save me now…

"The scroll, he stopped conjuring from it. I can barely feel his nous. Did he…?" Evren said in a low voice.

Leandro advanced to the top, carving through all in his way in a carnivorous manner; many from Klaring leaped to their deaths from the top floors. Tekla, gravely injured, tried to get to Milos, ignoring the aristarch's request to stand down, but Klaring's Mairu held them back. Birati's own men struggled with the pushback. Sibi released an onslaught of spells, but somehow they just kept coming.

The World-Eater, now at the gates, prepared its charge, leading Klaring to victory. No amount of spells, ballistics, or cuts could bring it down or even slow it. The sheer speed of regeneration was too much for the warriors. Udalann's banner army couldn't do anything to resist them.

Holding the line as best they could.

Drained eyes; losing color. The scroll reverts back to its original format. Falling onto the ground. There was no way he could do it all over again. The vision of the world blurred too much to focus. Pain: too great. Missing most of the vitals. A slow death.

His veils tried to keep him awake.

"*WHERE'S THE DAMN CALVARY?!*" Mulberry screamed.

"*It is us, and we have failed...*" Aquamarine replied.

"*The Heralds won't have us or the Primes,*" Cobalt declared.

"*We are together. To the end...*" Auburn whispered.

The scroll of Goldenrod shakes. She's trying to do the impossible. It does not work. The world is toneless. Crestfallen colors of the veil. Everything looks monochrome.

"I...guess...this is it," Milos utters, trying not to choke. With the last of his energy, he grabbed the scroll, held it out, and—

"NO!" Leandro shouted as he had finished paving the way to aid the dying scribe. His voice boomed throughout the world.

Milos ripped the scroll in half, instantly unleashing its power.

I see it all.
Your face.
Your words.
Your name.
I know.

The sky was covered with those same threads again, in a faster formation. Soporific incantations can take a backseat from here. A clockwork box covering Klaring's armies instantaneously. The Orkes, the Tarwini, the Mairu, Ard Rex, and the World-Eater are all caught inside the mystical box. Strange phantasm gears rolling. Rolling. Rolling. Faster. Faster. The box closes in on itself. Consuming within. Self-imploding. Nothing could escape. Everything is trapped in one go.

"Sorry to see you go, Father," Edling laughed, appearing outside the box's grasp. Sadie's unconscious body was held under his pit. The prince's grand prize.

"GET ME OUT OF HERE, WELP!"

"I'll continue your legacy," Edling finished, vanishing from sight.

The box squeezed everything inside. Lights scattering in all directions. Screams on mute. Then, the box just vanished, leaving no trace of life behind.

The armies of Gottlir: victorious.

The war is won, yet all is lost.

Chapter 14

†

Opus

Sunk low. It is all a blur. More like a prism. Colors splitting into every network. A beautiful sensation. Endless. Perpetual. But this is darkness. Wandering a desert blinded by achromatic vibrations.

The eyes need a place to fixate.

"A matter of time before we met again. Wrong to let you go. Maybe this is familial punishment. Can't check out so easily. How are your sleeping patterns? Is insomnia massaging your retinas? It's like staring into a chasm, right? Little pulls. Small tugs. Tempting, isn't it? Eternal sleep. There's music here. Who needs color when you can hear the notes, the tones, the melody—it's your theme! Fancy yourself an adapter? You're no composer. Striving for a manuscript culture? You're no librarian. You need freedom. It is your birthright. This land…it's yours to navigate."

"What nonsense is this noise?"

Sconces lit; ashes rising; smoldering; she pours truth.

"This isn't nonsense, boy; this is the grand quiet. You finally met it. Now we can speak in private. No distractions. No disruptions. Welcome to *The Black*. The White led you here."

"Is this the last door? Grand death? It feels tender…"

"Death? Yes, but not the last resignation. You went out like a true martyr. But it's no masterpiece to frame. Less than remarkable."

"Why? Am I not a hero?"

"Selfish child, this is failure—absolute failure! Do you really want this to be the last exit? No resistance? A husk on permanent furlough? Strange that no Prime is here. No Messengers answer either. Where are your beloved veils? Your little harem. Want this to be an eternal dream? We could make it this way. Your choice."

"I want out of this bleak geography!"

"Who are you kidding? Your black slumber just dropped a cataclysm greater than any of the Usurper's volatile experiments. You failed everyone—millions are dead because of your failure. Is this how you pay Iberitus? Her gifts give you bounty from the waters, friends in all zones, and a love that wants to bear fruit with you. You did her a kindness by melding into the void; you saved her great shame. No woman could ever love you again; great regret."

"Is this forever? No way to give back again? I remember…I have more in me! I am no joke! No court jester! I am on the verge of grand, now that I think about it! That's right. Grand! No imagination here. Xantho shines on me! Out of The Black. Into the light! Iberitus, always!"

Sconces brighten. Blind rage investigates the wandering pneuma.

"Do you think you deserve to stay a little longer? Maybe you just want to look into the past again. Maybe you crave some more sleepless nights under a tree atop that hill. Ever lackadaisical. Your mind is full of rashes you keep scratching. Crimson marks. How unbecoming. What would your brood think? Think that's a trait they need to acquire to be closer to you? Maybe you won't stay long enough. No one can keep you grounded, King of Skies. You are cruising over every element for your own amusement. A rebrand: skylark. That is what you are!"

"Spin your tales for lame ears! I'm getting off this ride."

A smile so bright, shining, and blinding the wandering pneuma.

Maybe this is the way after all.

"You think you got this?! Fine. I snatched you before envious Sulfur sniffed you out. Or Salt's viciousness. Or Mercury's tyranny. Chroma? Oh, you're an item for auction; without exception, every shade, hue, and tone seeks to claim you in perpetuity. None know of this little escapade. And they never will. Save for the Palatial Usurper, but it won't utter a syllable. Clandestine plots. Others—legends—know also. We pave new roads beyond the stars. Made of crystal and burning rainbows."

"Release me! I am duty-bound! All for the greater good! Far more critical than I! Service to the girl! Home…somewhere we all need to be. Warm and cozy and full of laughter. The passions of sex, of adoration, of kindred. The natural passing of time. Purpose. Before it all ends up here. Before the gloaming…the departure of daylight…"

"Let the rivers flow through your veins. The mountains rebuild your bones. Our grace upon you."

"Our?"

A faceless figure emerged from the void, beside the other of vicious words. Clothes and armor imbued with everything that personified color. Beautiful in every measure. Moving pigments.

"I feel I know you…"

"Flourish," the figure said. A voice like no other.

The sconces blew out. A cold wind joined to shake the nerves. The limbic system's cup overflows—this is a good place to stop.

No more words to be said.

Only acquiesce; finalized; paid in full.

Nerve endings fought for attention. Each chord struck a note of pain for each breath taken. Horizontal lights seeping in. This is a good sign. Voices in the atmosphere. A small draft comforting the skin. Hints of warmth. Two windows to the mind open, then a blink.

This is a place to be. Alive.

A little golem saw the eyes flutter. They strain to stay open. Mouth, earthbound, to the poor visage. No words, but a quivering smile. A quick roll to the door to garner attention from the guard. They stepped in, peering at the sad sight; a smile at first, but...

"Impossible...We...We saw you murdered. Felt no pulse. Saw no soul," Tekla said, her words breaking, overjoyed. "What did you have to do to come back to the land of the living?"

"...I just...needed to keep walking. The blind leading the blind," Milos winced, his lips parched and chapped from dehydration. She poured some water over a cloth and dabbed it along his bleeding cracks.

"You just got back. Don't want to accidentally drown you," Tekla said in a voice *too* gentle to be true.

She'll make a good wife.

Members of Clay and Powder arrived: an aristarch and a composer. The alchemist checked his vitals, brewed some potions, and changed his dressings while the composer played a song on her violin, healing his spirit so that body and soul could synchronize. She remarked on his mental stability for such a traumatic experience. Even the aristarch was speechless—technically he was declared dead by blood loss.

"There are wonders that go beyond my own understanding, but this is all I need to understand," Leandro said, entering with the Newts. "You. Alive. 'By the composition' is what you would say, right?"

"Did we win?" Milos asked.

A temporary silence. The Newts' rambunctious behavior was not aligned with this current state of affairs.

"Yes, but the one you call Sadie has been taken captive. Scouts of mine spotted her with Edling's remnants that were heading back to The Mouth. My son, Prince Ramirus, of my kingdom, my heir…catatonic."

"…"

"Milos," Sibi approached, "Nature's blessings upon you firstly for whoever resurrected you wholly. Goldenrod was displaced from your person when you collapsed, and most of our healers tried to bring you back to no avail. I am sure she and the others will be happy when they see you again.

"But…it has come to our attention that the king's scouts have discovered the remains of The Ternion Pilgrims. They sealed the few breached entrances with Singer and F&C, but we need to go as there are reports of stragglers roaming about in small bands. We *cannot* let Grand M, Kabir, and Nagy's deaths become public. Only to those closest, like the village. Poor Riha and Kosey.

Embrace education   Mentor the incapable   Pursue balance

CLAY & POWDER

"We fear it could rile up The Mouth, sending multiple levels all at once if they know, or bolster the Usurper's private force. If they catch wind and feed this critical information to their liege…who knows…Lusura might come to finish the job, and they have the tech to minimize casualties."

Leandro stood quiet.

"I understand," Milos softly said, "I need to get back to Riha…after I retrieve Sadie."

He tried picking himself up, but the aristarch held him back.

"You're in no condition, fool!"

"I thank you for keeping my pneuma afloat, but I have to leave as soon as possible. The fact I ripped a Cerulean scroll means trouble is already on the way from Celanjung—Evren knows my every move now. Every wrinkle in my face, every word I speak, every little sensation I feel, she knows firsthand."

Milos looked around for his quiver. Daru excitedly handed it to him. "They all scrambled, but I know how many you keep and found them all! I even tried to patch the ripped Ceruleans, but it wouldn't work…"

Milos smiled, thanking him for his tireless efforts. His hands smooth over the patched holes in his quiver; a paraplegic, at best, if he had survived. *I guess the blessing goes when my pneuma goes. Prime's willing it is back so I may not lose any of the ladies. That'd be a sad day.* Every veil materialized, omitting Argent, and welcomed him back eagerly. Except Mulberry. She simply stares. Speechless.

With Goldenrod in hand, Milos uttered the ancient words, healing the remnants of his broken state. He sat on the edge of the bed, his back arched, and his belly ached. He thinks of the prince, The Ternion Pilgrims, and his now failing mission to someone he made a sacred vow to. He intended to keep his word. To himself. To Sadie. To Marisha and the enigmatic prism wielder.

The Newts withdrew from the castle to aid in the cleanup. They weren't sure how long they would be about the realm before returning home. Days. Months. Possibly years. What must be done *must* be done.

"Can I see Prince Ramirus?" Milos asked.

Leandro led the way to his personal chambers. There was an extraordinary surplus of soldiers guarding the doors, the windows—*by the composition of red salt!*—just about anywhere that had an opening to finish the job. On his bed lay the prince. Motionless. An aristarch's medicine failed to revive. A composer, singing songs for an empty world. Sibi, new to the title of magister, knew nothing of resurrection. And never will. An affront to the teachings of Nature.

Goldenrod should do the trick.

Milos conjured the golden-veiled woman's power again for the prince. She hovered over his body. Something is amiss. It wasn't that she would not heal but *could* not heal. Returning back to the scroll.

"That's…impossible!" Milos shuddered. His fists boil. He looked over. Leandro's face: overshadowed with deep lines of melancholy. Scowling. Pressing his tongue to the roof of his mouth.

What could be done now?

Enzu patted Milos, trying to go for the incantation again, but with his help. He tried again, partnered by the clay golem, whose many gems started to glow and amplify the scroll. The veiled woman appeared again, shining brighter than before. Hovering over the body. Still, she couldn't heal his mortal wound, but a message came back to Milos from authoritative Aquamarine.

Is this the extent of their power?!

"This isn't just a physical wound; his very essence has been both splintered *and* absorbed! The Pictfero in Klaring are capable of blunting the powers of Chroma should they make physical contact with the body. This could've happened to me...and there'd be no way to come back..." Milos explained, his voice trailing, seeing the terrible power these twisted cousins procured somehow.

"Are you saying...there's nothing we can do to bring him back?" Leandro asked. A balled hand at his side, shaking uncontrollably.

"Only one way: destroy the attacker who holds the essence within them. And since I'm already a hunted man, I'm heading straight into Klaring to hunt Calbhach's heir, soon to be king. Now."

Tekla protested the wild idea. Suicide, she called it. Leandro remained quiet until he ordered a contingent to go with Milos.

But he declined.

"If I go alone, it'll be easier to dispatch them in one go with this," he said, holding out the largest scroll he had: Auburn. The king of Udalann's power was concealed within. Its wax seal remains unbroken. It was also time to summon the powers of the prism. All or nothing.

"How much time has passed since the siege ended?"

"Half a day," Tekla said somberly.

He just noticed daylight had begun its transition to set for Melano.

Time and action were imperative.

"I'll need quick transportation. I know Klaring, they can't cut through to the desert just yet; I'm sure they're hugging the mountain path still for the quickest route.

Another day, maybe two, and I'll never be able to locate them in time."

Leandro ordered Tekla to give him the fastest jumart, but Milos required two, along with a cart to sleep in while they were on the move. Enzu would guide them while he slept in the back.

Preparations were made, rations were given, and wishes of luck were sent to the young scribe to go along into hostile lands. Tekla protested the idea of sending him alone. He just rose from the dead, but only they can rest in peace.

"We did all that we could, all that he asked…we place our faith in him," Leandro said, watching him, with his Essent and vehicle, disappear from naked sight. Then, he walked back to sit by Ramirus's side. The only thing he could do now before returning to the castle. There were still piles of bodies to account for and an empty royal court with only fatherless heirs. Numerous scribes arrived to send letters of regard to any living relative to the fallen that could be identified.

Tekla stood there, looking out to Klaring, alone. Something clicked in her head. She did something that she never dreamed of doing: she prayed to whoever might be listening. The words were crude but sincere. Gravel, shoots of vines, and blood sprouted from the ground. A strange shape molded before her, not unlike a human, not unlike a beast. Chimeric. The coagulated blood burned into an orange liquid. It dripped profusely from the pervasive nature.

"What is this?!" she said, eyes wide, cold water in her veins.

"This is your testament, newborn," it said. The makeshift pipes in its throat vibrate, echoing out the words. Ultra. Rare. Revenant of carnage. A voiced scripture of blood letters. Birth of the prodigious. Her faculties are open for truth. This was no pseudo "third eye" of the mind awakening. It is a revelation. Or maybe it was a revolution. Either way, the perversion opened a path to the principle of plenitude.

Her newfound guide. Vakienda.

Hunger. That's the universal thought here. Better not collapse from starvation, or you'd be next on the menu. Fat, short, thin, tall—doesn't matter; protein is protein. Fat is fat. Bones? Scrumptious marrow. Filled with collagen. Stuffed with glycine. Topped with conjugated linoleic acid. All that regenerative cartilage just waiting to be consumed!

Just a spark. That's it! One. Little. Spark. Then, we can resume the party. Smell that? That pungent aroma is reminiscent of butter. Deep breath now. Oh, yes. Delicious tension.

Spittle and drool descend behind the cart's path. *Never tasted a calf like this one. Oh, she's so supple; look at that soft skin. Just a taste.* Hands clutch the bars. A rancid tongue reaches in for living sweetbreads.

How can one savor when its organ is greeted by the fifth-degree?

Uniform cackles along the line.

"Serves you right!" a Tarwini shouted, revealing broken fangs.

The lecherous Mairu fell on his knees, holding the mouth that once held a tongue. Green and angry eyes enjoyed the sight.

Suffer. More. Bastard! Go to hell!!!

Ears picked up the sounds of gallops. An acrid odor arrives; large, terrible, beautiful. Some sort of Capra, with screwed horns and long hairs, bashed the ogre, much smaller than this creature, off the edge of the path. Down into the snowy trees, eaten by mist and altitude, a gift for those who dare touch the property of his lordship. No one questioned it.

Shrugs, and the march continued.

"I hope you bring that same fire to my chambers later," Edling said, sneering at the cage's occupant.

"Touch me, and it won't be your tongue I'll set on fire," Sadie retorted, looking below his beltline.

"Don't threaten me with a grand time."

A glob of spit ejected from the cage, only to land on the beast's foul fur. It remained unfazed. Dumb and indifferent.

"Well, I'd love to stay and serenade you, but I have to declare my ascension to the throne. This loss is a win for me. Best prepare yourself in your new home soon. You'll give me many heirs until you're old and dry…then I can give you to the Tarwini for breeding. Maybe you'll lose consciousness before they grow tired and toss you for nourishment to the Mairu. They'll at least ensure your body won't go to waste; save for fecal matter," Edling concluded, "Keep that fire stoked."

The goat monstrosity felt his heels kick in. Full steam ahead. Rats and ogres and grayskins leaped out of the way so as not to become victims of gravity like the one they witnessed. No way to tell if it was a fast death or slow one. Strong anatomy might delay the inevitable. Broken bones might just offer paralysis instead. There are ravenous Winzangi in these parts. Stalking, bottomless pits. No evidence; you won't find a knuckle left behind. Or excreted.

Green pearls catching jaundice orbs. They may have lost this battle, but they were ready to snap into another. The ones escorting the cart kept their vision forward at all times. No words, no peeps, no snorts. On their waists, an array of small arms, ruby and glistening in the light. A fly gliding onto one for respite. Cut with no effort. Split into two.

No coin purses here or geodi. Only blood-knives and cutthroats.

I wonder if he's looking for me...He made me a promise...

Knees to the chin, she buried her face, trying not to weep. Heaven knows what'll happen if she makes any sounds of desperation. There are a million ways to make someone shut up; a billion if you're a woman.

Whispers in the ears; vicarious transmissions from one mind to another. Each directs a scene while another continues the play—only one was absent. She was *always* in absentia when the going got tough. Sure, she lashed a few sharp words and used her lovely fingers to try to garrote the mind, but he still kept her around despite the others' protests. Small affirmations from his veils. Stressors subside.

Hormesis breaks. Hormesis rebuilds. Slow and gradual. Stronger.

The mind hones in, lapping up the sweet, endearing messages with curiosity of its own. An inherited trait picked up from the girl.

His words to his rainbow:

"How come I haven't fallen apart yet?"

"You're an impregnable fortress of diamond atoms; always in the pink, sir," Aquamarine transmitted. *"The savagery of 'fero' doesn't apply to you like distant cousins—yours is of iron."*

"Do you remember your tribe? Are they as authentic as you?"

No more transmissions. Best see for himself when he appeases, or locates, her hierarchy. He assumes a well-founded pilgrimage is in order.

Another color waits.

"Am I strong enough to finish this?"

"Your celiac plexus is much tougher than when the Zebecan struck it," Cobalt transmitted, *"as is the rest of your sinews and tendons—strong, able, a physical instrument of capability."*

"Do you remember your tribe? Are they as fearless as you?"

Again, no more transmissions. Best to see for himself when he appeases, or locates, her hierarchy. He assumes a courageous pilgrimage is in order.

Another color waits; what an intense look this one has.

"Reminds me when I'm near the boiling point."

"You best believe it, and I love watching those colorful discs burn a hole into your target," Mulberry transmitted. *"I've seen you at your worst, more than the others. All your organs are angry, wanting to spread out to voice—sometimes fight—for their rights, only held by some robust, unwavering lynchpin keeping them all held together!"*

"..."

"Don't waver on me now, scribe. Hierarchy won't respect that. We curse the wicked, the vile, and the ignoble for drowning! You're currently racing to evil, but they have no love for one another after that display before; you cracked wide previous strengths. But your character has weakened...I'll refuse your existence if you continue this way."

"Why?"

A sultry reply emanated, *"Because you let that silly Mozmina kiss you and get away. You waited too long to pull back; a privilege only for Princess Natalina. Naughty. But no matter the sex, we can't help ourselves from keen interest. Every first is always a last. Every relationship begins to die the moment it has begun."*

Silence. Another color waits.

She cannot speak. She reminds him of blooming flowers, gentle zephyrs, light rain, and laughing babes. Tetri, that's the season within—no doubt in his mind. No questions for this one:

"Hey."

She smiles at him. Goldenrod. Little gold bunny. They continued to stare at one another. He couldn't resist her smile. Identical to Natalina's. More childlike, perhaps. Then...a question did come to mind:

"Will we ever converse?"

A little shrug, a roll of the eyes to act coy, then a brighter smile.

One day, I hope, he thought. Always mending. Afraid—but unafraid—when Sulfur came into play. Hopeful. Wanting the best.

The last color waits.

He felt her aura. He never got a chance to really know her. Then, another color was beside her. It surprised him, but not them. They *were* sisters after all. Their contrast was a sight. Meteors and comets orbiting one's head. A strange, wild, horned mask over the other. He didn't want to talk anymore. He isn't sure what to say. Discomfort. Shy. Yeah, he was definitely bashful of the wild one's empty gaze. Until...

"Don't," Auburn transmitted, looking over to the masked one. *"What if it was only for that one time? You might blind him. I won't forgive. I cannot!"*

His eyes see her sister's hand reaching for his body. Just like her mask, wild looks from adjacent veils. Cobalt and Aquamarines: peeled. Goldenrod panicked. Mulberry…

"Reap his pneuma! Desecrate it! Foul his body!" Argent roars.

More antagonism from Silver-White.

"Learn your place," Aquamarine transmitted.

"Withdraw your predatory hunger," Cobalt transmitted.

"Let me rearrange her syllabary," Mulberry transmitted.

Beams of light swirl around Goldenrod; no merriment here.

"Quiet!" Auburn transmitted, *"ALL OF YOU!"*

They all looked in unison at Milos, a blue hand over his heart, physically touching his chest. "I can still see."

"They're coming," Cerulean transmitted. *"Steel yourself. Almost there. They've crossed the border already. Utilize my ability before we are separated. This, right here,"* she emphasized, putting her hand on his heart, *"that is potential—don't misuse it. Inscribe a new direction in your tapestry. Break the cycle. I—no—WE are with you. My Masters, they have watched you since you came to the Spire. I will tell you my name."*

Cerulean strokes the back of her hand against his cheek, and whispers her identity to Milos. An enormous honor. Auburn sighs in relief and tries to do the same, but her hand goes through him, and cannot remember who she once was before the sacrifice. She hates this.

"We'll find a way. I've never broken a promise!" he nearly shouts, saying to the rest, "I will locate the tribes, appease the Primes, and make Iberitus safer!"

Some laughed. Some stayed quiet; they nodded proudly.

And some...

"You better, or I'm going to turn you into a lovely 'ice-floe' for several days in the pelagic!" Mulberry barked.

His vision watched as the kaleidoscope circulated in the air—back into the quiver they go. The vicious words of Argent become moderate.

"Ask me that same question."

"...I know your tribe. I'll keep my promise to them, but I'll never summon you. The lustrous Prime will never claim me!"

"I have seen your disembowelment. Your silly Goldenrod will be useless when the time comes. Your veils will be useless against them, but not me. It is inevitable. My queen will come to claim before Cerulean."

"Against who, liar?!"

"The Sleep..."

No more words to transmit. A man left alone with infinite thoughts. *Neither Argent nor the spiders, or Sky Blue, will ever claim me! Marisha...she could revive me again. And the other...*

An oily breeze pushes strands of hair over his face. Too distracted to move them. That's alright. Cerulean's hand remedied the distraction. A little caress on the cheek as a bonus. *Lucia, what are your sister's names?* Back into the parchment. Enzu, concerned the entire time, kept a close watch on Milos's condition. He pinches the bridge of his nose. "Don't look at me like that. Well-intentioned promises should never be broken. I really have to stop making so damn many. No more after this."

This cart is hauling a heavy load. When does the tension get relieved? Rolling, rolling, rolling. Little vapors come out to play. Brisk air. Edging into the dry desert. Scorched skin earth. Rain fails to land a single drop before drying out.

Let this kingdom burn unto itself.

"What do you mean it's stuck?! Wedge it out already, idiots!" One Mairu ordered a group of Tarwini's in the distance.

Flames spurting in excess. Human flamethrower. An angry veil to assist, but she was beginning to fade.

"Keep using her! She's at her limit anyway! Then, I'm coming in there to see how tough you *really* are, fake-Somdirian," the Mairu said.

"Are you alright?!" Sadie asked the fiery spirit.

Opaque, translucent, murky, transparent. Blurred, crystalline, dim…gone. *Don't leave me now!* A voice like no other enters her mind. It is distorted, but small visions of a prismatic entity appear in quick flashes. Her hands shake, and her fingers transform into unnatural metals briefly before reverting. Amnesia wipes clean the ancient enigma.

Gargantuan movements draw near. A frightened girl turns to look to see the causation, the dread, this eclipse! A missing eye, broken tusks, burly, hungry, *horny*!

"Dad…help me," Sadie whimpered.

"Father is here, child," the ogre replied pervasively, grabbing a handful of "lower meat."

Green eyes: wide and teary. Near bloodshot. A death cry erupts.

Startled beyond all measure. His upper body shot up. Head spinning in all directions. The jumarts neighed, halting to a complete stop. He leaped out with Enzu. There they were, the surviving remnants of Klaring, far off on another trail, while he was on his own mountain path, and a grand chasm between them. He had the higher ground, the element of surprise still on his side. Searching, searching, searching…*a walking bridge?* On his side, the only way over. Pensive thoughts of ensuring the gear isn't depleted before the end of the showdown.

Let the Heralds hear my call, the Primes announce my grandeur, and may all villains know no peace!

"ENZU! *NOW IS OUR TIME!*" Milos shouted, holding out his arm. The bracelet's gear charges an uproar of electrical shockwaves. Raw elements, among them: glowing, whining, flowing into Enzu to absorb. The clay man's gems beamed in a frenzy, dispersing into Milos's gear, networking into the diamond. The artifact of Sesathoth. Golden-amber energy crackled from his fingers, flowing up his arm, slowly transforming his skin into unnatural metals. His teeth grit, silently cursing the power that began to envelop him whole. *No way of backing out now!* Ancient symbols awaken. Markings on his apparel. Tight. It was so tight! Tubes, gears, plates—this was too much! Where did his face go?! What mask conceals it?! There's no scribe here…

"*Flourish under Spectrum and Shade. Unite the Clans,*" a deep, ancient voice reverberated inside the mask.

The animal of chroma and automation sprints across the edge of the cliff. Transformed into something fantastical described only in fables. Lost identity. He has forgotten all his aches, the voluptuous voices that tug at his heart, and all antiquated musings. This fashioned organism creates its own terrifying screams from hollowed-out lungs.

Where finality resides.

"What is that sound?!" a rat-man squealed, covering his ears. An ogre saw it across the way, high up, jetting along the cliff's edge, with puffs of steam and electromagnetic colors chasing after it.

"Enemy sighted!" it shouted, pointing it out to the others. Orkes lined up to prepare a volley with any projectile that wasn't broken. Tarwini archer's assembling—nocking.

Who could say what this spectre was that inhabited Milos's body, contorting his skin into strange glyphs? Untamed machinations. It was beyond riled, however, and the quarry below could not comprehend the incoming magnitude of its power.

One hand up, no need to remove the quiver, a scroll telepathically flung into the palm; the first strike: Lucia of Cerulean. Stretching its length across the air, with no need for incantations, *this* power made Chromatic abilities materialize instantly! Waves of wild, masked skeletal archers appeared—their aim already true, and their arrows wanting. Unending flurries from Sky Blue's wave! Each needle finds its target. Each dart evaporates its targets pneuma, vita, and nous! The physical dropped without marks. Strangely close to that of Argent's.

The cage exploded in a fit. Sadie was held by the waist by the stirred ogre under his pit. He watched the chaos unfold. A quarter of their strength is down. By one man? Was this a man or a new species of the mountains? What fury birthed this carnage? "Kill him! Kill him, already! The first to strike him down gets five of my own blood-knives!" it roared. Saliva frothed from the mouth. Pins for pupils.

Endothelial cells line up blood and lymphatic vessels, signaling nitric oxide to the muscles for vasodilation—a pump for the ages.

One band of Orkes set aflame the bridge.

No way of crossing now by foot.

A blast of steam from the shoulder's dreadful pauldron. Ripples cross the geared eyes. Visual calculus with strong odds. Plenty to go around. Slow. Time took some rest. The fires raged quietly. One could appreciate the range of colors that ate at the breaking wood. Heels sprung; calves tightened; quads holding it all together with core; King of Skies on the move! He surfed over the burned bridge on his nimbus transport. Instant conveyance. Nimble. Agile. The gears whining cooled down by the activated diamond. The ancient voice repeats. Stronger.

More volleys scream their arrival through the wind. Weaving and bobbing. Two scrolls unravel in the hands simultaneously. Strike two and three mixing together: Cobalt and Mulberry. Savage apparitions shot out like a frenzied mitrailleuse, tackling down the rats, the tusks, the half-bloods, beaten into oblivion, encased in beatific glass to suffocate inside of. Call of The White.

"Retreat!" a Tarwini bawled out.

The roaches tried to scramble for cover, for sanctuary, for anything that might save their hides! The path was too narrow. Too open! Why did they go this way, to begin with?! Many cursed the Pictfero prince for leading them astray! Like a falling star, *he* was upon them. Blinking. Teleporting. Aether-walker! Hurling his solid, braced fists into their faces to contort. Main target: discovered and locked for strike four. ***Ka-boom!*** Another blast of steam from the pauldron. More voltage from the diamond. Geared eyes calculated a one-hundred percent success rate. Categorical. Incoming damage of seismic proportions. Metal collided with bone and tusks. Neck broken. Ninety-degree angle. Time took another rest. He could see The White overtaking the Mairu's being. Limp.

Another blink!

Grabbed the frantic parcel in time. No marks, bruises, scars, or violations. "Milos! Is…that you?" Sadie asked in his arms. In her eyes, this was half-man, half-machine acting in place of the scribe. But he came. A promise kept to uphold. Burdens to carry. Refuge till the end.

Her champion.

He remained quiet, focused still on the many who still had courage in their battled hearts. Another scroll hovered. Its wax seal breaking—a satisfying sound. Armageddon appeared.

"Let me return the favor. Justice, my sword," she transmitted. The scroll flew into the sky. Higher. **Higher!** Longer. **Larger!** It overshadowed everything on the cliff. Arrows stopped shooting. Boulders stopped flinging. Attention—all—to the sky. Sadie studied the situation. Recalling images from the Book of Revelations. 6:8.

It was an awesome sight.

Red burning energies encompassed the frame. The ancient letters vibrated. Angry whispers in the wind; Auburn's. Soot flakes off the parchment. The letters inflamed. Terrible ejections! Directionless. The comets came! The meteors came! Fire! Sadistic love falling from the sky! Burning asteroids colliding with upheld boulders, hesitant limbs, all around! Wave after wave after wave. Grand anarchy! Bodies falling into the chasm, greeted by soft snow and edged timber, and who-knows-what waited at the bottom with vacant bellies. So ravenous. Cold-blooded apexes slithering in layers of snakeskin, quite possibly. Hypnotic eyes. Sipping on aperitifs. What an extraordinary day for a free meal that comes tenderized, crisped, boiled, baked, oh, *sweet* marinades of steaming gore in a variety!

Forget the geodi, the dungeon artifacts, the powders, the scrolls, the powders *on* the scrolls, the dumb Primes, the stupid Messengers, the crowns, the maps, the treasures, and the guilds. What's this new word going around—God? Right, forget that too. True nature is restless. Oh, and who gives a damn about pneuma-vita-nous?!

True nature offends.

Indiscriminate. The final flame came upon those who would prey on the weak. Conflagration takes its bow before the curtain call. Blinding. Leveling. Just another piece of history, of this war, to warn the children not to play with matches or angry tempers.

Or sleepless writers.

The diamond's power started to subside. The vision of body horror returns to its reasonable state of lightly marred—and tired—flesh. Familiar eyes. There they are! One auburn, and one…half blue and half purple? Undertones of red? Strange sort of burgundy.

"You alright, lass?" Milos asked, looking down, half awake. Immense power had taken a toll on his body. Little strands of white peeking from the sideburns. She further tightened her grip around his neck, her voice cracking, the words unintelligible, but he could hear her gratitude. Enzu hopped on her head, smiling. Glad to know amplification worked so well on his accessory.

So many miles together. Even more, as they crossed the sky. What a lovely vision of the land. It seemed so peaceful. Sadie became further envious of the birds.

Whispers from the quiver.

Milos looked behind. Then back. No need for a double take on these homing missiles. He was too exhausted to care. Happy to know he at least got her far away back to Gottlir's realm.

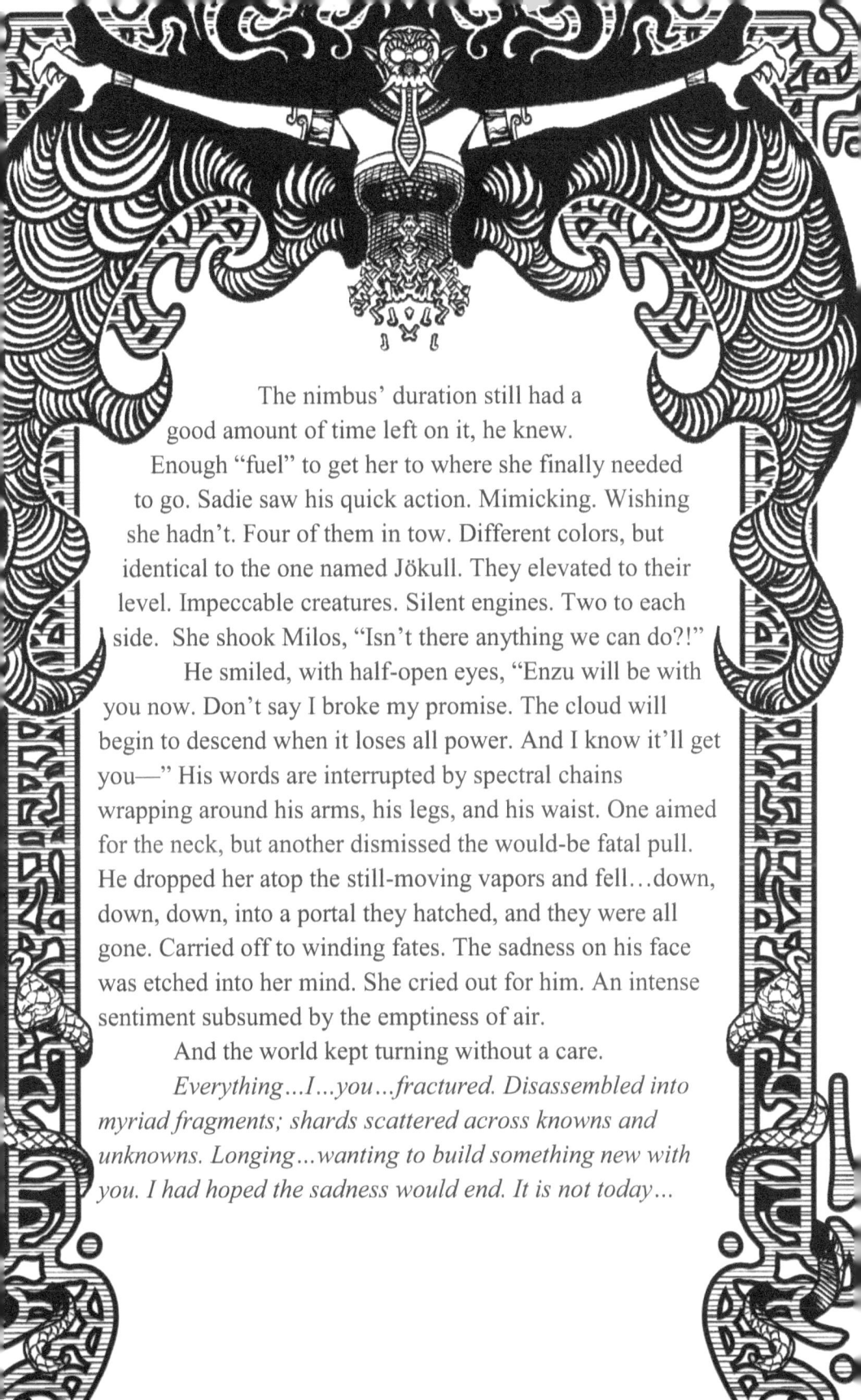

The nimbus' duration still had a good amount of time left on it, he knew.

Enough "fuel" to get her to where she finally needed to go. Sadie saw his quick action. Mimicking. Wishing she hadn't. Four of them in tow. Different colors, but identical to the one named Jökull. They elevated to their level. Impeccable creatures. Silent engines. Two to each side. She shook Milos, "Isn't there anything we can do?!"

He smiled, with half-open eyes, "Enzu will be with you now. Don't say I broke my promise. The cloud will begin to descend when it loses all power. And I know it'll get you—" His words are interrupted by spectral chains wrapping around his arms, his legs, and his waist. One aimed for the neck, but another dismissed the would-be fatal pull. He dropped her atop the still-moving vapors and fell…down, down, down, into a portal they hatched, and they were all gone. Carried off to winding fates. The sadness on his face was etched into her mind. She cried out for him. An intense sentiment subsumed by the emptiness of air.

And the world kept turning without a care.

Everything…I…you…fractured. Disassembled into myriad fragments; shards scattered across knowns and unknowns. Longing…wanting to build something new with you. I had hoped the sadness would end. It is not today…

Chapter 15

†

Platinum

They exited from the blasted crater grounds. Feet kicking up mud, blood, urine, and other lost organs the fray accomplished to scatter. Lifeless eyes with earth-caked faces. These are the new minerals to fertilize the land. But they will get destroyed soon enough.

A warrior fell on one knee, gripping the chestplate. Second time within a day. Untouched by their foes. This peculiarity agitated the commander. Weakness, like this, should never exist in front of others.

He raised his voice, cursing at the fallen fighter. No remorse. Verbal diarrhea. The line kept marching while the crusty, cantankerous, yawping commander showed no signs of slowing down—over and over and over, feeling like one was about to become tarred and feathered.

One lone flash of light vertically came down on him. The marching line stopped to look. One cough, two gags, then division. Piles fell down the middle.

Drips, splats, and thuds.

The fallen warrior stands with a bloody ax in the same space where the commander's center of gravity once stood. Someone from the line was about to confront the nightmare, but a fellow comrade placed his hand on the shoulder, shaking his head, and the march continued.

Good thing too, because inside the fallen soldier's other hand was a large serrated sword that didn't mind a soak. It was apparent this was not only a Mairu but a woman with long silver hair protruding from her helmet. She stood inside the pool of gore—desensitized—to gaze at the stars. Utterly heartbroken. Some part of her had died long ago. She felt that same affliction again. Worse this time. No words. No fluttering eyelids. Just irregular heartbeats. What a cruel rhythm it kicked to. What she would give to enjoy another day of rainbow trout, wild leeks, and morels with that once-scared little boy with the fancy eyes.

She turned back around to join her brothers-in-arms, thinking to herself, *If only I were there...*

South, that same feeling caught another ticker. Yes, a second time too, within a day. Even royalty dissolves—some faster than others, tragically. Pain, the kind that longs for anesthesia, that's what he felt. His towering body buckled under its own weight. The ground quaked, and everyone fell with him. Flight license revoked, for now, sire; it's time to see the aristarch. Or the ossuary...

"It hurts!" he cried out in pain. A terrible, terrible torment. Hot, searing blood comes in for a cooldown. Dynasty collapse. They ran to assist him. This wasn't in the cards! The wall is still up. Flaming about! News came regarding the grand victory Gottlir attained at the fort.

So, why was *this* happening?!

"Sir, speak to me. What's wrong?!" Aruna exclaimed, her eyes looking for physical injuries unknown to her.

Pain sprints in like a torrent. Waves accumulate in succession. Ten thousand needles lancing the heart. Fast and sadistic. No mercy here for linked ones. This must be what sad violins go through.

He clenched his chest some more, his hat fell, and he was sweating—yes, sweating!!! His race doesn't sweat normally! Only the gravest of ailments cause such a reaction. The captain was petrified. The adapter was petrified. By the composition of red salt, *everyone* was petrified!

Thunderstruck!

Heaving with labored lungs—what's one to do?

"Milos! **My son**! Gone! His spirit is *gone*! The tethers have severed!" Birati howled in pain. Nerves feeling the sensation of cold; a new experience. Windbags collapsing, barely expanding. He felt useless. The body worked against him with lurched spasms. It was better to toss his body as chum into the Akrav than continue living.

Victory came at what cost?

One life, for the many, never bothered anyone until it was one close to home. It's always the same. Earth. Iberitus. Uranus. They all posited a system of non-equilibrium scat.

Horror? Now that's what *every* plane of existence gets right!

Chapter 16

†

Quinone

A light rain washed over her hair. Flecked with an amalgamation of sand, clay, and black ash. Fingers combing through it, eyes closed; this was a small moment of respite to be clean for once. She missed her old school clothes, but considering the attention it garnered, this robed garb was becoming on her.

The little clay man keeps a vigilant watch on her shoulder. His gems lightly beaming—on, off, on, off. A lighthouse overpassing with the gulls. Poised and stalwart with eyes to the West. Where home once was. There remains no homecoming without his best friend. If he had bones, if he could shed one drop, if he had a trumpet for a voice, then they would break at the knees, create new oceans, and wail songs that would make those of the Abyssal weep in solidarity. Essents are eternal, if undamaged. To develop emotions for those touched by impermanence…hope evaporates.

Altitude wavers. Her eyes looked below to see the lawn of green turning back into its shape of forestry as perception adjusted to its original height. The cloud—his— losing, for lack of a better word, steam. Gently. Very, *very* gently, the feet touch the ground again, and the fluff of clouds disperses back to the sky.

Wits kept about them. Was there a sulfuric monster woman hiding in the swamp? Sniffing. No rotten eggshells here. At least for the moment. The pair landed in the middle of the strait, her feet mushing down on the soft moss. Nothing extraordinary here. Dull, but peaceful. Celanjung still was a ways away. *This could take days,* Sadie thought. Still, she walked. Still, she prayed for a sign of hope. Any sign, really.

Well…not anything that wouldn't try to eat them. She had no food in her belly, but nature did decide to call on other organs. No peeping Toms around—God willing. Grabbing fistfuls of lightly damp leaves, she headed behind a large domed rock, shooing Enzu away to have her privacy. Lifting up the robe halfway, with one more look around, she gave in to nature—a satisfying shiver running over her porcelain skin.

Sadie looked beyond the marsh, out west. Then, to the oceans that hugged the land. Small dotted islands. Her curiosity tuning out the world, wondering what beings lived out there. If they were violent or kind. Not enough kindness these last few days.

She pondered about the scattered dungeons she heard from the others. Nefarious creatures that do not climb from their bleak nests. Independent treasure guardians. Valuables that put to shame every country's natural resources. *Sibi's tomebook,* she thought, *I wonder what they had to face to get just one book? Was it worth it?*

Cattails rattled about. Close. *Too* close. On her *very* ass close! How could one be so deaf to the movement beside her? Silly girl. Daydreamer. Couldn't blame her; it was pretty quiet, and despite its size, without any light to shine over them, there were no shadows to cast over from gray skies. It could easily end her journey right here, right now. Especially with its sullen look. This monument to stromatolites, covered with cyanobacteria, blue-green algae, under-the-hood teeth, and horrendous slimy limbs, stared intensely at her.

Defecating on its doorstep.

Still, she did not look. Nothing of its presence snapped her to just take one small peek over the shoulder. Maybe her faculties just didn't want to be bothered during her water closet break. Enzu, on the other hand, was apprehended by the monument's cohorts. Slipping into the reeds. He tried to escape with his little arms flailing, his little feet kicking, wishing he had a voice to warn with. They were about his size. Facsimiles. Female. Fecundity on the mind. It's been too long since they have had company. Didn't matter if he was an Essent; where there's a will, there's a way to polish his jewels.

Business finished after wiping clean—as one can be. Just as Sadie was about to turn to face the organic monument, small waves in the distance caught her attention. Nothing at first, but she saw the waters turning suddenly from blue to red. Foreboding thoughts circulate.

"So long as you're here, they cannot harm you," the monument carefully pointed out.

Frozen. In place. No sudden movements. *Is this what gravel sounds like? Just don't try to look. Maybe a surprise attack?!* Her bladder played prankster. The bracelet garnered enough energy to regenerate on the way over. Little sparks ignited off her fingertips.

"Had I wanted to kill you, I wouldn't have made myself known."

Maybe this is true, she thought, *or maybe it's another trap!*

More domed monuments sprout from the ground. One by one, they turned to face her with those sullen eyes. Thick, jelly fluids dripping down their bodies. Gauntlets for hands and trunks for legs! Little capped mischief-makers running around playfully. Sloshing behind her, she felt the booming weight of her latest conversation piece. Well, Sadie let that old curiosity lead the way into dangerous territory—again—by turning to face it head-on. "The pelagic was too calm for the new brood today; a population explosion," it said.

Her internal response: *Quiet! Just listen! This thing is bigger than one of those Mairu! God knows what it's capable of!*

Verbal: Inaudible. A little "eep" caught behind her tonsils.

"Dinoflagellates…temperamental plankton," it explained, like teacher to student. A student who drizzled leftovers hidden away in the bladder. It heard the trickling sound under her robe. Its thought process was interrupted by toilet antics. There was a bad joke somewhere here…

This is it!

"Finish your movements, then climb on my shell. Evren awaits."

Still shell-shocked—was this her mind still making jokes? She uttered some words. A little incoherent. Jaw slacking and tongue-twisting, but still, words. "Is it safe? Is…Sulfur here?

"Her power has been disabled by my kin, but the waters are still contaminated. A problem we are still defusing…wretched Prime. It will take years for our ecosystem to return back to normal."

Enzu jumped out of the reeds with impressions of lips on his clay body. Giggles were heard from the wetlands. He quickly rolled onto her shoulder, tapping profusely, as if to say, "Let's go, damn you!"

The giant creature sunk back into the soft, damp ground. Noise was nonexistent. Dangerous. To be able to buffer, or muffle, the sound impeccably. They could ambush or ensnare anyone or anything with no effort. Curving her body to its round shape, clenching the hood, trying to avoid the teeth, she told it they were ready. No response, except a speeding rock slicing through the ground, like a turtle on speed.

Her ampoules are lost, accidentally, without notice.

The ride was cut short when they arrived at the border. Marshland turning into another world; enchanted. Polar opposite to the strait. A great tree, far too great to not be seen, blocked the path. The creature advised Sadie to dismount until it was cleared.

"Cleared? Can't we just go around?"

Massive branches, timbers, and splinters fell to the ground. A face, one contorted with fury and age, looked down at the party in contempt. *It's impossible to miss a face on a tree this large! It's greater in size than one of those World-Eaters! Just how?!* Vines came from the ground, bejeweled limbs, one about to sink its sharp edge into her head. She took a step back, bracelet readied.

Will it be strong enough? That's the real question.

"That won't work here; trust it won't harm you, like I," her monstrous transportation said.

"Trust…" she trailed off, "Who can I trust now?"

"I can always bring you back."

"No! No! I…fine. I hate this. Everything," she replied, defeatedly.

The vine twirled. Gems glowing. Something familiar about them. She saw another glow, but from the shoulder: Enzu. The vine swiped at him, splintering, jutting its needles into his precious stones, but not enough to crack or render them useless. Thoughts absorbed. Experiences transferred. Spiritual words exchanged. Then, the vines were pulled out and dug back underground. The giant face only snarled.

But a path cleared in the forest.

Hurry before it changes its mind!

Little fuzzy faces popped from their groves, their homes; lush and wonder abodes. *Welcomed? By her majesty?! This must be a very important guest.* Hop, hop, hop, alongside its colleague. Gold feline eyes watched. Scratches to the chin. Then, a tug at its harness before carrying on, back to the woods of Gottlir, with its cotton-tailed partner, fishing branch over the shoulder. She saw them and wanted to wave but was afraid of falling off the marsh creature's shell. A slight bit of somberness; it might be the last time she says goodbye.

She didn't get to say that to Milos.

More Wandrians were walking around. A lot more than she anticipated. They didn't come off as reclusive to the ones she met. These little beings came off much more relaxed. No tiger kings here. Or Khrosgar. Hopefully, no malicious Primes of rotting yolk.

Deeper
they went.
Eyes glued to more
massive trees with faces,
but none like the first. She
did notice three others far off in
the land. These four must be the
real guardians of Celanjung. Then,
human life came into the picture. A
young girl rests under a tree, half-asleep,
stretching out like a cat under the warm sun. When
they drew closer, the tree broke out of the ground—
almost defensively—to watch them go by. The
young girl, looking up at it, said, "Evren said *not* to
harm her," and went back to her catnap.

"What are all these tree creatures?" Sadie
asked.

"Vicara," the creature replied.

"Are you one also?"

"No, we do share a symbiotic relationship,
however. I am something your kind cannot
pronounce by tongue. We communicate by
mycelium and signaling our nous through the
underground network. We are the
Assinikoda." Underground, an electric
current of signals is directed in all
corners of Celanjung to the latest
arrival. They never slept.

A bit of nutrient sharing goes a long way to ensure the survival of the realm. What's mine is yours; willingly. No jealous minds here. No sharing of bedfellows. Everything needed to be pure. Pollutants were filtered by the marsh reserves before entering the realms, and, if high enough, the Vicara took care of cleaning the ozone. Nothing reached the pristine castle where the queen resided—never leaving it.

Sadie's eyes beheld the opulent architecture. The sweet smell of pinewood turned over. She couldn't place the fragrance. The gates opened, and veiled women appeared, but physical ones.

At the front, one dismissed the marsh creature, acting accordingly before Sadie could praise it for the safe journey. The lead looked over Sadie: tired, slouching, disheveled, with oily hair, torn garb, bruised, cut—a small wound weeping on her upper lip she probably wasn't aware of—and pungent. *Very* pungent.

She also gave off an air of rebellion. They could feel the pent-up rage of the woman in her bracelet that was at the ready. Probably knew it would take some time before the poor girl would allow someone to touch her again, without acting in defense, instinctually.

One of her half-opened green eyes held a flame inside. Answers—that's what she wanted. That's *all* she ever wanted! And justice for Milos.

"Welcome, Sadie Harper," the lead spoke with gentleness.

Still, the flames grew; she knew that these people were not to be trusted. It didn't matter how beautiful they were, how gentle and calm their demeanors exuded, or if they were a part of the royal class.

Inside this enormous castle of ivory and glass was a woman who, at the very least, was honest with her intentions.

Each woman glared at her, noticing the crackling of fire around her wrist. They had their own tricks. Each one closed their eyes, bowed their heads, like a mass silent prayer, and in seconds, became spectres of Cerulean. The veil of Alaea appeared behind Sadie, transmitting a stratagem, but the lead would not allow this to go further. An aggressive clap of the hands. Those behind her returned to their normal states, and Sadie's fiery companion—dispelled, back from where she came.

The lead said with sternness, "We'll have none of that. Inside…please." Sadie looked at Enzu for an answer. A little nod. That was all she needed, and so the young girl walked inside, and the gates closed, and now she would find her answers.

Or die trying…

Chapter 17

†

RGB

Pacing. Asking a multitude of questions. For every answer she received, she denied its honesty. It was all a lie! But it wasn't. They spoke truthfully. Earnestly. It's not in their nature to lie. This was, after all, a requirement before blessedness took hold of their essence, their…final breath. She hated the answers.

Riled in a chamber with her mother's sacred tree.

"An example will be made!" Evren shouted at them.

They knew she was powerful—a young woman her age—but they still made the choice of coming to his defense. In concert. The young queen was dissatisfied with all of this rubbish. One of Evren's corporeal veiled women entered the large chamber. The lead.

"We're having her washed. Please be gentle with her."

A crooked hand to the lead, blue crystals surrounding her, "Don't ever tell me how to behave…*ever!*" Evren growled, her face blackened with hate.

The lead looked calmly at the powers around her, "Remember: this was once your mother's chamber—don't break the oath," and she left. The crooked hand tightened into a ball. Her grip: vicious. You could see the blue veins clear as glass. Ready to shatter every artery.

"Uptight this one," Mulberry transmitted.

Evren returned her dark gaze back to the captured scrolls. Each one was held inside a glass reliquary, separated from one another, with their faces bleeding out like small constellations.

"Just one rip—that's it!"

"Go on then!" Mulberry continued her barbs, *"Who would ever want to stay with a tyrant like yourself! Even your own wants nothing to do with you. Pathetic isolationist. You tend to this sacred tree, and it bears no fruit! You are killing it!"*

Evren opened the case, taking the defiant scroll in hand to observe. Mulberry goaded her to shred her into a million little pieces. The others tried to calm the situation. Transmissions falling on a blocked mind. One would insist on the art of shredding. Argent.

This caught the queen's attention.

"I *was* going to save you for last, but now..." Evren hissed. A deep-seated hatred for this color. Mulberry was tossed aside, with Argent taking its place. Psionic communications from the others ceased. None of these beauties wanted anything to do with this color.

Small at first, but the rip started to lengthen; deeper, longer, spectacularly vertical without misdirection. Small rumblings in the castle begin. Argent liked this; she made no protests.

"Stop!" transmission from one that was not encased by the angry queen. And she did. And so did the terrible tremors. Looking out of one of the windows, she saw that not only did the castle shake, but also the realm. Scores of birds migrated to the East, the South, and some even to the West to take their chances over the storms of the Akrav.

The queen's voice became gentle. "Why...of all of them...why?"

"She is neither enemy nor ally, but the only one who can return your mother. A bargaining chip. Rip her and all is lost. And memory goes, too," Lucia of Cerulean transmitted.

Memory? Return of Mother?

Teeth bit the lip to draw a dental imprint on the skin, almost drawing red. The Cerulean woman continued to tell Evren to settle her thoughts. Evren placed the partially torn silver scroll back into its case. The blood pumping in her heart settled to normal levels. Adrenaline subsides. She walked over to her stolen heirloom and summoned the woman. The wild masked veil appeared, holding out her arms, looking for an embrace from the queen.

But Evren rejected it.

"You are about to fall off that moral cliff," Lucia transmitted, *"I will not force you. This is your choice to make—not mine...or ours."*

Evren heard their whispers around the room. They watch in the background, trying to hide from her sight, always afraid of the book in her possession. Whispers of how to break free like those encased. Nomadic life seemed wonderful. If *only* he had just stolen the book instead, then they would all have experienced the wonders beyond the lonesome castle. Never having to deal with the coldness of the princess. The queen looked at it, above the stairs, behind the tree.

They refused to come out to her commands.

Refusing to ever come out, until now, from the Cerulean Codex.

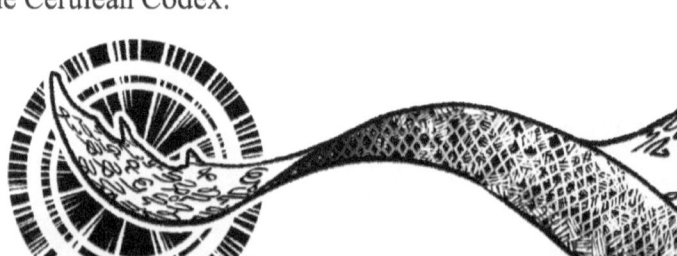

Droplets ran down her cheeks. Her mouth is partially open. Eyes looking at the ripples of her distorted reflection. She hadn't seen herself in a mirror in some time, forgetting what she looked like—this was not her. This was someone ugly, in her mind. That upper lip is going to scar nicely. Split apricot. The tip of her tongue prods it. Stinging. Every prod woke her up. Fresh jolts. No need for pinches of the skin. This was enough to realize she was still alive. Bags of stress under the eyes. Christ almighty. All she needed was bloating to the face, and voila: the face of a binge-drinking alcoholic! She touched the bags, realizing now how rough her hands were: calloused, leathery, is that a broken nail? Several.

Reflections call over a new face. This apparition has lost its usual intense expression. The girl's bracelet warms up the water, and curiosity becomes her again.

"You look…different," Sadie said.

"I am concerned for your well-being," Alaea transmitted.

"I'm trying to stay above water…Were you always like this?"

"No…I was forced into this state. Some memories left intact."

"Against one's will?"

"Yes, the veils of Mulberry and Goldenrod have undergone this same transformation I believe," the fiery veil replied, floating over to face Sadie. *"Would you like to see how the 'Ritual of Blessedness' occurs? And the ramifications of one who wishes to not be a part of it?"*

Sadie always wondered how these women became like this, always thinking of why they would want to serve out the rest of their days much like the pious. But to be subjugated against their consent?

"Will it be bad?" she asked.

"It will…This will come from my experience. You don't have to."

"I want to understand."

Alaea blew out a wave of flames over the girl's face. It transported her to various landscapes, but all in someone else's eyes. Someone else's voice. And it is bitter. It protests against another woman's demand that she is the only one strong enough to satisfy the Prime's request. A lie. Primes personally choose their sacrifices. They never liked her. Shackles clamped over the wrists. Nails sink in to disable. The lamb curses her captors to oblivion. All in robes, in a circle, around the lamb in this cave of magma rivers. She hears their incantation. She agonizes in pain. Levers pulled. She sees the flowing heat going through small mazes in the ground, leading to her station.

Voices from beyond transmit into her mind. Overlapping one another. Hard to translate. Fiery tendrils rise from the bubbling pathways. They grasp at her flesh. Burning without marks. Searing without evidence. Enveloping without love. She wants out of this hazardous fire blanket. It is killing her to new heights beyond euphoria. From the ceiling, a new face reveals itself to the suffering lamb. Like a celestial constellation of fire, it speaks to her, describing vengeance will come to those who have gifted this ruin. Her body melts into the rivers, but a star rises from it. Eaten by the constellation. Placed into a false skull for safekeeping. Comatose until she meets someone who can free her.

And the flames were extinguished.

"Was that really you?" Sadie exclaimed, "Who were those women?!"

"I do not know. I believe it is my own tribe. Memories wiped."

"...Even if it wasn't forced, why would anyone embrace this kind of horrid practice? What purpose does it serve?"

"War, and blessings unto the living kin from the Primes. Chromatics and Alchemists vie to be the winning rulers of this reality. The Naturals are caught between the two. I have heard of veils who regret their decision to serve. Your world—and others—will succumb once a victor rises. This has happened for eons. Call it a stalemate, a minor victory, but it's changing with the role of certain players."

"Like who?"

"The blind Barangda, Marisha...If the scribe went with her, it would be a decimation between the factions. No color, no science, nothing, would ever exist again! The same goes for the Lusuran slug king, except Alchemy and its Primes would declare victory. They would absorb the others. An existence without color or organic creation..."

"Why do only women become veils? Don't men prefer the role of soldiering and sacrifice?"

"Most do, but the Primes barred them, seeing as it would be a fast track for the Chroma's extinction. Something the Alchemists don't have to worry about. Kin are blessed with plenty of bounty by the Chroma they worship. So long as the next spawn follows the path of the family's color or colors. Certain Chroma have truces, while others want to be the dominant color in the grand wheel.

"The Messengers? There are tales that men who dedicate their lives to the Chroma become one just before death claims their pneuma. Perhaps your scribe has joined their ranks?"

She dropped her face into the water, bubbling like a crab, with no care in the world. Time, where was it going?

A hand grabbed her wet red hair, pulling it up, "Silly girl! Are you trying to drown yourself?!" A veiled woman shouted.

Unreactive. The lead was notified and came into the washroom to review the situation. A naked, catatonic adolescent with a proclivity to passive suicidal ideation. Slouched in the large pool. This was a different person compared to the one from the entrance. Where was that fiery spirit? Washed away? The woman took hold of a sponge and began to cleanse Sadie's back. Maybe that'll bring back that fire. But it didn't.

"Before, you looked like you wouldn't let anyone touch you, and now, you're unbothered."

"..."

"You know, I've been with Queen Evren for as long as I can remember. Even when she banished the men—my father and brothers included—I still remained by her side; thick and thin. You remind me of her when she took over the realm."

"...How can you stay by someone's side that makes you choose service over family? She and I are *not* the same!"

Sponge rinsed. Observance of the back. Small cuts turn to scars.

"She needed me, needed us; had we left, the realm would've looked far worse. No trees, no beauty, almost like Lusura, but without all the craters. She needs to feel love. It's all we, the Order of the Veil, can give her. Seeing her father slain, her mother sacrificed…it ruins anyone. The moment the Prime of Argent took her mother, the Grand Queen *Simay*, she snapped. It was either her own suicide or succumbing to the anger. A double-edged sword held to the neck, with feet sinking in quicksand. Anger…it can be remedied. I can't bring her senses back. But," she explained, stopping the wash, "maybe you can."

Sadie laughed to herself, "Fat chance...She tried to imprison me when I entered that garden realm of hers. I'm no one's slave to interrogate. Plus—" she stopped short, his dumb, sarcastic grin appearing in her mind, "he's gone..."

"The thief?"

"He was more than that! He made his amends! He was even going to come here with me before your irrational queen decided to send more of those faceless things to ask for mercy! He could've stayed away forever. But," Sadie let out a small, tired cry, head upwards, in a pleading fashion, "he just wanted to make things right...in hopes he could live a normal life. Settle down. Live quietly. Kosey has no idea he's gone..."

"Gone?"

"IS THERE AN *ECHO* HERE?! YOU BASTARDS TOOK HIM! I SAW THEM HAUL HIM AWAY INTO THAT CRAZY PORTAL!" Sadie screamed out in anger, standing up to confront the woman, no shame in showing her her birthday suit.

The woman, unbothered by the nudity in front of her, smiled at Sadie, "You *are* like her," she grabbed her hand and pulled her out of the water, "Keep that energy. Don't lose it! Off we go!"

A clean robe was handed. "Where's Enzu?!" Sadie demanded.

No replies. Horse blinders through all the excitement. She tried tugging away, but the lead gripped her wrist tighter. "Trust me, girl! No more questions...Save those for the queen."

They entered an empty room full of symbols, glyphs, and other strange markings carved on the walls and floor.

The same ancient text she saw on the scrolls. A blue light emitted from the ground. Flashing. Exploding upward. Gone. Teleported straight to the top.

To the Mene's Spire.

Lost compass; maybe broken. Was this the way? No. Maybe...*this* way! Wrong turn again. Tracing. That's what he was doing.

And cleverly sneaking.

"WHERE DID IT GO?! FIND IT!" A veiled woman shouted to others. Each transforming into their secretive powers of Cerulean. The halls were on high alert. Good thing he knew about the secret passages.

Where, oh where, are you? Someone needs to dust these passageways—far too mucky. Is that a rat's nest? She won't like this. Oh no. She just might very well burn the entire building down if she were made aware. Probably too busy with all that rage pent up inside. Fresh air. That's just what she needs! A walk on the green. Barefoot. Each blade would send a tickle to her nerves. Yes. A walk on grass is part of her prescription! What else? Cobwebs...this passage is rife with antagonists. Rats are easy to dispatch, but the spiders?! These are not the benevolent kind. These are cousins—sentries possibly. The Sleep. Banners of Black and Green. Better clean this up; pro bono. And the nest for good measure. All done. Nice. Oh! Maybe she needs a bedfellow? One does go stark mad if untouched for too long. Touch starvation is a cruel thing for these humans—simple or extraordinary. Granted, she isn't prudish.

Picking up the signal again. Run, run, run; away we go. Up the tubes, down the pipes, along the crevices—*Oh look, a flower! Hello, sky blue aster! You look wonderful today!*—over the hinges, into the vents, and...made a wrong turn. Rusty navigational skills. Detecting; detecting; detecting; pointer magnetized to this point of interest—southbound.

Please be there.

Entering a dimly lit room, a little companion searches for treasure. No torture devices here, but quite grim. *Where's natural light? No windows? How cruel. This only hastens depression and misery.* Split, splat, split, splat, were the tunes of it walking in curiosity. Keeping a low profile, the gems on its body were sparsely illuminated to see in the starless room. It had never been here before. Actually, this room had a vastly different persona compared to the rest of the castle.

Was this part of an older foundation? Oh dear, I hope it isn't part of some unmarked dungeon. We are not looking for that kind of treasure! Why is there so much dirt in here?! Little worries on its face, arms on its temples, pacing back and forth in such a worry. **Clink!** There's something in here with it! It's the signal! Drawing closer to it, behind a wall of metal tubes, it gazed at its sad features: blinded, shackled, weak.

No time to be worried now; the cavalry's here!

Spinning. Collecting. Retrieving. It got larger and larger, and, yes, larger. Two tons of fight from three pounds of soma.

She gazed at the crystal floor, the paneless windows, and the barrenness of the room. The lead had left her there with only the words, "Good luck."

Sadie walked over to one of the windows. Enthralled by the vision of what looked like a peaceful country, led by some twisted monarch. Green ores, blue gems, and other mineraloids conjured in the room. From the walls, the floors, even floating in the air.

On the throne, a sleeping bustard awakened, flapping its great white wings with black tips. Behind the gem-stoned piece, a staircase, and the footsteps of another.

They stared at each other for a moment—or was it an eternity?

Blue electricity popped into the air. Chain-linking with green currents. Ores acted as conduits. Perpetual motion of charges that surrounded the room. This was no ordinary tempest. Evren started to hum at first, and then that high-pitched operatic coloratura contralto melody began. Energy emanates, scattering in the sky, where voyeurs watched.

"Are we too late?" one said to her mentor.

She stopped the gamijah and lifted her straw hat. Looking up at the Spire, saying, "Just on time. Let's welcome ourselves in."

One Vicara's roots jut out of the ground, energies jittering about, bending its face. It will kill without hesitation. The mentor held out a thick scroll. "Are you going to let us pass, or will you be the one to tell her how you failed to let me, a composer, in with grand news?" Reluctantly, it ceased, allowing the party to enter the realm, unharmed. "See, girls, come with official terms, and all roads lead to the promised land. Onward!" The novitiates agreed wholeheartedly.

Evren's four elite Essents joined her in the room at her sides. They were armed with pole weaponry and had no care if this was overkill for one little teenager. Fealty above all else.

"Finally we meet. Ever since you invaded my private garden, tore one of my mother's works—my lineage—and practically gallivanted all throughout Iberitus with that thief, I couldn't wait to see what turned the realms upside-down," Evren declared, sizing Sadie up, "Not much."

Evren

Her hands released a quick bolt into the girl's stomach. It stunned her. A small throbbing pain, but enough not to have her collapse.

"What have you done to Milos, *witch*?!"

The queen detested that word. So much so, that she didn't bother to send any more harmful energy to inflict on Sadie's skin.

But the back of her hand.

Then a punch to the solar, knocking the wind out of the teen. Evren grabbed her by the hair, lifting her entire body up, pressing her forehead against hers, "You're *nothing* special! They told me the Usurper was trying to apprehend you, but I learned that the pelagic mad dog wanted nothing to do with you! I saw you in your little cart. Only the twisted folk and the depraved giants sought you. The rats would rather you be slaughtered." She dropped the girl. Sadie was heaving on the ground, holding her stomach, trying to figure a way out of this. "Why don't you cry? Go on! Compose me a song fit for a bird with broken wings," Evren taunted, "Don't put on a brave face; a costume! Show me your real pathetic identity!"

Sadie looked up, remembering the bustard. It looked as if it was about to die from panic with the madness in the room. One leg up, one foot in front of the other, lurch with gusto, see if it's alright. Evren continued to yell at the girl, walking past her, as if the queen was nothing, even walking past the four who awaited to attack, but the order never came. No. Sadie fell in front of the throne, trying to calm the bird. It was hopeless; it didn't understand what was happening. Evren had forgotten about the bustard in all her terrifying anger. Never crossed her mind. She lifted her hands and sang, much more delicately, and the ores stopped glowing, the gems stopped crackling, and the gales stopped flowing.

"Leave us…" she ordered the Essents.

It was quiet. The ambience, from outside, is put on mute. Only now, spilling out in a great flood, was the request the queen asked for.

To see Sadie cry in an ugly manner.

"From burning villages to the face of war, why are you people so cruel?!" Sadie yelped out, crying profusely, snot and all, "Everything is so goddamn despicable here! One after the other *after* the other! Thank God Almighty I wasn't born in this world! I thought everything was bad in my world, but nope, all of you *live* for war! At least where I come from, there are people trying so hard to bring unity…even when it puts them in harm's way." She tried to wipe her face, but it didn't work.

Too many fluids to keep up with.

"I don't know how I got here. I didn't make that choice. But I do have a choice in taking a stand against this heartless violence! Not like you. You *chose* this path. So what if Milos stole from you?! I don't know what his reasons were, but he was going to bring them back and throw himself at your mercy for forgiveness. But I see you have none…You removed the very person who looked out for me here. I'm all alone now. I'm all alone…" Sadie's words trembled, she searched for the medicine.

Lost to the unknown. Her sights turn to the outside.

Evren had no words. What was there to say? She had lived in solitude with her servants, never one to understand rationalization. Anger. That was her language in rhetoric. But it wasn't rhetoric; it was intimidation. A more bombastic version of the one who killed her father. She just wanted to protect the realm from those who would contaminate and defecate on her family's land. A way to uphold their memory everlasting so that others may gaze, from afar, in awe. By sending off the politicians, the beating-heart soldiers, the priests, and anything that had male qualities, she never learned how to delegate a country, except through the use of force. Never knowing the Wandrians or fair women that still resided here. And the women, their population was shrinking at an alarming rate. Natural causes on one side of the spectrum while others migrated to neighboring lands seeking warm companionship.

Maybe if she just…

Where's the girl?! Evren thought.

Standing on an open ledge, pressing her hands against the enclosure, and looking down, initiated vertigo. Why did she have to look down? Sadie closed her eyes, cleared her mind, and…dropped. Let's end the questions, the spirit of inquiry, hell, the problems of demarcation.

Wandrians saw the girl jump to her death, falling fast from a great height. Nothing but flat earth at the bottom. She doesn't care. The words of Alaea failed to reach her. In Sadie's mind, this is all a bad dream.

Anywhere, but here…

A woman screamed in horror at the sight. The new party, just arriving, watched the horror unfold. The mentor quickly ordered her novitiates to soften the ground and apply a dampener while she released an unfathomable power from her hands. Sigils covered a wide range below the target. She didn't know if she would complete the spell in time.

There's nothing for me here. It's just a nightmare. I'll wake up again, in my home, in my bed. I'll hear Mom call out from downstairs about breakfast being ready. Maple bacon, silver dollar pancakes, hash browns, fresh juice. Dad, reading the paper. Making up some corny joke he just thought up. That's right. I'll wake up at the bottom. I hope this dream dies. I never want to have it again…

Sweet release. The downfall felt amazing. Peter Pan, immature antics aside, you're quite lucky to be able to fly. Forget about how to land. Tears appeared. Not of sadness. Or joy. Gravity's coldness was just doing its part. There are so many trees here. Home. Back in the New England region. The East Inlet with balsam fir. The bogs of *Heath Pond* and the *Spruce Hole*. She managed to raise her eyes to see that immense face on the Vicara tree. *"Old Man of the Mountain," let me show you a picture of Franconia Notch.* Flying beside her, at great speed, the bustard, trying desperately to figure out a way to aid her.

"You'd like *Pondicherry*; lots of birds there," she said somberly.

Nothing gold can stay...

From above, still, in the Spire, a painful sound of the soul spiraled out of control; four Essents were ordered to intercept but lost in the race.

To one of their own.

"You..." Sadie said, exhausted yet surprised. It journeyed a long way back home. It had never been defeated before, and when the time came, it would accept its fate. But it was given a second chance.

This is all it had to give back.

Shivering. It was nonstop. Fingers, toes, any digit with nerves quivered with anxiety, with fright, tremendous apprehension.

Veiled women appeared in the throne room to see not their queen but a young woman, full of emotions not seen since childhood. She threw the crown across the crystal floor, sobbing quietly, unable to understand why the girl with red hair would commit a crime against herself. The lead, with her hand out and a grave look of worry, saw above the staircase to the private room's doors. Busting wide open. A unison of colors flowed into the room, veiled women of the Chroma, offering support—even recalcitrant Mulberry. Following behind, filling the room, looking at the lamenting Evren, all the women of the Cerulean Codex. Soft energies flowed into her pneuma, comforting her, waiting for this to happen, eventually. The lead helped her onto the throne, wiping her face. She places her hand on Evren's. She was absolutely destroyed.

"I didn't want her to kill herself…truly! I have no right to this crown, this throne, or this realm. I must abdicate it. I am no different than the Usurper…"

Entering the room, the two novitiates and the composer from Somdir, who were supposed to aid Gottlir, had other plans of recourse. The physical illuminated, charging their powers, thinking this was an invasion from the uninvited; an act of war about to be committed! The Somdirian composer lifted her arm, scroll in hand, and unfurled it to read aloud. "Queen Evren, Somdir received your message for an alliance, but, in light of current events, I'm not sure that will ever be possible now."

"I do not care anymore. Though I sit upon this throne, you can plainly see the crown at your feet. I have misused my power, all for the sake of blind revenge, and as of right now, I forswear my authority of Celanjung…"

"Are you responsible for throwing the girl to the quietus?"

A nerve struck, "Never! I raged, I hit, but I never planned to doom her to The White! Service! Loyalty! That's what I wanted in the end!" She stood up in an uproar.

"You have a funny way of showing it…It's…very tyrannical," the Somdirian composer said, "Are you willing to reform? It would come at a greater cost, but—"

"There's nothing else to discuss," Evren interrupted. "I am taking responsibility for this heinous behavior of mine. Speak to my lead on new prospects."

The rage de-escalated, and angels descended in the throne room.

With lost cherubs in arms.

"She's—" Evren faltered, with relief exposed.

"Alive," the Somdirian composer finished.

Sadie, cradled in the arms of her savior: Jökull. It placed her down. The novitiates were thrilled to see her, as was their composer. She placed her head against Sadie's, like at the Fort, listening. A finger to the girl's nose, "Never, ever, *ever* do that again, silly girl! You weren't able to send the message to the queen here, like you were instructed, so now's the time. Too weary, I suppose."

Evren looked on. Perplexed. Actually, she can't remember the last time she spoke to outsiders. Too cooped up in the castle, afraid of how she would be perceived with all the stories circulating about her "witch-like" qualities. Sadie, looking at the wide-eyed queen, stood before her, "Somdir accepts your alliance wholeheartedly, but only if you quiet the rage inside you, return me home, and forgive Milos. Is he—?"

The Somdirian composer snapped her fingers, and emerging through the portal was the oversized Enzu in his brutish form. Sadie, relieved to see him, tried to run over to embrace him, but the composer advised against it, saying, "Just watch."

Everyone gazed at the massive Essent. The queen looked at him, shocked, "It is Mother's creation!" He felt no animosity from her. Sadie was safe. The queen's personal guard showed no signs of attack. Veiled women, spectre or physical, remained in place.

Now.

He dug his large bejeweled hands into his chest, ripping it open, unveiling the contents within: Milos. Alive. Sadie screamed out in joy, rushing in without further delay to embrace him.

"Did you miss me?" he asked, softly.

"Never!" she giggled out.

The Somdirian composer grinned, looking at Evren, "I felt his pneuma immediately when I entered the great hall. Of course, I had to 'persuade' your subordinates to release him. Don't worry, they're still alive. A bit seared at the moment. The fact you kept him alive is enough to know you haven't succumbed to the ways of the king of black sulfur or the mad queen of Klaring; maybe better treatment for prisoners, but still, an 'E' for effort since this is still new to you."

Milos bent down, grabbing Queen Evren's crown, wiping some of the debris off, and handed it to her, "I believe you dropped this."

"I…I don't deserve it."

"We all screw up. I stole from your family, and I want to make it right, please?" he replied, lifting the crown up to her, "I believe in second chances, sometimes a third."

Hesitation. But some of the Cerulean, direct from the Codex, whispered thoughts into her mind, "*Start over; for Celanjung; for Iberitus; for mother and father.*"

She took the crown upon her head. It felt different this time. Light, and not so heavy. New perspectives. Open opportunities. The error of ways is seen. Something her lead tried for so long.

"Won't you follow me upstairs?" Evren said to Milos and Sadie.

They followed behind, and Enzu, back in his small body, rolled back onto Sadie's shoulder, nestling against the cheek. The others stayed behind, spectres of the veil dispersing, Somdirians talking politics with the physical. The Bistarira-Sanshan composer shot one last look at the others, smiling, "A new era has just begun," she said to herself.

In the room, they saw the grand mulberry tree, the tomb in the center, the Codex on the podium, and the trapped scrolls from Milos's quiver. Evren allowed him to take back his property, and as he was leaving the Ceruleans behind, she offered Lucia's service to him as a gift. The veil wouldn't have it any other way, and so he accepted the scroll as his own.

"Who's inside the tomb?" Sadie asked, not seeing any inscriptions.

"My father: Grand King *Dieter,*" Evren replied, ashamed to look at it, "Taken by the Usurper, who I will never name until I have it in my sights again."

Sadie remembered the dream. It all led back to this point. Better not say anything; Evren will dwell on it forever.

"This…this is how we get you home," Evren said, placing her hand on the massive tree. "My mother told me it was a portal. I didn't believe her until I once leaned on it to weep in her memory. It consumed me whole. I *have* seen your world, but only for a moment. There are others out there. They say there's one far below the borders of Udalann and Lusura; pray that the Usurper hasn't found it yet. Whenever you are ready. Sit, lean, and meditate. It will do the rest."

"I remember waking up in a closet, and before that leaning against a tree near my school. I'm sure I was reported missing by now."

The missing rectangular imprint. Could this be…?

"An accident when I first started practicing the arts. I suppose now that piece became someone's closet door. I doubt anything can come of it. The piece and the tree, in your world, must be connected to this mulberry. Time works differently here. It'll be as if you never left. We are not of the same universe. You can return if you want…to chat. Let me make my own amends with you," Evren said sheepishly.

A friend. Isn't that what most of us want?

"But I've seen plenty of people rest against the one I was on; how come none of them got transported here?"

Evren looked at Milos. "You and he…and I share the same enchanted blood. You are Pictfero. As is your birthright. This tree, and the one connected to your world, will only permit our blood through. But, for your family's sake, keep this a secret—I wouldn't want them to come over unprepared like you, and die," she warned, "As for the other portal's…Anyone can go through them, but rarely are they ever found considering they have their own guardians protecting their locations. They rival the dungeon guardians." No one would believe Sadie anyway. They'd call her mad and send her to the loony bin.

"…Do we have Klarinite in our blood?" Milos inquired.

"Don't be ridiculous, only the deranged do! We are either pureblood, like me, or have one of the saner realms flowing within us."

Who am I…really…

She looked around the room, then at the tree, then at Milos and Enzu. "I…I guess it's time. I honestly didn't think I'd make it out alive. And it's all thanks to you two, and the Newt brothers, and Birati and Aruna, and—wow, so many to thank—Natalina, send her my thanks. All the best for you two. Riha and Kosey…Give him one big hug for me…may The Pilgrims rest in peace. I heard about it when I was captured by Klaring's forces. Awful."

"They saved many lives. They're legends now. As for you, get some rest, in your own bed, and you enjoy all the simple pleasures you missed, and hug those closest. There is no future. We only live in the now," Milos said, "Keep that bracelet close if you plan to visit again. She's kept you from harm's way when I wasn't around, although I never could quite figure out how you could summon her full power without incantation."

"I can help with that," Evren said.

The queen asked Sadie to lift her wrist up to them for a closer look. She hummed a little tune, waving her hand over the bracelet, revealing inside, the Chroma was mixed in with a large chunk of the prism of Sessathoth. Greater than Milos's.

"That sly bastard," Milos whispered.

"The king of Udalann must have found this broken piece somewhere. I wonder who disguised and shaped this for him…"

He wonders if Sadie hears the ancient voice too, but dashes the thought since she never succumbed to the prism's raw power. "Eh well, that's something for me to ask the giant bloat. Let's get my favorite lass here home before his 'royal belly' catches wind of my pneuma coming back from the void. Your wards are…terrifyingly strong, Queen Evren."

"Evren is fine."

Sadie squished Milos's cheeks together. "I'm your favorite?!"

"Behind Natalina, and Katya, and Riha, and maybe the Mozmina girl, and who else? Maybe some of those village gals I saw in Gottlir with their round rumps and buxom tops! Give a Winzangi woman a run for their geodi!"

"Oh, just shut up! Smartass," Sadie pouted.

He laughed, "I am going to miss you something fierce. Don't come back to the Iberlands until you're strong enough on your own. We'll have lots more adventures to do when you've reached new heights. What a grand day that will be, eh?"

Evren summoned her lead into the private chamber. A gift for the girl. "When you ripped the scroll, I remember seeing you in different clothing. I assume your world. These should fit. The robe will arouse suspicion when you return."

"You never met a cosplayer..." Sadie said under her breath before going to change into her replicated uniform. When she returned, Milos rubbed his chin, saying, "Just like when I first met you. All you need is a chicken in hand to start tossing around!" he laughed.

She rolled her eyes and embraced him. One. Last. Time. Then, thanking Enzu for everything. A sad expression on his face, but he understood the situation. Homesick. A terrible feeling. Sadie sat against the mulberry tree and closed her eyes, a warmth surrounding her. The tree illuminated. Its silver-edged leaves shone radiantly. Her body was glowing suddenly, and just then, Milos shouted out, "Don't forget to write!" She managed to laugh, and just like that, she was gone.

Teleported back home. Like she never left.

"So...what now?"

"Let's talk in my chambers. I have a great view of the realm. There are many questions I wish to ask," Evren said, leading the way.

He picked up his quiver, hearing all the heartfelt messages the veiled women transmitted to him, but something caught his eye from the tree: a silver woman.

Despair on her face, realizing this was the mother: Evren's!

"Well?" She turned to him.

The visage was gone; was it an illusion? Who could say?

"I'll have a feast prepared for you,"

"I don't mind some rusk and—"

"Dried biscuits?! You are my guest, and you'll feast on no such subsidies fit for a pauper; wait until…" her voice trailed off.

His mind was busy with the vision of the woman.

What could it mean?

Chapter 18

†

Saturation

Back in its kingdom of strife, it gazed out of the glass window. It watched the soldiers have their drills, the citizens trading in the market, and slaves being sold off. Another day in Lusura.

How mundane, it thought.

Knocks on the metal entrance door, strange creatures enter the chamber room. Some are enigmatic, like the messengers sent to Udalann, and some are horrifying, like the pale rider.

"We've found all the pieces, my liege," one said.

It turned around to see a Mairu warrior lug in a cart of deadwood. Nothing remarkable, to the naked eye, but priceless to their ruler. They started to place the pieces on a table, assembling it, until it was completed. The king walked over to observe, silently, until it saw the thin lines of hypnotic energy swirling about its broken cracks and veins.

Grand picture puzzle.

"Tremendous, so this is what brought the girl over. I cannot wait to study this. Now, I'll be able to have my own kind of power that Celanjung holds, and so much more," Ashokara said, tracing its hand over the broken pieces, once a closet door—the original piece from Celanjung's royal family tree. Energy unfolded below the Prime Aeolid's hand.

Its eyes discerned the power. The others watched in silence as it formed around the gauntlet. First: warm. Then: hot. Searing. Ashokara tried removing its hand back, but it was glued in place, when suddenly...

"I am the turpentine to your canvas, Usurper! You will never bloom! GIVE YOURSELF TO THE WHITE!" A female voice boomed from the furniture. The surge formed into a silver-white hand; breaking Ashokara's armored limb like putty. Others went to assist their king, pulling the arm back along with the door to no avail. The pale rider shattered the configured deadwood, and the silver-white hand disappeared, but not before taking the Usurper's hand with it. It held up the dripping stump to its face and laughed with amusement.

"The joys I am going to have studying this discovery!"

Tentacles shot out of the stump; regeneration.

His belly was about to burst. "No more," Milos managed to say. The queen offered more, but he insisted he was at his limit.

She looked at Enzu carefully.

"He went with you at his own request?"

Milos looked over, nodding, "Couldn't keep him away from me at first. Just kept finding ways of latching on. Impossible to shake off."

A small smile on her face, "This is the last thing my mother created; I am unable to replicate its power. A secret buried with her: to shape Prime Matter. My Alephim are still neonates of my creation. Thank you for sparing Jökull, it brought back the Cerulean you used, the veils spoke sweetly of you. Jökull was my first Essent. It's very dear to me."

"The Alephim...the Vicara...how?"

"On the Crescent isla," she pointed to the west, "A dungeon. My father managed one there: jewels for mother. Now on Enzu. I lost all hope…saw nothing to lose, and went down to die there…I forgot how to die, and the artifacts of power gave me the ability to raise them. Slow, but worth it. How else do you think I can keep everyone at bay?"

He asked a daring question, "Are you responsible for the beasts in the Akrav?"

"No," she replied, "I believe the Usurper's kin, in the Abyssal, are responsible, but I have no proof."

"I remember Birati telling me there used to be another realm there in the middle, before the great swallow."

"…Do you serve under him? Or Leandro's banner?" she asked, sipping the tea delicately from her cup, not breaking eye contact.

He was caught off guard by the question, "I don't serve under any banner. I just provide help for some geodi, and move to my own beat." Enzu looked at him, pouting. "I'm sorry, *our* beat," he corrected himself.

"And, is it true you have decided to wed the princess of the Euphotic Nation?"

"How'd you come across that?!" He was taken aback.

"Wandrians talk, and they tell me *many* things."

He shook his head in disbelief—maybe fish was off the menu for now and he should go carnivore to keep his secrets to himself.

She placed her cup down and stood up to walk to the edge of the balcony, watching her realm. "You're the first man up here in years," she said, turning to him, "Are you aware?" He didn't know how to react to that. Just a shrug. And filling his mouth with a pastry to muffle words; really it was just sounds to make it seem like he was shocked.

"Don't speak with your mouth full, it's unbecoming," she said sharply. She watched; studied; gazed; he was not sure where this was going. For years, she was trying to apprehend him, to do whatever unspeakable things she had in store, but now, he's having tea time with her, as if nothing happened.

"Are you interested…" she walked over casually to him.

His eyes bounced around. Enzu watched the show. A hand on the table, close to his, her hair falling a bit, before fixing it behind her ear. Her cleavage is exposed. His heart was racing. Blood to the head.

Rushing to *another* "head."

"Would you be my first…" she asked, gently.

Natalina, forgive me!

"…man, to serve under my banner?"

"Denied! You jackass!" Mulberry transmitted with a hearty laugh.

She explained how this could help fix relations with the other realms, especially since his name carried immense weight. She hadn't replied to Gottlir's messages. Milos was too flustered, letting stupid "man" thoughts get in the way, and decided to just accept the invitation…anything to get out of this mess once and for all!

Evren announced the good news to her veiled women and everyone in the realm with the telepathic use of her crown. A small insignia patch, of Celanjung, was stitched to Milos's coat. She also declared that Jökull would assist him whenever the need arose. She did not mind lending out its services since she had the others.

"Your attending veils…How can they swap into the spectres like those after the sacrifice?" he asked with intrigue.

His veils hovered in to hear her answer. This was groundbreaking.

"Another artifact from the dungeons…I have conquered many."

"The Primes see this as an affront. Even Cerulean should have you banished for this!"

Evren curled her lips, looking like an absolute demon, "Cerulean sanctioned this in the first place. Just because I dashed the Chroma does not mean I would dash the one who would unite the others under Her banner solely. I still hold loyalty to Her. My Codex veils tell me She has permitted a grand blessing on you. I am sure Her Herald will come to seek you soon…maybe Herself too."

"This is dangerous news to us, sir," Aquamarine whispered.

"She'll have us permanently killed!" Cobalt shouted.

"…I don't want to die again," Auburn said tearfully.

"NEVER! NEVER! EVER!" Mulberry screamed.

He felt the scroll of Goldenrod tremble under his coat.

Evren heard his variants clearly, "All of you can be converted like Auburn. Don't think I never noticed. I glimpsed into her history when she was encased. Tragic, but you and Birati saved her nonetheless. I can always convert her back."

"This new color suits me," Auburn replied.

"Even if your new leadership has failed to reach out to you? *Any* of you for that matter?"

A long silence.

"Maybe…I can help unite the colors," Milos insisted.

"Don't joke like that. In the end, every Chroma wants to be the grand leader of all the colors. Better to meditate on this more. It is a heavy weight that will require focus and lifelong participation."

"I can still try. My travels take me everywhere. It could lead to the unity of Iberitus, and the Primes. Not just the Chroma."

"Don't let me down, I love you," Mulberry accidentally muttered.

"What was that?!" Milos twisted his head almost owl-like.

Back into the quiver. Evren scanned his other veils. They were fiercer than they looked when she held them captive. His possession of Argent caused a volatile reaction inside her, but she remained steadfast. *Mother.* She dismissed the impossibility of the Chroma uniting as a rainbow without hierarchy. But not entirely. Alchemy, however…

After the short celebrations, he prepared to take his leave, first to Haven's Mark, to check on the king and prince, before heading home, to Riha's tavern.

"Here…I'm sorry about what happened, but I had no choice," Milos said, handing her the Ceruleans he ripped in half back at the fort and the one Sadie did when facing the Khrosgar.

"I can mend these. So long as the pages aren't burned, they still survive. Thank you for this, truly," Evren said, handing the split parchments to her lead. Just as he was about to lift off into the air, holding the grand bustard, she gave him a message, "Tell Birati he can stop sending me letters of scorn…I will contest him. Goodbye, little one, thank you for the company." Milos shot off into the air, heading back East. Exhilarated. To think he survived it all. Miracle of miracles.

But, not everything was right with others.

Upon his return to the Capital, Leandro, amazed by the journey and tale, still had a son who remained catatonic. Edling had survived the onslaught of Auburn's wrath. Gone before the ambush, unknowingly to Milos. He vowed to make it right by planning to figure a way to enter The Mouth of Klaring to defeat him. An impossible task at the moment. They still had to clean up the countryside that was littered with small groups of raiders that came through the mountainside.

And there was still talk of the rogue Herald.

Many signed up for Flint and Coin, and the king's army, to engage the new threats.

New names rising in the ranks. Determined. Memorials were held for The Ternion Pilgrims who protected so many. Word in the city was that Kotsudas was preparing a regiment to speak to Leandro and Birati. And there was the matter of an important group from Grenvalk who were supposed to aid the fort but never made it past Lusura. The country was in an uproar when they learned of their and Grand M's fate—someone had to pay. Many Trasno resigned from Leandro's army to head back to the main island. No kins murder remains unavenged. There was nothing else he could do now, and so, Milos made a pit-stop to Udalann. Birati nearly broke Milos's back when he came with his bustard. Aruna, she didn't say anything, except, "What took you so long?" She had a peculiar way of showing concern. Old ways of the pirate. Milos imparted Evren's message to Birati.

"Hmph! Let her contest me any time! I'll best her in anything!"

Milos and Aruna just sighed. *Pigheaded, ogre,* they both thought.

The king saw Milos's new insignia. Completely taken aback. He sent orders for a fresh patch to be sewn onto Milos's jacket…above Celanjung's. "Better! I should have done this long ago. That is no ordinary royal badge. It's only fit for the prince of this realm!" Birati boasted. "And don't you dare fake your death on me again, boy! Two times? Food just doesn't taste right."

If only he really knew…

Milos looked at the patch, then looked over to Aruna with a raised brow, "How's about a congratulations kiss for the prince?"

She stepped in front of him, standing on her tippy-toes, with the most feminine face he had ever seen on her. Milos blushed intensely, not thinking this far ahead. He never noticed, until now, how beautiful she looked. Her full lips parted a bit.

Then a seismic punch into the gut. He succumbs to gravity.

"I'd sooner kiss the backend of a Khrosgar," she growls.

"Haha! I love it when my children play with each other in jest!" Birati said in high spirits. Milos craved for air while on the ground.

Should have known better, Milos thought, gasping in pain.

They traveled together to some dolmen, giving thanks to the Chroma before Milos departed again. He would ask about the deceptive bracelet at a later point when he settled all his accounts.

Time to deliver the final grave news he was not prepared for.

He sat on the stones, outside the small tavern, pondering to himself. A puddle of water by his feet. He kept staring at it until a new face appeared next to him. "Milos! You're back! It is a blessed day!" Kosey exclaimed, going in to embrace him. Riha came out to see the fuss. Immediately going back inside in a hurry. He was confused, Kosey was his normal self, did she not tell him yet?

"Just a moment, Kosey, I need to speak to Riha real quick..." he said with a low voice.

"Oh, okay then," he replied, sitting back on the stones again, kicking his feet, humming to a little tune he just made up.

Milos rushed into the tavern, bursting through the door, "Has the news not travelled here?! Does he still not know?!"

"You have no right! *None!* I kept the village from saying anything! You can't tell him!" Riha shouted, her voice starting to break.

Kosey turned his head to the tavern wondering about the commotion.

"I have no right?! Damn it all, woman! She was there too! What if I kept Nagy's death a secret from you?! Do not answer that! That's rhetorical," Milos shouted with anger.

The argument continued for some time until they heard the Tarwini below shout, "Enough! Both of you! Scribe, you need to understand the boy's mentality to this; he's still growing. This could very well alter his mindset forever. Innocence could disappear. Antisocial behaviors. A dark personality change. An instrument of surrender. And Sanshan...it's time."

"But—" she tried to talk.

"It. Is. Time. The boy must learn this is how the cycle works. You cannot shelter him forever. He will grow up to regret you."

The two stared at each other. Riha, a woman of strength and ability, couldn't bear to see what was about to happen. Fluid dripped from her nose. She held it in. A sadness so blue.

"Let's…just tell him," Milos said, reaching out, "Together."

She agreed.

The pain on her face started to give rise to a migraine. The two stepped outside, walking over to the affectionate child, who was staring at them, wondering what was happening. "Kosey…there's something you must know," Milos said.

Black-eyed mutts wanted no part of this revelation; sprints made to the forest. Shutters closed. These neighbors want no part of this.

Knots, in the tapestry of sanity, slacken in pitiful reverence.

It went on for hours. No end in sight. The small boy bawled out his entire being. His greatest hero: dead. He never met another of his kind, and Kabir was the only one he came across. Riha held onto him for dear life; both weeping into each other's arms. Something *did* shatter inside Kosey.

It will never return.

His perspective of the world became skewed. Colors all around started to mute one by one. Bleak and gray. It was a dark day for the boy. He had forgotten about loss before. Where does it all go? To the sky? More cries. An ugliness. They kept watch over him all night; vigilant.

There was no rest here.

*I wish I could take away your pain, your sorrow, your grief. I want to help, but all I can do is hold you. I'm trying. That's all I can do. The rain keeps falling on us. It pours from us. Never ceasing. Let me hold you as long as you want me to—I won't let go. I'll never let go. Please, believe me. I'm trying. It's all I can do…it's all I **can** do…*

At first light, Milos looked at the boy; asleep from all the dreadful emotions he let out. Riha was on the bed with him—cradling. He left the tavern, and ventured to the coast, telling Enzu to stay behind, "I'll be back soon, I have to see her." The tavern would stay closed for the day.

Relayed messages sent to sea.

Waiting.

Waiting.

Waiting.

The saddest feeling in the world.

Waiting.

Soon, she arrived, all smiles, until she saw his face. Sheer gloom. He throws light on everything, and she listens attentively, holding on to every word like little prayers for a Prime. Then, he finished, and she placed her head on his shoulder.

"Will we make it?" she asked him.

"We have to."

"I'm always afraid I'm going to lose you…and it sounds like I almost did; multiple times. Do you want this?"

"Of course I do."

"Will you stay?"

"…"

She sat up, and turned his head to hers, "Look at me, Milos! I want you to stay…otherwise, why continue…"

"Don't say that, Natalina. We've come this far."

"But look at yourself! Bedraggled; washed; hung to dry! And now you're under *her* banner?! Their banner?! Where does it end? Leandro sees you as another soldier: expendable. Birati sees you as a street urchin. And the rest want to murder you! When does it end?!"

He kept silent, he was not ready for this discussion.

"My father, Glaukós Imperator *Almaric*, has acknowledged you! Do you realize he never once gave permission to a human before?! As does my mother and my hardheaded brother. I'm not asking you to choose us over the rest, but you need to stop wandering all the time. I want a family! Kids! Grandkids!"

Milos heard a soft hum in the wind. Calming. Voices of the Chroma sent their signals to him: "*You can't save the world, but you can always make a home to build upon.*"

He took her hands, kissing them passionately, "I'm not getting any younger, and all of this started because I was too poor to buy a ring for you. Should've never stolen those damn pages to begin with to pawn. Too hot to barter. My account with Celanjung is officially settled. I'm still keeping my promise to Leandro. I will do what I can to help bring back the prince, but that's it. Let me keep that and my contracting work as contribution to the Nation; no war work…unless it threatens all of Iberitus. That's all I ask." A hard pill to swallow, but she agreed to the terms. Sealed with a kiss, and a group of veiled women watching them, "Do you mind?!" he shouted at them.

He returned to his old spot to rest for the day. So much to plan for in the coming months. Who would be his best man? A wedding on the beach…that sounds…just…right…

And he fell asleep under the shade of the tree.

And nature came along, watching him, guarding him.

Let him rest. He deserved his reward of peace, finally.

Epilogue

✝

Tincture

Her rambling ceased, at last, "Hey! Did you hear what I said?" Mary shouted at her. Sadie opened her eyes again, shaking her head. The girl was really annoyed with Sadie but still repeated it, "So Felix was drugged by two weirdos! They dumped it into his thermos, and his parents found him wandering by one of the mills! Good thing they found him in time. Who knows what would've happened to him! They at least caught and arrested the guys that did it. Did they not know there are cameras in the classrooms now?" she explained, looking at her watch.

"Crap, I gotta go! I'll see you tomorrow!" and she ran off.

To think, Sadie had just returned back home, in the same place she rested before. Time stood still while she was gone…or did it? It didn't matter. She survived. It was time to head home. Her *real* home.

One deep stretch and off she went.

"I look forward to seeing how you live in this realm," Alaea said.

"Much more peaceful here. Same annoyances with different cultures and technology. Wars in other countries no doubt, but we have our own peacekeepers. Just stay out of sight because it will cause too many problems, and I don't need to be taken away by the suits."

"Who are they? Villains?"

"Yeah…not much we can do about them. Law is power around here, but it's not black and white like your world. It's more nuanced. Just like how in your world there's Chroma and Alchemy and Naturals, we have this thing called separation of church and state. Color and science are very different. Nature is just nature for most of us here on Earth."

They continued talking: Sadie giving the answers, her veil becoming the curious one, basking in the warm rays of the sunlight.

The dwarfed cottontail kept watch, and so did its feline companion, tugging on its harness. Munching on some salmon.

Come back anytime…

𝔖𝔬𝔲𝔫𝔡𝔱𝔯𝔞𝔠𝔨

1. Therion: Birth of Venus Illegitima
2. Amorphis: Mermaid
3. Spiritbox: Secret Garden
4. Skyforest: Autumnal Embrace
5. Novembre: Zenith
6. Alcest: Écailles de lune – Part 1
 ("Moon Scales – Part 1")
7. Alcest: Écailles de lune – Part 2
 ("Moon Scales – Part 2")

<u>Closure</u>

Unreal. Done and done. I am going to go and try to get as much air as humanely possible before starting the next project: Lost Aristocracy. Like other works, this series will be 18+ ONLY, but unlike other works…it's going to be me delving into the horror aspects, from my personal experiences, on sex and addiction. Always stirring trouble. Can't take me anywhere.

I hope you enjoyed the read as much as I enjoyed finishing it because I was ready to start tearing my hair out on this book after losing who knows how much vision, brain cells, and time when I was doing research work.

Don't forget to call/check on those you haven't spoken to in a while. They might be struggling in silence like yours truly and will really appreciate the wellness-check.

Be safe, and pet some animals to rid your blues.

All my love to you.

-Ryan

Disclaimer

Copyright © 2025 by Ryan Kreiner

All rights reserved. No part of this publication may be reproduced, distributed, or transmitted in any form or by any means, including photocopying, recording, or other electronic or mechanical methods, without the prior written permission of the publisher, except in the case of brief quotations embodied in critical reviews and certain other noncommercial uses permitted by copyright law. For permission requests or other inquiries, please reach out to Guy Maybriar on either Facebook (@gmaybriar54) or Instagram (Guy Maybriar).

This is a work of fiction. Names, characters, businesses, places, events, locales, & incidents are either the products of the author's imagination or used in a fictitious manner. Any resemblance to actual persons, living or dead, or actual events is purely coincidental.

Under no circumstances does this story condone the acts of homicide/torture/kidnapping/drug use/racism! Do not attempt to recreate these scenarios in real life. The author is not responsible for the actions that are beyond his control. Seek professional help/medical assistance when circumstances of life might cause a violent behavior in your life that could jeopardize the lives of others/yourself!

ISBN (Paperback): 978-1-7336856-8-9

Lil Puddin Taters: *Incipit Widdershins*

IN THE VILLAGE OF RIFFS A SMALL TEAM OF WARRIORS ARE COMMISSIONED BY THE VILLAGE ELDER TO LOCATE THE "TREASURE OF SILVER MOUNTAIN."

WHAT WILL OUR HEROES DISCOVER IN THE DANKEST REGIONS OF FARTLANDIA?!

AGES THE ZOOMIE

MCTOUGH THE FLUFF

BARE, THE GOOD BOY

SIR DIDDLES THE WADDLER

CHUMBA THE WAMBA

DUDE, WHAT IS UP WITH THIS TALL ASS GRASS?

I THINK I FEEL IT SHAKING.

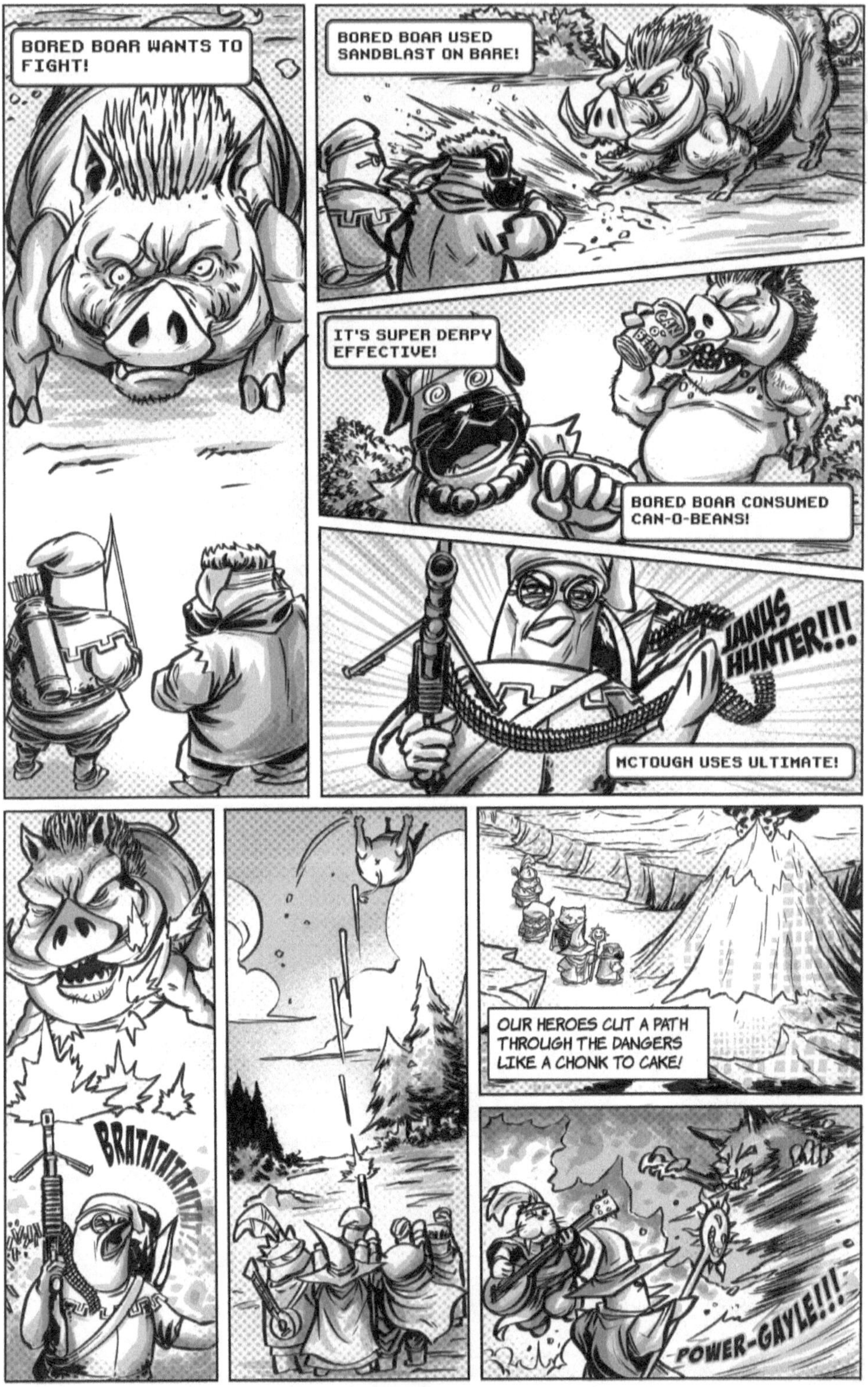

UNBEKNOWNST TO THEM THEIR GREATEST FOE HAS NEVER BEEN DEFEATED!

IT'S THE LORD OF VERITABLE EMOTIONS!

MY CHILDREN, LET NOT ANGER FILL YOUR HEARTS AND MINDS! LET HE WHO IS OF HARMONY BRING ITS SOUND TO THE UNIVERSE!

MY SON, USE YOUR WONDERFUL STRENGTH TO UNVEIL YOUR GIFT TO ALL!

GO! MY LITTLE WARRIORS! FEAR NOTHING!

EXCEPT CHOCOLATE.

LUTE OF BLACKMORE ACQUIRED!

HISSS!!!

TSOCSP

THE SOUND OF CHUCK SCHULDINER'S PERSEVERANCE

LET OUT THE DANKEST OF RIFFS CHILD!

ABBOT FROM HELL?

DESPITE THEIR BUMPS AND BRUISES THEY NEVER GAVE IN TO DEFEAT! NEVER SURRENDERING TO EVIL! NEVER GIVING IN TO THE FEAR!

STOIC

MAY YOU AND YOURS ALWAYS TRIUMPH OVER THE DARKNESS, MAY YOU AND YOURS BE SURROUNDED BY LOVE UNTIL WE MEET AGAIN...

0	1	2	3	4
5	6	7	8	9

100	1000

ALPHABET

A	B	C	D
E	F	G	H
I	J	K	L
M	N	O	P
Q	R	S	T
U	V	W	X
Y	Z		

UDALANN

GOTTLIR

GKENUALK

KLARIN

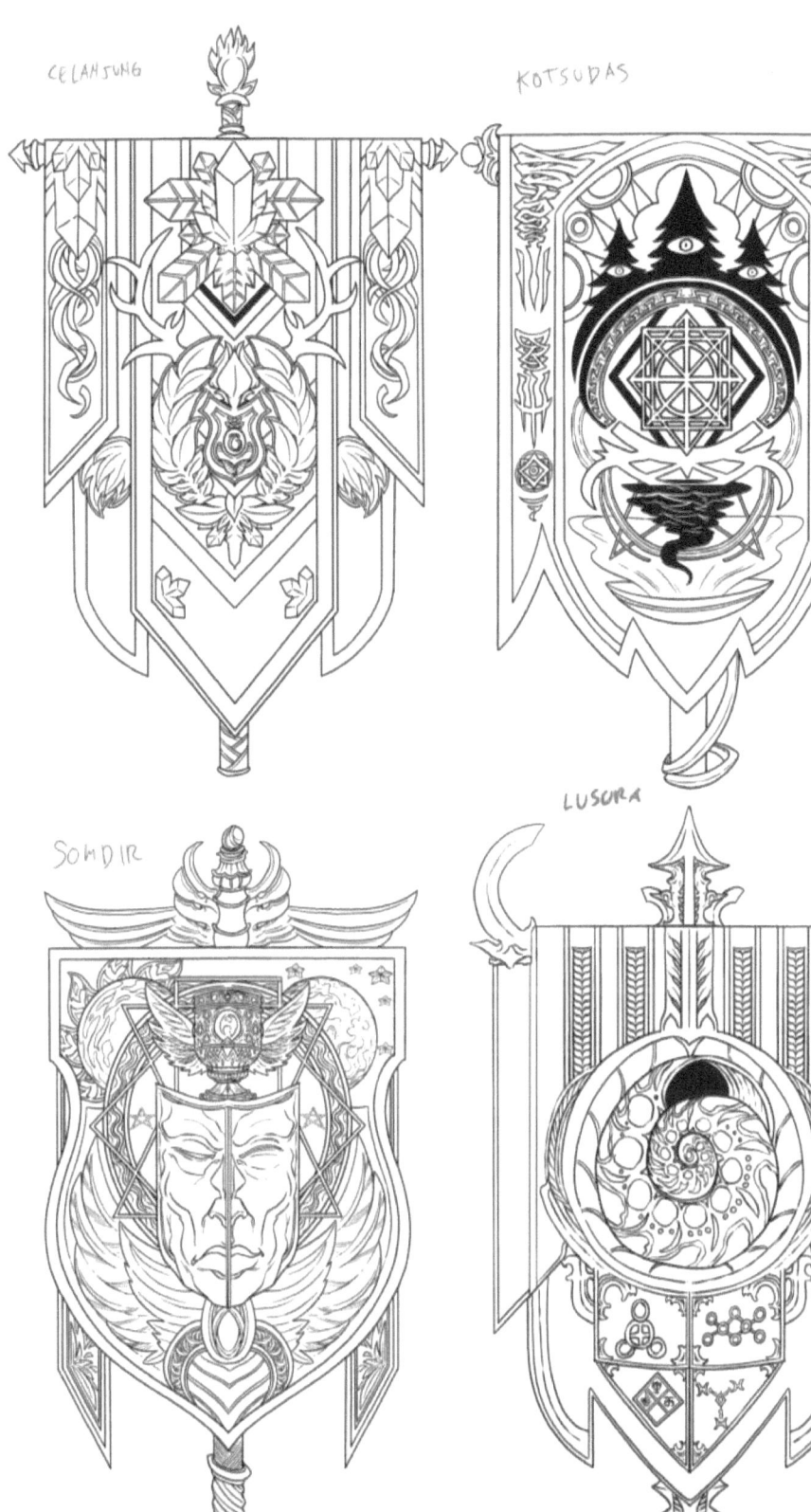

CELAHJUNG

KOTSUDAS

SOMDIR

LUSURA

Stories by Guy Maybriar

Never Being Me

Brother Roman

Miasma

Brother Roman: Tribute

Martyrdom: Insurrection

A Town Named Dulcet: Carnival

Foundlings Nest

www.ingramcontent.com/pod-product-compliance
Lightning Source LLC
Chambersburg PA
CBHW030543020726
47494CB00005B/1470